GHATS

Joshua Amses

Fomite

Burlington, VT

For Sam

I.

> *"Haven't you noticed how we all specialize in what we hate most?"*
> —Kingsley Amis, *Lucky Jim*

I MOVED INTO CARISSA AND BUCK'S attic in Acheron, Vermont at the end of August; this was a mistake. My room overlooked the backyard where Carissa gardened in a bikini most afternoons, pruning tomato plants and spooning compost into the raised beds as I watched her through the window above my desk. I could no longer tell if she was beautiful; her limbs blackened with soil to the knee and elbow, and more of it caught in a rill of sweat between her breasts. Beauty didn't matter because there was nothing to compare it with; the cataract of my diminished world included only Carissa, myself, and the window separating us. She taught art classes at a summer school program, and wouldn't usually appear in the garden until midafternoon. This gave me the mornings to swing in a hammock on the front porch, and haunt myself with her afterimage from the day before. I hoped recognizing my behavior as unhealthy meant I could just monitor it like an atypical mole rather than change anything about myself.

I had been unemployed since June, and was beginning to notice my time had no value. I refused to allow this to depress me; the money I'd saved from managing the produce section of Grover's Market might see me through Labor Day if I stuck to two meals a day and didn't leave the house. I wasn't paying rent, and Carissa and Buck usually included me in whatever they did for dinner. They were good, eager cooks and always served too much wine with their meals. After eating, we usually finished our wine in the backyard and burned things in a fire pit ringed with stones from the Wendigo River. I watched them be in love through the flames, imagining myself staring out at Buck and Carissa from inside a woodstove, the two of them feeding me lengths of dry evergreen wood until I burned white and steady as the moon.

My only obligation was finishing my thesis. Or beginning it, I should say. I knew I no longer wanted a master's degree in military history before moving in with Carissa and Buck; no one else knew this except my advisor, Norman Downing, PhD., and only through osmosis, in his case. When we met in his office in Holmes Hall on the Acheron College campus before summer intercession, I tried explaining how afraid I was of becoming just another welfare academic, before floating a half-baked thesis idea about Belisarius his way as a kind of olive branch. Dr. Downing had worked with me for years. I didn't want him to think it had been a complete waste of time.

"Welfare academic," he said, the term unfamiliar to him. "What might that be?"

"Right," I said, happy to explain it. "I'm afraid I'll end up living on food stamps and teaching intro classes at a community college in Arkansas."

"Is that the best you can imagine for yourself, Oliver?"

"I don't know, Norman. It's certainly not the worst."

He shrugged and green-lit whatever I'd suggested with the cozy smugness of someone who no longer saw me as competition and glanced at his notes on our meeting as if they were threatening hieroglyphics before combing them into the wastebasket beside his desk. Meanwhile, I was fascinated to the point of distraction by his resemblance to Tolstoy; always had been. An old-growth beard the color of peppery snow curtained his mouth, chin, and chest, and he wore blousy, homespun clothing made by his wife. He had also been spotted wandering barefoot on the quad between classes, not so unusual, but also downtown, leaving a bar on Clamence Street, and doing his shopping in Grover's Market shortly before I quit working there. I was on duty at the time, managing the produce section and hoping I wouldn't have to kick my professor out of the store for failing to comply with the dress code.

The collision of the personal and the professional is probably the closest I will ever come to actual warfare, I thought then, watching Dr. Norman examine a bushel of red Russian kale as if he expected to find a microphone hidden in it. Rather than confront him over the footwear issue, I slunk through the plastic drapes at the rear of the store to the break room, feeling as if some inner Maginot line had fallen. I'd always thought bravery was just stupidity seen from below, and tried to apply this to my new life as a coward. I wondered: How can someone so afraid of conflict say anything important about it?

This moment inadvertently galvanized my desire to learn nothing else about how long and how well human beings had been killing each other; I was weary of it. I couldn't tell Dr. Norman or my parents or anyone else and considered faking a nervous breakdown to buy myself some time, but knew my life wasn't stressful enough to make this convincing. I lived alone on the edge of town in a comfortable shoebox beside the Wendigo River where I slept and graded papers for Dr. Norman, ate out for most meals, read Robert Graves at the bar after dinner, and was paid a livable wage to work thirty-five hours per week at a food coop. I made extra money I didn't need writing press material for a tour company co-managed by the owner of the grocery store, Grover Ratliff. Nothing about my lifestyle spelled disaster and everyone I knew at Acheron College was completing a degree they either didn't want or couldn't use. It felt like a zeitgeist of some kind coalescing and the coward in me didn't want to be left out.

I'd used the figure Flavius Belisarius as kind of human shield since June, sheltering in his long silhouette whenever anyone asked what I was doing, including Carissa and Buck prior to moving in. I spun out some disorderly nonsense about the Vandalic War of 533 A.D. and the deposition of Pope Silverius at the order of the monophysite empress Theodora, none of us really knowing or caring what I was talking about. But they seemed excited by the idea of something esoteric brewing in the attic, the way a feudal lord might install a tubercular poet in an unused tower of his castle to see what he would come up with. Since they allowed me to live in the house for nothing, I felt I owed them some part of this *mise-en-scène* and tried to appear earnest and academic as I hovered over the desk in my garret each afternoon, pretending to take notes while Carissa gardened, essentially bored stupid with myself. But I sat with Procopius' *Secret History* anyway, or the third volume of Edward Gibbon in the Penguin edition arrayed in my lap, feeling like a defrocked priest as I watched Buck stride across the yard toward Carissa with a beer for her, she mostly naked, and he shirtless among the bean poles and tomato cages. They looked very happy together.

Adam and Eve among their crops, I thought, trying to steer my way through the bitterness I felt without admitting I was lonely;

this felt like defeat, and years of studying with Dr. Norman and his colleagues in the history department had given the word a severe gravity. Defeat meant: summary executions, mass graves, life amid ruins. I knew they hadn't invited me to join them for a beer in the backyard because they didn't want to disturb my work. There was no reason to feel left out; I'd exiled myself. And I wasn't sure I could handle being much closer to Carissa and her soiled bikini without tipping what was left of my hand. So I settled into telling myself she wasn't beautiful, or the woman she'd become across the fifteen years we'd known each other wasn't beautiful. Either way, I hoped lying to myself like this would soften and confound the time I spent watching her from the attic.

I considered moving the desk away from the window, but was too afraid of scratching the pine floorboards if I tried it by myself, and too embarrassed to ask Buck for help. His landlord was apparently fussy about the upstairs flooring, so Buck asked me to keep an eye on the cat, a tortoiseshell pain in the ass named Agatha, with whom I shared the attic. I didn't know if she came with Carissa and Buck or the house itself, but banishing her from my room wasn't an option. I tried tossing her out into the hallway and locking the door shortly after moving in and spent the rest of the afternoon listening to her yowl and claw the wainscoting before she appeared outside the attic window, occluding my view of Carissa toiling in the garden as she scratched mincingly at the screen to be let inside. Buck described the cat as "troubled" and "a biter" and asked me if I wouldn't mind making sure she didn't scratch up the floorboards while tearing around the attic, since I was going to be spending a lot of time up there anyway. Considering how little he and Carissa asked of me, and how little I had to show for myself, this seemed like the least I could do.

*   *   *

Buck had a fondness for English novels, and once described himself and me as sharing the "free-masonry of male sensuality" to someone at a party, a woman he was trying to take home. I don't think I was meant to overhear, but the phrase stuck with me; it seemed to describe where our relationship landed after Carissa went to New York for college. It was hard to pin down exactly what we had in common without her nearby, though she'd left enough history behind to make it almost beside the point. Buck and I had been in and out of each other's lives for fifteen years, half the time we'd been alive, a thought that made me feel deeply vulnerable when I realized that he was my only friend shortly after we graduated from Acheron College together. I wasn't his only friend. I knew that. We sometimes walked up the Mt. Abandon access road to the fire tower with women he'd met in one place or another or shot guns with people he still knew from high school in a sand pit the county commissioner mined during winter to treat the roads. But I wanted to believe that whatever kept us friends after all this time wasn't her, or her memory, near or distant; it seemed too close to the way people stuck together after someone they both knew had died. Still, when Carissa moved back to town, I realized Buck and I had missed the opportunity to feel bad about the same things. Or he had. Even after our first conversation about her leaving Brooklyn, it felt like we were discussing the same performance seen from the best and worst seats, respectively.

Buck had supported himself since college by selling used books online and, in the past year, started distributing them to homeless shelters around New England, an initiative with the weirdly obvious title of the Homeless Library Project. This move got some attention, enough to earn him a set of interns from the college to mail books and help write grants, a steady stream of donations to a website they helped him create, and the place I would eventually move into at the end of the summer, the five bed, three bath Victorian home he rented on Winter Street. Buck said he was expanding and needed more room. This was all shortly before Carissa came back from New York; I assured myself there wasn't a connection.

Also around this time, he began referring to the HLP as a foundation, which sounded credentialed enough to me, though I noticed nothing different when I visited him at the house on Winter Street. Stacks of unshelved books listed from low-lit corners, spilled from a ziggurat of ruptured cardboard boxes in the center of the living room carpet, and blocked half the windows on the sun porch. It felt, or continued to feel, like a kind of intellectual preserve. The interns, Chelsea and Amanda, austere, indistinguishable brunettes ten years younger than Buck or I, prowled the aggregate shelving I'd helped him install around the house when he first moved in, watching me like a brace of bird dogs whenever I withdrew a book from the stacks they'd organized on the ground floor. Buck said not to worry about them and invited me to take whatever I wanted. I privately wondered if this included one of his interns. I would take either, I thought, and then: there is apparently a gulf in my life.

Now would be a good time to find someone to be an adult with, I thought further as we sat together one night in early June after the interns went home, wishing I could order loneliness from my life the way the generals I studied ordered divisions of men into the mandibles of irrecoverable doom. Buck was beside me, his beer resting on a menhir of books I'd taken from inside and

my own growing warm in my hand as we watched a sunset unravel above Mt. Abandon. This was my fourth visit to his house
that week and the ritual of it, our ritual, was no longer cloaking
the parts of my life I didn't want to think about. It may have actually been drawing them to the forefront. So when Buck told me
he'd spoken to Carissa, I was ready to hear something different
than what I'd been telling myself and the people around me since
meeting with Dr. Norman.

"She'll be back at the end of the month," he added. "Maybe
before then."

"Back where?"

"Here, she said."

I wondered why she told Buck this instead of me, but it seemed
to fulfill the tripartite pattern of our history together. He always
heard things first. I rarely got anything from Carissa she hadn't
already filtered through him. This may have been unavoidable;
they were both from Acheron, I wasn't, and they had a landscape
in common, reasons to be near each other. The only characteristic
separating me from being a townie was still being in school.

"Do you guys talk often?" I asked Buck. This wasn't exactly
what I wanted to know, but seemed near enough.

"Sometimes we do," he said, his speech toneless and beer-leav-
ened. "Lately we have. But I think she only called because she
doesn't want to stay at her parents' place, and she knows I have
the house now."

"Did something happen in New York?"

"She didn't mention anything. I think there was probably a
guy somewhere in the mix."

"Is he coming with her?"

"It didn't sound like it. Last person she mentioned like that
was someone from her program, a found form poet, whatever

that is. Seemed like an insufferable pain in the ass. But this was over the winter. I don't know if he's the same guy I'm thinking of. Either way, her friends sound annoying and I don't want them staying with me. I made that clear."

"I didn't know she was seeing anybody," I said, sheltering in the shade of the obvious, oddly relieved.

"I don't know if that's what it's about. Carissa just said she needed to get out of the city. I feel like I'm explaining more than I have to. I thought you two talked."

"We do," I lied. "I wish we did more."

"Well, she asked about you. I tried to tell her what you're doing, but I honestly have no idea, Oliver."

Counting Dr. Norman, that makes three of us, I thought, glancing at the books beneath Buck's beer: *The Songways, They Shoot Horses, Don't They?, The CIA and the Cult of Intelligence, Ride a Cockhorse*, a book of Kleist's short stories, and another about shark attacks. No order there. Nothing particularly warlike either. Reading confuses you into thinking you're doing something important. By this measure alone, my activities are quite valuable. I wondered if Buck's recent success in marketing himself had anything to do with why Carissa contacted him instead of me. His star was clearly ascending; if they spoke regularly, she couldn't fail to notice.

I flipped through my inner Rolodex, seeking someone to compare him to other than myself, a successful sort of person would be best, but succeeded only in conjuring the near memory of Henry Hoffmann, boy king of Acheron County, emerging from Grover's office at the beginning of the month as I stood outside, tucking a sheaf of order forms awaiting signatures into an accordion folder taped beside the door. His face, handsome and uniformly villainous, hung in a barrel of shadow beneath the brim of an outsize straw sunhat he'd taken to wearing since purchasing a derelict Boy Scout camp on Mt. Abandon with money from the estate he managed for the remaining members of the Castle family. Apparently, he'd repurposed the old camp buildings, and was marketing the place to people from Boston and New York as a retreat of some kind. This was only the most recent in Henry's line of acquisitions; he'd been working for the Castle household since we were undergraduates at Acheron College, in what capacity, no one knew, but it was generally assumed he was up to no good. Not even Grover knew how much property he'd acquired around town, but since the passing of Joshua Castle, the family patriarch, the subdued commercial district along Clamence Street was informally known as Hoffmann Strasse between residents, a sobriquet Henry was probably aware of and appreciated.

He didn't say anything to me when he came out of the office, but even before he scooped the order forms out of the accordion folder and signed them with an arrogant flourish on the express line's black rubber conveyor, his expression suggested we would be seeing more of each other in the future. I watched him leave the store before leaning my head inside the office and asking Grover if there was something I should know. Unlike Buck, Grover was able to parse the real question recreating within what I'd asked. He said he'd made the decision to sell the store a while ago, but was afraid people would quit if he told them who bought it. He was right; even if I could teach myself not to fear Henry, I knew I never wanted to work for him. When I shared this with Grover, he mentioned the promotional material I'd written for a local foliage tourism company, Releaf Tours it was called, and asked if I knew Henry owned it. I hadn't known this, but told Grover I did, said luring leaf-peepers to Acheron with brochure copy was as involved as I wanted to become with the Castle monopoly, and made a remark about how freedom from spookiness and cruelty was important to me. Grover said he didn't think Henry would spend much time on site, but if I needed to leave, he understood. By the end of our conversation, it wasn't clear whether I'd quit, or been laid off, but I agreed not tell any of my coworkers why I was leaving.

And as I sat with Buck on the porch, drinking his beer beside a passel of books he'd given me and talking about Carissa, I realized I was trying to make a nemesis out of him by stacking his imprint against Henry Hoffmann. Aside from displacing my sense of comfort, their separate successes had nothing in common. But no one else I knew was up to much of anything and I was determined to leave the porch feeling wronged. I wanted to blame Buck for the privileged relationship he maintained with Carissa, a relationship I was afraid of watching blossom once she moved back, the way I'd saddled Henry with the responsibility for my unemployment. So I prepared for war, combing Buck's character for something I could comfortably hate, trying to tally the ways he'd harmed me during the tenure of our friendship. Carissa's bare back seen through a tent flap rose to mind, the shape of her in ecstasy, or so I imagined, fifteen years ago, the summer I met her and Buck on Kranion Pond. But this was nothing new, hardly the kind of war crime I hoped to hang on my friend and the three of us never talked it over, so there wasn't much I could blame on him or Carissa without including myself. And I also remembered running out of logs for the woodstove in my shoebox during a particularly bitter stretch last winter and Buck showing up in the middle of a Sunday afternoon with a pickup of cordwood, helping me stack it as the mercury in the thermometer outside my bedroom window dipped past zero. Or last summer, when he was still living in a crummy studio full of books out by the town dump. I'd stopped by to return some camping equipment he'd left in my car and found him too sick to do much of anything, so dehydrated his skin behaved and felt like dough when I took his temperature with the back of my hand. He refused to go to the doctor, so I slept on his kitchen floor for three nights, making things he could eat, helping him shower and get to the bathroom, feeding him a few times when it became clear he couldn't hold a spoon without dropping it. I worried in an abstract way that he might die, the way I worried about prostate cancer, or the envelopes that arrived in my mailbox from student loan companies, things that threatened from afar, but I worried about it enough to call up the clinic in town and rattle off his symptoms; flu was the tentative verdict on their end. As I made the call, I watched Buck sleep on the couch through an avenue of books across the single room he lived in, a dismal place with a drop ceiling, vertical blinds, and Formica cabinets; I imagined him suffering in it alone and when he awoke an hour later, I wanted to tell him he wouldn't ever have to because I would be there. But I clammed up at the last minute and went to make soup in the kitchenette, afraid he might see that caring for him was an unconscious action for me, like love or an offshoot of it, the sort of thing that doesn't come up in conversation between middle class North American men because of what it might be mistaken for, as if there isn't anything worse. I still don't know if we were best friends, whatever best friends means to adults, but I knew the slings and arrows of male intimacy over the years had often left me wondering if I knew enough about men to be one — at least in the common arena, the place where batting averages were discussed and engine cylinders counted. Still, I knew I never felt like caring about Buck as much as I did made me any less of a man, even while trying to find a reason to hate him on the porch the night we talked about Carissa coming home.

So: memory has the power to absorb conflict, I thought, as a fresh beer hissed and clucked in his hand. This is one thing warfare does not teach us.

"You should call her," he said, passing me the can he'd opened. "She'll probably be able to tell you the stuff you want to know."

If only that were true, I thought further, wanting to apologize to Buck without explaining why I was sorry.

*   *   *

Before she moved back to Vermont, I hadn't seen Carissa since visiting her in New York City the year before. My grandmother died in her home in Nutley, New Jersey, on a Wednesday in October and I volunteered to help my mother clean out the house. We drove down on a Saturday afternoon, past antique malls and farm stands selling pumpkins, through the battered, post-industrial ghettos of upstate New York. I tried to parse my mother's grief from the passenger seat, wondering what my father would have said to make her feel better, but I hadn't lived with my parents in nearly a decade and couldn't guess how they solved things without me around.

And I shall be the custodian of my mother's sorrow, I thought, as Whitehall and Fort Ann crept past the windshield, shabby, declining towns, quietly gruesome in the twilight. A viridian beer sign winked from the window of a roadside bar as we waited for a single traffic light to change. It looked like the sort of place where a person like me would stop and never be seen again. Part of me was itching to lighten the mood, so I said something about how I'd heard Whitehall was home to a Sasquatch and immediately-felt like an imbecile as my mother, obviously in pain, yet infinitely decorous, asked me to pass her a banana from a cooler behind the driver's seat. This is your mother's way of asking you to be quiet, I thought, helping myself to some companion fruit, defeated, but grateful to be muzzled by something as simple and polite as eating.

We stopped for dinner at a pizza restaurant in Lake George, a place we'd visited many times as a family on our way to and from my grandmother's house for Christmas or Thanksgiving. When we arrived on Saturday evening, the dining room was festooned with Halloween kitsch. A string of glowing plastic skulls hemmed our booth and an animatronic grim reaper howled from an alcove beside the bathrooms whenever a customer passed by. A pair of foam rubber tombstones upheld the napkins and ketchup between us. The place was clearly getting into the spirit of things.

None of this had a noticeable effect on my mother. We sat with plastic cups of domestic beer and moist slices of reheated pizza, trying to say nice things about my grandmother. She always remembered birthdays. She was kind to animals. She loved us all very much, in her own way. These were true, but didn't dispel the calculated isolation my grandmother had built around herself since the death of my grandfather five years earlier. No one in the family expected her to live so long after him, and yet, there she was, year after year, lucid and furious, withdrawing into the dark little house on Princeton Street and generally turning away from the world, even the small one containing her family. Holidays became a bastinado. Phone calls were always brief. She was in near constant pain from osteoporosis, but still tried to move an air conditioner on her own the summer after my grandfather died. Doctors were managing it. My mother drove to New Jersey once a month to take her to appointments and always returned to

Vermont behaving like she'd spent the weekend volunteering at an asylum. My father did his best not to sound relieved when he called me on Wednesday morning to say my aunt had driven in from Highland Lakes to take my grandmother to ShopRite and found her on the floor of the upstairs bedroom, at rest, perhaps even at peace; no one would ever know. Even if she wasn't, it was nice to see my mother sad about something irrevocable for a change.

"She thinks the house is cursed," she said, meaning my aunt. The reaper by the toilet whooped as if it agreed. "Won't go near it. We spoke this morning and I asked if she wanted anything. She said she didn't, of course, but wouldn't take something even if she did. Too afraid of being haunted by the ghost of your grandmother."

"Maybe she's being metaphorical," I suggested, wondering if the décor might be influencing our conversation. I wanted my mother to feel relieved, but it seemed we were a long way from that.

"I don't think so. Your uncle fell off a ladder yesterday. He's fine, but she said something about how it must be mom, coming to take her revenge. This is a grownup, Oliver. My sister. Between her and your grandmother, I feel like I'm losing the ability to communicate like an adult."

"I think it's hard not to want things to be normal when they're not. We have an unusual family," I said, a little spooked by my mother speaking about my grandmother as if she was still alive. Was that normal? Probably, at this early stage. I'd run it by my father if it continued.

"I wanted to ask: revenge for what? We're talking about mom, not some poltergeist," said my mother. I scanned the dining room for something unrelated to mortality. Through a window beyond our table, the lights of an outlet mall occupying both sides of route 9 had the distant, transitory luminescence of an airport at night. "Then I started wondering if there was something my sister hadn't told me and whether I can ignore her pathology for a little while, at least until the house and everything else are sorted out."

"I think you can," I said. It seemed like a hopeful answer, and I wanted it to be true. My mother gave me money for the check, and left the table to use the restroom. On her way back, I noticed her stooping in the alcove to unplug the yodeling reaper.

I began thinking of Carissa the next morning, after it became apparent the house was something my mother intended to sort out on her own. I awoke around midday in my grandfather's bedroom, beneath a painting of a circus clown weeping on a barrel. My mother had been up for hours, emptying drawers and bookcases, cleaving everything into two piles on the living room floor; one for donation and one to bring back to Vermont. When I came downstairs, she was weighing a bag of buttons in one hand, and legal pad in the other; my grandmother had written out sequential sets of instructions for nearly everything in the house, including the buttons. Decoding them was an impossible task. Relics lurked in every corner, their origins answered by photographs of my grandparents in North Africa, Red Square, the Galapagos Islands. They'd been everywhere; the house spoke to that.

The more places you go, the more difficult your life is to organize after you're gone, I thought, serving myself a cup of coffee in Woolworth's china from a percolator on the dining room table and nibbling a paczki from a bakery in Montclair; yes, my mother had been up early. I opened the liquor cabinet to see what was what and found bottles still in boxes from the duty-free. Is it too early to spritz some Rakia in my coffee? I wondered. And would my mother notice? A long day was beginning. I had no idea how to fortify myself.

After sifting through books, souvenirs, and boxes of photographs for several hours, my mother seemed to have absorbed the full burden of my grandmother's loneliness during the last years of her life. She survived the killing fields of Poland during WWII and escaped the Russian occupation afterward, before settling in France with my grandfather. Based on photographs I'd seen, these seemed like good years for the family. They immigrated when my mother was nine and my aunt was five to live in what is now a million dollar condominium in Jersey City across the street from Lincoln Park. When they moved in, it was a cold-water walk-up with a privy in the backyard. They bought the house in Nutley after my grandfather retired and traveled until he got sick. For my mother, the impersonality of my grandmother's death felt bathetic beside what she had lived through in order to die here, alone and angry, on the floor of her empty exurban house.

After finishing my coffee, I helped my mother load several boxes of books into the car, destined for a Polish community center in Passaic, and walked back inside to see if I could make myself useful without her around to direct traffic. Making sense of the clutter on my own seemed unlikely, but the rooms were beginning to show signs of anonymity. That felt like progress.

I managed to wait until around noon to get stoned in the backyard, rolling several joints in a row out of a large bag of weed Buck gave me as a type condolence before I left town, along with two books of puzzling short stories by Julio Cortazar, one of which, *A Change of Light*, was fractured over my knee as I puffed away in the shade of some kind of pine tree my grandmother had transplanted from a national park out west. The day was a tepid seventy degrees, the sky a buff monochrome, the sun wreathed in gauzy stratus. I tapped my ashes into the birdbath, and watched a pair of rabbits dishevel the remains of my grandmother's garden. Life seemed to be approaching a standstill and the house was still a disaster in situ. I wanted to project something other than remote bleariness when my mother returned from Passaic.

I left the yard with some vague idea about checking the mail, but walked in a pleasant fog to the end of the street instead, where some trees had been cleared from a small ridge to make space for power lines, and sat on a guardrail. A meadow of roofs, satellite dishes, and covered pools with beds of orange leaves undulating on aquamarine tarpaulin stretched below. Beyond this, the irregular delineation of New York City annexed the horizon. Before I had time to really think it through, my phone was pressed to my head and Carissa was on the line, sounding a bit nervous when I explained where I was, but inviting me to spend time with her later that evening anyway. I listened with a kind of clerical obedience as she dictated an address in Brooklyn and asked me to call her if I got lost.

I now have plans with a woman, I thought transparently as I walked back to the house, pleased with myself even if I couldn't locate the origin of my sudden decision to contact Carissa. We hadn't spoken much since she began attending the Pratt Institute and I had no clear idea what she studied there. I stopped calling on her birthday because it made me feel like a relative rather than a friend or whatever I'd become over the years, a nuisance, perhaps. Later, when I told Buck we talked frequently, I wanted to say I never had any real reason to call her except to find out how much we had grown apart.

My mother drove me to the PATH station in Hoboken after dinner without asking where I was going or what I was doing. She had other things on her mind. We'd spent the most of the afternoon dismantling the dining room and my presence was beginning to feel redundant. If I hadn't made plans, the possibility of my mother needing a break from me would have been upsetting. And later, as I exited the PATH station on Christopher Street and began heading in what I hoped was the general direction of Brooklyn, I realized this was the first time I had visited New York City without her and my father. Whenever we stayed with my grandmother, my parents usually took a day to get away from her and escape with me into the city. We'd take the ferry from Hoboken, a bus uptown from the terminal, and eat pretzels on the steps of the Met or at the base of the equestrian statue of Roosevelt outside the American Museum of Natural History. This rich, entirely closed experience constituted most of what I knew about New York, but even as I crossed Hudson Street, heading toward the river, I didn't want to admit I was lost. I expected to be able to see Brooklyn from where the street ended at the water, the way a man lost in the wilderness will climb a tree to gain better vantage. I realized I was looking at New Jersey when I noticed the ferry terminal I'd used many times with my parents across the water. As I crept back up the street, toward the interior of the city, I considered taking the train back toward something more familiar. I wasn't certain what I wanted from Carissa and my mind was too disorganized to figure it out.

By the time I crossed the river toward Brooklyn, I was nearly two hours late, which didn't seem to bother Carissa when I called her from the train over the Manhattan bridge. She gave me the address of a bar on Dekalb Avenue. She was there, which was good, with friends from her program, which was bad, or had the potential to be. She went to art school, so I assumed her friends were artists; studying history had left me suspicious of creativity, and somewhat awed by it, but I hoped we might all have something that wasn't alienating in common. As the train was subducted back beneath the earth, the sun began setting behind the parabolic rictus of the Brooklyn Bridge; a loopy, unsettling grin at dusk. I wanted New York City to make what I was doing feel important, but a brush with mediocrity seemed imminent.

I got lost again after leaving the subway station at Classon Avenue and wound up getting high by myself beside a large sculptural head on the Pratt campus — something by Philip Grausman Carissa told me later, as I sat beside her in a booth at the bar on Dekalb Avenue, trying to reinvent myself for her and the people we shared it with; two men, both painters, and one woman, some sort of performance artist. Our composite ratio troubled me, and the light in the bar made me feel like I was going blind. One of the men at our table was responsible for a painting on the wall above it and several others scattered around the room. I couldn't tell if this was an opening or if the paintings been there for some time. Either way, I figured my duty was to appreciate what I saw. Carissa hadn't seen me for four year and I wanted to seem vulnerable to whatever was important about her life in New York without making a bumpkin of myself.

"Nice paintings," I said, gesturing at the canvas above our table after Carissa seated me in a corner of the booth. The paintings were part of series and all of them appeared to be of someone who looked very much like her climbing apple trees in a short skirt without underwear. The overall effect landed somewhere between Adolf Koch and a comparative anatomy textbook.

"It's basically about how the higher you climb, the more you're exposed and objectified," said one of the painters, his eyes flitting over Carissa with an aspect of hunger. "I mean, as a woman. It's basically a feminist statement, but you could apply it to anyone. The idea of exposure and vulnerability, how we become weaker in the public eye as we ascend according to their standards, hoist ourselves out of the shared depths, the cultural gutters . . ."

"Pedestals are made to be toppled," I supplied, trying to helpful.

"I think the overall idea is that Rudolph and his vaginas have nowhere else to hide except behind a kind of thinking man's pornography," said Carissa, twirling her empty wineglass at the waiter, ordering another. "I mean, seriously, Rudy. How many hours did you make me stand on that fucking ladder for you?"

"Who's Rudolph?" I asked, glancing around me.

"I am," said Rudolph, the painter, looking like he either wanted to kiss Carissa or bite her face. "I think it's important not to give in to what attracts us without making an intellectual commitment to understand why."

"It's okay to just be a talented pervert," said Carissa, mildly.

"Apples, temptation," I said, feeling like I no longer had a place in the conversation.

"I don't need to defend myself or my work from you. You're just showing off for your friend," said Rudolph, patting himself down as he stood up from the table, withdrew a pack of cigarettes, and walk outsedide. I glanced around to see if any of this appeared unusual to anyone else, feeling a little like a yokel visiting the stock exchange, but glad I was worth showing off for, if that was what Carissa was up to.

"So you study war heroes or something?" said the other painter to me. Apparently, Carissa had made some effort to explain me to her friends before I arrived and hoped I wouldn't repay her by demonstrating exactly how narrow the domain of my studies had become. Essentially the distance between my bookshelf and front door of the shoebox I rented by the river back in Acheron. Let's get this over with, I thought.

"War doesn't have heroes, unless standards for heroics are drastically lowered," I said. The joint I'd smoked earlier by the statue appeared to be tugging me toward a litany. "Otherwise, it's like lighting a house on fire to rescue the people inside or patting yourself on the back for performing valorously in a dangerous situation that wouldn't be dangerous if you weren't part of it. War has figures. Full stop. Take, for example-"

"I'm not going to spend too much time trying to figure you out," he said, searching himself for cigarettes. I was two beers into what felt like a four beer evening and Carissa and I had already cleared out half the table. The odds for getting her alone looked good, even before Carissa's hand began combing my thigh beneath the table somewhere toward the middle of drink three. The conversation had left me behind, so I couldn't tell if she was trying to comfort or seduce me.

Possibly both, maybe neither, I thought, my attention locked on her profile, fixed in a nimbus of light from a sconce above the table. As she spoke with what remained of her friends, I scoured her face and body for what I knew was already there. Not a beautiful woman, I decided, assuring myself then as I would years later while watching her garden from the attic and nodding weirdly to the performance artist across the table as I confirmed this privately. But what right do I, or does anyone, have to expect beauty? I wondered, my mind in retrograde as I recalled the supple expression of her bones beneath the skin of her back as she slipped one foot through the loop of a rope swing, her features sharp and distracted, continually attending something off stage as Kranion Pond beckoned past the treeline and her hard, capable body suspended above it a moment later, black hair fanning cape-like above her broad shoulders as she plummeted evenly to the surface of water, the rope slapping wet against my hand as it swung back to Buck and me through the trees, where we waited for her on the ridge above the lake like two chamberlains. An image from the summer I came in last and a memory somewhat answered at the bar in Brooklyn when I saw how little she'd changed according to what I remembered. And from this, I thought, I somehow derived concupiscence. Beauty was never a benchmark. Knowing her was enough.

As we walked to her apartment after leaving the bar, I briefly wished Carissa had left me enough space to wonder what was going to happen next. Somewhere along the line, the element of anticipation had withered on the vine and here we were, overdue. Even after we kissed deeply beneath a sodium vapor security light on the Myrtle Avenue side of Fort Greene Park, I couldn't shake the sense of us as equally low-hanging fruit. I wanted to ask how long she'd wanted to do this with me, but managed to keep the question to myself, even after smoking some of Buck's weed with her at the base of the Prison Ship Martyrs' Monument. I didn't tell her he'd given it to me or why.

How many different ways do I need other people to confirm how much I matter? I asked myself later as we climbed the stairs to an apartment she shared with two other women, both not at home. She towed me through the kitchen toward her room at the end of the hall. The bed was the only surface not given up to the artsy feminine squalor in which Carissa led her life; tubes of paint oozed onto the carpet, glasses of muddy water barricaded the windowsill, and brushes stiffened beneath the radiator. Dresses, underwear, and high heels lay in irregular piles around the floor, as if Carissa's outfits had sprung off her body as soon as she walked into the room. Novels, textbooks, and library material had become a sort of furniture for withered houseplants, flaking cosmetics, and hirsute plates of incomplete meals. An easel supporting an ironical blank canvas protruded from a snarl of carpet like the mast of a ship soon to be lost at sea.

"Your friends seem nice," I said as we lay on the bed, wanting to draw the conversation away from the ruin where we were having it; mentioning the obvious is always impolite.

"His paintings were awful, weren't they?" she said, tilting a magnum of lukewarm Australian chardonnay against her lips, flourishing it toward the part of the room where she thought I was. The night had bumped along at pleasing, uncomplicated speed after I realized Carissa was probably taking me home from the bar and I wasn't entirely sure who she was talking about. The other faces around the table were tufts of animate shadow, waving treetops in the dark. I couldn't remember the paintings, or anything said about them.

"They didn't leave any impression on me," I said, verily.

"This is what I do most nights," she said, gesturing at either me or the room, I couldn't tell which. "Celebrate the shabby art people I know make. I think they keep making it so we all have an on-hand excuse to drink more than usual on a weeknight. We're all a little too old for Thirsty Thursdays. It's normal to have a few glasses of wine at an opening, right?"

"I'm the wrong person to ask," I said, my hand scuttling over her breasts; larger than I remembered, softer than I imagined. We kissed again and both took another sip of foul white wine. It felt like a toast.

"I'm think of moving to Portland," she said. I couldn't tell if this was part of the conversation we were having or entrée into a new one. I had never visited Portland, but I imagined it as a place where two thirds of the population is always on its way to a costume party. "Hypocrisy is a lifeway there. I think I'd fit in."

Our talk was roaming toward self-examination. How many half-smart people in their late twenties are having a form of this conversation right now? I wondered, undressing both Carissa and myself, our clothes joining the detritus on the floor as her hand fluttered to the bedside lamp, cloaking us in the near dark of the street beyond the window.

"You stopped calling on my birthday," she said, as our mouths separated for a moment. We lay side by side, slipping our hands over each other, exploring what we had passed over years ago.

"I didn't think it mattered," I said. "To you, I mean."

"You were my only friend who did that. When you stopped, I noticed."

Carissa slipped her leg under my hip, and locked the other around my back, her hands simultaneously tweaking both my nipples as she rolled her pelvis against mine. Urgency suddenly existed between us, a welcome change from whatever we'd been careening toward. Her breath was hoarse with smoke and humid with wine as she spoke.

"Please fuck me now, Oliver."

"I don't have a condom."

"I know you, it's okay."

I wanted whatever happened next to be joyful, but our bodies did not fit together the way I'd imagined. The vigor and consequence of a decade earlier was beyond recapture; we were strangers who knew each other once. Adulthood should have softened the part of my brain that still believed in pivotal moments; studying warfare likely kept it alive. And we hadn't spent much time catching up between the bar and her bedroom. Though I was fucking Carissa in a nest of clues, I still didn't know what she studied at school, or even how she'd spent the last four years in Brooklyn and the window for usefully applying this information had closed over an hour ago. Focus on what you're doing, I told myself, as Carissa quaked and shuddered beside me. Rather than on what you're not doing. Or haven't done. Or won't do at all.

A door opened, footsteps drummed in the hall, and another door closed. One of her roommates had arrived. A moment later, the opening bars of 'Make It Easy On Yourself' filtered through the thin wall between our rooms and Carissa began humming.

I didn't know what to make of that and decided I wouldn't spend too long trying to figure it out, but broke this promise fifteen minutes later as Carissa wheezed softly in bed beside me, and sirens wailed from the direction of Crown Heights. The roommate upshifted; 'I Gotta Dance to Keep from Crying' bleated next door, making sleep unlikely. I rooted through Carissa's purse until I found cigarettes, wrapped myself in a curtain, and stood by the window, tapping ashes in one of the befouled glasses along the sill, wondering if anyone passing below might look up and mistake me for a cutout of a man of the great wide world surveying his realm. I considered calling my mother and giving her an idea of where I was. She was the only person I knew who might care. But I'd left the bar on Dekalb Avenue around 1AM. Whatever time is was now, I hoped she was asleep and not still rooting through my grandmother's possessions. I checked my phone; no messages. Clearly, she wasn't worried.

Carissa had an early class and left a note apologizing for this and the lack of food in her apartment taped to the center of the blank canvas on her easel. She recommended a cafe down the street and said it was good to see me.

Carissa wants me to take myself out to breakfast after our

big night out on the town, I thought, trying to tamp down the bitterness of being left alone with myself once again while fishing my clothes out of the gutter beside the bed. In daylight, Carissa's room looked as if it had been abandoned in hurry and roughly searched afterward.

Even if her note hadn't urged me out the door, the roommates might have done the job. Two women around Carissa's age, a pretty brunette and a dumpy blond, neither with anything to do at 10AM on a Monday morning except watch me sip from a mason jar of tap water as I put my shoes on by the coatrack. A TV or radio was on somewhere in the apartment, though it appeared to interest neither of them. I tried to guess if their behavior meant Carissa often brought men to the apartment for them to study. Was I unusual in this context or only the most recent specimen of knee-jerk decision making? I caught myself once again scouring the commonplace for reasons to feel special and felt vaguely disgusted with the way I'd chosen to spend the past eighteen hours, even before I called my mother from a Q train stalled over the East River, with the Brooklyn Bridge once again grinning like the Cheshire Cat across the water, and asked her to pick me up in Hoboken.

She arrived outside the PATH terminal with the same weekend at the madhouse expression she'd had when my grandmother was alive. I figured she'd probably been talking to my aunt. My mother asked if I'd had a nice time, without asking what I'd been doing when I said I wasn't sure. She told me she'd found a donation bin by a gas station on Brookfield Avenue and had made so many trips there over the past ten hours that the Syrians who owned the place had started helping her unload the car. Her priorities were set in the moment and immovable; mine were generally amorphous and entirely occupied with the problem of who was lonelier; Carissa, or me?

Cattails nodded on either side of the road as we drove through the Meadowlands toward Nutley. My grandmother's house felt like a raided tomb. Things I'd spent my entire life looking at were gone. Closets were vacant. Shelves yawned. But the backyard still held a familiar shape. This is where I retreated with a bottle of Spaten I'd found in the back of the refrigerator and an album of photographs of my grandmother and her family in France, camping on the beach at Normandy after the war, riding a motorized scooter around the village where they lived. I hoped showing respect and interest for this self-evident material would appease the potentially restless spirit of my grandmother and excuse me for having abandoned my grieving mother to the empty house and the Cassandra-like spookiness of my aunt.

I had some lingering questions for Carissa, but wasn't sure I wanted answers and calling her was out of the question. She appeared to be leading a rich, indeliberate life in New York. I'd managed to shoehorn myself into it for an evening, but her note made it clear any longer would have been an interference. I decided I would feel fine if we never saw each other again. I remembered this moment years later, watching her garden from the attic in the house she shared with Buck, remembering what believing I wasn't in love with her felt like, and relying on time and distance to excuse me from the responsibility of my unclear emotions. A good strategy, I thought. If she and I hadn't moved in with Buck a year later, it might have worked.

*　　*　　*

Since I couldn't hate Buck, I settled for cultivating distance between myself and the house on Winter Street after the night we discussed Carissa on his porch. This felt like practice for the future. I wanted to avoid reliving what I'd come to think of as my adolescent heart of darkness or the journey into the part of myself I like the least over the long summer on Kranion Pond. Carissa's return seemed like an advent of some kind, the incorporeal hand of our compound history circling back to swat me in the groin. People who self-mythologize are usually creeps, but I was beginning to wonder if I wasn't one of them. The possibility troubled me; did my inability to view my past without being either afraid or ashamed of myself mean some essential part of me was still fifteen years old? I looked at the loneliness I felt then and compared it to what I felt now. Was there a difference? Absolutely. Did it matter? Not much, as it turned out.

I spent most of the next week sitting in a sun-bleached director's chair beside a stretch of the Wendigo River fronting my yard, trying to distract myself from thoughts like these with the books Buck gave me. *The Songlines* lay open in my lap; I envied Bruce Chatwin's mobility. When he wanted to escape, he ended up living with nomads in the Sahara, buying them goats with publishing advances. When I wanted to escape, I hung out with myself in the backyard, reading about him.

My bare feet rested on a cooler filled with Polar seltzer and Champlain Boathouse Ale and I wore nothing except a pair of paint-stained Carhartt cutoffs. When the sun grew overwhelming, I removed these and slipped into the river, paddling naked out to a sandbar splitting the current to stare at the green wall of Maybrick Peak in the near distance. My closest neighbors were a quarter mile away, hidden from view by a crabapple orchard and the collapsed remains of a hay barn. The only people I saw bobbed past in inner tubes or slid along the rushing surface in canoes or kayaks. Overnight, my life had become one long Labor Day weekend.

At high noon, a garter snake the length of a bicycle chain emerged from a rock wall dividing the property and sunned itself at my feet on a contoured slab of sandstone. This made me feel a bit like a demigod. I was enjoying this feeling and watching the snake, curious if there was a way to tell whether it was a boy or a girl without bothering it, when I heard pebbles popping beneath the tires of a car as it turned from the main road into my driveway. A high-performance engine purred to a halt, a door opened and closed, footsteps mashed gravel.

I wasn't at my best; I knew that. But I wasn't expecting company either, so if whoever it was knew me well enough to drop-in unannounced, they'd likely pardon whatever I'd become over the past week. I was briefly terrified it might be my parents, dropping by to see how unemployment was treating me, but as Carissa turned the corner of the house and spotted me on the riverbank I felt the degenerate equipoise of the past week shift into a lower gear. She crossed the lawn on slim white legs retreating into the frayed cuffs of her shorts, cutoff black Carhartts like mine, a sort of uniform around Acheron, her black hair gathered beneath a leaf-print mesh baseball cap, and her broad torso sheathed in a sleeveless white t-shirt with a Disrupt logo crookedly screen-printed across the chest. I remembered her buying it at a show in someone's barn down in Warren, watching her from the top of a mini ramp beside the stage as she negotiated the price with an older guy running the table, his cheekbones veined with blue-green ink like the open page of a road atlas leading nowhere. She must have done some deep digging through the closets at her parent's house to turn that up. I never expected to see it again.

"You're not who I was expecting," I said, as we embraced midway between the house and the river.

"Who were you expecting?"

"Well, no one, now that you mention it," I said, catching my reflection in the kitchen window. Haircut needed.

"You look good," she said, surprising me. I'd been drinking a lot of beer, but had taken to walking the mile and a half into town to go buy it and was tan from this and doing nothing out in the sun all day. Swimming in the river had toned me enough to make it look like I cared more about myself then I actually did. In any case, she looked better.

"I'm so glad you're here," I said, over my shoulder as I removed a second chair from beside the fire pit Buck and I had dug last summer and dragged it toward the river. I meant it, in a way. I'd been spending a lot of time alone and I could sense it making me weirder than I was comfortable with. And the possibility of seeing Carissa without Buck around hadn't occurred to me when we discussed her moving back. I wondered if I'd misjudged the situation and hoped I had. Whatever happens next may be complicated, I warned myself. Consider: lowering the ante, trying to have fun.

"It was time to come back," she said, her gray eyes suggesting something vestigial and immoderate from beneath the brim of her hat as she settled in beside me on the bank. I showed her my snake and she removed her t-shirt, adjusting the bikini top underneath as I fished around in the ice water in the bottom of the cooler for a beer, fencing with the urge to dump the entire thing over my head as kind of reset. Things appeared to be moving forward despite the small effort I'd made to keep them in limbo. An argosy of wood ducks gave me something to comment upon as they glided past.

"Those ducks," I said, like we all knew each other. As I sat down, I noticed my pubic hair tufting over the crest of my cut-offs, and hoped this was sexy because there was no way to hide it. "When did you get in?"

"This morning," said Carissa, arching her back over the flimsy, canvas rest, stomach taught, breasts aloft. "Left Brooklyn around 3AM, dropped the van at Buck's place, and took his truck up to my parent's house to get a few things."

"How are they?" I asked as a kind of placeholder. "I see your dad sometimes around town. Not your mom, oddly."

"We had brunch. Dad made eggs benedict. They seem disappointed I'm not staying with them until I get a job. But they're both retired. I imagined us all hanging around the house each morning, in no real hurry. Sounded too much like living with Chelsea and Astrid."

"I don't think I know them."

"They were there when you visited, in the morning. They said they saw you."

"We didn't introduce ourselves."

"They're both narcissists trolling the back-channels of the bar scene in Cobble Hill for men to get them pregnant. Their euphemism for this is: being an actress. Doesn't matter. Buck has space and things to do. It's a better arrangement."

"When I heard you were coming back, I thought of asking you to stay with me," I said, cooking this up on the spot. The conversation was drifting toward neutrality and I wanted to remain relevant.

"You have no space," she said, eyeing the house over her shoulder, or cabin really. A studio with a river view, in realty speak. Her gaze returned to me. "And clearly nothing to do."

"I'm between important things," I said, wondering if this might be a good time to give Carissa a tour of the Potemkin village I'd erected around my thesis, but a quick scan of the yard turned up no signs of Belisarius. Inside the house wasn't much better. I'd given most of the smart, conflict-oriented books I owned to Buck a few weeks ago and a tonnage of jaundiced mystery paperbacks, their print raised and flaking, was all that remained. Warfare had anchored my library; I saw it now. Without Willaim Shirer or Michael Herr to hide behind, my shelves looked like they belonged to someone who came by most of what he read at the airport. I didn't want Carissa to see the same thing. "And I'd give you a tour, but I think you've seen most of what's relevant."

"Relevant to what?"

"I don't know what I mean, Carissa. I wasn't expecting to have you here today."

"I know that. Buck said he told you I wouldn't be here for a few weeks. But I managed to offload my lease on a member of Astrid's coven. And New York in June is like a city preparing for war."

"Ragusa on the march."

"I had no reason to still be there, Oliver. Discovering that sucked."

"I wondered if something changed for you. It sounded like something did from what Buck told me."

"I don't know if anything changed. But when I got into town this morning, I realized I knew my time in New York was over when you visited me last year. I thought my life was impressive. You were unmoved."

"It was a messy weekend for me, Carissa," I said, filling space. I appeared to have some power over whatever we were talking about, but no idea how to use it. "I was far from home and wanted to be comfortable."

"I wish you'd told me that. After you left I couldn't see why you'd come in the first place. When you called, I thought you wanted to catch up. But we didn't really do that. I wanted you to call again and explain it. But you didn't."

"I called you on your birthday."

"I can't remember what we talked about."

"I can't either," I said, echoing her diffidence. This wasn't true; I remembered the conversation perfectly. But I was trying to grope my way along the bow of our current conversation without scuttling the possibility of her staying the night in my cabin. We seemed to be moving in that direction; our joint narrative began shaping itself into something with possibilities, the kind I hadn't considered when talking about all this with Buck, or speaking with Carissa on her thirtieth birthday. What did I learn from our colloquy? She was rounding the bend on an MFA in painting and writing a thesis on Franz Marc, a person I had never heard of. I tried to conceal this from her during the phone call, and was relieved when she began telling me about her job as a receptionist at a midtown yoga studio across the street from Bryant Park. The clients were all lonely, affluent, metropolitan psychopaths who looked like they spent the interim between classes gnawing the tatami mats in the dressing room. She told stories about them, and I listened, embarrassed by how little I knew about making or understanding art. The physical evidence of creativity occupied the center of her academic life the way the passionate destruction of it and more sat at the bull's-eye of my own and as she spoke about Marc, I felt as if I'd entered the kind of specialized company I was too ignorant to appreciate. I couldn't imagine her wasting her passion on me and decided the distance between our lives was probably a good thing. Still, after she hung up, I walked to the Acheron Free Library, checked out a book of Marc's paintings, and studied them in a bar all afternoon, glad to have found something I couldn't relate to intellectually. The sensual contour of Marc's blue horses and the sly geometry of his foxes soothed the part of me left feeling like a default philistine after our conversation. Perhaps Carissa will continue to expose me to new things I appreciate, I thought then. If not, I had one less subject I needed to avoid the next time we spoke. This turned out to be the afternoon she appeared in my yard.

"I was glad you called anyway," said Carissa, levering one foot into the river, the nails painted an unfussy, terrestrial green, and stirring it amid the shallows. "After we talked, I began noticing everyone I met in New York was fleeing something. But I didn't know what I was running away from and that bothered me. When I saw you in Brooklyn, I envied whatever you were going back to even though I didn't know exactly what it was. So, when I got in this morning, I figured why not come up here and see how you're living?"

"Not much to look at," I said, gesturing at the foreground and a little bit of myself. "But the truth is that no other way of living occurs to me."

"Well, Buck didn't know what you were up to whenever we talked. And I was curious," she said, her green eyes sweeping the property with an eerie specificity, as if seeking something to paint. "I like what you have here. It's comfortable. I want to be comfortable, too."

I hoped we'd reach a point where the conversation between us would become less expository and self-referential, but as the day began ebbing toward evening, I realized this was unlikely. Carissa had been through many recent transitions and seemed to be in an examination phase. It's impossible for people to think they've changed without talking about it, I thought to myself while I mostly listened, worrying I'd become a caricature or personage to Carissa during the apparently crucial period of self-work prefiguring her choice to leave Brooklyn. New York City, she'd decided, was not a very nice place to live. Even as a child shuttled through the uptown museum circuit by my parents, I'd reached a similar conclusion. I'd never visited a place so needlessly threatening. The city always seemed to be trying to outdistance its own menace. Carissa was tired of living under the aegis of Brooklyn beta-male arrogance, she said, and the reckless, a priori chauvinism of people who believed they were lucky to live there and smarter because of it. I didn't understand this particular point at all, but was tired of having to appear as if what she said was new to me and suggested dinner as a kind of compromise. It seemed about time. Willows genuflected toward the river as we sat in the long shadow of Maybrick Peak. The feeling of being a stage presence in Carissa's life wasn't going anywhere, but her decision to make me part of a pivotal moment felt dehumanizing. I was a sexless cog buried in the clockwork of her choice to leave New York.

An epiphany can occlude as many things as it clears away, I thought, as we left our chairs and walked toward the house. Carissa mistook my suggestion of dinner for an invitation to eat out somewhere in town. She noticed an Ethiopian restaurant on State Street and asked if I'd been there, and when I said I had, she asked if the food was any good. The question stumped me. I knew the family who owned the restaurant as well as I could without actually trying their cooking. When they opened the place last winter, I'd spent most of Christmas break tucked into a serviceable bar in the rear of the dining room, drinking tej, a type of honeyed mead the owner made in the basement and served in what looked like a volumetric flask. This was called a berele, I learned later. The front of the house staff may have thought I was depressed, when in fact, I was glad, grateful even, to find a place to have a drink after work where I wouldn't see anyone from the grocery store. Even so, the wait staff occasionally brought me desserts they needed to get rid of at the end of the night, cups of coconut crème brule or wedges of baklava, things I hadn't asked for but was weirdly touched by and uncomfortable receiving. The entrees leaving the kitchen as I sat at the bar smelled and looked delicious and I was on the verge of telling Carissa this, but made a joke instead about how most people in Acheron hadn't gotten used to having the U.N. drop their dinner order through the ceiling and retreated inside to see if I actually had anything to feed her.

Things picked up a bit as we prepared the rudiments of a meal together. A balmy wind blew through the kitchen window, rustling the pages of lowbrow books stacked against the wall at our feet and mingling the sunned, riverine odor of our bodies as she sautéed Brussels sprouts and garlic in olive oil and I rolled some trout filets in sesame seeds and red pepper flakes. The fish had been in my freezer since March, an ice fishing catch a friend of Dr. Norman's had given me as payment for tutoring his son, and I hoped eating it wouldn't kill us both, but was willing to take the risk for the fine meal Carissa and I were stumbling toward. I didn't know anything about wine, but had several bottles Grover assured me were good mellowing in a box by the front door, a kind of severance package from earlier in the month. Carissa fussed over it when I asked her to select something to go with the meal, choosing some kind of Riesling and pouring us each a generous glass as we plated the food.

"I knew this was how you must live even if I didn't know it," she said, plinking her Mason jar against mine. I didn't own wine glasses. She looked almost beatific and song-ready, like an actress in a musical. "I'm reconsidering your offer to bunk up."

"All yours," I said, trying to include myself in the gesture I swept toward the single room in which I made my home, the unmade, narrow bed, the acrylic, faux-Persian carpet I'd taken from my grandmother's house, and the single wheeled chair in cracked green leather drifting like a carelessly tied dingy from the bollard of a writing desk beneath the living room window. This was the only furniture that suggested a table. There wasn't even a second place to sit unless we went outside. I live like I'm recently paroled, I thought, watching her long-boned, heavily beautiful face assess the situation, glad she had found something in it to idealize. We weren't drunk, but we'd had enough to drink to make knocking into each other while we prepared dinner in my tiny kitchen seem prefatory and familiar. At one point, I'd cupped her hip like the cap of a newel post while skirting around her to reach the stove and felt her pelvis incline slightly, enough to make the pragmatic side of me glad I hadn't bothered to put on a shirt. Love didn't cross my mind, but we seemed to have made each other happy in a short period of time. She believed whatever chased her out of New York wouldn't find her here and I was happy to support this notion if it meant I wouldn't continue being alone.

We carried our plates outside and ate in the day's last light with our feet and the wine cooling against the river bottom, watching a family of deer grazing in the meadow across the water. I'd dragged my speakers to the kitchen window and put on a Weston record, melodic punk rock with a doo-wop component, a band we'd discovered together shortly after I got my driver's license. I remembered the afternoon we'd spent in Burlington, rooting around the music shops off Church Street before meeting Buck at a show in Winooski. We had our war paint on; Carissa in a studded leather jacket with a Mob-47 logo painted on the back, a miniskirt made of band patches, her black hair bleached an off-white and spiked into an urchin-like configuration with gelatin. I wore a black denim vest with a Nausea back patch bristling with conical studs, a Misery t-shirt, and black jeans smelling vaguely of the mint-impregnated dental floss I'd use to peg them, something my dentist gave during my last check-up. The uniforms of our unfixed dissent made no secret of what we thought we believed in or the kind of maximalist aesthetic that spoke to us. People looked at us. We enjoyed it. What I remember most from the day was listening to *Got Beat Up* in my car on the way to meet Buck in Winooski and later that night, after the band didn't show up. As he and Carissa went back to Acheron in his car, I drove home to my parents house outside Montpelier, glad to be alone because it meant I could sing along with songs like 'Retarded' or 'Teenage Love Affair' or 'Heather Lewis' without feeling embarrassed and commune with the desperate part of myself feeding off the close memory of the afternoon with Carissa. Everyone assumed we were a couple when Buck wasn't around. They said we looked right together. Our outfits even matched. Wasn't that enough? Though I grew into my shallowness as an adult, I wanted to believe this was the most superficial I'd ever be. And later, when the three of us lived together, I recognized this memorial, adolescent longing returning as I lingered in the hammock on the porch, waiting for her to get home from work and put on her bikini.

"I spent years not doing anything like this," said Carissa, shelving her plate on a stump, and pouring more wine into her jar. "I wish you'd told me what I was missing when you visited."

"I mistook you maybe for someone who had everything she wanted," I said, liking the sound of this, wondering if it was true. I tried to reanimate the memory of our night together in Brooklyn and remember what I felt; mostly nothing with an underpinning of grief for grandmother, but I wasn't going to share that. "I didn't think I had a place in anything you were doing, so the opposite was probably also true."

"I'm sorry we had sex," she said, abruptly, startling me. I'd made the mistake of assuming this wasn't going to come up. "Or I'm sorry if it made you feel useful in a bad way. I wanted to feel close to someone who remembered me for longer than a couple years. People I knew in New York were starting to get married. Everyone around me was a bridesmaid or part of a wedding party. No one ever asked me to do that for them. But I always thought you would whenever you found someone to marry. It was a small, weird comfort for me to remember that you remembered me."

"I never get invited to those things either, Carissa. If I had one, I'd want you there. But I don't see it happening. I've been alone for a while," I said, trying not to sound as if I was proud of this or didn't expect it to change. The average woman my age in Acheron had a nose ring, a degree in something I knew nothing about, and HPV, not an unworkable, or even unwelcome state of things. I didn't want to date myself and I sometimes worried I'd been doing it accidently for years. I had a defined urge to have my heart broken as an adult for the experience of it and had been wondering lately if there wasn't something about me preventing the women I saw from getting the job done. They usually mentioned my niceness and predictability after we agreed to remain friends, so I'd learned to treat the sense of comfort Carissa seemed to crave as a kind of envoi. If things end before they begin, I wondered, do they still exist in a way that might benefit me?

"I wish you weren't alone," said Carissa, brushing the back of my hand with her fingers, not taking it. "You should have someone steady to share your shack with."

"I'm not expecting much to happen until the marriages of the couples I know who met in college begin to dissolve," I said, trying to be funny again. "We're all in our thirties. It should begin any day now. When it does, I'll be there with my eye to the keyhole, scratching to be let in."

"When you say awful things about yourself, do you believe them?"

"I don't know. I think I say them to see if other people do."

"I bet most of the engaged couples we know haven't known each other as long as we have."

"So let's get married," I said, slurring a bit, but essentially aware that I was living through the result of a spell I'd cast over the evening just by showing up and doing what I would have done anyway. The dinner was nicer and the wine was open; all other details remained the same. I didn't have much else to show for myself, but neither did she and I hoped we were both equally impatient for something to begin, if it was going to. Could we fall in love this way? I wondered, as an engine coughed on the road behind us and frogs belched along the water's meridian. Carissa's foot nudged mine beneath the river's surface, a non-answer.

"Maybe we should wait until we're both not afraid of being alone," she suggested. I couldn't tell whether or not she meant it.

"I'm not afraid of being alone. Just tired of it."

"You know, after you visited, I imagined being pregnant and calling you to tell you about it. I wanted to know what you would say."

"Rearranging my life because of stuff I can't avoid always irritates me. But I think I would have been basically fine with it."

"I think I hoped you would invite me to come back here."

"That would have been the first condition of carrying my child."

"I've probably had too much to drink," she said, drawing the edge of a green-bladed fingernail down my sternum, an unzipping motion. "I'm not sure if you're saying the right things the wrong way or the other way around, Oliver."

"Let's get married and find out," I said. This was fun, dangerous talk. She adjusted her bikini top, testing the possibility of removing it, I imagined and hoped. Her hand continued to travel the raw peninsula of bone above my heart.

"Stop," she said, meaning the opposite.

"Small wedding. We won't invite anyone who didn't invite us. Long honeymoon."

"Stop it, Oliver."

"We'll try new things. Have a baby. Travel to exotic places with it. Make sure it learns a second language."

"Please. Enough."

"French lessons. Cello lessons. Imagine Bach's G major suite played by someone who came out of your body. Our first house will have a minimum of ten acres and things wrong with it. You'll garden. I'll cook. Our child will dance naked around a bonfire."

"I am," she began, her voice suddenly hoarse, her eyes serious and milky beneath the brim of her cap, "so wet right now. I don't think I can keep listening to you."

The distance between us closed as the bell above town hall struck 9 and redounded off the wall of the valley cupping Acheron, finding us on the riverbank lurching out of our seats, toward timelessness. I have reached the center of a labyrinth, I thought, as Carissa's fingers slipped beneath my waistband, tugging it like a dog's collar. Her mouth hung partially open, her bottom lip slightly jutted, her hot, vinous breath pillowed against my face. She said something vulgar and open-ended as I coiled my fingers in the black hair piled beneath her hat, rolling her jaw to a mantel of stars just beginning to show above the trees. She repeated herself, louder, skyward, and her eyes sank to mine. The channel between us remained open; we wanted to look at each other more than we wanted to kiss.

This distinction turned out to be important, because it gave me time to realize I was marching blindly toward something I might regret later. I suspected I was only supplying Carissa with a temporary idea of what she wanted out of all this, allowing her to expediently reinvent herself through a specious characterization of me as someone who had something vital figured out. How long can I maintain this falsehood before we both end up disappointed? I wondered, as she popped the top button of my cutoffs with a kind of flourish. I didn't fear emotional pain so much as emotional mediocrity and worried about once again finding myself at its nucleus. Except for things Carissa would get used to, I had nothing to offer her. And beyond an appreciation of my shabby lifestyle, what did she have to offer me? Admitting I didn't know her well enough anymore to answer this question deepened my suspicion of how easily everything had happened, though I was comforted by the possibility of us both being equally vulnerable to bad ideas. I tried settling into the role Carissa had prepared for me: I am a debased hillbilly scholar, I told myself, cupping her left breast. And tonight I will ravish a nubile city mouse in my rustic hermitage beside the river.

Within this shtick, I sensed the opportunity to become a person I didn't like very much, but was oddly fine embracing it. If love is indeed around the corner, I should practice compromising, I thought, as my eyes travelled from Carissa writhing beneath my hand, searching the dim apron of sand and grass around us for something to spoil the evening and found the outline of an average man half-revealed in the cabin's porch light, the creak of his utility belt, and the glimmer of a badge on his chest as he crossed the dusky lawn toward the riverbank.

Officer Roland, Acheron Sheriff's Department; I didn't hear the cruiser pull up.

"Evening, Oliver," he said, and, after noticing Carissa: "Ma'am."

"Ma'am?" she said.

"Roland," I replied, thinking: I will never want to kill a man more than I do right now, as we shook hands and instantly feeling bad about it. I knew Officer Roland from around town as a mild, gentle policeman who everyone always expected to join the seminary. We'd also spent some time together in a Byzantine art class as undergraduates at Acheron College. I remembered presenting on the Arian baptistery in Ravenna and being distracted by how closely he resembled the unthreatening, hermaphroditic mosaic portrait of Jesus in the church's ceiling. Before I quit my job, I sometimes ran into him at the grocery store, his coxcomb of red hair nodding over a library copy of Herodotus or Ovid as he waited with his cart in the checkout line, absorbed, in full uniform. Nothing offensive about him existed and knowing this made me feel cornered in every interaction we had, as if I was always on the verge of establishing myself as a truly bad person.

"I didn't mean to bother you both or interrupt your dinner," said Roland, intuition ticking in his eyes as they took in the dirty plates, empty bottles, Carissa's loosened bikini top. "But I was passing by, Oliver, and it occurred to me that --"

"Do you not recognize me?" asked Carissa, shifting in her chair to face him. Roland squinted, clearly uncomfortable having to figure out who he was talking to.

"Maybe I do," he said, seeming to brighten. "Carissa, right? When did you get back into town? I don't think I've seen you since high school."

"This morning," she said, looking almost disappointed to be

so easily recognized. "From New York. I'm back here now. For good, I think. I hope, at least."

"I heard you were in Brooklyn," said Officer Roland. "Though I can't remember what you were doing there. Someone may have said painting."

"You could call it that," replied Carissa. Apparently, Roland knew more about her life than I did until recently. How could that have happened? I retreated into my chair, watching the benign movement of the river in the early moonlight and listening to the sound of them catching up, talking about people they both knew and I didn't. I felt like I was on a break of some kind, glad not to be of service for a moment, curious what Officer Roland wanted, but not worried about it. Like most people who have never been in trouble, I didn't expect to be and when I felt his cool hand on my shoulder, it seemed apologetic, urging me back to whatever he'd interrupted by dropping by.

"Listen, Oliver," he said. "Could we speak privately?"

"About what?"

"Why don't you walk me back to my car? We can talk about it."

"We all know each other," I began, hoping Carissa would see my choice to include her in whatever happened next as a step forward for both of us. Her eyes glittered curiously. "Whatever you need to say, you can say right here."

"Well, if that's what you'd prefer," said Officer Roland, hesitant, puzzled, probably ready to go home. "We've had some complaints filed downtown. People out on the river for the day have been seeing a young, naked guy hanging out on a sandbar. Some people were upset by it. A few had kids with them. But most of them seemed worried the guy was a little off and he might need help."

"You think it was me?" I said, hollowly, trying to remember how many times over the past week I'd fallen asleep naked after swimming out to the sandbar. Uncountable. At least daily. The chance of someone having a problem with it never occurred to me.

"I don't think anything, Oliver," said Officer Roland. "But I told Sheriff Blivet I'd address the complaints. Aside from that elderly couple across the meadow, you're the only person living on this particular stretch of river, so I have to talk to you. We also have a description of the naked sunbather. Do you want me to share it with you?"

"No thanks."

"It's vague enough to be kind of redundant anyway."

"So he could still be out there?"

"I also wanted to make sure you're okay, Oliver," said Officer Roland, ignoring me. "I need to know if you think you need help. If you do, please tell me and I will help you."

"You're doing a welfare check on me."

"People just reported what they saw. I'm responding to it. Please don't assume this is personal. Most of them were from out of state."

"Most of them?"

"Unless you want to admit to something, I can't really tell you any more about it."

"Well, thanks for letting me know there's a pervert on the loose," I said miserably, trying to gauge whether or not the dim outline of myself scowling back at me from the river's surface resembled any of the pictures of sex offenders I'd seen on the bulletin board at the town post office. Most of them needed haircuts too. "Thanks for dropping by, Roland."

"I'm afraid this is my duty," he said, sounding reflective. "I sometimes hate my duty."

A tangle of pubic hair still reared over the crest of my shorts as I walked Officer Roland to his cruiser, trying to reassure him I wouldn't continue spooking the tourists without admitting anything. He thanked me for my patience, looking embarrassed and sad, but made a roundabout effort to let me know I wasn't in trouble without actually accusing me of a crime. It was a weird conversation, most of it hidden from view. Carissa had followed me to the driveway to say goodnight to Officer Roland and I hoped the implications of it would escape her. But when I looked at her for the first time since he'd arrived, standing in the vermillion halation of his taillights as the cruiser eased onto the road, I knew the spell was broken. Urgency had abandoned us and our frenzy was at an end. Everything had suddenly become too real. I wanted to blame Officer Roland for this, but he was only the man who bumped the pedestal, not the person who put something on it to admire. A tourist. Nothing to be done about him. Meanwhile: I was a frequently naked mental defective who lived alone in a rural shack filled with books about violence. I would understand if Carissa no longer wanted to sleep over.

"It's late," she said and I mostly agreed, though it was only 9:30. I knew what she meant. The quicksilver outline of her father's BMW hooted as she tapped a button on a ring of keys held below her waist and out of sight. The car was expensive and new; I recalled a point when borrowing it would have embarrassed Carissa. The summer before she left for college, she'd worked unnecessarily hard waiting tables at the Herrenhof Inn to pay her own passage to New York, refusing to take her parent's money for reasons held over from the time when she and I and Buck spent weekends flirting with the patchy ideology of gutter life. Even then, I never understood her reaction to her parent's money. Her father was a cardiologist and her mother worked on the administrative end of pediatrics at Central Vermont Hospital. Carissa acted as if they were war profiteers. And her parents were comfortable, happy people, amused by their daughter's indignant reaction to the prosperity they'd cultivated around her, like people watching a new pet find its way around the house for the first time. Buck and I also seemed to amuse them whenever we visited their home, a rehabbed New England cape sunk in the Mt. Abandon foothills outside town. Though Carissa tried to keep us from hanging around her house, we still spent enough time up there to be regular dinner guests. Her parents were curious about her friends and were probably glad to see we shared their daughter's inability to escape our respective middleclass upbringing. Buck and I unlaced our muddy jackboots by the door and removed our patched vests before sitting at the dining table so the studs wouldn't scratch the finish on the chairs. Costumes were what they were; our manners betrayed us. Her mother surveyed Buck and me from the island in the kitchen as we loaded the dishwasher in socks and bullet belts, her hands joined around the stem of a wineglass, chatting to us ironically about how nice it was to have two young revolutionaries to clear the table and offering us dessert. After dinner, her father sometimes played Clash albums from the vast library of vinyl he collected as a hobby and tried to parse Strummer's lyrics for us, since neither Buck nor I were alive when most of what made the songs important took place. Buck once played him a Spazz record. Carissa's father said it sounded like redneck jazz and asked to hear more. Buck still went up there occasionally to have dinner with them, play records, and drink wine. I'd been invited along more than once and declined, fearing awkwardness without Carissa nearby to contextualize me. I was also afraid her mother or father would ask what I was doing and I'd tell a lie they found interesting enough to expect a follow up. Buck never worried about appearing in the proper context and didn't have to deceive anyone to be interesting. When propped beside him, I imagined it would be easy for Carissa's parents to see how little I'd matured over the years. Avoiding dinner with them altogether was also a symptom of immaturity, but seemed like the less rigorous of two bad options. Dr. Norman had tricked me into associating the ability to make this distinction with victory. But as I watched Carissa prepare to depart, I only wondered if trying to convince her to stay rather than letting her go would lead to a less robust stalemate and tried to focus instead on living with whatever happened next.

"I'm sunburnt," she said, and yes, her arms were dry and hot around my neck as she hugged me farewell. A faint beachside odor clung to her. "And very tired. I haven't slept for thirty-six hours."

"Should you be driving?" I asked, hoping I didn't sound like an older brother and wondering if I could leverage myself back into captaincy of the evening's outcome by swiping her car keys.

"I think I should be more worried about you," she said, unclasping and stepping back. Her voice was uninflected and it was too dark to know if this was a joke.

"You don't owe me anything, Carissa," I said, struggling not to sound used to this kind of thing or made bitter by it. "If you changed your mind about something just now, you don't have to pretend it's because you're worried I'm living up here like some kind of maniac. You can just change your mind."

"In New York . . ." she began, but trailed off, reconsidering. Then: "I need to remember how bad my instincts are, Oliver."

"I'm not whoever you're talking about."

"It's not about you; I really love you a lot."

"Then come inside. I have an Aloe vera plant and more wine. We can listen to 'Heather Lewis.' "

"That sounds so good, great even," she said, stepping forward, keys jingling, lips pressing the corner of my mouth, and then retreating once again. "But maybe too familiar. Part of moving home was about me promising myself I wouldn't crawl back into the womb."

"What's wrong with my womb?"

"Is that a real question, Oliver?"

"I think so."

"I'll try to come back up here and explain it to you when I have some sleep," she said. It sounded like sleep meant at least two things to her. I wanted a second departure kiss or something else to happen, something to clarify whether I was being rejected or forborne. A door opened and closed, the car hummed to life, the headlights capturing me for a moment, standing beside my shack like something out of a German fairy tale before Carissa angled the BMW onto the road and darkness reclaimed the property. I walked back to the river to gather the dinner plates and finish the wine, less depressed than I probably should have been. Whatever self-work Carissa was in the midst of had nothing to do with me, but I sensed her time in New York had left her with clever ideas about sexuality. Would I be a victim of whatever these were? Or was I already? Imagining the artsy kennel of unstable, bottom-fed men she probably wasted her time with in Brooklyn made me feel better. I was nothing like these fictional people. Good for me. At least one of them had left a mark. That was obvious. If he'd lowered her expectations enough, it was probably safe to just be myself. I tried to define the boundaries of this person to prove they weren't fictional as well and arrived at: kind, patient, and available without getting much further. Is that was Carissa saw? I asked myself as I bent to fish the wine bottle out of the shallows. No way to tell. I'd try to find a way to ask for an explanation without inviting her to judge me when she visited again.

It took me another week of fiddling around in the yard and paddling in the river to realize Carissa would not return to explain anything and whatever her visit had been about was over. The mail came; I listened to the sound of carrier pulling away on the road, warning myself against associating it with disappointment. Nothing had gone right with Carissa, but nothing had gone wrong either. The scene remained set as I idled in neutral: A stack of Eric Ambler's novels arranged on a stump beside my director's chair. The cooler under my feet freshly stocked. The river beckoned. But the hold most of this had on my daily life had slackened. If swimming meant going up to the house to change into a suit so people floating past wouldn't call the police to come check on me, I'd rather cede the river to them for the time being and set an example of minding my own business on dry land. The beer seemed to be buttressing my sangfroid rather than pleasantly clouding my attention and the spy stories I read ran together, clotting into a bolus of dissociative dread, like a dribbling comic strip raincloud blooming above my head. I knew I'd read something to make me paranoid, but had no idea what it was. And the snake never returned. I began to think of it as an omen.

I hadn't seen Buck for almost two weeks and was glad he didn't mention this when he called on Thursday morning. After the evening with Carissa, avoiding him and the house on Winter Street made more sense than it had before, but solitude was beginning to feel like a general state of affairs rather than an option for me. I didn't have enough close friends to make hiding from them seem eccentric and was beginning to feel like my presence in Acheron was only noticeable when I did something weird. Unemployment was getting the better of me. I knew that. Except for mealtimes and beer runs, I didn't have much to order my life around without visiting Buck in the evening. And even if he and Carissa were living in the same house now, I'd have to face whatever that meant eventually if I wanted to avoid becoming the sort of person Officer Roland needed to check on.

The call was brief. Buck bought out an estate sale in Randolph and wanted help loading the books into his truck and company during the drive. I'd been planning on visiting my parents over the weekend and he said he didn't mind dropping me off in Montpelier on the way back. An hour later, we passed the Middlesex exit on I-89, the moist wind roaring in the cab of the pickup and a paisley handkerchief cossetting a wedge of jalapeño smoked gouda and a bag of dried prunes spread on the bench seat between us. So far, Carissa hadn't come up in conversation.

"I'm glad you were around to help me out with this," said Buck, the inchoate character lines beside his eyes puckering against the glare as he slid a hand beneath the visor, searching for a pair of sunglasses hung by one leg from the collar of his t-shirt. I pointed this out and he thanked me. "I didn't want to spend all day in the truck with Amanda."

"We both know I wasn't busy. What happened to Chelsea?" I said, still unsure which of his interns was which.

"Back to Massachusetts for the summer. Her parents have a place somewhere. She explained it. I wasn't listening. But I'm holding her position till term starts."

"So it's just you and . . . Amanda?" I asked. Buck nodded. "Just you and Amanda for the summer."

"Maybe that's the problem," said Buck, rummaging through a box of tapes in his lap. "Or part of it. We're alone together a lot and there's now no one from her class at the college to provide a counterpoint or a good example. After Chelsea left, Amanda started camping out at the house. I'd come down in the morning and she'd be asleep on the couch in the living room, in her underwear. Fancy stuff. Not worn accidentally. Said she'd stayed late listing books and didn't feel safe walking back to the dorms alone. It put me in the position of being able to say almost nothing in response except to suggest she only work the hours she gets credit for. So she stopped staying late and started arriving early. I came in from grocery shopping earlier this week and she was already there, taking a shower."

"I probably would have done the wrong thing in that situation," I said.

"It's easy to do when you don't know what the right thing is. I had no idea. I just dropped the groceries in the kitchen, grabbed a beer, and sat on the porch until the water stopped running. I was just about to go back in when she came out in a towel and asked if I was hungry. She'd noticed the bags from the market and possibly gone through my shopping. Would I like her to fix us something to eat? Meanwhile, I'm trying so hard not to call attention to the obvious that I say something about how I was planning on making dinner in a moment anyway rather than telling her to get dressed and go home and suddenly, she's prepping a spinach lasagna in my kitchen, still in her towel, which she keeps adjusting whenever I walk in to get a beer. I considered abandoning the house entirely for the night and coming up to see you, but I was worried she might burn it down to get back at me."

"How was the lasagna?"

"It was fucking delicious, Oliver, thanks for asking," said Buck, as if Amanda was a plague of locusts or a similar and dire inevitability, something he needed help preparing for. He may have wanted advice, but I wasn't the right person to give it to him, and was surprised he didn't know that. Buck was handsome; over six feet tall, broad-shouldered, dark-haired, green-eyed, with the kind of robust, woodcutting appearance the women of Acheron seemed to like. He could afford to worry about doing the right thing.

"Sometimes I make dinner naked," I said. "It's a pain in the ass. She may have been doing you a favor."

"That's not how favors work," said Buck. "The foundation is in a good place right now. I don't need a reputation around town as one of those creeps who starts a non-profit so he can have a seraglio of college girls working for free."

"White slavers and their internships," I said, trying to mute my lack of any real insight into his problems. Thank god this friendship seems to get along just fine without me contributing anything, I thought, and then: I am clearly a bad friend. But perhaps it wasn't my fault. Buck was outsize and hard to keep up with. I always felt a little like a ventriloquist dummy beside him when we were out in public, especially at a bar, where everyone is usually at their most accidentally honest. Women chewed straight through me in order to reach him, looming over his beer from the neighboring stool as if he'd just finished a log drive. After one particularly bad night last winter, when a girl rushing to talk to him spread her coat over my knees as if the stool I occupied was empty, I told Buck being out with him made me feel like an obstacle. I could tell he felt bad, but wasn't sure whether an apology was appropriate or even something I wanted. He suggested we try going to bars with fewer students, so we ended up at the Ethiopian restaurant, drinking tej by ourselves. This was a better arrangement. The wait staff seemed relieved I'd brought a friend and may have mistaken us for a couple. I was fine with that, even flattered by it. If strangers imagine us having sex, I thought, maybe we look like we're in the same league.

"Since I turned thirty, it feels like every opportunity to enjoy myself is a cautionary tale waiting to happen," said Buck. At least we have that in common, I thought, as he plunged a Leatherface cassette into the tape deck. The opening bars of 'New York State' reminded me of a weekend he and I spent together when we were still in high school, camping and bait fishing on the lake near my parents' house or the Friday evening beforehand. I met him in Montpelier and we were walking back to my car from the food coop with supplies for the trip, roasted almonds, dried apricots, a tub of New England clam chowder from the deli counter. I remember the food we bought because I was rooting through the bag as we crossed the lot where I'd parked behind the movie theater on State Street, when I heard someone say something about two faggots having a picnic. Ahead of us, three guys from my high school were hanging around a lowered Honda Civic with a crooked spoiler and a thumping bass can in the trunk. I knew all three, Jake, Cole, and Creswell, but couldn't remember which of them it belonged to. The faggot thing was something I'd gotten used to; I heard it in the halls at school and whenever we ran into each other in town, but never had much to say back. Cole and Creswell lifted weights and played football, and Jake didn't do much, but was naturally large enough in a fat way to make intimidating him a problem for someone like me. Occasionally, after being thrown a shoulder by one of them or knocked into a locker, I'd retreat to the school bathroom and look at myself in the mirror, trying to imagine what about me threatened them: the twice-bleached, nearly platinum hair, black denim vest scalloped with conical studs, Econochrist t-shirt, circlet of empty cartridges around my waist, and black spandex jeans my mother had worn when she was in college sewn into a patchwork of political slogans and band names. Even though this was the person I thought I wanted to be, I wondered if I wasn't inviting outside punishment. Revenge crossed my mind, but never gained a foothold. I didn't know how to use firearms and was too afraid of getting caught to make a school shooting work. Being a coward meant I could continue doing what I wanted most of the time. The other choice was putting it all on the line in one way or another to prove a point to a bunch of proto-dropouts and there was no reason to believe I would succeed where all our teachers had failed. So I took what came my way, silently hoping an asteroid would flatten the Civic and its retinue in the parking lot behind the movie theater before Buck got a better idea of what I considered normal.

He asked me if I knew them and I didn't say anything, but may have nodded. I'm not sure what happened next, because my face was buried in the grocery bag, as if I'd lost something at the bottom. When I looked up, Buck was ten feet away, standing in front of Jake, talking to all three of them. He asked what the problem was about. One of them said something threatening in response. I don't remember who it was. Buck laughed and told him they would probably need help. I don't know what effect he expected this to have, but Jake gave him a hard shove in the chest. Buck took a small step back and slapped Jake in the face hard enough to pirouette him back toward the Civic. Cole and Creswell stepped forward, but appeared to have second thoughts, their minds suddenly freighted with the seriousness of what had just happened to Jake and their resultant responsibility to him. Scales creaked as they watched Buck; loyalty in one pan, doom in the other. Jake turned around and said something situational and generic. Buck grabbed the front of his shirt and slapped him twice more across the face; I thought of a scene in an old film I'd watched with my father of a man with a handlebar mustache and dinner jacket trying to revive a hysterical woman. The blows fell like misplaced applause.

Buck raised his hand a fourth time and watched Jake wince, anticipating the blow, beyond the point of defending himself from it. I wondered if this was how I appeared in the hallways at school, scurrying between classes like prey waiting to be devoured, waiting for things to happen to me instead of trying to avoid them or defend myself at any rate. How infuriating that must look. I'd probably pick on me too, I thought, as Buck released Jake's shirt and rejoined me. Jake stood by the Civic, leaning on the palsied spoiler, shaking his head. Cole offered him a large can of iced tea and a mentholated cigarette. Creswell watched us across the lot with a kind of dog-like, a posteriori apprehension of the state of things. But they didn't leave. They were probably waiting for a movie at the theater behind them to start.

Meanwhile, I felt safe beside Buck in a way I didn't like. He'd proven how incapable I was of defending myself, but I wasn't his prom date or younger brother. I didn't need a champion prodding me away from passivity, presumably toward righteousness. There was nothing gratifying about watching Jake cringe in front of someone bigger and stronger or get what the sort of people who mistake the world for an orderly, moral place would say was coming to him. It was an equitable transference or a shift in the balance of individual cruelty; a changing of the bully guard. Nothing new there. The sort of thing you expect to see when young animals fight. The long arm of stupidity never breaks off a hug, I thought, as Buck waved to Jake across the lot before ducking into the passenger seat beside me.

Still, as we drove out of town listening to 'Pandora's Box', I wondered what it must be like to see a door where people like me generally found only a wall. If a triumvirate of provincial morons hanging around a parking lot wasn't anything to be afraid of, did I have anything left to fear? Buck had slapped away the only source of empiric friction in my life casually, like a man brushing snow off a windshield and shown me how unimaginative my nightmares were. Despite how I felt about the situation overall, I seemed be on the other side of it. Even when Jake showed up at the skate park a week later with Cole and Creswell, I wasn't afraid. I was alone, but glad Buck wasn't there to interfere. They needed to get something mutual out of their systems, but whatever it was, their hearts weren't in it. Everything between us felt like the closing stage of a pasquinade. They pushed me around by the quarter pipe, said I was a faggot, and threw my skateboard in the elbow of river flowing past the park. Then they left, three large young men crammed into a ludicrously small car like inmates of a third-rate travelling circus. I was too annoyed by what I'd learned from all this because of Buck to tell him about it.

Carissa wasn't mentioned until after we'd picked up the books in Randolph and were on our way back to Montpelier. Storm clouds cushioned the horizon as we passed the Berlin exit and the temperature lingered around eighty degrees. Our shirts were soaked through from hauling twenty boxes of what turned out to be mostly popular novels out of a windowless root cellar down the street from Gifford Medical Center, the hospital where I was born. When we'd finished, Buck stood on the lawn, counting out twenties from a bank envelope and pressing five of them into the hand of the executor, a thin, pretty, avian women in her thirties who ran a cosmetics company in New York City, and lived around the corner from where I'd gotten lost while trying to visit Carissa. The house we were emptying belonged to her grandfather.

The executor was curiously chatty and told us she had just

patented a lip-gloss with a hoodia berry base or extract or something that acted as a natural appetite-suppressant. The San people in the Namib desert, she said, clucking her tongue appropriately, used it to stave off hunger during long hunting trips. Buck said something about how he didn't realize hunting was so popular in Manhattan, while I walked off to smoke a joint on the hospital lawn. The point of the day was getting away from me and I thought visiting the place where I first entered the world might dispel some of the parallels between the executor's life and my own I heard in her conversation with Buck. Her clumsy self-promotion was also getting to me. It felt macabre, under the circumstances. And misplaced; we were just there to drag some crap out of the basement. I was confident nothing about the way we'd gone about that suggested shinier lips and reduced waistlines were a day-to-day concern for either of us. And yet, the spiel on the lawn continued as I sat beneath a shade tree by the hospital entrance, watching Buck nod to me ironically from a block away as the woman handed him some lively-colored sample cases of her product: Plump Lips / Tiny Hips. You'd think a death in the family would stem the urge to shamelessly plug yourself, I thought. But then: I remembered calling Carissa a year earlier from the street outside my grandmother's house and didn't really see much of a difference. At least the executor had something tangible in mind.

As we closed in on the Montpelier exit, Buck suggested we grab a beer, or some beers, as he said, in town while I waited for my mother to pick me up. I was going to do this anyway, but it was nice to have him invite himself along. We unmerged from I-89 onto the exit ramp and Buck changed cassettes; The Queers churning out 'Teenage Bonehead'.

"I keep expecting myself to outgrow songs like this," he said, raising the volume as we turned onto State Street, the golden dome of the Capital building ahead dulled beneath a graying sky. "But they only become more vital as I get older."

"I collected bottles and cans out of the swamp by parent's house so I could redeem them for cash to buy an Amebix record," I replied. "I can't remember a time when I thought anything was that important."

"Points of departure, I guess. They are many. I put on *15 Counts of Arson* while I was making dinner one night last week and Amanda thought I was playing a practical joke on her. It was the how-can-you-listen-to-that? conversation, but between an employer and an employee. Made me feel all grown up."

"Well, she's how old? Twenty? What do you expect?"

"She'll be twenty in September, she claims. I wouldn't mind her hating my music if the stuff she played while she's working for me didn't suck so much. It's all bands from Austin singing about beaches, asexual charlatans trying to sound like Ian Curtis, or haircuts from Brooklyn with laptops but no instruments specializing in non-era musicality. I know I sound like one of our dads talking about a time when music meant something, but when you borrow from everything you end up with nothing."

"You sounded more like King Lear just now."

"Music is a canary. People like Amanda are the coalmine."

"Don't get it, Buck."

"If art isn't sincere, what the fuck is, Oliver?"

"Carissa and I were listening to *Got Beat Up* the other night," I said, not really thinking about what I was saying, but aiming for a shift in subject. The pot I smoked in Randolph had suddenly superseded my active role in our conversation. I wasn't necessarily trying to keep any secrets, but didn't like the foggy sound of my voice sharing this information. "And I realized I'm still expecting to find out what most of the songs on that album are about. When I was fifteen, I thought I knew."

"Every few years I rediscover how little I understand about the things I think I like the most. It's almost like having no memory," said Buck, sliding the truck backwards into a parking spot at a rough perpendicular to the bar he'd chosen. "I didn't realize you saw her. I'm glad you did."

"She came by the day she got into town. We had a fish dinner on my lawn."

"How's she doing?" he asked. The question confused me. How would I know?

"It's complicated," I said, verily. "I'm sure you noticed."

"Not really, Oliver. Her mom got her a job doing art stuff at a summer school program a day or two after she moved in. I haven't seen much of her."

"It must be hard on Amanda."

"She's been visiting her family down in Brattleboro for the past week. Came back late yesterday, I think. I'm hoping the entire problem will take care of itself now that Carissa's living at the house."

"What do you expect to happen now?" I asked either Buck or myself. I couldn't decide what kind of answer I wanted. But he was already out of the truck, crossing the pitted sidewalk toward the barroom door and I was glad he didn't hear my question. Even if he was interested in Carissa, he wouldn't tell me about it. Buck maintained a kind of omertà regarding the women he saw; he had nothing to prove and therefore nothing to brag about. Every few months he introduced me to someone new without clarifying her role in his life, leaving the guesswork to me. I never knew where he met these women; certainly not with me. None of them resembled the coeds who used me as a coatrack whenever we were out on the town. The last one, a sensuous, sporty redhead named Shelly, taught geology at the college and brought her rock pick along on a hike with us last Spring, vigorously tapping at things and explaining them as we wound our way up and down Maybrick Peak. It was the most enjoyable afternoon I can remember spending with a woman I didn't have a chance with, though the experience made me wish I spent more time around people who knew exactly what they were talking about. When Shelly left town after a term to do fieldwork somewhere out west, Buck took it in stride. There was funding involved. She needed to go. He helped pack and drove her to the airport in Burlington when it was time to leave. Both of them seemed determined to be adults about everything. No one had any reason to ask how I felt about any of this, but I recall being embarrassed by how much I missed her after she'd gone.

We finished a set of beers and ordered another as thunder rumbled above the building. The front door was propped open by an ashcan; purposeful seeming gusts of wind fluttered beer mats and stray tips on the dappled surface of the bar. The clock above the register ticked toward mid-afternoon. Buck went outside to throw a tarp over the books in the back of the truck. I said I'd join him after I called my parents to come get me. For the time being, the conversation about Carissa was on an indefinite hiatus.

"We weren't expecting you until tomorrow," said my mother, sounding excited after I explained where I was and what I wanted. She'd retired earlier in the year after the sale of my grandmother's house was finalized and was still casting around for interesting ways to occupy her time. "What a nice surprise! I'll leave the house in ten minutes. Where are you?"

"At the bar by the pancake restaurant," I said, glad I could make someone happy by just showing up unannounced at their house and expecting to be fed. Like a stray dog, I thought, wincing internally. In the background, I heard my father dropping tuna steaks into a colander in the kitchen sink, running warm water over them. Despite the weather, he was determined to barbecue.

"Do you mean the creperie?"

"I think I do, yes."

"Are you there by yourself?" asked my mother, a remote quartertone of concern shading the question.

"No, mom. Buck is here with me."

"Oh, good," she said, transparently relieved. "Would he like to come to dinner? We haven't see him in a while."

"I think he has things to do," I said, unilaterally deciding to excuse Buck from the meal. "But I'll ask."

After I hung up, I watched him for a moment through the front window. He sat on the dropped tailgate of the truck with his beer glass resting beside him, a carton of books partially visible beneath an ochre tarpaulin stretched over the bed and a copy of *The Long Day Wanes* balanced on his thigh as the sky roiled above. Too much evidence of self-containment in one place, I thought as I joined him on the tailgate and relayed my mother's invitation to dinner. He declined, citing the load of stuff he needed to sort out in the back of the truck when he returned to Acheron and replacing the book he'd been reading in the box it had come from. I was mildly irritated with myself for not having more to do as I watched him root through the carton between us.

"Oh, look: Raymond Carver," he said captiously, withdrawing a copy of *Where I'm Calling From* from the box like a tray of burnt cookies from an oven. "Or the reason undergraduate creative writing classrooms suck to be in. Someone will buy this. What else? *True North*. Okay. Jim Harrison would have us believe a pedophile lurks behind every old-growth pine North of Marquette. His friend Thomas McGuane is like Evelyn Waugh in spurs. But here's something: *Antwerp*. Roberto Bolano was the only real genius to appear in the Americas after Faulkner. The throne is now vacant. Next: Ian McEwan, habitué of the Booker prize shortlist with his penny dreadfuls for the petit bourgeoisie. Next, James Ellroy, a cosmetically insane gossip in wolves' clothing . . . "

This will continue with or without me nearby, I thought, feeling prop-like and unlettered as I sipped the remainder of my beer beside Buck, listening to his riddles. I knew he had an English degree he didn't use, but he'd also read enough to make people of a similar background and education level feel stupid. He may not have been aware of it. I suspected and partially blamed his family. Buck's father was the head librarian at the college library and lived with his girlfriend, three dogs, and thousands of books in a kind of chalet up the Mt. Abandon access road. His mother wrote young adult novels and lived somewhere in Connecticut. Buck always looked as if he'd fallen off the top rung of a siege ladder whenever he returned from visiting her and his stepfather, also a novelist. His mother did well after the divorce and several of her books had been made into films. Carissa and I once went to see one of them without telling Buck, but left halfway through, feeling nosy and disloyal. As far as I could tell, the movie was about a romantic trilemma between three pubescents, two boys and a girl. The title, *The Wolf*, made no sense to me at the time. Later, I learned it was derived from the controversial penultimate scene: Both boys awkwardly sucking on the girl's half-formed breasts in a pup tent on her parent's lawn, like Romulus and Remus nursing from the teats of a wolf prior to founding the Roman Empire. Several theaters around the country refused to screen the film because of this and certain children's advocacy groups, made up of the sort of obsessive, idle people who use minors as human shields to disseminate their neuroses with impunity, pushed to have the book it was based on removed from school libraries nationwide. None of this made my radar until years later, when it came up in an early Roman history class Buck and I took together during our junior year at Acheron College. The professor either wasn't aware of his connection to the material or didn't care, but it ended up not mattering. Buck tucked his copy of Livy's *Ab Urbe Condita* beneath his arm and left the classroom. When we met up afterward and he asked me if he'd missed anything important, I had to pretend I didn't know more about his family life than he was comfortable with. But I never told him about Carissa and me seeing the movie in the first place, so this mostly felt like a different aspect of the same lie.

"When you asked me what I expect to happen now," said Buck, sliding the box of books he'd been digging through back under the tarp. "Did you mean something specific?"

"I can't remember what I meant," I said, thinking: Carissa. "I didn't think you heard me."

"I was trying to figure out an answer between my first and second beer and time got away from me."

"We have other things to talk about."

"Sure we do. But maybe I don't fully understand the question."

"Forget it."

"I thought maybe it had something to do with Amanda."

"No. That's self-evident."

"Or Carissa."

"I'm pretty sure we don't know as much about her as we used to," I said, feeling as if I was being corralled toward a conclusion Buck had settled upon. "At least, I don't."

"So how can I know what to expect from her?"

"I'd start by examining what I want and guessing based on that."

"So you're asking what I want," said Buck, staring into the sour froth bottoming his beer glass. "It's hard to know what I want when I don't know what someone else wants."

"I'm pretty sure Carissa wants something, but has no idea what it is."

"Maybe I was talking about you, Oliver."

"I don't want anything," I lied, uncomfortable with how easily Buck had rolled the responsibility for leading the conversation toward coherency back on me. I considered repeating myself.

"You sure?" asked Buck, tossing one of the Plump Lips / Tiny Hips sample cases into my lap.

"I don't want this," I said, trying to give it back to him. Buck leaned in, rolling the ugly little box over in my hands until a phone number printed on one side of it appeared, and beside this, a name: Karen. "This is the woman who sold us the books, right? And you got her number. Good for you. I still don't want this."

"Not me, dummy," said Buck, as if nothing could be more unusual. "She's in town for the next week and asked me to ask you to call her. If you're not too busy, she said. I tried not to run wild reassuring her about that last part."

"Why didn't she just give this to me herself?" I asked, even as I tucked the box into my pocket. I suddenly felt very good about myself and was beginning to patrol the boundaries of this feeling, testing it for weaknesses.

"Probably because you were off getting high in the hospital parking lot," he said, not without affection. He finished his beer and walked inside with our empty glasses as rain began clucking against the tarp. The storm had established a bivouac directly overhead. I closed the tailgate and sat in the cab, examining my reflection in the mirror behind the sun visor, trying to determine what Karen saw there. Dark brown hair, already graying at the temples. Nasolabial folds in the preproduction stage of someday becoming mighty jowls. Puffy hazel eyes, bloodshot and crinkling at the corners and glassed behind the kind of spectacles that were obviously picked out before the prescription was filled. Clearly someone tipping toward thirty or not young enough to be fetishized for it, at any rate. But Karen had obviously seen potential there or something to be desired, I thought, as my mother's car drifted into the parking spot beside the truck. What had it been? I wondered. And how do I show whatever it was to Carissa?

An hour later, I sat on the deck attached to my parent's house, discussing my student loan payments with them as the midevening sun crept beneath a palisade of fir trees on the property line. The cosseting scent of postprandial espresso, wild apples cooling in the orchard across the meadow, and the bog menstruating at the foot of the lawn reminded me I was home, not in some kind of public assistance office, and waylaid the impulse to continue topping off my wineglass during the discussion.

This is serious talk, I told myself. Stick with mostly coffee. Your mother and father don't want slurry assurances they've heard before. The grill on which my father seared our meal, tuna steaks in a balsamic reduction, red onions, yellow peppers, and Adirondack Blue potatoes, ticked in the background and a loon hooted on the lake down the road from the house with an aspect of abandonment. My father loved birds and I hoped evidence of one nearby might draw his attention from the subject at hand. Of course, even in that event, my mother was still present and accounted for, looking worried across the table. She didn't care enough about birds to leave my financial illiteracy unexamined. An archaeopteryx flock could blot out what remained of the sun, and we would still be here, exchanging the morose grammar of

American debt slavery: cosign, interest, principal, consolidation, forbearance, deferment, default. These words all seemed to have two definitions; one good, one bad.

Right now, we're focusing on the bad, I thought, feeling guilty and embarrassed, but good, otherwise. Up until this point, the evening had gone well. The storm haunting the sky above Montpelier churned the countryside to a green and brown pulp past the car window as my mother and I drove the twelve miles to North Calais, but had veered off toward New Hampshire by the time we arrived at the house, where my father was setting the table on the deck in a leg of late afternoon sunlight like a dutiful saint, oblivious to the tempest raging a few miles South. My mother and I walked down to the lake while he prepared dinner, cheerfully discussing the sale of my grandmother's house, a class action settlement she'd received over a bungled hip replacement, and what began to sound like our mutual retirement the more we talked about it. While I boozed by the river, waiting for Carissa to show up and explain the obvious, my mother read a lot, painted, took photographs and long walks with my father in the afternoons. They were planning a vacation, a walking tour of Cinque Terra in September. And the lake had warmed up enough to swim in each morning. I tried to summon a euphemism or two, hoping to graft a comparable well-roundedness onto the little I was able to share about my life without worrying my mother. I read a lot and swam too, according to me. And sometimes I saw Buck in the evenings. She appeared to be waiting for something more, but moved on to questions about Buck and what I was reading when the silence following my summary became embarrassing. I mentioned Buck's trouble with Amanda and spoke a little too emphatically about envying Bruce Chatwin's shiftless lifestyle. I sound like I'm determined to remain unemployed, I thought, watching a motorboat in the center of the lake dispatch a ribbon of surf toward where we stood on shore. I wanted my mother to be proud of me without having to lie to her, but found this was becoming harder to expect the longer I talked freely about myself.

At least we're getting all this out in the open, where it belongs, I thought then and again, two hours later on the deck, unevenly digesting the meal my father had served as I pawed dimly through a fluttering bushel of account statements from the Vermont Student Assistance Corporation. My mother brought them to the table shortly after we received a phone call toward the tail end of dinner, a call my father answered. The man on the other end didn't immediately unmask himself as a debt collector, but said he was looking for me and needed my social security number to complete some paperwork he was sending my way. Could my father also provide him with my current mailing address? My father asked if the guy had a pen and gave the address as 1-2 Fuck You Avenue, before slapping the phone back in its cradle. He sat back down at the table and my mother immediately stood up, returning a few minutes later with a binder I mistook for one of my grandmother's photo albums and set it heavily on the table, rattling the espresso cups in their respective saucers. The storm that missed the house had returned, I imagined, in the unremarkable guise of an amoral loan shark in a plastic headset and yellowed shirt collar, plying his trade beneath a drop ceiling and hissing fluorescent lights in some anonymous middle-American business ghetto. The only devil worth caring about wants my social security number, I thought, imagining him picking his hooves in his cubicle with a nicotine-rouged finger as an auto dialer plugged away in the background.

"We should talk about this," said my mother, gesturing at the binder, and I agreed, lifting its cover like a man baiting a trap.

In a way, I was relieved to be caught in the midst of a tangible problem rather than a prospective one. It was theoretically solvable. My parents didn't share this relief. They'd cosigned what they needed to in order to get me through my undergraduate education. Now they were on the verge of paying the price for it if I didn't. Even if I died, they would remain on the hook. If I can't fake my own death, I thought, examining one of the pages. Maybe I can sell an organ or two. There has to be something I'm just carrying around and won't miss.

"You can't afford to be unemployed right now," said my father, grimly. He understood my reasons for leaving the grocery store, but didn't want his retirement endangered over scruples. "I don't like to get calls like that."

"I thought you handled it well," I said.

"Rest assured, Oliver, he will call back. The scum of the earth seek your personal information. This should worry you."

"It does," I said, hoping it didn't sound like a question.

"We can't afford it," added my mother, emphasizing the pronoun. "So let's figure a way to deal with this before it becomes a bigger problem."

"We'll help you in any way we can," said my father, still grim. He hated discussing money matters. "But we can't make these payments as they are."

"I'm sorry I can't afford them either," I said, clinking an empty wine bottle against the rim of my empty glass as I blindly tried to refill it, looking like I was toasting myself. "I wish I understood how I'm supposed to manage this or what I'm doing wrong. Even when I was working full time at the grocery store and writing stuff for Grover, I couldn't pay them anything. I could afford everything else. Food, rent, amusements. Just not this. Remaining ignorant would have been so much cheaper."

"They're bastards. It's not your fault. Call them on Monday," said my father. "Try to negotiate a lower payment or something that seems like you could afford it based on the kind of job you expect to get in the future. The near future, I hope, Oliver. We'll sign off on whatever you decide."

"Try to see if they'll allow an unemployment deferment," said my mother, speculatively. "You're working on your thesis still, right? Maybe you can buy yourself a little more time for that."

"How's that going, by the way?" asked my father, stripping the cellophane from a cigar, sipping his espresso, glad to be moving on. "It's on Bell . . . Belly. . . Bellycyrus? . . . What are you writing about again?"

"Belisarius, first of the Romans," I said, wading into the first stage of a soliloquy that would become more familiar to me over the next few months. My father silently puffed his cigar and my mother gathered her documents, closing the topic for the time being. We were all worried about the same thing, so the evening sailed toward common ground as we began clearing the table. I dropped plates into the dishwasher as fireworks clattered down by the lake and my parents watched the news in the living room. I'd insisted on cleaning up because I felt deeply guilty for endangering the wellbeing of the people I cared about most and it was the least I could do while still doing something. I also thought I should practice using the dishwasher in case I had to move back in with them. In that event, it would be too late to seriously begin pulling my own weight, but I hoped arriving on their doorstep with an arsenal of small gestures might offset this. Going forward, I resolved, I will strive to appear at least semi-capable in familiar surroundings.

The news ended as I finished the dishes and I joined my parents to watch Jeopardy. One of the categories was related to the

First World War, an area I should have known something about and did, at one time. I stopped answering aloud after getting the first three questions wrong and flubbing a Daily Double, glad to see I'd managed to unlearn some of the horrors I'd studied under Dr. Norman, but concerned my parents might notice I'd lost even trivial command of the education nibbling away at their credit score. I surprised myself with the questions I got right. They were mostly about things I'd read in the books Buck gave me.

My priorities have gone rogue, I concluded, as my mother set a tray of cookies on the coffee table and touched the top of my head to indicate they were mostly for me, not my father. I felt like an impostor or an epigone of the person she expected me to become after our conversation, but this was nothing new.

I couldn't sleep after my parents went to bed. The clock above the stove read 10:30 as I passed through the kitchen on my way outside, a joint I'd rolled on my mother's cookie tray stuck to my bottom lip and a tumbler of her gin cradled between my abdomen and elbow as I battled with the sliding glass door to the deck. It was a warm night. The lake was still alive with people blowing things up and having a good time. The worriless susurration of water-oriented fun had been in the background of every summer I could remember, but this was the first time it seemed to call attention to all the fun I wasn't having, water-oriented or otherwise.

Where are your fireworks? I asked myself, as one popped and spread above the treeline in a nimbus of red and gold. A good question. Could I live through an entire weekend of this? Carissa suggested herself as an answer, eddying upward from some subcutaneous grotto of self-pity. All this navel-gazing on my parent's deck seemed to echo the thing Buck said earlier in the day about maturing sideways. Maybe I should dig the studded vest and combat boots out of my closet, head down to the lake, see what people younger than I were up to.

I sensed my internality cruising toward a bad decision, but didn't immediately associate this feeling with Karen until I'd already dialed her number and she'd already answered. Something rattled in the sample box as I held it up to the guttering light of a single match, reading the digits aloud for some reason with the cordless phone sandwiched between my head and shoulder. Flee omphaloskepsis, I told myself, the atonal music of her voice ratcheting up the number of things I could reasonably expect of the evening. We were both pleased I'd called. No trouble about the hour. I felt excited and satyr-like.

"What are you doing right now?" she asked. Tricky question. I surveyed the radius of inactivity surrounding my deck chair. Not much was the obvious answer.

"We should meet," I said. "I can show you."

"Sly," she said, dryly. "Funny. Weird. Where are you?"

"North Calais. It's hard to explain how to get here from where you are."

"Is that a town?"

"More of a hamlet. The post office is actually in East Calais."

"What's there? Aside from the post office."

"My parent's house," I said, adding: "I'm visiting."

"Charming," she said, appearing to mean it. "Will I be meeting your family?"

"We hadn't planned on it," I said, thinking: Why not? "They're asleep. Soundly, I should think."

"Should I bring anything?"

"A swimsuit," I said randomly.

"Fun. Is there somewhere we can have a drink in between before I see how you live?"

We arranged to meet in Montpelier around 11:30. I had enough time to take a shower and dig through the closet in my childhood bedroom for something vaguely night-going. I didn't have a specific outcome with Karen in mind, but I felt solution-oriented, a good place to start. I am a willing participant in my own life, I thought, as I stood to go inside and get ready. Something clattered by the grill behind me, and as I turned to see what it was, a firework burst above the trees, shading the deck in a cool Tyrian purple. The color of imperium in Ancient Rome, I reminded myself, admiring my sudden command of this fact as the explosion's mulberry glare revealed a skunk rooting through a bucket of compost beside the sliding glass door. Handsome fellow, I thought, as we made ambiguous eye contact and shared an expression of regret. The skunk didn't have to maneuver much to spray me; a meaty cataract opening beneath the plume-like tail was the last thing I saw before the rocket's violaceous remnant burned out above the lake, returning us to darkness.

The skunk scampered off in the direction of the orchard, while I hung over the side of the deck in a sulfuric fug, dry heaving onto the woodpile. I smelled like a mass grave, but was determined not to cancel my meeting with Karen. I'm not going to allow some wayward rodent to get the better of me, I though as I lurched over to the kitchen window to check the time; the clock above the stove read 11:00PM, giving me between ten and fifteen minutes to solve my problem. It had to be possible. Even if it weren't, I would show up anyway. I am a willing participant in my own life, I reminded myself, as I removed my clothing on the deck and walked inside.

In the kitchen, I pawed through the refrigerator and cupboards in search of tomato juice, but found only a pallet of marinara sauce intended for lovers of garlic. I like garlic, I thought, trying to remain positive as I read the label on one of the jars like a nudist doing his shopping. Hopefully Karen does too. I walked to the bathroom with the pallet beneath my arm and set it beside the tub as I ran the shower. I wasn't sure exactly where I'd been sprayed; the odor seemed to be everywhere and nowhere at once, so I upended each jar over my head, working the sauce into my hair, beneath my arms, and across my chest. I was doing this, so I might as well be thorough about it. Bits of vegetable matter began clotting in the drain; muddy orange water flecked with wafers of garlic rose steadily around my ankles. I scraped it free with my foot, combing the biggest chunks of tomato and whatever else toward the aft end of the tub, and promising myself I would remember to clean all this up when I returned from the bar, with or without Karen.

I couldn't smell myself in my parent's car on the way to Montpelier and felt as if I'd gotten away with something until after I'd found a stool beside Karen and ordered a drink. She was prettier than I remembered from earlier in the day. Slim, beaky, intelligent and orderly looking. Very little makeup, oddly. The kind of person it didn't seem realistic for me to be around at the moment. Her hair tipped in an erubescent cascade down the back of a flannel shirt worn loosely over a bikini top as she rotated in her seat to summon the bartender. Her stoical gaze held mine while I nervously sipped my beer, trying not to look at two men and one woman shooting pool nearby. They had gazed across the felt in our general direction since I walked in, the nose of each player contorted in an anticline of disgust as it tested the suddenly foul air of the bar. I knew the triumph I'd been celebrating earlier in the car had eluded me before Karen spoke.

"Why do you smell like a burning tire?" she asked cheerfully, tapping her beer against mine. Cheers, pigpen.

"A skunk sprayed me as I was leaving the house," I said. The truth was more sympathetic than anything I could make up. "But I wanted to see you."

"That's sweet," she said veridically, her eyes locking on something either over my shoulder or attached to my head. "Is that . . . It is! Why do you have garlic in your hair?"

"Vampires," I said nominally, wondering if fearing the undead was more or less normal than bathing in pasta sauce. Would the truth remain sweet or begin to curdle as she learned more? I mustered my dignity and explained what I'd done to myself, monitoring Karen's expression for signs of trouble. She seemed to be on the verge of buying us both another drink.

"You did all that," she said, fanning some bills on the bar without removing her eyes from my face. Green eyes, like Buck's, I noticed. "So you could see me tonight?"

"Yes," I supplied, while also thinking: yes. Things seemed to be syncing up. Good. Yahtzee. "The outcome was important to me."

"What kind of outcome did you expect?"

"I think I just wanted there to be one," I said, and then, to clarify: "I'm working on not being consistently disappointed. Or alone."

"Is that related to whatever you were doing when you called me?"

"I'm not sure," I said, circling my finger at the bartender. "I was getting high and watching fireworks on my parent's deck."

"I can't tell if you're trying hard to impress me," said Karen. "Or not at all."

"I wanted your company," I said, narrowly avoiding using 'need' in place of 'want'. "Friday night in North Calais isn't the swinging scene you might expect."

"It's Thursday."

"Thursday," I echoed, trying to sound like this wasn't news

to me. I'd been drinking with a definite resoluteness since early afternoon and temporal boundaries were beginning to seem like a kind of chicanery, a needless anchor on my animal velocity. "I didn't know that. But I'm glad I do now."

"Why are you so honest?" asked Karen, poised, bewitching, still somehow curious about me, and probing the rim of whatever axiom she believed I represented.

"I think it's working for me, at the moment," I said. An affirmative gesture sweeping toward me from the direction of the pool table caught my eye. The sharks were evidently beginning to circle. "Can I ask you a question?"

"Aside from that one, yes."

"Why am I here with you instead of Buck?"

"Is that your large friend who paid me for the books?"

"Yes," I said. Dimorphism wasn't the usual way I separated Buck's character from my own, but it was serviceable enough to get the point across. "He's normally the one people, women, can't wait to find out about."

"You looked like more fun," she said. That can't possibly be true, I thought. Good liar though. Point awarded. "Like you're maybe still learning about yourself, and a little vulnerable because of it. Your friend has himself mostly figured out. He projects the kind of self-knowledge that always ends up being an example of something enviable. I don't want to have a drink with a role model."

"We've been friends since middle school. I wish I had the strength of character or whatever not to feel like I have something to make up for when I'm around him."

"You skulk around in his shadow. Do you know that?"

"I don't want to hate someone I like because they're better than me. But you're right about the shadow. No matter where I stand, I always seem to be in it," I said, watching one of the pool players, the woman, vigorously discussing something with the bartender and pointing with her cue toward the end of the bar where Karen and I sat by ourselves. For the first time I noticed we were at the center of a proscenium of empty stools.

"Want to get out of here?" she asked, also watching this over the horizon of a glass as she finished her beer. The question seemed to have two meanings, both rhetorical, under the circumstances. I excused myself to use the men's room, feeling impressive as I micturated, like I was in the midst of a dress rehearsal for living the dream, but missed the flusher on the toilet and ended up on the floor beside the bowl, wondering how I'd gotten there. Three beers on top of the gin and pot seemed to have triggered a kind of timed release; the distance between thought and action had narrowed and now I wasn't in any condition to drive anywhere or even walk across the street by myself. This is not a big deal, I thought, steadying a hand on the tank and hauling myself to my feet. We can figure this out. I am a willing participant, etc.

"I think you should drive," I said categorically, flourishing my keys at Karen when I returned to the bar. A string band beside the fire exit seemed to be on the decaying end of a madrigal. The bartender was clearly rehearsing an apology under his breath and looking our way as the company of pool players formed a kind of picket by the door. Dr. Norman would say they're preparing to charge, I thought, watching them over the top of Karen's head. Or tendering an ambush, by the looks of it. I didn't want to be the focal point of a scene, but avoiding one was beginning to feel unrealistic.

"We'll take my car," said Karen, pushing the hand with the keys back toward my body like she was closing a cattle gate. Aside from plucking a nodule of garlic out my hair, this was the first time we'd touched and even the mild discursion of her hand against my wrist was enough to remind me what was at stake. Danger and embarrassment were beginning to feel interchangeable. I wanted to avoid both, if not with grace, then an approximation of fortitude. This must be what it's like having a manager, I thought as Karen conducted us past the rattling cues and out the door. Or common goals, at least. She'd wanted a drink and we'd gotten through three before the choices I'd made earlier in the evening cannibalized the possibility of having another. I wanted to celebrate the bar I'd set, but couldn't prevent myself from wondering if Buck would have made it through four.

Ten minutes later, I sat safely belted into the passenger seat of a newish Audi sedan idling outside an all-night gas station on the edge of town. As Karen grabbed a few things inside, I prepared to navigate. Somewhere between where I was now and where I had been a moment earlier, the evening had tipped back onto the rails. The clock in the dashboard read 12:45AM as semi-coherence loomed. I could smell myself again for the first time in a few hours, which wasn't great, but normal, at any rate. Burning tire *con aglio*, with a side of generalized anxiety disorder held over from the bar. So far for Karen, time with me had been persecution rich, but I was determined to prevent this from becoming a theme, even as I gazed around the plush interior of her car, feeling a bit like a yokel dropped on a throne, but less so after noticing what looked like an overnight bag nesting between my feet. Plans had been made without me, a gleeful thought, for once. I'm not the sort of person who needs to go through that, I told myself, even as my hands tested the zipper. Karen emerged from the halogen glaze of the storefront with a briefcase of wine in her hand and a plastic bag of something dangling from her wrist, and I reared up in the seat with a Cat's Cradle of filmy underthings tangled between my hands. An explanation turned out to be unnecessary.

"I don't blame my dog when he eats the slice of pizza I leave on the coffee table," she said, throwing the car into gear and spinning us out of the parking lot. Montpelier looked like it was under martial law as we drove down Main Street, empty and silent, and up the hill out of town, cresting as the opening salvo of 'Electric Blue' roared from the stereo, a song that always made me feel like I was skipping school. Karen liked her music loud, not that unusual. She also drove like a maniac. As we merged unsteadily onto the County Road, I wondered if these two observations were related. I'd rolled us a joint, assuming this might slow her down a little, and it may have, though by the time the car dropped onto dirt in Maple Corner, I was warbling along to 'Bette Davis Eyes' with my head almost hanging out the window. Who is this person I'm having such dangerous fun with? I wondered, looking over at Karen in time to see her face change as we reached the top of the acclivity leading to my parent's house and the lake fell into view. A scimitar of moon hung above the water, its shape remapped on the undulate surface beside the stray lights of summer homes on shore.

"It's beautiful," she said, mercifully slowing the car as we drove past. "You live here?"

"I'm visiting," I repeated, from earlier. "I grew up here."

"Where do you live now?"

"Acheron, the town where I went to school. Where I continue to go to school, I mean."

"This makes me miss where I grew up," she said. "New York's all right if you like saxophones."

"Fear. The Record," I said, titillated and impressed. Lee Ving shitting on middleclass sensibilities with equanimity. Buck and I, aged sixteen, used to listen to the tape on our way to the skate park in Montpelier, but what was Karen's relationship to this devilish music? Whatever the answer, her reference pit was a deeper and lusher place than I suspected. Marry me, I thought experimentally. I had to interrupt myself asking her where she grew up to point out the turn to my parent's house or the hole in the forest I called home.

As it turned out, Karen was from rural Maine, a pocket of country in or around the woods where Thoreau made a nuisance of himself a hundred and fifty years earlier, but she didn't tell me this until after she'd removed her shorts and flannel shirt in my parent's driveway and stood for quiescent moment in her bikini beside the Audi, the plastic bag from the gas station reslung around her wrist. This felt like a strange place to be mostly naked, but I assumed seeing the lake had made her want to go for a swim. That sounded nice to me, so I said I'd run inside to grab my suit and some towels, but she made a gesture of forbearance, crossing the moonlit patch of lawn between us like a sylvan glade-walker, something peeled from the corpus of a Baroque fountain and cast into life.

"I like you Oliver," she said, pointing to me. I sensed myself being added to some internal roster. "But the smell is going to get in the way of me demonstrating that."

"Right, of course," I said, backing up a few steps, not really sure where to go. "Frankly, I'm amazed we made this far, all things considered."

"First thing's first," she said. "I need a bucket of water. Warm water, if possible."

"Right, of course," I repeated, walking around house's flank, and entering through the basement. I stood at the utility sink beside the washer and drier, sniffing absently at myself while the bucket filled. My frame of mind was difficult to get a fix on, but appeared to enjoy taking directions. I have a little job to do, I thought, feeling merry and whistling internally at my work as I hauled the bucket around the house and placed it at Karen's feet. She removed several items from the bag, and began mixing them into the water as I watched, fascinated.

"No tomato juice," I observed, brushing away the panic I felt as I suddenly recalled the disaster I'd left in the bathroom after my pasta shower. I made a tentative plan with myself to solve this problem by dawn, depending on how things went with Karen.

"One quart three percent hydrogen peroxide," she said, stooped over the bucket in her bikini, and stirring the mixture with a twig like an occultist centerfold. "A quarter cup sodium bicarbonate. One teaspoon liquid detergent."

"Will it take any skin off?"

"No, Oliver. It's what we used to use on my dogs whenever they came home smelling like you do."

"Thank you for deciding to solve this problem," I said, gesturing loosely at myself. "What do we do now?"

"You get naked. No, wait, actually. Do that after you find me a garden hose."

My mother had been spritzing her flowerbeds earlier in the day, and the hose remained coiled beside them. I ran the business end of it over to Karen, waiting in the yard beside the bucket, and loped back across the lawn to open the water valve by the basement door. Something hooted impassively in the lintel of trees bordering the property as I removed my clothes and folded them with needless delicacy on the woodpile beneath the deck. I wasn't nervous about Karen seeing me. After smelling like an open sewer for most of the evening, being naked in front of her felt redundant. Still, I tried to look proud of myself as I crossed the grass toward her in the moonlight, a brave nudist touring the mineral spa. Carissa said I looked good a week ago. Maybe this was still true.

"I'm sorry, Karen," I said anyway, stopping short beside the sudsy bucket. I wasn't ashamed of my body, but I felt the need to apologize for showing it to her all at once.

"You look like you walk a lot," said Karen. "No one in New York looks that way."

"Still, I'm sure this isn't what you expected when you gave Buck your number."

"Give us both a break, Oliver. We have the same outcome in mind. Haven't you noticed by now?"

"I suppose you wouldn't have driven us all the way out here and decided to clean me if our motivations weren't compatible."

"And if you were going to murder me and sink my body in that lovely lake of yours, you wouldn't have met me at the bar smelling like you took a dump and rolled in it. I think we can trust each other a little bit."

"It is possible to do that and still enjoy ourselves?"

"Are you kidding?" asked Karen. "I haven't had this much fun since my first month of college. Now, dump the bucket over your head. In stages, is probably best. Scrub everything in. Then I'll rinse you with the hose. Let's begin."

These ablutions took less time than I expected. Karen giggled to herself and made jokes at first, but this faded into a relaxed, intimate silence as the chemicals leeched the horrible smell from my skin, resettling us both on a plane liberated from obstacles to the outcome we ostensibly shared. Need emerged between us undamaged. As I rotated in place during the final rinse, the water ceased abruptly against my back and Karen was suddenly there, like an actress hitting her mark, her mouth cupped against my scapula and her arms winding dendritically across my stomach

and chest. The warmth of her body pillowed against me reminded us both how cold I was and Karen suggested we build a fire
in a pit she'd spotted by the flowerbeds. While I dragged an old
sleeping bag out of the basement to wrap myself in, she plucked
kindling from the woodpile, and arranged it into a tripod, stuffing the space between its ribs with newsprint from a box beneath
the deck. She asked for something to drink, so I went back to her
car for the wine and inside the house for two glasses. By the time
I returned, Karen sat staring into the blaze she'd ignited on my
lawn, wrapped in the sleeping bag like an Indian brave at rest.
The disunited halves of her swimsuit hung over the back of a lawn
chair nearby, snapping in a dewy wind rolling up from the lake. I
poured us each a glass of wine and eased in beneath the sleeping
bag, saying something about how I should have brought food
and asking if she was hungry. For what seemed like the first time
that evening, I realized I was Karen's host and probably had some
making up to do. She didn't answer the question about food. Her
body was alive in the firelight for a moment as she shrugged the
fabric from her shoulders, threw a long, shadowy leg over my
own and vaulted into my lap. I still held two full wine glasses
belonging to my parents and had to fight down the impulse to
toss them away into the night. Karen took one, sipping regally as
I passed my newly free hand from her armpit to her knee, testing
the unknown contour of the antumbra she constituted, her back
hot against the fire, her body in shadow.

"So, no food," I said, feeling like a stewardess. "Anything I can
do to make your stay at my parent's house more comfortable?"

"I really just need to get laid now, Oliver," she replied, rolling
her stomach flat against mine, rocking her pelvis into place. I am
a willing participant, I thought as something hooted again from
the underbrush. It sounded encouraging this time. A cloud fell

across the moon and the night closed in. I briefly imagined the skunk, my skunk, watching Karen and me from his home in the orchard; two figures bucking, shuddering, mating beside a rippling point of light, castled against the darkness.

I awoke the next morning with the pommel of Karen's elbow digging into my sternum as she leaned across my chest to shake hands with my mother standing beside the bed. I am either witnessing the tail end of an introduction, I thought, or the opening stages of a French farce. Greyish sunlight shaded the room and rain tapped martially beyond the blinds, as Karen did her best to answer my mother's questions about what took place in the bathroom and where my parent's car was. Her summary of the liaison with the skunk and resultant unpleasantness at the bar made me sound like a rudderless imbecile left in her care, but I was glad to have someone speak for me. Explaining myself without sharing the wrong kind of information was nonviable and I didn't want to say anything to further embarrass my mother. She and Karen seemed to be getting along anyway, possibly bonding over what they couldn't avoid having in common, like two people discovering they both have a relative at the same prison. All is well, I thought, or wished, opening my eyes experimentally and meeting my mother's steady, concerned gaze as she stood in the doorway listening to Karen, but watching me, possibly for evidence of something she wouldn't have to give up on.

"Is this your grandmother's?" she asked me, plucking an ornate leaded glass vase off the bedside table. Water rocked in the base; I'd been drinking out of it three to four hours earlier. None of the glasses in the kitchen cabinets looked large enough to quench my thirst when I came in from the fire and the vase seemed like an obvious solution, centered as it was on the dining room table, home to a quartet of yellow tulips. I'd repatriated the flowers in a beer bottle from the recycling beneath the kitchen sink, figuring I'd fix it along with the bathroom in the morning, though it had been morning at the time, 5AM by the clock above the stove. Now it was nearly afternoon and there was still work to be done. I may have nodded, though my mother didn't need an answer and wasn't waiting for one. She tucked the vase beneath her arm and backed out of my bedroom like a robber leaving a bank, telling Karen how nice it was meeting her, and that there was coffee in the kitchen whenever she was ready, before closing the door.

"Your mother seems like a strong woman," said Karen. I didn't know how to interpret that, but thunder murmured outside, suggesting divine agreement. She kissed my face as I laid the side of it between her breasts, determined to cocoon myself there for at least another hour. Fingers stirred my hair in a grooming pattern and her heart beat woodenly against my cheek. Because I didn't know when Karen would leave, the bliss of all this felt efficient and unspoiled. Even when I awoke some time later to find her gone, the bed empty and her imprint cooling in the sheets, the sense of having achieved something far in excess of what I actually deserved left me with a curious sense of wellbeing. My expectations were dialed way back since the rendezvous with the skunk; anything that didn't go wrong from then on felt like a happy extra, or needless bonus.

I assumed Karen had gone back to Randolph or her apartment on Christopher Street and expected a communiqué stuck to the mirror above my dresser or a message left with my parents. Perhaps a call later, when she was safely out of reach. Instead, I found her sitting at the kitchen table drinking coffee and discussing New York City with my father as my mother slid an apple cinnamon pancake the size of a manhole cover onto her plate. As far as I knew, Karen's overnight bag was still in her car and the bikini had been unmoored somewhere around the fire pit and never reclaimed; she'd helped herself to whatever was available in my bedroom closet. A Dystopia t-shirt sans sleeves, her nipples extruding around a screen-print of some anonymous dissident in a gas mask and a pair of bleached Wrangler cutoffs I used to skateboard in. Nothing else I saw in the kitchen suggested immediate action on my part. I joined the table, exchanged greetings with my parents, and nibbled a quadrant of the pancake set before me. All is well, I thought again, a little more convinced this time, even as my father and I exchanged a look of disbelief. Nice girl, he seemed to say; you've disturbed your mother.

Who are these kind people who let me use their nice house in the forest as a place to bring women? I wondered. It was the most academic question I'd asked in months and reminded me I'd managed to make it through an entire evening with Karen without having to pretend I was doing anything noteworthy. Belisarius hadn't come up once, a good thing, but relief over this seemed to indicate how much I relied on avoidance and omission to buoy my relationships with the people around me. Hopefully, last night won't become a metric for success going forward, I thought, as Karen dropped a few sample cases of Plump Lips / Tiny Hips on the breakfast table, trying to contextualize what she did for a living for my parents as they examined the variegated boxes.

"Does this stuff work?" asked my father, sniffing one of the canisters released from its packing.

"It's snake oil," said Karen blandly. "But that seems to be where the money is."

"I feel like I should disagree with that. But I assume the Audi in my driveway isn't a rental."

"When a joke relies on irony to be funny, there's something like a sixty to eighty percent chance most people won't get it. Profiting from that just means pretending you don't get it either. The person I expect to buy my product lives beneath a suspended punchline."

"Is it hard to be good at something you don't like?" asked my mother, sliding into a chair beside me, attracted by the sound of hubris. She seemed earnest, perhaps even interested in helping if she could.

"No one has ever asked me that before," said Karen. Thunder gurgled overhead.

"The most eloquently cynical people I know," said my mother, sounding vaguely oracular, "spend a lot of time doing things they hate to eventually do things they enjoy. What do you enjoy, Karen?"

"My dog," said Karen, looking at me for some reason. "Or dogs; animals in general. For a while, I imagined what it would be like to have a shelter somewhere like where I grew up or like where we are now. I liked the idea of doing that when I got tired of the whole New York thing. This was a few years ago, but I still think about it."

"I have a friend who does that," said my mother thoughtfully. "She's very content."

"I know who you're talking about," said my father. "She always smells a little wolfish to me."

The storm outside began a second act as breakfast drew to a close. Everyone seemed satisfied. My father went out to check the mail dressed like a watch stander during a typhoon. Karen stood at the sink in my clothes, helping my mother clean up after the meal. I looked on, worried about allowing her to be cross-examined by my parents, but glad they'd saved me the trouble of hashing out Karen's hopes and dreams on my own. I never know the questions

I want to ask until after I hear them answered, I thought a little later, watching the gloomy weather batter the landscape through the Audi's windshield as we drove back to Montpelier to pick up my parent's car. Our hands were clasped over the console as we listened to 'Boys of Summer' in generative silence, allowing the adenoidal voice of Don Henley to imbue the time we had left with an unearned epochal aspect. Opening credits rolled jauntily through my mind. I was beginning to imagine us rusticating with a pack of feral dogs, inviting myself into the future plans Karen shared over breakfast, when she said something about needing to get back to Randolph to pack and apologized in a jokey way if I felt used. The credits began rolling in reverse.

"Buck said you were in town for a week," I said, as we descended the hill toward Montpelier, socked in beneath an aggressive-looking cloudbank.

"I am," said Karen. "This is the end of that week."

"He made it sound like I had all the time in the world to make up for last night."

"Fun, Oliver," she said, kissing my hand and dropping it back in my lap as she turned into a parking lot behind city hall. "I'll be back in a month to deal with the estate. Try to stay harmless and weird in the meantime. Where did you park?"

Wherever I'd left the car constituted an opaque patch in my memory, so we had to drive around the municipal lots within a logical radius of the bar until we found it, parked at a creative angle beside the police station. I thought I noticed a soggy ticket flapping in the wind beneath the wiper as I got out of Karen's vehicle, but this turned out to be an invitation to a Reggae Church Supper, whatever that was. I returned to the Audi to say goodbye, and handed Karen the flier through the driver's side window, glad of any prop I could use to promote myself, at this point.

"If you stay tonight," I said, making a prefatory, magician-like motion with my hand over the paper. "We can go to this thing together. I'll call ahead to get some idea of the menu. Reserve a table."

"Reggae," she said, glancing at it. "Polka for black people."

"I think you would go with me if you could, but I don't know why I think that."

"I think we have the potential to appreciate each other in interesting ways, Oliver."

"So I can see you again?" I said, trying to rephrase the question before she could answer it. "So you want to see me again?"

Instead of answering, she reached through the window and cupped the crotch of my shorts. This evolved into an obscene sort of kiss, and a promise to call me when she returned in the next few weeks. The window ascended. The imminence of her sudden departure was no longer sudden or imminent. Credits continued rolling to the same soppy, self-serious tune as I stood in the rain waving until the Audi vanished around a corner.

As walked to my parent's car, a dog shitting pacifically beneath a shade tree barked at me mid coil, something I had never seen before, and didn't consider possible. What else have I learned today? I asked myself, wondering what it was about grandparents dying that made me more attractive to women like Karen and Carissa, a crossed wire or crooked spring somewhere along the line, but realized speculating on questions like this was unprofitable. Even if it were true, what would I do differently? I couldn't answer this question without imagining my life becoming appreciably weirder, so I let it drop.

*　　*　　*

When I returned to Acheron on Monday afternoon, I found a note from Buck flapping against the door of my shack. Would I like to have dinner at his place whenever I got back into town? An immanent time frame followed. Something new and weirdly formal was afoot. It wasn't as if he'd left a calling card with my butler, but the note suggested freshly mingled priorities, his and hers. Buck and I ate together often enough before Carissa reappeared, but never planned around our meals or made playdates out of them. He worked odd hours and I didn't work at all, so eating together felt like a good way to witness ourselves living like well-adjusted people.

This is clearly what it must be like to be married, I often thought, looking up from a plate, watching him chew whatever we'd thrown together to bookend a trip to or from the bar. I was usually hanging around his house when it happened to be dinnertime anyway and was under the impression I didn't need an invitation to have my meals there. The note felt a little like an eviction.

I leave town for a weekend and everyone grows up and starts throwing dinner parties, I thought, snatching the note off the door and walking inside to fix myself up for the evening. Hopefully there wouldn't be other guests. The act of conversation seemed like something I would have to lay siege to and my mind felt like a sluiceway of wartime photographs and soft-core pornography. I tried to shake it off, but ended up showering with a wine bottle within easy reach on the bathroom sink, hoping my nervousness would cloud up a little before I had to leave the house. I hadn't seen Carissa since the night Officer Roland came by to check up on me and didn't like the general direction things were moving anyway, but was relying on my success with Karen to get me through the next few hours, confidence-wise. I was getting used to the idea that my self-esteem had a mind of its own, but getting sprayed by the skunk threw everything into alignment long enough to make this seem like something I had to work around rather than live with. Syzygy, I thought as I dug blindly through the box of wine in my kitchen for something appropriate to bring. Is that the word I'm looking for?

All the windows were open in the house on Winter Street when I arrived and the place smelled like a library. The wind made a papery sound as it drew through the rooms, leaving a damp residue behind. Music we all liked played from a stereo Buck had moved onto the back porch, *Pink Flag*, I think it was. The dining room table sat beneath a willow in the backyard. I was relieved to see only four chairs around it. I assumed the fourth was for Amanda, who was helping Carissa make dinner. The two of them seemed to be getting along when I arrived and went into the steamy kitchen to say hello. They were making tapas, Carissa explained as she kissed a part of my face too far from my mouth to make any real difference in what I expected from the evening. I made a mental note to myself to drink enough to make the walk home seem short before remembering I'd driven.

That will definitely be a problem later, I thought, watching Carissa remove a pitcher of sangria from the fridge and hand it to Buck when he asked if she needed help with anything. He handed it to me and I followed him outside to the table beneath the willow. The dirt in the raised beds beside us had been turned over, and the yard smelled like fresh soil and the cut fruit bobbing in our glasses. Carissa spent most of the weekend getting the garden ready, Buck explained. I didn't see why I should care about this then, but later on, after moving into the attic, it began to seem like an obvious warning.

The food arrived in stages. Amanda sat beside me on one side of the table, and Carissa sat beside Buck on the other. Plates rotated. I ate without really knowing what I was eating. Most of it tasted like sangria, from what I could tell. I looked at the napkin spread across my thighs and wondered how it got there. Wine-logged fruit sat in the bottom of my glass, drawn and quartered. Everyone appeared to be having a nice time. Carissa was determined to be a good hostess, a development that set me speculating as I knocked back the meal she'd prepared, wondering how long it could possibly take a single shoe to drop. One of these things is not like the other, I thought, looking at the three people sharing the table as Carissa talked about her students and their art and how much better it was than most of the work she'd seen at school in New York. This had a flavor of noble-savagery about it, the sort of thing people say to make apathy seem whimsical. I watched her talk instead of listening and noticed she wore makeup and had stopped shaving her armpits. A briny odor hung in moist night air above the table. I began associating this with Carissa as the sun sank among the hills to my right, her left. The napkin twitched in my lap and I scooted further under the table so Amanda wouldn't notice. As if on cue, Buck asked about Karen.

"Nice," I said. "Smart. Efficient."

"So you called her," he said, glancing at Carissa as if this settled a bet between them.

"Efficient," echoed Amanda.

"I'm glad you met someone nice," said Carissa, sounding relieved. I'll bet you are, I thought.

"We just had a drink," I lied, wondering what sort of ground, if any, I needed to cover to make her jealous of someone she didn't know.

"You going to see her again?" asked Buck.

"She lives in New York," I said. "I don't know."

"You visited me there," said Carissa, her eyes smirking above the rim of a wine glass, clearly up to something. "You could probably visit her."

"I probably could," I said, irritated with myself for having nothing else to say back, or return fire with, and wondering if Carissa was trying to flirt or gently edge me out of town. A foot nudged mine beneath the table. This was encouraging. I nudged back.

"Are you kicking me as a signal or something?" asked Buck.

"Might be time for the other pitcher," said Carissa, eyeing the quarter inch or so of red wine in her glass.

"Do you like her?" asked Amanda, still interested in Karen for some reason.

"Yes," I answered a little too fast, my eyes locked on a tuft of tawny hair beneath Carissa's arm as she stretched over the back of her chair. I stood up, loudly volunteering myself to fetch the other pitcher of sangria from the kitchen and immediately sat down again to retrieve the napkin sailing out of my lap beneath the table. It was good cloth, more like a serviette, and could have matched the plates. Before tonight, I hadn't known Buck owned this sort of thing. Perhaps he never had a reason to trot out his linen chest and china set for just you, I thought to myself as I dropped beneath the table, raking the grass for the wayward linen, and noticed Carissa's hand clasped over Buck's knee like a starfish about two feet from my face. I stood up too fast, and smacked the back of my head on the bottom of the table hard enough to rattle the plates and silverware settings and dispatch a grackle roosting on the top rail of my chair.

Everyone looked worried above the tabletop and asked if I was all right, in canon. The pain at the base of my skull settled into a pulsing, livable vibrato as I assured them I was fine, trying to use as few words as possible, because I'd also bitten into my tongue when I hit my head and my mouth was filling up with blood. I felt a little like Count Dracula as I gestured opaquely at the empty pitcher and stalked off toward the house, resuming my errand with the sort of discipline I was used to envying in other people.

Being disappointed by things you expect is the same as expecting to be disappointed, I told myself, as I stood in a wedge of light before the refrigerator, cooling my head against the topmost rack and dribbling blood into the napkin I'd pulled out from under the table and brought along for some reason. She had chosen him. Historically, this made sense. How else? Geographically. Same town, same house, why not? Symmetrically. Can't forget that. Large, beautiful, important people belong together, don't they? Buck and Carissa were part of the same outsize world, a place I knew I didn't belong from hanging around both of them. I felt like the protagonist in one of the tragicomic English novels Buck was always quoting from, pointlessly adjusting myself to unfavorable circumstances beneath an umbrella of dim martyrdom and wondering whether Amanda and I had been invited to dinner as emotional factotums of some sort.

There must be a clever and painless way to not care about this, I thought, sipping directly from the pitcher of sangria as the cat, Agatha, I would learn later, twined herself between my legs, mewling for acknowledgement. The recent evening with Karen was beginning to feel like a fluke, an outlying coordinate on a map of uniform misadventures, beginning with the first afternoon Carissa and I spent together on a dock in the northwest cove of Kranion Pond, fifteen years earlier. She'd noticed my Clash t-shirt, a recent birthday gift from my parents, and I'd spotted her pink hair when she rose from the depths of the lake in the same bikini she gardened in years later and walked onto the strand of beach assigned to the summer homes our families had rented for the month. We clearly had things in common; I've never had an easier time knowing this about someone. I don't re-member who spoke first, but we passed the rest of the afternoon on the dock discussing music, shows we'd seen in Burlington and elsewhere, an upcoming Warped Tour at Suffolk Downs in Boston. I recall being only mildly let down when she mentioned a boyfriend in Warren who built a stage in his barn and had bands play pretty often. She said I should drive down there with her and Buck sometime and when I asked who Buck was, she said his dad had a place on the other side of lake. He has a record player over there too, she added. We could paddle across in her parent's canoe and see him that evening, listen to some music.

When I shared these plans with my family over dinner later on, they seemed glad I'd made a friend outside the circle of inveterate pot-smoking morons I skateboarded with in Montpelier or the older dropouts who hung around on the State House lawn and sometimes drove me to shows. I didn't tell them that when Caris-sa stood up after we agreed to meet later, excusing herself for the time being to change and eat with her folks, the towel threaded beneath her arms and fastened across her breasts fell away, re-minding me for the first time since she sat down how beautiful she was, yes, but also how much she resembled a woman. Long-limbed, broad-shouldered, buxom, the same figure I eventually explored years later in New York City, clearly at a different point of development than my own spindly, bird-like body shrouded in a t-shirt with the cover of *London Calling* on it. After dinner, I stood naked in front of the bathroom mirror before meeting Ca-rissa, examining myself for signs of retreating boyishness, or the possibility of one day looking less like myself and more like her or the kind of person I imagined her boyfriend in Warren to be.

This imaginary person turned out to closely resemble Buck when I met him for the first time later that night and we sat on the deck at his father's camp, listening to the Varukers and drinking his mother's coconut rum. The alcohol didn't dispel the feeling of being babysat by the two of them and seemed to enhance the dog-in-a-costume novelty of my presence in general. He and Carissa went to school together and knew each other well enough, but didn't know me at all, so the evening was mostly given over to resolving the question mark I represented for them. Things quickly grew jocular to a point where it began to seem like I was chasing after a bus they had boarded, so I settled into listening to the music and watching them be attractive, while fencing with the idea of what being well on your way to growing up must feel like. At the time, I assumed I would never again feel as outclassed as I did during the inaugural night of our friendship. But a decade or so down the line, as I stood in the open door of Buck's refrigerator, drinking sangria out of pitcher Carissa had prepared, I caught myself once again wishing puberty would go ahead and finish up with me.

Carissa was clearing the table when I returned to the yard with the half-empty pitcher. Buck was building a fire in the corner of the garden while Amanda gathered kindling from a woodpile on the back porch. My mouth felt bronzed, but the hole in my tongue had stopped bleeding enough to permit speech. I told Carissa I would help clean up and began gathering plates and glasses. With Buck and Amanda occupied, this might be my only chance to get her alone and I wasn't going to allow it to pass me by. There were certain things we needed to talk about, I thought. Or things I needed to say to her. Or things I wanted to say aloud and hoped she would listen to. I had some confessing to do, at any rate, and was hoping I could get through it without being sloppy or sounding as if I thought she owed me something. Whatever you do, I told myself, following her up the back steps with a jittery tower of dishes swaying in my hands, don't be smug. Smugness roosts beside mediocrity.

When we reached the kitchen, I realized Carissa would go right back outside again unless I said or did something out of the ordinary, so I ended up kissing her a little too hard beside the sink. She didn't scream or run away, but she didn't respond either. I briefly imagined my mouth as a remora probing for commensalism with something large and uncaring, the bottom of a boat or belly of a whale. Dirty plates trembled against my chest as I reached blindly for her hips with the stack balanced between my elbows. I was afraid of what she would say if I stopped kissing her long enough to put the dishes aside and hoped sending them cascading to the kitchen floor would look like a passionate symptom, if it came to that. Love and property destruction go hand in hand, do they not? I thought or prayed, as Carissa backed out of the kiss to scoop the entire creaking mess out of my arms and dump it in the sink.

"You taste like blood," she said, her eyes measuring the distance she'd drawn between us across the kitchen tiles. "Are you okay?"

"I know. It's bad," I slurred through a mouthful of gore. "I'll stop."

"Why are you talking like that?"

"I bit my tongue when I hit my head under the table. I think it's maybe a little swollen from that."

"I wouldn't kiss anyone else until you have it looked at by someone. You sound like you had a stroke."

"I won't kiss you again. I just expected to see you before now. I wanted to, I mean."

"I got a job, Oliver. I've been working a lot. Teaching."

"Can I give myself a break here and admit I'm not too blown over by that as an excuse?"

"You lead an imbalanced life."

"So the fuck do you," I said wearily. I would have given up one of my eyes to be taken seriously in the moment. "You can't possibly not know that about yourself."

"If I didn't, you probably would have seen me before now."

"I had this idea of us being pretty happy together without having to drain an ocean or move any mountains to get there."

"I feel like you're offering me a shortcut that isn't a shortcut because the beginning is the same as the end."

"Why work when you can travel?" I suggested meaninglessly. I was beginning to feel a little like a tent missing a pole and worried I might collapse on the floor unless I found somewhere to sit. Plates barricaded the counter and the kitchen chairs were taken up with the collected works of some Marxist freeloader Buck had purchased at a church sale in South Royalton. Falling over will mean the end of your side of this conversation, I told myself, listing slightly in a gentle breeze from the window above the sink.

"I wish you reminded me more of how much better I can be at the things that matter to me," said Carissa.

"Buck does."

"He's starting to."

"I think I've been trying to love you for a while," I said, lowering myself to the tiles at her feet, trying to look as deliberate about it as I could. "Years, maybe."

"I think you want someone to piss away your time with," she said, towering overhead. "That scares me."

"Eleanor Roosevelt said you should do something that scares you every day."

"Did you read that off a fridge magnet somewhere?"

"I think I saw it on a bumper sticker on the way over. Still, maybe we're on the right track here."

"I'm worried you'll only remember the parts of what I'm saying now that I've confirmed what you already think about me."

"If you mean, will I help you close out the topic in a way that leaves you feeling like there's nothing more to talk about, then you probably should be worried. Just not about that."

"Why are you doing this, Oliver?"

"Because I still want you to come back with me tonight, even though being near you right now makes me feel a little stupid for wanting that. Why are you doing what you're doing? With me, not him, I mean."

"Because we're old friends, and I wish you didn't have to try to love me. I love you without trying. I always have."

"I know what you think you mean, but I won't allow you to repaint me as your eunuch or best friend, whatever your aiming for here. I'm sorry, Carissa. If that was okay with me, I wouldn't have helped you clear the table."

"You said it was okay if I changed my mind."

"It is. It always was. I'm sorry you have to listen to me talk about how I haven't changed mine."

Carissa may or may not have been about to speak, but her eyes shifted over my head, clocking someone in the kitchen doorway. Amanda, seeking beer on behalf of Buck, who had finished with the fire and was changing records. The smell of wood smoke swept through the kitchen on a breath of wind as 'Somebody Got Murdered' roared from the porch. Carissa ran a finger beneath her eyes and checked her reflection in the upper pane of the window above the sink. I couldn't tell if she was combing away tears or reworking her makeup and didn't have the opportunity to find out. She left the kitchen with Amanda, each of them bearing a tinkling six-pack as they passed me sitting on the floor, staring fixedly at a nebula of cracks in the tile between my feet and suppressing the urge to do the dishes as a cover for smashing a couple of Buck's matching plates.

I never expected to get what I wanted out of the conversation with Carissa, so leaving it incomplete didn't bother me. But I disliked how comfortable I was becoming with bitterness. Trying to blame this on her didn't make sense. I was clearly a self-made victim. For the second time that night, I felt a little like Count Dracula, parsing the vulnerability of those closest to me for something to siphon off and internalize, something that would allow me to act like a casualty of their choices instead of my own. Who would choose to be the way I naturally appear to be? I riddled myself, resting my back against the kitchen cabinets and closing my eyes. At some point I must have wandered outside, because I came to two hours later in an Adirondack chair beside a bed of smoldering coals with a tepid, foaming beer crushed between my thighs, and Buck cupping my shoulder as he said something through the smoke about a spare bed in the attic, all made up if I needed to stay the night. Nothing in his demeanor suggested Carissa had told him about our earlier conversation in the kitchen, but I couldn't imagine waking up sober in the same house as both of them. Buck walked me to the front porch and listened as I did an oily job of asking him to thank Carissa for the meal. He seemed to understand what I meant, though not how I felt about it.

"I'm not going to take your keys," he said, before closing the door. "But if I hear your car start, I'm calling the sheriff. Walk home, Oliver. But come by tomorrow if you want a Bloody Mary and couple of Maigrets. Someone dumped a box of them on my steps over the weekend and I thought of you."

How kind you are to me, all things considered, I thought as

I marched raggedly down the stairs, toeing the empty air for the next step as if I was crossing the front yard on a tightrope. No wonder she likes you better.

I don't know if Amanda was specifically waiting for me, or something better to come along, but she must have watched me drop my keys five or six times trying to unlock my car before detaching from a belt of shadow across the street and asking for a ride up to the campus.

"I was just getting some books to take with me," I lied. Before she appeared, I had every intention of driving myself home, but I wasn't comfortable plopping her into the pool of risks I would have to court in order to do that.

"Maybe you can walk me to my dorm then," she said, her expression unreadable in the dim light thrown from houses up and down the block. "It's late. I worry about being by myself at night."

This reasoning rang a warning gong from some remote part of my memory of the past week, but I ignored it, curious to see what I was getting myself into. I wanted to tell her how little protection I expected to be if a carload of depraved perverts showed up, but it was nice to find we had something in common aside from garden-variety loneliness. I, too, worried about being by myself at night and also sometimes during the day, though the reasoning behind this ranged far and wide and was hard to isolate. My guess was most of it stemmed from the interactions I'd had or hadn't had with Carissa over the past two weeks or fifteen years, depending on how I looked at it, but I wasn't about to disentomb the topic in front of Amanda as I trotted beside her down Winter Street. She was objectively very pretty and had called on me to escort her home. The evening was suddenly awash with possibilities I was determined not to ruin.

Focus on what's in front of you, I advised myself, meaning this both figuratively and literally. The sidewalk had taken on a schismatic, tidal quality, seeming to draw away as I lifted my foot and rushing up to meet it when I stepped down. I managed to work myself into awkward, loping rhythm beside Amanda, but not before she asked why I was walking like a dinosaur. The question stumped me, but I noticed the lights of the Ethiopian restaurant beckoning across the street and suggested we get a drink.

"You should take Carissa here," said Amanda after the hostess greeted me by name and escorted us to the bar. She set out a plastic jug of tej and two glasses, not even bothering with a menu. The dining room was nearly empty, and the waiters hung around the kitchen door, watching us and nodding conspiratorially whenever I glanced in their direction. Something had recently been cleaned; the back of the restaurant smelled like bleach and red lentils.

"You think she'd like it?" I asked. Behind Amanda's back, one of the waiters made a feminine shape with his hands and gave me the thumbs up.

"It would be something she doesn't know about you."

"How much did you hear?"

"Enough to not feel like I'm taking you away from anything important by asking you to walk me home."

"Please don't tell him anything I said."

"She might."

"She won't."

"I think it would be good for you to make friends with people you actually like," said Amanda, thoughtfully cracking the glucose shell of a Crème Brulee one of the waiters brought her with the edge of a spoon.

"They like me," I said. "That's close enough, isn't it?"

"Resentment, Oliver. Envy. Love. One of these things is not like the others."

"I think all strong feelings are actually the same prevailing feeling with minor variations."

"You're a slob."

"Can I borrow your lasagna recipe?"

"You heard about that."

"He's treating it as an open secret."

"I can want things without being obsessed by them," she said, gesturing with her spoon, offering me the last bite of the dessert. "Can you?"

Good question, I thought, as we veered out of the restaurant a few minutes later and continued winding our way up the hill toward the college. I couldn't tell if I was headed for trouble or away from it, but the vaguely oracular conversation with Amanda left me wondering if it mattered, at this point or any other. I had plenty to lose, but nothing I would miss for very long. Reminding myself of this had the strange effect of cheering me up; it seemed to prove I was preoccupied with Carissa, rather than obsessed, as Amanda claimed. I tried to explain this distinction to her as if she was part of the conversation I'd been having with myself since leaving the restaurant, but I didn't get very far. I tripped over a sprinkler mid-sentence and collapsed in a heap on the lawn outside the Acheron College library. I didn't realize I was laughing until Amanda asked what was so funny. The moon slid from behind a cloud, making the campus look like a necropolis; this was my final memory of the evening. But Amanda told me later that instead of answering her question, I requested the lasagna recipe again and began loudly singing a Sinatra song about the French Foreign Legion in a Bela Lugosi voice until a campus safety officer emerged from the colonnade of Holmes Hall and asked me to stop.

I awoke shortly after dawn the next morning face down in a pile of dirty laundry at the foot of Amanda's bed. My skin was grass stained and my shirt had blood on it. I noticed my glasses inside a terrarium across the room, guarded by a red and white-banded milk snake sunning itself beneath a heat lamp. The day looked murky and fogbound beyond the dorm room window. Condensation slid in vertical streaks down the pane as if the building was weeping. My first impulse was to strike out for home. I sat up sharply and locked eyes with a young woman sitting beside the window, Amanda's roommate presumably, as she restlessly stirred a steaming cup of noodles and scowled into a textbook broken over her knees.

"Nothing happened," she said flatly, returning to her meal. This answered most of my questions. I had the sense she'd been examining me for long enough to fill in any gaps in the narrative explaining how I ended up in her room and had some opening remarks prepared if I didn't leave now that I was awake.

Threat-maker, I thought, excusing myself with a fling of my head in the general direction of the door. Amanda purred evenly in bed. I didn't remember enough of what occurred the night before to know if I should have learned a lesson from it, a troubling note to leave things on. I considered waking her up to fill in the blanks, but decided I might be happier with a few scenes missing until further notice. What I didn't know could hurt me, I knew that, but at least I wouldn't see it coming. Under the roommate's supervision, I retrieved my glasses from the snake pen and left the room.

Students were already milling around campus outside the dorm, rushing through the brume toward class in the early morning humidity. Summer intersession had begun. This is something I should have been aware of before now, I thought as I crossed the quad at an acute angle to the cafeteria, hoping I blended in, though my reflection in the window of the student union suggested someone a little too old to be waking up in a coed's laundry pile. At best, I looked like a caddy who slept on the links between shifts, awake now and up to no good.

At least I look like I have a job, I told myself. Threshing the positive aspects of my recent decisions from the negative ones might have occupied me for the rest of the morning if Dr. Norman didn't hove into view from the fogbank, barefoot, grey-bearded, imperious, wearing some sort of homespun caftan or bed shirt. He looked like he drove a chariot to work and his generally upright mien drew an unavoidable lifestyle contrast between us even when I was at my best, which I hadn't been for weeks. My thesis advisor noticed me and halted like he was leading a parade. I tried to remain downwind to keep the sour wine smell from wafting over him.

"You're early," he said. "But I can see you now."

"See me," I echoed, not understanding what he meant. His getup always directed me toward a mystical interpretation of whatever he said. Most of our conversations devolved into a kind of toneless counterpoint if they went on too long.

"Yes, Oliver. Last time we met, we agreed to see where you were with Belisarius and whatnot when intersession began," he said, his eyes wandering over the bloodstains on my shirt.

"I've been painting the shed," I said. It sounded experimental.

"Is that a euphemism for something I don't want to know about?"

"I'm nearly done," I said, either about the shed or the thesis. It didn't matter. Both were untrue. My tongue was still swollen from the night before and it sounded like I said 'dumb' instead of 'done'.

"Why don't we meet when you're feeling better?" he suggested, gliding past me, back into the murk. Pedant in the mist, I thought, as I stalked off toward town, feeling the way a crab must feel when it's scooped from the ocean and dropped on a rock by seagull. A Bloody Mary sounded necessary.

But after descending the hill from the college and bypassing downtown Acheron, I stood on the corner of Winter Street, staring up the block at my car parked outside Buck's house, wondering if there was a way to reclaim it without running into him or Carissa. After last night, a cocktail with the two of them might as well have been the coda of a passion play. I promised myself I'd come back for the car at more convenient time, whenever that might be. Possibly after the acrimony circulating in my brainpan had cooled off. No time soon, at any rate. We need some space from each other, I decided, setting off toward my riparian shack on foot. Even if they don't know it.

I didn't expect things to get better, but I assumed they would eventually get easier. One of the writers Buck had told me to read said something about all horrors becoming routine with time.

This ended up becoming true when I moved in with him and Carissa later that summer, but at the moment, it sounded like something to look forward to.

II.

"He was a good loser—at any rate an experienced one."
—Evelyn Waugh, *Men at Arms*

A WEEK AFTER THE DINNER AT Buck's house, I left town to caretake a summer home in North Hero. The property belonged to an acquaintance of a family friend, a woman my father met at a solstice party in some outlying region of Woodbury. She'd mentioned the job and he'd accepted on my behalf before calling me about it, as if he not only sensed how little I was up to, but knew how skewed my priorities had become as a result. I hadn't gone farther than my driveway since skulking home from Amanda's dorm and when my father called, I was casting a length of sewing thread into the current of the Wendigo, hoping to save myself a trip to town by hooking something I could eat for lunch. I'd baited the end of my line with a cube of cheese speared on a repurposed paperclip, and wound the slack around the wrist of the hand I wasn't using to read through a John Barron book about the KGB.

If beer grew on the trees, I thought, specifically, the stand of box elders beside the mailbox, I would be all set. Reminding myself that I wasn't afraid to leave the house was becoming a fulltime job, so I had decided to treat avoiding Buck and Carissa, or anywhere I might run into them, as a hobby or something I did because I enjoyed it. I felt positive about this decision, but didn't expect the feeling to last and noticed it starting to wane when my father called about the caretaking gig up north. My ersatz fishhook whirled anarchically in an eddy as he spoke, the cheese crumbling away in the sun-warmed water. It seemed, no matter where I looked, my life was rich with symbolic invitations to feel sorry for myself at all times and I was a little tired of it. On the phone, my father mentioned a change of scenery, a phrase I associated with the kind of self-recovery and work to be done I hoped I didn't need. But shifting my holding pattern to a new theater would solve enough immediate problems to make whatever was left over feel normal and might even remind me how I spent my time before Carissa moved back to town. At the moment, her reemergence in my life constituted a godhead of sorts and I was struggling to look past or beyond it.

The job didn't pay much, my father explained, but I didn't have to do much either. The owner wanted someone around through July and August to prevent teenagers from kicking in the window screens on the back porch and having sex on the three-season furniture. Aside from this, responsibilities sounded normal. The house sat on a quarter acre of cliff top overlooking Lake Champlain and I was expected to mow whatever this meant in terms of a lawn. A landscaping crew had been working on the veranda the month before and they'd left behind a pile of brush the owner wanted me to immolate in the yard. There might or might not be a dog to feed and walk. This was clearly work I could do, no getting around it.

"Plus," said my father, sounding a little obligated, "you'll have plenty of time to work on your thesis."

"Sure I will," I replied, wishing we agreed on something that wasn't mostly made up. I hadn't made any effort to reconvene with Dr. Norman since he cruised out of the mist earlier in the week, so as far as he knew, I was still painting the shed. But how long could that take? Should have told him it was a barn, I thought, wondering what my father would make of all this if I wasn't too afraid talk about it. I thanked him instead, set my line adrift, and went inside to see what packing felt like. My car was still outside Buck's house and most of the stuff on Belisarius was coffined in a banker's box on floor behind the passenger seat, so I considered it ready to go. But how had it gotten there? I remembered combing the notes, books, and loose papers off the desktop, not in a fit of rage, but in an ellipsis of paranoia after having half a bottle of wine with dinner and dozing off for an hour on the carpet. I dreamed of Mt. Abandon unmoored from the landscape, stalking purposefully through the dormant hills of Acheron at night, the war drum footfalls throbbing against the valley wall as they drew closer. I'd had this dream before, but not for years, and when I was younger, applying it to my waking life didn't seem important. But when I awoke on the floor in a neurotic fog with the tumulus of source material on the life and times of Belisarius looming above me on the desk, I listened for the thud of the juggernaut approaching my house and heard nothing because, I thought, it had arrived. So I dumped everything in the banker's box, adding a few good-sized stones plucked from the river bottom, intending to drive the entire mess up to Kranion Pond and scuttle it in the shallows off the fishing access. But as I was preparing to leave, Buck called from the supermarket downtown to ask what kind of beer I wanted and if I owned a shovel. Apparently, I'd forgotten we had plans to excavate a fire pit in the backyard of the house he'd just moved into on

Winter Street. I don't know what I said, but I remember his solitary voice sounding much more sane than the impetuous choir of hoots and screeches rocketing around my head as I rested it against the steering wheel of my Volvo with the weighted box on the floor behind my seat. Whatever alternate reality I'd been flirting with fell away, leaving me without anything to flee from. A deer rushed through the headlights as I rolled the car out of my driveway and turned left, toward town.

*   *   *

The owner of the house in North Hero was waiting in the yard when I arrived almost an hour late to pick up the keys. She introduced herself as Anne as I stepped out the car, concatenating different parts of the apology I'd rehearsed since becoming lost after exiting the interstate at Swanton. She immediately put me at ease by ignoring me and talking about herself as we toured the property beneath a gloomy brocade of storm clouds. She indicated the patch of lawn I was to tend and several piles of sticks around the yard she expected me to collect and burn in a hibachi she alluded to, but didn't show me. The teenagers weren't mentioned, so my duties seemed to end there, but she continued talking as we walked around the house to the back deck overlooking the lake. Anne was a dishy, active-looking woman in her mid-forties who taught poetry at Middlebury and was preparing to spend the next two months attending a series of residencies or symposia or artist retreats or some analogous combination of these. I didn't know anything about poets, but they seemed to lead busy lives. When I told her this, she laughed, an oddly musical snort like a French horn, and swept her slightly vulpine gaze away from my face, toward the cobalt surface of Lake Champlain rolling away at the foot of the cliff. I looked over the side and saw a skeletal staircase leading down to a thin slate ribbon of private beach. Small waves knocked against the hull of a canoe tipped against the rocks, manacled to the trunk of a waterside conifer with a clinking length of log chain.

"I used to come here to write," she said, running a thoughtful hand across the topmost slat of split rail fence dividing the yard from the face of the cliff. "Now I come here to get away from it."

"Then I've come to the right place."

"Sure you have," she replied, misunderstanding me. "Your father mentioned a thesis, though he couldn't explain what it was about."

"I don't think I can either."

"Try. It's good practice."

"No, thank you. I appreciate the invitation, but I don't want to pollute your sanctuary or anything by reminding you of one your less bright students."

"How considerate," she said slowly, hoisting an eyebrow. "No ivory towers in your future, Oliver?"

"A tower sounds nice. I don't need it to be made of anything in particular."

"Academia always has a place for people who don't want to be part of it."

"Can you recommend something else?"

"Unless you want to be a thrall to the MFA industrial complex, spending your summer shuttling between conferences in middle-American hellholes like Cleveland and Kansas City so you can listen to people half your age moan about combatting the kyriarchy at 9AM while you try to think of something not utterly disingenuous to say about their relentless hybrid forms and slam poetics other than it all being very topical, which most people are beginning to realize means the same thing as disposable, only to return home to a classroom of students who think poetry is the same as memoir and are willing to pay fifty grand a year for a degree to prove they're right about that, then no, I'm sorry, I have no suggestions. Let me show you inside the house."

Her dog, a boxer with the curiously sober name of John, broke off rooting around the base of the neighbor's fence to follow us inside. He would be my companion over the next few months, she explained, as the three of us shared a polygon of grey light from picture window in the living room, watching the distant surface of the lake and the humpbacked shape of a small island a quarter mile off the beach. Two cell-like bedrooms opened onto the living area and a narrow kitchen encompassed the corner beside the front door. A bathroom was presumably somewhere nearby, but didn't immediately suggest itself. It was both a disappointment and a relief to find the house wasn't all that much different than what I was used to.

Still, as Anne gestured at the window screens, reiterating the thing my father mentioned about teenagers, I began casting around for amenities. A bookshelf beside the picture window held a small, dreary library of poetry; Georg Trakl, Ezra Pound, Paul Celan. I didn't expect any of them to do me much good. But I noticed a wine rack in the kitchen with several bottles that looked expensive from across the room and the keys to the canoe were on a hook by the door. A blueprint for my existence over the next two months began coalescing. I imagined myself paddling out to the island with a bottle of wine uncorked between my knees, and the pages of *The Cantos* flipping wildly in the wind as John the dog sat in the forecastle, barking at a merganser. The beach was cloaked on three sides by the cliff, and private in any case, so swimming naked wouldn't be an issue. I'd passed a small liquor store and even smaller library on the way here and was pretty certain I could find at least one of them again.

114

So the important things in life are under control, I thought, following Anne and John outside and glancing back at the house. And the mountain will never find me here; it can't cross open water.

This thought seemed to have unhealthy origins, particularly the last part. Where had that come from? I wondered if having all of my immediate needs met had left me with enough spare time to redefine my relationship with paranoia. A sloppy syllogism began brewing as I watched Anne boot John back inside, and latch the deck door behind him: if real people have real problems then I am not quite a real person.

I followed Anne around the house to the driveway, anticipating a long evening of keeping watch through the picture window in case Mt. Abandon showed up. But she surprised me by asking if I was hungry when we reached her car and suggested we get something to eat when I nodded. We drove off as night closed in, our way lit only by the crepuscular glow from neighboring homes strung along the cliff. The car windows were down and the interior was humid with the smell of the lake and the swarthy evergreens bulwarking the lane. Periodic gusts of warm, sinister wind burst from somewhere over the water, buffeting the side of my face tauntingly, like one gentleman slapping another with a glove; the natural elements seemed to be tendering a prank of some sort. I kept turning toward Anne to avoid it and must have looked like I had something I needed to say. Our eyes met a few times, hers expectant, willing to listen, and mine probably alarmed and slightly febrile as I jerked my gaze back toward the headlights fanned ahead of us without saying anything.

"Are you okay?" she asked, finally, probingly, when we reached the main road.

"Why not?" I replied, mishearing her.

Anne chose a restaurant on the bay in St. Albans with a nautical motif; charts on the wall, sheets of rigging nailed to the ceiling, a disembodied ship's wheel propped in the corner beside an unlit fireplace. The waiters were dressed like luckless buccaneers, and one of them led us to a table on the deck at Anne's request, where we split a bottle of white wine and shared a joint between a guttering enfilade of Tiki torches, looking out over the winnowed face of the bay while we waited for our food to arrive. Anne was in the middle to late stages of talking about her divorce from another poet whose latest book, *Arranging Second-Hand Furniture with my Third Ex-Wife*, had just won an important literary prize I had never heard of. There were no children involved—a good thing, according to her—but enough territorial splintering between the recondite encampments of writers they both knew to make the entire thing seem like an Anschluss falling in his favor.

"Divorce is not generative," she said, smoke pluming between her lips, drifting toward the bay. "If he had died, there would be something to work with there, an authentic tragedy. But he already won a prize for writing our story. I can't publish my own thoughts on the subject, his subject now, without looking like an apologist. I feel silenced."

Her problems had no access point for me, but the resentment was familiar enough to set me at ease and seemed to summarize the resigned, careless mood of our surroundings beyond the seafaring embellishment. It reminded me of the dinner I'd had with my mother in the pizza restaurant in Lake George amid the Halloween ornaments shortly after my grandmother died.

I am the sort of company misery loves, I thought, witlessly passing the joint to our waiter when he arrived with two identical plates of fish and chips. Anne looked mortified and I felt a little stupid, but he surprised us both, glancing over his shoulder toward the dining room before taking two quick hits, nodding his thanks and withdrawing inside.

"Tough job," I said, flicking the joint into the mouth ofa small wave breaking soundlessly against the shore below the deck. "Big tip."

"I think I expected you to be more of a geek after talking to your father," said Anne, thoughtfully rolling the stem of her wineglass between thumb and forefinger, watching me across the table like I was the most challenging exhibit at a petting zoo. "But you're more like a—and don't take this the wrong way please, Oliver—you're more like a tramp. No offense. I mean it nicely, or as nicely as possible."

"None taken," I said, smiling redundantly. I liked this new idea of myself.

"Is there another word for someone who wanders around without any particular destination? Nomad?"

"Wanderer?" I suggested.

"Peripatetic," she decided, quaffing what remained in her glass and fixing me with a fox-faced, indulgent look, a real sizing up. It suddenly occurred to me that we were both single with nothing to do. "Have you ever read Li Po?"

"Is that a poet?"

"An eighth century Chinese poet. Tang dynasty. Wandered around the Yangtze river valley and hung out in the mountains and forests, drinking wine and visiting friends. And women, I suspect; he was married four times. Reading his work and talking to you makes me wish I could find more joy, or any joy, in aimlessness."

"I don't read much poetry."

"You should try. It might strike at the heart of whatever you're not sharing with me."

"I doubt that," I said, recalling the upright cone of Mt. Abandon strolling through Acheron at night, seeking me, or whatever I represented. "Why do you assume I'm not sharing something?"

"No one lets anyone else talk for as long as I've been talking about myself unless they have something exquisite or horrifying to mull over. Tell me what it is."

"It might be both," I said, figuring I may as well tell her about the dream, the mountain, the paranoia, just to see if everything sounded less hopelessly maladjusted in the wide open, empty air of the deck, thick with the oily smoke from the torches and the neutral sloughing of Lake Champlain against the beachhead. Anne had a flight to some middle-American toilet in the morning, Tulsa or Cleveland or Indianapolis, so firing me wasn't an option, even if she ended up thinking I was a lunatic. Who would look after John the dog? I wondered, trying to reread her expression and speak rationally about an irrational topic at the same time. I thought I was doing a decent job of it until I allowed the moon to startle me as I turned in mid-sentence to look out over the bay it hung above like an unripe, self-evident pumpkin, waxing nearly full. Had it been there the last time I looked? No way to tell now, but there was something emphatically creepy about imagining it surreptitiously racing up from the stygian horizon behind my right shoulder while I unwound the skein of my dread for Anne, as she had asked.

Apparently, I take requests now, I thought, tearing my gaze away from the moon, whose fixed position I was beginning to envy, and returning it to her, scribbling something on a napkin across the table. Our waiter materialized from beyond the reach of the torches and took the plates. The meal appeared to be finished. Anne asked if I wanted coffee and I just looked at her.

"Well, I'm getting some," she said, dispatching the waiter.

"And I need to ask if I can use what you just told me. It's a poem, I think, or the beginning of one."

"You'll do what you want with it no matter what," I said, noticing my reflection in the mirror behind the bar through the restaurant window; I looked a little tired and very vulnerable. "That's why no one trusts writers."

"You're right, of course," she said, smiling, tucking the napkin away in her handbag. "But I'd prefer to proceed in good faith, if possible. The mountain moves at night. It's like a sacred image, Oliver."

"I wish I shared your opinion."

"Maybe you will. I hope you will. Either way, we don't own our experiences."

"Maybe I'll write about your divorce then. Blame you for it."

"I'd be flattered if you knew what you were talking about."

"Scavenger."

"Tramp."

Her lips were moist with coffee as she pronounced the epithet and resettled her cup in a saucer, stirring it with a finger, smiling, amused. We were getting along well, I decided. And it had been a nice enough evening, objectively. The idea of sleeping with Anne began to take shape.

My soul is a murky place, I thought as she finished her coffee and paid the bill. A clock above the bar read 11PM as we left the restaurant, meaning I had until 11:30 or thereabouts to make myself worth sleeping with, unless she decided to take a short-cut or something back to North Hero. I wasn't quite sure how to do this on such short notice and wondered if I wasn't working against myself after sharing my fear of Mt. Abandon striding across the landscape to punish me in some way. Poetics aside, there was an inconvenient person attached to this raw material, a tramp, in her words, and obvious conclusions to consider. I circulated in the practical world, but stood apart from it in a way that I assumed would have made me the ideal rebound after a difficult divorce if my mental health wasn't such a crossword puzzle.

Still, we managed to hold hands and share another joint on the deck when we reached the house, as the dark lake chewed the base of the cliff somewhere below. Anne read aloud from a book of Li Po's poems in the light of a storm lantern and didn't ask what I thought of them, though I think she was encouraging me to locate myself, or the idea of me she'd developed over dinner, somewhere in his work. I attempted to resist this parity, but several lines into a poem about drinking wine and talking to the moon, I became a little spooked and lifted her hand to my mouth, kissing it as kind of nervous reflex. She didn't quite respond, but closed the book firmly when the poem was finished and stood up.

"Maybe when you're feeling better," she said, echoing Dr. Norman as she inclined her chin toward my pelvis and leaned in to kiss my cheek.

Like that's going to happen, I thought, watching her turn the corner of the house. A car engine erupted a few minutes later; tires creaked and receded down the gravel drive. Despite the ardor I'd been tunneling toward since leaving the restaurant, I was a little relieved. I wouldn't have to learn anything new tonight, thank god, or Mt. Abandon, whichever showed up first.

When I went inside the house to check my phone, there were several messages from Buck, and one from Carissa, all wondering where I was and inviting me down to Winter Street for the evening. Another dinner party no doubt. Did they know I'd been there earlier in the day, staking out the house from behind a hedgerow as I waited for them to leave so I could reclaim my car? She appeared first, striding down the steps and out into the day in paint-flecked work clothes, a reusable bag of art supplies bouncing jauntily against her calf as she passed within ten feet of my hiding place. Still beautiful, or what I thought that meant, not that I needed to check. It was impossible to imagine myself on her mind. Buck appeared next, forty minutes or so behind her, leaving the house with several boxes of books in the back of his pickup, destined for the post office, in no real hurry. I expected them to have no idea I'd watched them leave and assumed Amanda, who'd appeared on the porch while I was getting into my car, wouldn't say anything. I waved. She nodded. That was it. There wasn't much to discuss after the night I'd spent in her laundry, but I wanted to believe we could somehow be friends, even as she watched me ferry my bags from behind the hedge into the trunk of the car. I hoped Amanda was smart enough to realize not all my friendships ended this way and was on the verge of inviting her out to North Hero for the weekend just to see what would happen, but realized there was no way to formulate this invitation without sounding needy and indiscriminate. Any port in a place with ports, I thought, starting the car and turning to wave once more to Amanda, but she'd already gone inside.

* * *

Toward the middle of July, the homes along the cliff filled up with families from Massachusetts and Connecticut. Boats dotted of the formerly vacant stretch of water between the island and the shore, canoes, bowriders, an occasional catamaran. The evenings were thick with grill smoke; conversation and music wafted over the fence separating me from my neighbors. Passels of teenagers roamed the lane at all hours beneath the hooded conifers, looking for trouble. I watched them pass from the yard, hunched over the squealing, medieval reel mower, feeling a depressing greed for the company of people half my age.

This must be how the witch in the candy house felt, I thought, creaking my bitter way across the patch of lawn beside the deck. There was no way to participate in or escape the merriment surrounding me. I knew that. After the evening with Anne, living deliberately, or less indiscriminately, seemed worth a try, but my new job conferred the kind of rudderless solitude I would have worried about more if I hadn't been in such a hurry to get away from Carissa and the results of this were becoming apparent. During the last week of July, I nearly mowed my way off the cliff while watching a group of girls about Amanda's age flounce past the house on their way to the beach, a slow reel of bikinis, suntanned skin, and one or two navel piercings, and realized the three or four beers I'd gotten into the habit of enjoying over lunch would probably be considered a problem if anyone other than John the dog was around to notice. He and I got along well enough as it was, though he'd begun giving me overlong looks of what felt like professional concern from between his paws as I swayed in a rocking chair in the living room late into the evenings, reading Li Po aloud over and over and perennially glancing out the window toward the lake for anything large and mountain-shaped lurching out of the middle distance.

John seemed bored, but content, a mood we shared and which I considered a job well done on my part. The rest of my duties seemed almost honorary by comparison. I'd been mowing the lawn everyday just to have something to do and it was getting a little threadbare. The teenagers hadn't come anywhere near the house after I'd found a collection of Wagner CDs in one of the bedroom closets and started playing the operas on repeat throughout the night and day, a little too loud to be ignored by anyone passing by or standing too close to the fence. I still had to burn the sticks the landscaping crew left behind, but was waiting for a special occasion and hoped one was on the horizon. I felt a little like a lighthouse keeper overall, but without any sort of essential duty to animate or ennoble my reliance on alcohol to shoot down the hours of the day, one by one, like targets in a carnival game, the sort that spring inevitably back into place after the prizes are awarded.

Still, the possibility of doing anything differently seemed remote until the afternoon I nearly strolled off the cliff while watching the girls walk to the beach, and only then because the clerk at the liquor store in town looked at me the same way John had started to when I approached the counter later in the day with a case of beer he ended up refusing to sell me. I think he suspected I was drunk, but knew he couldn't prove it and cited the store's policy requiring shoes and a shirt instead when I tried to pay him. I wanted to argue, but noticed my manifold reflection in a spinning plastic display of sunglasses beside the register, shirtless, sunburnt, unshowered, with a mean-looking thatch of pubic hair coiling over the waistline of my cutoffs, and queue of friendly-looking tourists backing up behind me.

I've become one of those people who cause scenes, I thought, dropping a twenty on the counter and leaving with the beer beneath my arm. The clerk protested limply at first, but was glad to see me leave and even said something on my way out about how I could come back for my change tomorrow morning, but he wasn't having me in there three times in one day. Three times? I thought on way back to the house. Had I been there this morning? I couldn't remember, but didn't see why the clerk, who knew me by name, would make it up.

What else have I forgotten? I wondered, crossing the scalped lawn with the case of beer beneath my arm, a little mortified with myself when I noticed I smelled tangy, in addition to everything else. I stood on the edge of the cliff in the place where I'd nearly tumbled to my doom that morning, watching a yoke of purple clouds settle over the shoulder of the island occupying the near distance. I sensed an incomplete answer across the water, or something ineffable and distracting, at any rate. Except for my mostly made-up obligation to the lawn, nothing prevented me from exploring it, so I went inside to grab John and the keys to unlock the canoe down on the beach.

Forty minutes later, our hull knocked against a bank of rock in small cove on the island's flank and we debarked. I dragged the canoe ashore and tied it off, while John disappeared into the underbrush. The island was no more than two acres of scraggly trees and mossy rock, but it was new terrain for us both and provided something unusual to explore. When I saw how happy this made John, I recalled something Schrödinger wrote about achieving consciousness, "becoming is conscious, being unconscious," and I felt deeply guilty for how unedifying the past few weeks must have been for him. I hoped spending time around me hadn't made the dog stupid.

But later on, as I sat with John on a tongue of pitted limestone reaching out from the corpus of the island into Lake Champlain, sharing a tuna fish sandwich I'd brought along and looking at where I'd come from, the house on a cliff across the water, I suspected the dog and I shared a renewed sense of mutual wellbeing. I was weirdly grateful to myself for remembering to take advantage of my surroundings and wondered if this was what it felt like to live deliberately. I am a willing participant in my own life, I thought, as John nibbled the remains of the sandwich dangling from hand. It had been a while since I had reminded myself of this.

*　　*　　*

Through the remains of July and the beginning of August, John and I canoed out to the island every morning. In the afternoons, we took long walks along an old railroad bed running parallel to the cliff, part of a former service between New York State and the Canadian border. The tracks were removed sometime after 1948 and the walk terminated at a narrow isthmus between a beach and a marina where there had once been a trestle across the water. I sat on the slabs of granite remaining from the bridge, smoking a joint beneath the trees and watching girls swim off the beach while John rooted around in the cinders. Having a dog nearby seemed like evidence that I wasn't a creep, or that I was a discrete one, at any rate, a gentleman creep. I decided to treat this distinction as a mark of progress. Watching women at a distance instead of begging them to randomly participate in my life had to be a step in the right direction.

In the evenings, I worked on what was originally intended to be the opening sortie of my thesis, but over time had become a letter to Carissa composed of a series of semi-related vignettes— or an autobiographical novella with her name and a salutation at the top. After returning from my maiden voyage to the island, I'd removed the box of material on Belisarius from the car as if it were a reliquary or an urn holding the ashes of a particularly imposing relative, cruel in life, I imagined, and still somehow holding sway after death. I intended to do something purposeful with it, whatever that meant, but ending up tossing the stones from the river bottom off the deck and dumping the box under-the dining room table after removing an unopened package of yellow legal pads from it. I remembered buying them in good faith, intending to take notes, many notes, notes of all kinds, or enough notes to throw Dr. Norman off my trail for a while. At this point, the idea of receiving an advanced degree in anything had all the gravity of a practical joke.

But, I wondered: how much raw, academic sewage would come churning out of me if I actually sat down and tried to write something? I had the time to find out, though after two hours, three joints, and almost the entirety of *Das Rheingold,* I realized I didn't know enough about my subject anymore to produce even a mediocre outline. Perhaps I never had; the title I'd written at the top of the page, 'The Campaigns of Belisarius,' was nothing to get excited about and clearly an Appian rip-off. Am I thinking deliberately? I asked myself. As if to answer this question, my phone vibrated on the tabletop with a text message from Carissa. She missed me, she claimed, and thought we should talk.

"I disagree," I said aloud, crossing out the title, the only real headway I'd made on my thesis in two months, and replacing it with 'Dear Carissa.'

From this point on, filling a page or two each night wasn't a problem, and became something I looked forward to after walking John down to the former bridgehead and back. I was drinking less beer, but smoking more pot, a changing of the guard that often left me in an expansive mood after sunset, as if someone had cast a very mild spell on me. I felt like sharing my feelings on things, but not with anyone in particular. Writing about them diked the compulsive void left behind after I stopped needlessly shearing the lawn each day. Whenever I needed a break from the novella, I loaded John into the car and drove hazily into town for a treat. The clerk at the liquor outlet appeared less worried now when he saw me coming. He'd become used to me showing up late at night with food stains on my shirt, eyes the color of a harvest moon, and watching me leave with only a pint of ice cream or package of cookies, a jar of raw honey, on one occasion. Driving back to the house with whatever I'd bought open on the seat between John and me, and the steering wheel sticky from my fingers, I'd recurrently lapse into tallying all the indications over the past few weeks that eudemonia was at hand.

*   *   *

Karen called one morning during the last week in August. She was in Randolph to settle some details of her grandfather's estate and sleeping on the floor of his living room on an air mattress. All the furnishings had been cleared out, she said, and the house was for sale. She had wine, some grapes, and cheese. Would I like to come over?

"Yes. But if I leave the house, teenagers might break in and have sex all over the place," I said, without explaining where I was, or what I'd been doing for the past month. At a glance, the recent details of my life and work seemed self-evident. When I looked back on the conversation, Karen surprised me by taking this prohibition in stride.

"Well, okay, Oliver," she said. "Why don't I just go where you are then?"

I liked this idea, but the day ahead was shaping up to be messy through the picture window. The sky above the lake looked contused and the chop between the cliff and the island was starting to rock and swell in the wind. Randolph was a ninety-minute drive in good weather. I offered to meet Karen in Montpelier, but she had meetings with two lawyers and a real estate agent

127

and couldn't commit to a time, so she offered to drive out when everything was finished.

"I thought you lived in Acheron," she said when I gave her the North Hero address. "I was looking forward to seeing your Kaczynski cabin."

"I'm housesitting a place on Lake Champlain," I said. "It has a dog and a private beach. And a canoe."

"I see about the teenagers now," she said, excited. "Should I bring anything?"

"A swimsuit," I said, meaning it differently than the last time she'd asked. We hung up, both a little giddy. I glanced at John, sitting like a gargoyle by the front door, expecting a canoe ride. "We're having a guest."

On the way down to the beach, I noticed the pile of sticks Anne wanted me to burn stacked in a corner of the now overgrown lawn. Karen visiting seemed like the kind of special occasion I'd been waiting for; I made an unreliable mental note to drag them over to the hibachi when I got back. Also: buy something that can be reliably cooked over an open flame. Clean the bathroom. Wash the bed sheets, or at least shake them out. Locate a shirt without a chocolate stain or hole burnt in it. Buy Visine.

It seemed I suddenly had a lot to do before Karen arrived, more than I was used to, which was enough to keep me from noticing the lack of other boats on the water as I shoved off into the bucking surf toward the island. Waves slapped the keel as the canoe reeled along, breaking across my lap and rolling John all over the bow as the clouds murmured above. It had already begun to rain by the time we reached our embayment, the wind sweeping through the palsied trees as I tried to find one sturdy enough to tie off the boat. By the time I'd gotten everything more or less squared away, the squall had completely obscured the house and beach where we set off. John and I sheltered inadequately beneath a low rocky outcropping, sharing the sandwiches and coffee I'd brought along and watching the static curtain of rain and wind buffeting the island toss our canoe around the bay. We weren't going anywhere soon and the possibility of dying from exposure was growing steadily less remote as water dribbled down the wall of rock I leaned against. My clothes were soaked and heavy and my teeth clicked in my jaw as I chewed and swallowed. Still, there was something funny in the chance of the joyful little routine I'd cultivated over the past few weeks killing me, a gallows irony, the sort of thing I hoped to share with Karen if John and I made it home alive. He seemed fine, a little disappointed, but enjoying the food and not all bothered by the concussion of thunder overhead. If I died first, he would probably eat me and I was fine with that and strangely at peace with whatever else might happen. I'd be sorry to make Karen drive all the way out here for nothing, sorry to upset my parents, and the idea of never seeing Buck and Carissa again troubled me, but freezing to death on an uninhabited island with a dog and a cup of coffee sounded better than steering my car into a tree after one too many drinks at the bar. I knew this wasn't an either/or proposition, but it seemed like firm evidence that I was beginning to expect better things from myself.

Good for me, I thought cheerfully as I broke from the shelter of the rock and began untying the boat. The storm wasn't over, but had settled down enough to make crossing back to the beach less of a fool's errand. I strapped John into the only life jacket, and pushed off, secure in the knowledge that I wasn't going to get any wetter and even if my appendages were beginning to lose feeling, they probably still had enough vitality left to get us back to shore. A sudden dendrite of lightening pointed toward home as I began doggedly scooping my way across the water.

When the house on the cliff finally appeared through the coverlet of rain and wind, a light glimmered from the living room window, a development that would have seemed cozy if I'd left it on before leaving the house. Hormones wait for no one, I thought, feeling a little old as I pulled up on shore, rethreaded the log chain beneath the thwarts and rolled the canoe against the base of the cliff. I expected trouble as I mounted the steps up to the house, but wasn't really in the mood for it. The muscles I could still feel ached with a kind of animus, as if my body was furious with me, and I wasn't certain I had what it would take to kick a bunch of rutting kids out of the house. When I dropped off the life jacket and paddles in the shed, I considered taking a short nap beside the lawnmower, just to regroup. But there was nothing to wrap myself in other than an old tarp and I began wondering if this idea fell under the heading of normal everyday dithering or hypothermic judgment in action. Hot shower, dry clothes, kick everybody out, I thought as I locked the shed and crossed the soggy yard to the house. In that order if necessary.

Karen stood in a bikini at the sink, filling a kettle when I rose above the sill of the kitchen window like a periscope breaking the surface of an otherwise placid sea, intending to take whoever had invaded my home by surprise. We shared an expression of shock. I couldn't hear her scream over the weather outside and she probably couldn't hear me apologize for scaring the bejesus out of her.

"What the fuck is wrong with you, Oliver?" she asked earnestly, holding open the front door for me as I hauled John inside and began removing my clothes. "And where have you been? When you popped up in the window I thought it was the Creature from the Black Lagoon."

"I'm sorry," I repeated over and over again from beneath a jet of boiling water as I stood in the shower stall I'd planned to clean earlier in the day. I'd expected to find a coterie of five to six licentious adolescents drinking my beer and smoking my weed in a nest of ashes, empties and used condoms, and wanted to explain this in way that made sense.

"Why are you so fascinated with the sexuality of people half your age?" asked Karen, thrusting the curtain aside and wedging herself into the stall.

"It's my job," I said gravely. Apparently, my reasoning ability was still thawing from the brush with exposure. I caught myself about to ask where her bikini had gone, but managed to reroute this into a question about how she ended up at the house while I was still skirmishing with the elements out at the island.

"Everyone cancelled their meetings," she said, resting her face against my neck, her lips moving against my collarbone. "Storm's a-comin'."

As if to punctuate this remark, the light in the bathroom went out and the water grew cold.

The storm I'd paddled through to get back from the island was actually part of a hurricane system making landfall up and down the eastern seaboard, battering Boston and New York and leaving Karen temporarily homeless.

"Last I checked my street was under water," she said, as we lay knotted together in bed later that night, listening to wind howl against the bedroom window, rain sloshing onto the roof. I'd found some candles beneath the kitchen sink, not many, but enough to keep us from banging into things until we could get more. Several guttered on the nightstand, brokering the darkness. Whenever I looked out a window, I had the impression we were at sea.

"So stay with me until it gets swamped out," I said, hoping she would, but trying to sound casual about it. Karen didn't say anything, but drew herself deeper into the mattress, coiling against me. Neither of our phones was getting a signal and the house's router was on the fritz, leaving us without the means to contextualize the threatening events outside and abroad.

So, for now, we're trapped, in a good way, I thought, drooling a little on Karen's forearm as I imagined the coming days passing in a languid haze of sex, pot smoke, and the poetry of Li Po. Perhaps walks with John along the railroad bed and trips out to the island when the storm cleared up. Maybe she wouldn't even want to return to New York once her street was drained; we could set up shop somewhere back in Acheron, start taking in strays and donations, live like two people who have it all figured out. There was nothing to get in our way, so why not?

"I'm seeing someone," she said, abruptly. It sounded almost like a cough.

"Someone else?" I asked.

"Someone back in New York. I thought you should know if I'm going to be here for a little while."

"How do you know they haven't been claimed by the tempest?"

"He has a place in Connecticut and he's out there now, so I don't think so."

"A place in Connecticut," I echoed, toying with all the possible permutations of this. Most of them seemed to indicate a disparity on my part. "Can we maybe roll the conversation back a little, maybe to a time before I didn't know about that?"

"Sure, if you want. I just thought I'd give you the chance to kick me out in the storm, make me sleep in my car so you don't feel used, whatever you need to do."

"There's a second bedroom if I get around to it."

"Oliver," she said, hoisting herself up on an elbow, her face half-mooned in the candlelight. "I'm here with you now. I was under the impression that was good enough."

"No, it is and I'm happy about it. I want you here as long as you'll stay," I said, meaning it, but trying not to sound martyr-like as I extinguished the candles on the nightstand. I thought we were settling down for the night, but Karen began steering things toward coition in a way that felt almost apologetic, obliging me to accept conditions as they were unnaturally fast, shelter in her body and dry my tears on her laurel wreath or risk spoiling the moment.

Traps travel in pairs, I thought obliquely, measuring the sides of her torso with my hands, until I found her hips, trying unsuccessfully to shake the roving, renaissance image of the Connecticut homeowner I shared Karen with as the storm rocked the house and we panted rhythmically, heroically, like distant drums in the night.

Karen wasn't in bed when I awoke the next morning, still jealous from the night before, but glad to hear her grinding coffee beans, playing the radio in the kitchen, her bare feet sweeping across the wooden floor of the house. This was good enough, as she said, a kind of enclave in the isolation I'd been struggling to enjoy over the past six weeks, but hadn't really reached the other side of until she arrived. Despite the residual jealousy, happiness had fallen upon me like an air raid during the night and waking now to the minute noises of Karen nearby, it was easy to retreat into the illusion of a complete life or what I imagined one might look like.

Of course, our time together was temporary, a stable oasis in a desert of reckless neglect. No problem, I thought, fully expecting everything to slip back into its former disorder as soon as she left for New York and wanting to gird myself for this in some way. But how? I wondered, as my phone vibrated in a bed of wax on the nightstand; Buck calling, the second time that morning. Re-checking my recent anarchic treatment of him and Carissa might be a good place to start. I didn't answer the call, only because I wanted to ask Karen for help explaining why I'd ignored him since July.

Adults teach other adults to behave like adults, I thought, testing the weight of the apology I probably owed her after allowing bitterness to define my part of the conversation last night. I was a little disgusted with myself over it, but had begun to worry I came off as someone who was fundamentally happier by himself, even if I didn't know it. I tried picturing myself as a lone wolf plodding endlessly around the tundra instead of mating for life, but ended up wondering what it would feel like to gnaw my fore-leg out of a trap. Not good, I decided. This wasn't the kind of entropy I expected to thrive in. I left the bedroom naked, scared, but not alone, for the time being; this turned out to be important.

Karen was on the deck wearing a t-shirt of mine with nothing underneath, sipping coffee and reading through one of the legal pads I'd left on the dining room table with her feet elevated on the armrest of the chair I sat in. The shirt rode up over her butt just enough to give me a slightly zoological view of things as we said good morning. For some reason, I wondered if I'd ever own a home. She flipped a page and looked at me over the jaundiced horizon of the legal pad.

"Is this something I should worry about?" she asked. The question caught me off guard.

"I'm not," I said, or decided, just then. "Why should you be?"

"Sometimes it sounds like a memoir," she said, in a way that made me feel like we were in the early stages of solving a crossword. "Other times, like a last will and testament."

"A memoir," I repeated, a little insulted by that more than the other thing. Over the radio inside the house, the local public station broadcast on the residuum of the storm. Rainfall of three to five inches statewide, with some higher, eastern areas getting up to seven. Floodwaters choked with debris inundated two hundred and twenty five municipalities and rivaled, some thought, the damage wrought by the historic flood of 1927, a kind of high water mark, apparently. Experts were calling it a disaster for the state of Vermont. This made me briefly nervous, but I glanced around the yard and didn't see anything to worry about. The sticks I was supposed to burn had been blown around the yard. The hibachi I was to burn them in lay against the split-rail fence on the edge of the cliff. A mutilated tree leaned a little cravenly toward the house. But no shingles were missing from the roof. The lawn was overgrown, but healthy. The lake appeared silver and mottled beneath the tired grayscale sky. The day risen up around Karen and me on the deck was damp, humid, and looked a bit moody, but no longer sinister.

"Is Carissa a real person?" asked Karen, closing the legal pad and setting it aside. She smiled, something I wasn't expecting.

"Maybe not as real as I made her out to be in what you read. We used to know each other better."

"Buck is."

"Yes, Karen," I said, trying not to sound like I had something to defend as a I gestured vaguely around the property. "Do you think I just make these people up to pass the time out here?"

"I'm talking about fiction, Oliver. Literature. What are you talking about?"

"Maybe I don't know. I mostly read mysteries," I said, as my phone buzzed on the table between us; Buck again. I had to answer, if only to show Karen I wasn't cooking up phantoms to wile away the hours. "In fact, that's him now, Buck, I mean. Mind if I take this?"

I stood up without waiting for her answer and strode naked off into the yard as if I had private business to attend to out there, something sketchy I couldn't share with her. I was embarrassed for automatically assuming Karen was questioning my toehold in reality by asking if I'd made up Carissa, but figured this was the kind of trouble all authors must encounter when their only reader is also the person they're fucking. And, in point of fact, I made things up all the time—the itinerant shade of Mt. Abandon being only the most recent example—but didn't write any of them down. This was the only real difference between what she'd asked and what I thought she meant by it, a hair split at least three ways, and counting. Maybe I should start keeping track of this crap, I thought, leaning on the fence and looking over the cliff as I took Buck's call. There could be a thesis in it for me.

"Oliver? Is that you?" said Buck. He sounded a little frantic, which didn't match the mood I'd settled into before answering the phone. "Where are you? I've been trying to reach you since 5AM! I don't exactly know how to say this, but-"

"Listen, Buck," I interrupted, feeling ennobled by the contrition I assumed he was waiting to hear. I slid down the fence, closer to the deck and raised my voice, wanting to give Karen an example of myself owning up to something. I imagined the title: Oliver Himmel Addresses Those He has Wronged paired with a portrait of me naked and remorseful above the slow, silver roll of the lake, with the island in the background suggesting itself as a place of banishment or exile. Hang that above the fireplace in Connecticut, I thought, pretending to not to notice Karen nearby as I launched loudly into the opening movement of my threnody.

"I know I've been a bad friend since Carissa came back to town and I think you know why, even if she hasn't told you. I talked with her about it, but I wish I'd had the nerve to talk to you and I'm so sorry I'm only able to do it now. I love you both; I think I always have, but I don't know how to love the two of you together, without me. I can't explain it any better. It's not the kind of situation anyone gets to practice describing. I knew what would happen when she came back, so I have no right to pretend I'm surprised by it or to take my jealousy out on you. But I knew you wouldn't abandon me over it, so I knew I could be shitty about it. I wasn't so sure about her, because she had you. In a way, it's possible she and I want the same thing, even if our reasons for wanting it are different. I thought you were a singular person before any of this, Buck, but after allowing me to be petty and cruel to you over her, I'm humbled, and I don't know what to think. I want to feel lucky, but I don't know if it's too late to feel that way and I miss you guys and want to-"

"That's all fine," said Buck, wearily. He'd been trying to override my monologue since it began, but managed to succeed when I paused to shoo a confused honeybee away from my genitals. We were both impatient to get our separate points across, but I figured I should probably allow him to talk a little, if only to remind Karen I was capable of listening. "But wherever you are, you need to come back now or at least call the sheriff's department. Roland showed up here at like 4AM with Sheriff Blivet, looking for you. I didn't know what to say, and no one could reach your folks-"

"They're in Cinque Terra," I said, adding: "Italy."

"Great, good for them. Look, I wish I didn't have to be the one to tell you this, Oliver . . ."

The conversation didn't last much longer and mostly involved Buck talking and me listening, though based on Karen's expression when I returned, she overheard enough of my side of things to know something was wrong. She stood up as I sat down, gathering her cup and the notepad from the table, tugging my shirt down to cover herself. Being naked now seemed absurd, almost infantile under the circumstances; my own nudity made me feel like a newborn set adrift.

"I'll pack," she said, turning to go inside, but pausing in the doorway, worried, very beautiful, clearly planning to come along with me wherever I had to go next. "I'll get you something to put on."

"Thank you," I said, somewhat formally as she kissed me along the hairline and went inside. Dressing felt a little redundant at this point, but I sensed the obvious rising up around me like a kind of shelter, or a place to hide at any rate, and the mundane details of the day taking on a new and overpowering resonance. Poetry, I thought. This would be an excellent time to read some. I lurched through the deck door, nearly falling over John, who Karen had already cinched into his traveling harness, and grabbed at the bookshelf for something, anything, that might imbue my surroundings with a measure of ambiguity, or a reminder of something to hope for.

A shade I am remote from somber hamlets.
The silence of God
I drank from the woodland well.

Karen encountered me mumbling this stanza over and over

when she came out of the bedroom, trying to apply it to myself in some way. Beneath the overcast morning sky, the island seemed to beckon through the deck door. I realized this was something we wouldn't get to share while she struggled to get me dressed and out of the house, as if I'd become the overgrown child I imagined earlier on the deck. I wanted to ask why Karen was doing all this for me so I could hear something affirming, but worried her answer might come freighted with the sort of everyday humanist logic that had nothing to do with me and everything to do with inarguable principles, some general idea about helping people who needed help. So I sat quietly in the living room instead as she made us a quick breakfast, stroking John and whistling a reedy version of 'The Solemn March to the Holy Grail' from *Parsifal* until Karen leaned out of the kitchen to say the song was frankly creeping her out and asked me to stop.

Buck must have made some calls after he got ahold of me, because when Karen and I reached Acheron an hour later, several cars were in my driveway and a bored but solemn welcoming party was arrayed around my yard. Officer Roland and his boss Sheriff Blivet, as expected, and Buck, of course, talking to Henry Hoffmann, the surprise guest apparently, and the last person I expected or wanted to see in that moment. A couple of people matching the physical description of my neighbors and the fire marshal were preparing to pull out as we arrived. The sound of Karen's car drew their compound attention from the denuded smear of soggy land where my house had recently stood. Only a trellis of loose plumbing and a cairn of cinderblocks, which had supported the front steps, remained. As Karen parked between two cruisers, I noticed my front door pressed into the cut bank on the opposing side of the river. It didn't look good, I thought as

I stepped out of the car. But at least it looked complete. I'd hate to have an unfinished ruin on my hands.

Buck met us beside the somehow perfectly intact mailbox, re-introducing himself to Karen and hugging me, but not saying much else as he walked us over to Roland and the Sheriff. Henry sat on the heap of cinderblocks nearby, reading a waterlogged John Le Carre paperback he'd picked up from the lawn, waiting his turn, placid as a hangman beneath the brim of his sunhat. I remembered him from years ago stalking around town while Mr. Castle, his patron, was still alive, managing properties and collecting rents like the Sheriff of Nottingham, all the while with the collar of his pea coat turned up in what I always thought of as a needlessly threatening gesture, like a frilled lizard trying to scare something out of a tree. A few days before Mr. Castle died, Henry and I got into a doctrinaire disagreement over whether or not he could bring his dog into the grocery store, a moment I remember well because we were both clearly working through ineffable personal issues at the time, issues that found weird, circumstantial expression in the store's pet policy, of all things. I don't remember yelling, but I know my side of the conversation got loud enough to draw the attention of other customers and make the dog growl as Henry smugly scratched her ears, watching me sputter and unravel with tears in my eyes. Grover broke it up and sent me home before anything serious happened, a decision I hated him for at the time, since it made me look like unhinged clown in front of Henry, though later on, after learning more about his activities around town, I realized my boss was probably trying to keep me off the Castle family's shitlist. There were rumors of people losing their homes, jobs, personal property, of lifetime residents evicted from the entire municipality or living in a kind of sadistic indentured servitude for running afoul of Henry in one way or another.

And this was years ago, I thought, watching him page through the soggy Le Carre as Roland and Sheriff Blivet strode unevenly across the yard toward Karen and me. How has his power grown since then? And what is it doing on my doorstep?

"Glad you're okay," said Roland, shaking my hand, as his ape of a boss looked Karen up and down, like he was trying to get a bead on how someone like her ended up hanging around someone like me.

"Neighbors called it in after they saw your mattress, I guess it was, floating down through their pasture," said the sheriff, as if there remained some mysterious aspects to all this that needed clearing up. His gigantic russet hand absorbed my own, fluting the bones of my fingers in a kind of prehistoric greeting. This is how an illiterate says hello, I told myself, as Blivet continued speaking. "Course, we couldn't get up here until early morning what with the water washing out the road and by the time we did it wasn't clear if you'd been here at all, since the car was gone, but nobody seemed to know where you were. To be honest, it would have saved us a lot of manpower and worry and resources, if you see what I'm getting at, if you'd just informed maybe your friend here, or if not him maybe Officer Roland, where you was planning to be afore you went to there so we wouldn't have this whole runaround and get to worrying about whether you been washed away downriver in the storm while there's still folks out there right now who need some help getting swamped out. And I really don't need the wear and tear on my cruisers, if I'm going to be completely honest. Coming here I nearly lost a filling-"

"You want me to inform the police whenever I leave town, or just when the weather looks like it might wash my house away?" I interrupted, seeing no end to this. Karen squeezed my other hand, the one not being squeezed by the sheriff. Roland made no effort to avoid eye contact with me over the escarpment of his boss's shoulder, but his expression said: I know it's bad, but we all have to make choices.

"I leave that sort of distinction-making up to you," said Sheriff Blivet, raising the brim of his Stanton with furzy knuckle and peering around the yard. "And I can tell by all the reading material around here you're probably a pretty bright penny, but sometimes it's just the right thing to do to come down out of your crow's nest and take a good long look at how you're living and what that means to people down below who gotta sort through it all when you aren't around to keep us from wasting our time. Point of the matter is that I could have had this all wrapped up by 9AM if you took a minute from your studies or whatever to pick up the phone, though if I didn't know better I'd say you got the look of someone who's been hitting the peace pipe pretty hard lately. You smell like you been cavorting around the woods with those Bread and Puppet types and if I wanted to teach you a lesson about how to walk into a grownup situation, I might toss your car over there or just bring you down to town hall and have you stay in a cell for the night and let you thank me in the morning, since it'd probably be more comfortable than sleeping on the ground where your house used to be—unless you were planning to construct some kind of rough and ready shelter with some of these old books here, peel your front door out of the riverbank for a roof or whatever you need to do. Anyway, the point I'm trying to make is I feel like you ain't taking me or the situations I represent as an elected official of this town seriously enough to leave me believing you learned something from all this, so state-sponsored hospitality might be the way to go-"

"I won't do it again, whatever it was," I said, my hand still absorbed by the sheriff's up to the forearm with no sign of release on the horizon as his paranoia reached cruising altitude. Karen and Buck both seemed to be on the verge of saying something and Roland looked like he was hoping for a cake bell to drop out of the sky and contain Blivet until he could get his loyalties ironed out. The loss of everything I owned except the Belisarius box felt like an obvious answer to the question I'd asked myself not long ago about what it was like to be a person with real problems and a random night in jail was a logical next step. There was nothing to go back to, so a cell sounded like the perfect place to be. I was at the point of offering my wrists to the sheriff when Henry intervened.

"That will be all, Blivet," he said, suddenly rising up between me and the sheriff as if he had been conjured and tapping the wrist of the hand enclosing mine with the spine of the book he'd scooped off the lawn.

"Well, okay then, Henry, if you say so," said Blivet, releasing me like a gundog who'd been called off. "But I can't help feeling you might not appreciate the lesson I'm attempting to impress upon our mutual friend here, the kind of thing a man can't learn unless you teach him, and furthermore --"

"You had your turn, sheriff," said Henry, without inflection, his steady, slightly reptilian gaze leveled like an elephant gun at the haystack-sized shape of the police chief. "And whatever conversation you think you were having with Oliver here is now over."

"Well, I suppose I'll be on my way then, Henry, as soon as I make one more thing clear-"

"This is not a negotiation, Blivet. We solved the mystery of where Oliver is. You no longer have a role here."

"Well, I suppose I'll be on my way then," repeated the sheriff, apparently all out of words. Behind him, Roland gazed into the neutral distance, toward the driveway or escape. Henry's relationship with the Acheron police department was a kind of open secret around town, so the only surprising thing about any of this was the fact it appeared to be momentarily benefiting me.

"He's like one of those children who can't go anywhere without coming home with some kind of plunder or souvenir, something new to mark his excess," said Henry, watching the sheriff and Officer Roland plod across the lawn toward their respective cruisers before swiveling his entire body to face me. "I'm sure you're tired after listening to all that folk nonsense, so I'll keep this brief. On behalf of myself and Acheron Property Management, I wanted to offer my sincere apologies for what happened to your domicile. We have a few residences lined up for you to look over at your leisure, something in a similar rustic modality and price range, if you like, but meanwhile, we'd like to offer you an extended stay at the Herrenhof Inn as our guest, while you take whatever time you need to straighten things out."

"Wait, what?" I said, as Henry handed me a large envelope with the embossed and gilded seal of the Herrenhof Inn in the upper left-hand corner.

"Your room key, or card rather, is inside, along with all the standard information on the services, meals, luggage storage, though you won't be need that, I suppose. I believe you're in the Ethan Allen suite. Lovely view overlooking the winter garden. I think you'll enjoy your stay. Bring your friends over there. The bar tab will be taken care of."

"What are you doing this to me for at all?" I said, not really the question I wanted to ask, but there were several jockeying for primacy all at once and I got a little mixed up. Henry seemed to understand what I meant, though not why I wanted to know.

"You've been a valued and reliable client for many years,

Oliver," he said, factually, with zero warmth or consolation. "And you've been put in a difficult situation through no fault of your own. We would like to help and hopefully continue counting you among our customers."

"All the years I've lived here," I said, glancing vaguely, bitterly at the scoured patch of land where my house once stood. "And it was all going straight into your pocket."

"There are several ways to look at this," said Henry. "That's one of them."

"I don't want this from you," I said, trying to hand him the envelope, but Henry was already nearing the mailbox, beyond reach, as if the entire scene involving us had skipped a frame or two. "And I would like to formally renounce my relationship with Acheron Rentals, or whatever it's called."

"If you want to stay in this town, that might be tricky," said Henry over his shoulder as he opened the door of an impeccable maroon Saab hatchback. In the back pocket of his denim cut-offs, I noticed the Le Carre book he'd purloined from the yard. "Whatever you decide to do, hang onto that in case you change your mind. A person like you needs the kind of options a person like me can provide."

"Fuck you, Henry," I said, or heard myself say, as he started the car and sped off. I wanted to believe I fully intended to say thank you and the phrase got turned around somewhere along the way, that I hadn't wanted to reinvigorate the debate over the dog from years earlier, when I'd narrowly avoided landing on Henry's shitlist, though clearly, I was on some kind of list now. Buck had overheard enough of the conversation between Henry and me to be worried about the same things I was and may have explained them to Karen as the two of them walked around the lawn, searching for anything that wasn't completely destroyed.

"You're staying with me," he said, as Karen took the envelope and the two of them herded me toward the car. Since the jail cell was no longer an option, bunking up with Buck and Carissa felt like the next best thing. I rode with Karen as she followed Buck in his truck to the house on Winter Street with John the dog sitting lumpily in my lap, methodically licking the side of my face to the tune of 'I'll Do You' clattering from the car stereo.

"I could waste your words and turn and talk again," I sang to myself as we reached the house. Carissa was on the porch, her arms crossed as she watched us arrive. She flew down the front steps to hug me as I got out of the car, desperately, I thought, or in a way I could never remember her doing when the stakes were higher. Karen watched, possibly fitting all of this into whatever she'd gotten out of the manuscript earlier in the day. I decided to worry more about that later on. Carissa said she was glad I was alive or that I was okay, one or the other. Over her shoulder, I noticed the carpet I'd taken from my grandmother's house swaying on a laundry line in the side yard.

*   *   *

Though I stayed with Buck and Carissa for ten days after the storm, I didn't officially move into the house on Winter Street until after my parents returned from Italy. Marking time this way helped me treat my friends' hospitality as something I only had to deal with temporarily, a stopgap on my way to straightening things out, as Henry had said. But when I finally settled into the attic later in the month, I looked around my room and realized I didn't have much more to my name than I did during that first evening when Karen helped me carry my grandmother's tattered carpet upstairs and unroll it over the pine floorboards of my garret. There were several small, thoughtful items given to me by townsfolk, mostly people I didn't know who'd come by the house when they heard about what happened; an architect's lamp, a rocking chair, and a chess set, of all things. I didn't know how to receive these people and Buck had to act as a kind of doorman when they showed up, saying I was either asleep or out of the house, indisposed, any rate.

I am underequipped to deal with the kindness of strangers, I thought, feeling like the bridal half of an arranged marriage, receiving my gifts in seclusion until the big day. It didn't help that Buck was keeping a list of people I needed to thank whenever I stopped hiding from them. Where had all this goodwill come from? I wondered. Did a dam break? Amanda and her roommate showed up at the house with a box of dormy items they didn't need, a coffee maker, two or three houseplants I had no idea how to care for. Hodan, the hostess at the Ethiopian restaurant, brought me a jug of tej and a wicker coffee table I'd passed many times in the vestibule on my way to the bar, take-out menus fanned across its woven surface. Even Dr. Norman took time out of his busy schedule of doing god knows what to stop by with some books for me and let Buck know I shouldn't worry about the thesis; we could discuss deadlines and everything else when I was feeling better. That phrase again, I thought, when Buck passed this along. I was swaying in the new rocking chair by the window, watching my professor sail down the front walk as if he'd just completed a hunger strike. Life was rolling forward, at the usual rate it seemed, whether or not I was on board.

After a few days, Karen got tired of watching me fly up the steps to the attic whenever the doorbell rang and ended up spending a lot of time with Buck and Carissa, though mostly with Carissa. The two of them had New York in common the way people who have seen combat have war in common, a dominant topic for them and consistent point of departure for me. Listening to them talk about the city made me aware of what I lacked in terms of sustained, formative life experience, the sort of time on earth that really clears out your priorities and sets you up to know what you want out of being an adult. I badly wanted to be a veteran or survivor of something generative and knew having a houseful of crap washed away in a flood didn't count for much; I needed my own gravity.

Perhaps this is why my character often feels half-built, I thought, watching them, the two woman I wanted most in the world, share a bottle of white wine on the back steps as they discussed yoga studios in Park Slope and the best way to get to JFK without using a car service. The Long Island Railroad, apparently. Seeing two people I liked get along should have made me happy, but the impulse to reign in their sorority and refocus the conversation on myself was overpowering. The more examples of generosity I encounter, the more selfish I become, I thought further, wondering if I was too old to ship out as a cabin boy somewhere.

At some point Carissa and Karen went up to North Hero to get Karen's car and return John the dog to Anne, freshly arrived from some literary camel fair in the Midwest. I don't know what they talked about on the way, but when Karen returned, she told me she was leaving the next morning. She didn't say where she was going, but since New York was still underwater, Connecticut seemed like a safe bet. Even if it wasn't, whatever was going on between us was too new to continue flourishing in the shade of anything serious. And in retrospect, I was amazed Karen stuck around for as long as she did, a business week spent watching me fiddle around the attic, looking for things lost in the flood, things we both knew weren't there, listening to *Parsifal* on loop, and sipping periodically from the plastic jug of tej Hodan brought by as if was for refueling.

"I think you need a job," she said finally, the afternoon before she and Carissa drove back to North Hero. "I say that not in a mean way."

"None taken," I said, either mishearing her or not paying much attention, both were just as likely. I didn't want Karen to go, but I was beginning to realize this might be best. Summer was ending and I felt like a caricature lost in my own skin. She was at least half-right about the job. I had enough money left in my savings account to buy food and put gas in my car for a few months, but not enough to rent and furnish anything beyond Henry Hoffman's purview. I began thinking of myself as casually homeless, a phrase I assumed would make Karen laugh when I shared it, hoping it would remind her of what we had in common as result of the storm and make me seem a little more aware of myself than I probably was.

"It doesn't seem very casual to me," she said through the window of Carissa's Volkswagen. As the car pulled out, heading for North Hero, I locked eyes with John the dog through the rear window and cautioned myself against treating this as a pivotal moment. At least one of us was returning to the island, I thought, hoping I didn't look like I was retreating as I slunk back inside the house.

*　　*　　*

I went through several rounds of phone conversations with my mother and father after they returned from Cinque Terre without saying anything about what happened to my house while they were away. They'd had a nice time, three weeks hiking around the terraces of the Italian Riviera, and I wanted the trip's after-glow to fade a little before spoiling it. I was already in the early stages of becoming a burden to the people around me; I knew that. Karen had been gone a week and Buck and Carissa seemed unsure of how to absorb her role. Our dinner conversations had adopted a pathological undertone, as if the two of them had a depression checklist hidden beneath their placemats. I didn't think I was depressed, but I knew being around people who thought I was would eventually make me depressed. Paranoia, depression's squire, was already establishing its own inroads into my daily life. Every invitation to have another helping of whatever meal Carissa had prepared, or play chess with Buck afterward seemed like a clinical probe of my appetite and con-centration. Whenever Amanda was over at the house, I tried to practice being upbeat on her, hoping to sand down the parts of my personality that worried Buck and Carissa, but ended up in-viting her up to my room to drink what remained of the tej and listen to *Parsifal*, an offer she declined without really needing to explain why. While researching how I shouldn't behave around my new roommates, I'd bumped up against the term 'cycling' and wondered if this applied to the opera and honey wine rou-tine I had established in the attic, though I saluted myself for not pressing the issue with Amanda. The tej was nearly gone anyway by that point and I'd taken to peeing into the empty jug it came in to avoid answering any extra questions about how I was doing on the way to the bathroom. While emptying this out the attic window one morning, I realized that even if whatever was going on with me had arrived fully formed, there was always the possibility of adding a new stratum to it when I glanced over the sill and noticed Buck frowning up at me beside a withered flowerbed.

"I'll be visiting my parents today," I announced from the window, as if showering his marigolds with urine was a part of setting things in order before embarking for North Calais. Buck struggled not to appear relieved at this news and even showed up at the attic door a half an hour later with a satchet of marijuana and book about dinosaurs for me to take along. This was all the encouragement I needed to get out the door and on the road, weirdly enough. Neither of us knew whether I was coming back, or seemed worried about it. Buck didn't need a roommate, moneywise. I had nothing to pack, other than the carpet. Carissa was at work, so no need for any kind of guilt-ridden farewell, on her part or mine; I no longer knew who regretted what more. The opportunity to painlessly flee the house and all its nebulous associations seemed within reach for a moment until Buck followed me out to the car, clearly intent on imparting some kind of message—something he and Carissa had probably worked on together or agreed upon long ago—and been waiting for the ideal moment to deliver.

"Listen," said Buck, grasping my arm gently below the elbow as I stood within the acute angle of the car door. Oh god, what now, I thought. "What you said when I called you at the house in North Hero. It's always been like that for me with you and I know Carissa feels the same way. We didn't talk about it, or I didn't tell her, but I know we both want to help you, whatever that means, even if you can't be here right now. Just don't keep us at a distance to make a point. The three of us don't have anything to prove to each other. I think that's mostly what love is, Oliver. So I hope you come back and I know she would too if she was here."

These had the flavor of closing remarks, the kind I could have spent the next week stewing over if I hadn't already decided to bunk up with my parents until something better came along. I said what I needed to say to get out of there, lying minimally and trying to ignore the doleful, towering figure of Buck in the rear-view mirror as I surged toward the interstate with the book he'd given me on the passenger seat and a joint of his pot clamped between my lips. This felt right, momentarily, as if everything had been severed on a high note.

Nothing reminds you how vulnerable people are as much as when they reciprocate your crazy feelings, I thought to myself, wondering if the sense of wellbeing I felt was a result of the upper hand in all this somehow landing in my favor or the weed Buck had given me. A delightful combination of both, I decided, steering the car through the passing lane on I-89 with my knees as I spun another joint between my fingers, a kind of rinse and repeat cycle that didn't end until I arrived in North Calais with smoke billowing from the windows of my Volvo as if the car was on fire and 'Dancing on the Ceiling' playing way too loud from the stereo.

"The magic carpet has arrived," said my father tonelessly as I stepped mistily out of my car and waved in the direction I thought his voice had come from. This turned out to be the deck, where he sat with a doll-sized cup of espresso and a Cuban cigar he had smuggled back from Italy. "I'll bet you're hungry."

"You bet," I warbled through a mouth like a saltpan as I rounded the house to join him on the deck. At one point, an entrance like this might have worried my father. Now he seemed to find it amusing, even though I'd been too busy throwing piss on the flower patch beneath my window to let him and my mother know I was coming, though this didn't come up until after I was already bracketed by them on the living room couch, looking over their pictures of Monterosso and Vernazza or the gulf of Spezia in Porto Venere, which Byron used to swim across to visit Shelley, according to my mother. What would my life be like if I had to swim to visit Buck? I wondered hazily, stuffing an oatmeal cookie in my mouth and washing it down with a glass of sweetish white wine. Annoying, I decided.

"I should start dinner," said my father, watching me slurp my drink like a wino. "You said you were hungry an hour ago."

"If we knew you were coming, I would have picked up something special at the farmer's market," said my mother, following my father into the kitchen.

"Knew I was coming," I echoed, wondering how I'd managed to screw that up.

"Not that we don't like having you here," continued my mother. "But you usually call."

"Right. Yes. I'm sorry, Mom. It's just been kind of a busy week."

"Is everything okay?"

"Absolutely," I said, meaning it, confident I was being honest with my mother. I'd completely forgotten how little I'd shared with her or my father about my house being washed away in the storm. The information had been at hand for long enough to make it easy to take for granted, so I was proceeding as if we were all on the same page. "It's just been a while since I've shared a house with anyone, so that's a bit of an adjustment, for them too, not just me, I assure you, but everything's fine otherwise, in fact—"

"Wait, I'm confused," said my mother, worry etching itself into her voice. "What happened to your little house by the river? You're not living there anymore?"

Ah. Fuck, I thought, sudden recollection sweeping me into a pit trap. At least we've gotten through the vacation photos. The afterburn of Buck's pot had left me in a yarn-spinning mood and both my parents seemed a little disturbed by how passionately I related the story of my house and all my belongings being swept into the Wendigo River while they were in Europe, seriously appalled that this was the first they'd heard about it since getting back. Discussion of what I was doing now and what I would do next held sway throughout dinner and later, as we sat in the yard around a fire my father had made.

"You should stay here as long as you need to," he said, sending a brocade of sparks toward the emerging eyes of stars above as he dropped a fresh log on the flames. "Putting all this back together is going to take some time and you shouldn't be in a hurry. How are you for money?"

"Not great, not terrible," I said. A loon wailed from the direction of the lake as if it too was lamenting my finances.

"I have suitcase full of amber jewelry from your grandmother's house," said my mother, kidding around now that the bad news was out there, nothing to be done about it. "You could sell that."

"I'd be glad to," I said, trying not to sound too hopeful, but also not like I was joking in case my mother really needed someone to sell it.

"We can talk about this more in the morning," said my father, kissing my mother and touching the top of my head as he went inside to go to bed. "But don't worry overmuch about it, Oliver. There's nothing here we can't fix."

"I'm glad Karen was with you when all this happened," said my mother as the front door clicked shut behind my father. "She seems like a nice person."

"She's seeing someone else," I said abruptly, wondering why I'd chosen to share this information with my mother.

"That doesn't mean she isn't a nice person. How's Carissa?"

"Seeing Buck. They're living together."

"Is that why you don't want to stay there?"

"Yes."

"I see," said my mother, standing up. "I'm going to get us some ice cream."

If I'd inherited my mother's talent for stopping short once I have all the information I need, I thought, sitting before the fire, awaiting my dessert, then I probably would have been in my house when it washed away. How many other times has ignorance saved my life?

After my mother went to bed, I sat up in front the fire, gurgling through a half bottle of wine and what remained of the ice cream, at home with myself for the time being. I'd escaped most of what I needed to escape and what was pretty certain none of my recent decisions would come back to haunt me. I am once again a willing participant in my own life, I assured myself, stirring the coals with an old broom handle, hoping the sudden figure of Henry Hoffmann wavering past the flames was a mirage or the pot doubling back on me.

"Evening, Oliver," he said flatly, the sunhat tilted back on his head like a bonnet. "Mind if I join you?"

"That depends on what you expect out of it," I said slowly, a little spooked, wondering if mirages are supposed to talk. Probably not, I decided, as Henry settled into an empty lawn chair beside me. "You're a long way from Acheron."

"I own a few properties down at the lake," he said, gesturing vaguely toward the sound of fireworks through the trees. "And the local developmental review board met tonight to discuss some renovations I'm doing. So I came down to testify for a bunch of Luddite hayseeds, assure them I will respect their provincial ordinances and whatnot."

"So you were in the neighborhood, making a mess of things."

"Indeed."

"Thought you'd stop by."

"Why not?"

"Liar."

"Oliver: If it was important for you to know how I knew you were here, I would have explained it already. That's not what I came to talk about."

"Good. I'm glad, Henry. But before we get started with what you came to talk about, I'm going to have to ask you to get your creepy ass the fuck out of my yard and off my property in general, if you don't mind."

"I don't demand or need respect from you, Oliver," said Henry, calmly dragging a topsider through the coals. "But I would like you to listen to me for five minutes before we get all man-to-man about anything."

"I've thought it over and I think I could probably take you, Henry."

"I know you don't like me."

"No one likes you."

"But I think I can help you with your problem."

"What problem?"

"You have no money. I have a lot of money."

"I don't want your money."

"I would like to give some of it to you, even so."

"Or your hotel coupons."

"For a small amount of work on your part. Three weeks, four at the most."

"Go home, Hoffmann; this isn't your map."

"I wish I knew which of us is wasting the other's time more," said Henry, rising from his chair.

"You're fresh out of reasons to be here, either way."

"Not quite," said Henry, removing a short stack of letters

from the back pocket of his cutoffs and dropping them in my lap. Vermont Student Assistance Corporation, each and every one, the windowed address printed on shades of ascending urgency. "I stopped by your old place with some people from the insurance company. Thought I might bring you your mail. There are quite a lot of bills, Oliver. I hope you and your co-signers aren't having trouble making payments."

"Go shit in your sunhat, Henry."

"This is a nice property," he said, shifting his eyes from me to the shadowed shape of the house behind us. "Whenever it goes up for auction, I'll make sure to get my bid in early."

The tip of the burning broomstick described a perfect orange arc in the still air between as I yanked it out of the coals, aiming for no particular part of Henry, though he was already walking away, back toward the driveway, the upright halo of his sunhat bobbing and disappearing beyond the cast of the firelight.

Fucker, I thought, dropping the stick and picking up the wine, the bottle all but empty. Just when I begin to relax, Henry drops by to chew over my solvency. The night could only get more normal from here on out, I assured myself, a thought I would have found more comforting if I'd taken the job, whatever it was, rather than marching onto the Castle Memorial shitlist Grover had gone out of his way to help me avoid years ago. And now, Henry had taken an interest in me and the short story here was that all was lost. If I wanted to draw him off, away from my family and the property my negligence was putting in jeopardy, I would have to go back to Acheron, start making money somehow try to keep him and my creditors at bay long enough to achieve a stalemate of some kind. Things didn't look good, in the short or long term, but I didn't want to imagine a world in which making myself more trouble than I was worth wasn't an option for a rainy day. Henry was dangerous. I knew that. How dangerous, I didn't know, but if the stories around town were even half-accurate, I should expect to see him again. I suppose dropping by with my mail was a friendly way to remind me that my parent's house wasn't an embassy where I could hide from him indefinitely like some Champlain Valley version of Cardinal Mindszenty, living in endless fear of being abducted at the county harvest festival. No, at this point, the only thing worse than saying no to Henry would be working for him, or perhaps it was the other way around. After taking a swing at him with the broomstick, my only choice was to wait and see. We'd both made our points for better or worse, probably worse on my part, though an inadvertent side effect of our conversation had been to remind me of how I was beginning to feel at home as a kind of emotionally unavailable millstone to the people who cared about me; how after scraping the bottom of Buck and Carissa's goodwill, Karen's too, I had moved on with the hazy plan of living like a parolee off my parent's bottomless hospitality until I got tired of it or got a girlfriend; how I was thirty years old and setting myself up for a middle age of itinerant parasitism where the only question was about who I would burden going forward.

How do I feel about all this? I asked myself rhetorically, as the waning firelight measured the borderless shape of my childhood home, the place where I'd spent the first twenty years of my life and where I still believed I was most comfortable, though no longer safe. Not good, I decided. I didn't have enough money to do anything major like live on my own or take a trip to some far corner of the earth, hang around brown women on beaches, reinvent myself, and return with something to talk about. But I had enough to get through the end of the summer if I had to and repurchase a few basic real life amenities lost in the storm. Maybe I could save a part of whatever my future salary would be to someday do something independent or at least out of the ordinary. Meanwhile, if I wanted to live like a willing participant in my own life and keep Henry out of North Calais, all roads lead back to Acheron.

Since Buck didn't know I'd already made up my mind about not doing what I was doing, I didn't have to explain why I'd changed it when I called. Carissa murmured sonorously in the background. I'd caught them in bed together. No surprise there, and the sort of thing I needed to start getting used to. Even though I'd called Buck at weirder times for dumber reasons, I tried apologizing for the hour; I didn't know what time it was, but it had to be late. He said not worry about it or anything else. I could live in the attic as long as I wanted to. He was glad I'd changed my mind.

"About what?" I asked the cordless phone, the dial tone already humming against my ear. It was 3AM by the clock in the kitchen, too late to call back and get an answer to my question or call at all, really. I imagined them, curled together in the second floor corner bedroom they shared, curtains rippling against the open windows, pillars of books bracketing the headboard, a pile of clothes in a rhombus of moonlight. I hoped all outward expressions of how happy they were together wouldn't continue to feel like a kind of penance for me after I moved in—even the ones I made up—but I had trouble envisioning my life as a frictionless array of healthy relationships and offhand gladness for things I had no control over. Is this what people thought of as happiness? I wondered. And could I stand it if it fell upon me?

If I run out of things to feel bad about, there's always the thesis to fall back on, I assured myself, as I drank a shaky glass of water at the kitchen sink and tightrope-walked toward my bedroom.

III.

Towards the middle of September, Carissa got me a job working at a therapeutic day school for autistic kids. She seemed to think this was good news and not some kind of punishment. I tried to see it her way. I'd been living with her and Buck for nearly a month, swinging in the hammock on the front porch for most of the morning and watching Carissa garden in her bikini through the afternoon from the attic window, pretending to work on my thesis for the sake of dinner table conversation, and occasionally messing around with the manuscript I'd begun while housesitting in North Hero. My most important jobs were feeding Agatha and watering a philodendron I'd won at a Labor Day plant giveaway at the farmer's market, lucky me. It was the only thing I could remember winning as an adult and I was determined not to kill it. Meanwhile, my resources were dwindling; I no longer had enough money to put gas in my car or replace the cold-weather clothing I'd lost in the flood, so I walked everywhere and looked like a bum, though as the season drew towards autumn, I stopped going out as much and tried to find a route in direct sunlight if going out was unavoidable. Foodwise, I ate whatever Buck or Carissa cooked and if I got hungry between mealtimes, I went out back and uprooted something from the garden, a carrot, radish, squash, at one point, which I would consume on the spot like a ground hog, shivering in the shade of a willow bulwarking the yard.

I didn't think I was testing anyone's patience by living this way and even worried about what a regular job might do to the stasis I'd achieved since returning to Acheron, a Tao-like coexistence with my environment and the people who were part of it. I was proud of myself, happy even, or nearly, and wondering who I could share this feeling with when Carissa returned from work, tapping up the sidewalk and mounting the front steps to the porch where I rocked in the hammock watching her arrive, oblivious, and almost wildly ignorant of what to expect next. I was excited to see her for no reason and glad to be excited about this, a sort of self-propelled attitudinal buoy from which there was no escape, though I didn't find this out until much later. At the time, I thought of this period of hyper-motivated malingering as an enlightened stage. My mind is a empty mirror reflecting the world, I thought, glossing something I'd read while living in Anne's summer house, a line from an anthology of classical Chinese poetry. Carissa was looking less and less impressed lately whenever she saw me. I'd decided she was just tired from work as a kind of compromise between what I knew to be true and what I wanted to ignore. She sunk down beside me in the hammock, smiling as if she'd found a nifty use for something she was planning to throw out and told me about the job.

"I don't think that's really in my wheelhouse, Carissa," I said, after listening to her explain what was expected of me as an instructional assistant, whatever that was.

"Your wheelhouse doesn't have a wheel," said Carissa, abruptly, standing up, looking down at me as if I was at the bottom of a well. "I'm sorry, I know how shitty that must sound, but I've seen you in the garden, Oliver. We both have. We will feed you. You don't have to do that."

"I like to do that."

"Okay, great, I'm glad you have things you like to do. I don't know what you're afraid of nowadays, but this woman, Alice, she's the principal of this place and she's great. We knew each other in high school and she'll pretty much just give you the job if you go in and talk to her. It's hourly, but you have full benefits after thirty days, health insurance, paid vacation, all that real world shit. If you want to live here like a Trappist or whatever, that's fine, but realize you're going to make me look like an idiot for how much I talked you up to Alice. Also realize that this won't be the last time Buck or I try to get you to do something because we're both fucking terrified we're going to find you swinging from a rafter one of these days."

"This house doesn't have rafters."

"You know that's not an appropriate response."

"I promise you I'm not depressed."

"Watching you live makes me depressed. You need an income. And a girlfriend. Something to do."

You should fuck me again, I thought abruptly, ashamed of myself as I watched Carissa walk inside. None of this was her fault. My priorities were all askew, no doubt about that. I wondered if this sudden typhoon of candidness had anything to do with the telephone conversation she'd overheard earlier in the week between a debt collector and me. I hadn't had a captive audience in a while and when Dante Sloane called from somewhere between cornfields in southwestern Ohio, I took the opportunity to speak at length about my current lifestyle, as I saw it, and more or less explain myself to him. We were on the phone for forty minutes, but after the first twenty, Dante stopped trying to set the dialogue back on the rails and began talking about himself a little bit, a pleasing development. He studied archeology at Wright State and spent his free time driving around the Miami Valley, searching for Indian artifacts in open fields and construction sites. Over the past weekend, he'd found some arrowheads in a riverbank in the Glen Helen Nature Preserve, just outside Julian Falls. Exciting stuff, I thought.

Meanwhile, dinner was ready and Carissa had been dipping her head out of the porch door to let me know, not wanting to interrupt me doing something that looked normal at a distance. When I finally got off the phone and went inside to join her and Buck at the table, she asked who I'd been speaking to for so long and I told them about my new friend Dante from Ohio, his hobby, the arrowheads, all with a kind of wild floridness, as if he were joining us for drinks after the meal. They continued eating in speculative silence, listening to me talk, both stacking up observations to share with each other later on, I suspected, when I wasn't around to overhear. Say what you will, I thought then, watching the sidelong bulb of Carissa's breast through the armhole of a sleeveless t-shirt she wore, I'm the happiest person at this table.

Still, I followed her inside after she left me swinging in the hammock and asked when Alice wanted to meet me and talk about the job. We were in the kitchen, standing next to the sink, suddenly drinking beer and listening to The Smiths, normal people behavior. I felt like even this small overture on my part had moved things in a good direction. I knew Buck and Carissa worried about me and was comfortable allowing them to, but not thrilled with feeling as if I was inflicting myself on their household day in and day out, like some rudderless apparition dragging my chains around the attic. Getting a job probably wasn't the only thing I needed to do to be a good roommate, but along with curbing my forays into the garden and the probing, heuristic questions I put to Amanda whenever she came over to work for Buck, it was one of the most obvious.

Oliver Himmel, friend to the obvious, I thought, as Carissa wrote down Alice's number on the flyleaf of the book I'd been reading when she arrived, something by Cornell Woolrich I'd found in the upstairs bathroom, and explained when to call. I watched a tendon in the side of her neck shiver to the surface of her skin, remembering how it felt against my mouth when I visited her in Brooklyn. Through the window over her shoulder, Mt. Abandon appeared stationary for the time being. A good sign, I decided, for whatever came next.

*   *   *

Alice Lowell, the principal of the Acheron Learning Center, turned out to be a serene, put-together army wife a few years older than me, though not old enough to make the rockier parts of the interview seem like a generational problem. I'd forgotten my resume for starters and the oversized, semi-formal clothes I'd borrowed from Buck made me look like a tramp; the khakis cinched around my waist and ballooning from thereon out like a pair of harem pants, the stout oxford loafers slapping up the stairs to Alice's office like clown shoes, the collared shirt like a piratical blouse billowing over the ferrule of my belt. The necktie was the only part of the ensemble that theoretically fit. Walking over from the house, I'd taken a good long look at myself in a puddle of standing water outside a candy store, wondering if this was what me trying to get something done looked like. Was I encountering the best I could expect from myself? After meeting Alice, exactly the sort of person I would normally have avoided showing myself to, I hoped it wasn't true. I badly wanted to seem like I didn't know any better and was counting on whatever Carissa had told her about me to carry us through, in one way or another.

Alice's office was at the top floor of a craftsman style house across the street from the Herrenhof Inn, in what would have been the attic if the lower floors weren't given over to classrooms. So we're both attic dwellers, I thought, hopefully, unsure what I was hoping for. Not a job, not yet. It seemed too early for that.

"Normally, I'd be looking at your resume right now," said Alice, swiveling in her chair, a gallery of photographs on the desk behind her. Alice with her arm around a man in fatigues, Alice posing beside some kind of armored vehicle, Alice and several other women with more men dressed for battle. Apparently, she was accustomed to bravery, or heroism, rectitude at the very least. Hopefully, I thought, my scattered virtues won't speak too loudly for themselves. "But since we don't have that, I guess I'll just look at you."

"Sorry," I said, looking at the window above her desk. Could I make it through there and down to the yard without hurting myself? "I don't want to waste your time, but I feel like I might be doing that anyway."

"Not at all," she said, halting her swivel, fixing me with an expression that seemed charity-driven. "Carissa told me what happened during the storm. I'm sorry about that. She said you'd been a little scattered since then. That doesn't worry me. I mostly wanted to make sure you weren't a drifter. We've had issues. I won't get into it. Can you pass a background check?"

"I doubt it. What kind of score do you want? Mine is definitely below six-hundred."

"I think you're thinking of a credit check," said Alice, not sure or not caring whether or not I was joking. "I'm talking about fingerprints, drug test, criminal records. Any issues thereabouts?"

"I've never been arrested," I said, trying not to sound like I thought this was an achievement. Normally, the drug test would have been a problem, but I hadn't been able to afford any pot for at least a month and didn't want to ask Buck. He was already feeding and housing me for free. The least I could do was support my own drug habit.

"Fantastic," said Alice, retrieving a clipboard from the surface of her desk and rearranging her legs until the mouth of her skirt faced me like the bore of a cannon. "I'm going to ask you a few questions. Speak freely, I'll write down the answers. Don't be nervous. I need to do this for our employment files."

"I'm not nervous," I said, my voice hitching nervously, popping up an octave.

"Tell me about a time when you've tried to communicate something important nonverbally."

"Well," I began, shuffling through a patchwork of memories both near and far, remembering all the times I'd tried to offload my feelings and needs on the people around me, friends, girlfriends, relatives, without sermonizing about it or explaining anything, hoping whatever I wanted would become clear after enough hints and guesses on their part, how this way of suggesting myself had often left me wondering if I was invisible. A recent example: Allowing Carissa to catch me watching her garden, framed in the attic window like one of the German expressionist paintings she had tried to imitate all through art school, *Shirtless Man Malingering at Desk*, hoping she might drop her hoe and come upstairs, hang her bikini over the doorknob so Buck would know not to interrupt us when he came home. This probably qualified as trying to communicate nonverbally; Alice never said it had to be successful.

"Do you need more time?" she asked, not impatient, yet. Through the window behind her desk, the angle of sunlight falling across the whitewashed face of the Herrenhof Inn seemed to have changed. How long had I been sitting in silence, staring at the ceiling so I wouldn't look up my maybe new boss's skirt?

"I either have too many examples to choose from, or none at all," I said. "Maybe I'm misunderstanding the question."

"We'll come back to it," said Alice, writing something on the clipboard anyway. Subject may be mildly epileptic, I thought, hoping whatever came next would be less puzzling. "How do you deal with stress?"

"Espionage stories mostly," I said. Not the best answer, but with India pale ale and soft drugs off the menu, there wasn't much left. "Charles McCarry, Eric Ambler, John Le Carre, that sort of thing. Or I wait for something worse to come along."

"It usually does," said Alice, weirdly satisfied as she wrote out my answer, the clipboard flat against her thigh and her knee cocked wide enough to make her pelvis seem like a bottomless wishing well. "Moving along. Do you work best alone or as part of team, and why? Whatever your answer is, a situational example of why you think you're right is encouraged."

"I don't know. To be honest, it's been a while since I've had a goal in common with anyone else. But I think I'm teamwork-friendly . . . It's not a deal-breaker at any rate."

"Can you give an example of meeting a goal on your own?"

"Oh, sure," I said, thinking I'd share the story of getting John the dog and myself off the island during the thunderstorm on Lake Champlain. "It's kind of a long story, but I was pretty happy with myself afterward. In fact . . . "

"This is taking longer than I expected," said Alice, looking at a clock on the wall behind my head. "And we still have a few of these to go. Why don't I give you this to take home? Write whatever you want to write, and bring it with you on Monday morning, 8:30."

"Why so early?"

"That's when school starts."

"Oh. I see. So I've been hired?"

"Assuming you're not on a registry somewhere and can pass a drug screen, sure, why not?"

"Well . . . Thank you," I said, offering my hand without getting up from the chair, not really sure what to do. Alice was busy stuffing some documents in a manila envelope across the office and didn't notice, thank god. "Should I do anything to prepare?"

"Take this," said Alice, handing me the envelope. "That has everything you need for the drug test, fingerprinting, and background check. Get that done as soon as possible. Some of the clinics we use are open on the weekend, so make the calls when you get home. Also, a schedule of upcoming trainings: first aid, CPR, non-violent crisis intervention. A few professional development opportunities. Keep all the dates in mind. I'll try to remind you, but I have a lot on my plate generally and things slip through the cracks. We're also providing the hepatitis B vaccine for all our employees if they want it. You'll meet with our HR rep after ninety days to discuss health insurance, but you can go ahead and get inoculated whenever you want to."

"I'm not sure I know enough about hepatitis to make that decision"

"Well, do whatever research you need to do to feel informed. As your boss, I can't really advocate one way or the other. Your body, your choices. I will say, though, that we get more than our

168

fair share of bodily fluids around here. We serve students from elementary up through high school and generally they aren't promiscuous needle junkies or anything, but it never hurts to be on the safe side. Anyway, your choice, Oliver."

"Bodily fluids," I echoed, as Alice began tidying her desk, tucking things away, preparing to leave for the day. I slapped down the stairs behind her in my clown shoes, passing a bulletin board with some sketchy student art in the hall, self-portraits in construction paper and crayon, rows of empty chest-high coat hooks, and silent classrooms with chairs stacked against the wall.

This environment is not humiliating. But can I work here without humiliating myself? I wondered, as Alice closed a security gate over the front door and asked if I wanted a ride home. I said yes; it was Friday evening and students were already beginning to converge on downtown Acheron from the college on the hill. Even though I'd somehow gotten what I came for, I still felt a little like Charlie Chaplin in my interview outfit. I imagined myself traversing passels of hooting undergraduates with their entire lives ahead of them like some roving cautionary tale, a buffoon unable to say what he would do differently, but with a pretty good idea of having gone wrong somewhere along the way.

"You know," began Alice as we pulled up outside the house on Winter Street. "I realized I never asked you whether you want this job. Carissa said you aren't the sort of person who goes after what you want, so I just assumed."

What in the fuck does that mean? I wondered, as the truck pulled out, leaving me in a cone of light from the porch as thunder ebbed like footsteps from the direction of Mt. Abandon.

*　　*　　*

On Monday morning, Alice assigned me to a high school classroom with four young adult students, three guys and one girl.
Most of them were nonverbal, which suited me just fine. I didn't
have much to talk about anyway and was struggling not to appear like I was drowning on dry land after shadowing Tracy and
Pete, presumably the team Alice had mentioned during my interview, hustle the kids through the morning routine; meet the buses, go for a short walk around the neighborhood, unpack bags/
put away lunches, brush teeth/put on deodorant, swing on the
swings or play Connect Four until homeroom. It seemed simple
enough, but I couldn't remember the last time minimal expectations had left me feeling so far out of my depth.

Perhaps sensing this, Inez, the classroom teacher, immediately
put me with Dan, whose behavioral proclivities, she explained,
were confined to food-stealing and elopement, for the most part.
Dan had just turned twenty. His quarterly goals included brushing his teeth, ten strokes per quadrant, and playing a turn-taking
game for five minutes with a peer. When I asked Inez if I could
be considered a peer, she just looked at me. Dan and I spent a lot
time doing puzzles together—or I spent a lot of time doing puzzles as he rocked and laughed in an L desk beside me, sometimes
pausing to join two pieces I'd arranged for him. Inez had advised
me to sit close enough to Dan to prevent him from running out of
the classroom and onto the playground. Most of the time he went
for the swings, she said, though occasionally, he'd go up the fire
escape. So we sat like two gentlemen on a crowded bus, laboring
over a sixteen-piece jigsaw like it was a chess problem.

This suited me well enough; I occupied myself with thoughts
of Carissa, who was clearly waiting for me to tell her how much
better my life was now that I spent a significant part of it doing

puzzles with Dan. Buck didn't ask me about work, and I was grateful for his disinterest; it had more or less rekindled our friendship, now that I could afford my own beer again. Meanwhile, Carissa questioned me about the school as if she was searching for something to take credit for and as much as I enjoyed the extra attention from her, I didn't see it going anywhere significant. I was still her side project, something she was in the active process of fixing up in her spare time, no way around it. Some of the responsibility for this new dynamic was mine; I knew that. I was buying my own food again instead of pilfering it from the garden or waiting for someone to cook something and as September drew to a close, I walked to work through the chill autumn morning in new pants and a green and black checkered lumber jacket, no longer freezing on the vine wherever I went. As much as I tried to conceal these outward signs of progress from Carissa, I knew she had noticed me beginning to live normally again and was proud of her part in it. Since the problems in my life had always been obvious to me, I didn't understand how anyone could derive a sense of satisfaction from solving them; you see a crooked picture, you straighten it, unless you don't, and then it just remains crooked, harming no one. Still, I knew she'd sent out slides of her paintings over the summer, applied to shows in Waitsfield, Provincetown, and New York City and been rejected across the board, so I didn't discount the possibility that Carissa just needed something to feel good about on her days off. And as the weather grew cold and she stopped gardening in her swimsuit, spending my afternoons leering at her from the attic made less sense. I realized I also needed something to occupy my spare time in a way I wouldn't regret later.

Aside from my thesis, nothing immediately suggested itself. Earlier in the month, I received a weird letter from Dr. Norman's departmental secretary, informing me that he was on a walking tour of Chechnya, investigating atrocities on foot or something and would essentially be offloading his advisees on whoever would take them. I withdrew the Belisarius box from beneath my bed only long enough to drop the letter inside and stowed it away again, wondering if there was such a thing as neutral luck as I stared out the attic window at Carissa in dungarees and a cable-knit sweater of Buck's, harvesting what she could out of the garden before the first frost. The North Hero manuscript sat on the desk beside me, more or less complete; I had nothing more to add at any rate. My eyes scanned the titles of books piled around the room for something I hadn't read. I couldn't listen to *Parsifal* again without making everyone in the house miserable. My private life seemed to be idling toward a standstill.

What exactly do I like to do? I wondered then and continued wondering the next morning as I waited for Dan to debark the bus outside the Acheron Learning Center. An obvious, somewhat mocking answer seemed to present itself in the guise of a svelte redhead on fixed-gear bicycle pedaling past the school in a halter-top and yoga pants, her butt perfectly upheld in the saddle -- a hand cupping two quail eggs. I stared coolly, feeling as though I might have worked something out until I heard my name once and then again louder and noticed Inez looking behind me, pointing over my shoulder at what turned out to be the retreating, scarecrow-like figure of Dan, far enough down Loomis Street to be almost indivisible from the middle distance as he turned the corner and was gone.

The last time I could remember running anywhere was during my final game of middle school soccer before quitting the team and by the time I caught up with Dan, rattling the door of a closed bakery we sometimes visited on class outings, I was so exhausted

I could barely stand up. Inez found us sitting beneath a street-side Maple tree, my hand encircling his skinny wrist like a manacle as he rocked in place, smiling hugely at us both, while I wheezed beside him. She sent me to lunch early after we returned to the school and got through the rest of the morning. School employees ate in shifts, like people digging a secret tunnel, so I sat with the teachers and instructional assistants from other classrooms, all of them bruised and scratched up from dealing with students a lot more difficult than Dan. There was probably worse to come than having to run a quarter mile down Loomis Street. Dan and I had spent weeks together and I knew Inez wanted me to start working with Tyler next week, a twenty-one year old who was six foot four and outweighed me by sixty or seventy pounds. When angry, he would bite into a crenellated patch of skin on his hand, pinch, hit, kick, and pull staff around by their clothing. I'd seen him do it to Pete one morning during homeroom and I knew Tyler was the reason Tracy never wore necklaces to work. I imagined myself flapping from the end of his arm like a ragdoll in a hurricane and wondered if I could possibly convince Inez to set me up with Ellie, who was also twenty-one but looked about ten, who had Rett syndrome and spent most of her day in a wheelchair, spitting at Tracy and reading a laminated book about pasta one of the occupational therapists had put together for her. When not in the wheelchair, she walked around the yard like a zombie in a helmet and transfer belt, Inez or Tracy constantly at her side to keep her from falling or walking into anything. Her goals mostly involved socialization, choosing someone to talk to from a set of photographs, or asking Tyler or Dan how they were doing during homeroom. I was pretty sure I could handle that and being spit on had to be better than getting hit or dragged around by my collar.

Inez seemed to be saving Sasha for last, which worried me. He had just turned nineteen and, from what I could tell, seemed happiest eating dirt in the yard and peeing in his pants. His receptive language was excellent, but he didn't talk and communicated more or less with a binder containing laminated Velcro pictographs of things he might want or need, FRUIT, SONGS, BATHROOM, things like that. It wasn't a perfect system, Inez admitted and no one seemed to know if he understood any of the symbols. Tyler and Dan both had electronic tablets for this kind of thing, but teaching Sasha to use one had never worked out; he had a habit of playing with his spit, arranging strands of saliva between his fingers as if he was weaving a web and had shorted out the keyboard on the classroom computer enough times to make Inez hesitant to recommend anything more advanced at his IEP meetings. I'd often paged through Sasha's communication binder, wondering what my own might look like if my existence was boiled down to its most essential parts. BEER, LIBRARY, SEX WITH PRETTY GIRL. A life in pictures. Sasha's goals involved carrying his communication binder with him whenever he left the classroom and choosing between two leisure activities during choice time.

Even with my limited experience, that felt manageable, though whenever I tried to get myself excited about the possibility of doing something right with Sasha, I remembered prying his spit-slickened fingers out of Tracy's hair during art class as he sank his teeth into the forearm she'd used to block a headbutt. We were trained to push into the bite when this happened, though Sasha hadn't left Tracy with much room to maneuver, and I wasn't willing to force her arm further into his mouth on what seemed like a wild chance that he would let go. Inez was out of the classroom at the time, giving our tripartite tangle an aspect of reckless abandonment. Sasha ended up solving the problem for us by releasing the bite and changing his grip from Tracy's hair to the collar of my t-shirt as he dropped to the classroom floor all in the same movement, like an anchor unreeling from the side of a ship. By the time Inez arrived came back from wherever she'd gone, I was sitting bare-chested beside Dan attempting to solve a puzzle, while Tracy iced her forearm in the middle ground, and Sasha crouched in the sensory corner beneath a weighted blanket, strumming his lips and guarding what remained of my shirt like a fresh kill.

After school, Inez showed me the rubric she used to chart his maladaptive behaviors, a multi-page spreadsheet with subdivided categories for head-butting objects or head-butting people, biting himself or biting others, scratching, squeezing, spitting, hitting, grabbing, and stealing food. I wondered if this was her way of saying things could have gone worse or a warning that they would definitely get worse and I should prepare myself to act bravely. I thought of the pictures on Alice's desk upstairs, her husband blithely jetting off to war, a subject I'd studied closely enough to feel a sense of superiority over the people who actually participated in it, American heroes by default, I always thought, at least until the threshold of my own courage was tested by a hundred and ten pound autistic man no taller than the average free-standing mailbox. I imagined Sasha sauntering through a smoky battlefield, strumming his lips as platoons of soldiers dropped their arms and fled from him, stricken, terrified, hysterical; more than one of them seemed to have my face, I noticed, a little irritated by my own imagination seemingly betraying me. But, the early stages of rediscovering cowardice are always like that, painted in the broadest possible strokes.

When Inez returned from finding me a spare t-shirt somewhere in the school basement, I tried to spin off a jokey-sounding request in the form question about working only with Dan, or maybe Ellie, until Christmas break, but it came out sounding a little off kilter and beggar-like in the reconstituted order of the classroom. Chairs stacked, toys boxed and put away, floor swept, laundry sorted, desktops and tables sterilized, everything ready for the next morning. Inez seemed split between feeling bad for me and worrying about the wider implications of what I'd said. I toyed with the idea of asking her out for a beer, though I still hadn't put my shirt on. Reintroducing myself to her as someone slightly groovier suddenly seemed important; I found myself wishing I had a tattoo to show her. Instead, I went home and watched Carissa work in the garden dressed in Buck's clothing while Agatha yowled and clawed her way up my pant leg, into my lap.

Go to work, get bit by a student, I thought. Come home, get scratched by the cat. Symmetry like this cannot be forced; it will assume its own shape with time. Tracy wasn't up on her shots and had left school early with Pete, who gave her a ride to the clinic. When they called me on their way back to see if I wanted to grab a drink in town, I tried not to sound as if I'd been waiting to hear from them.

*　　*　　*

I stayed after school the day I nearly lost Dan at the bus stop, trying to write an incident report for Alice that didn't make me sound like a complete clown. Inez and I had gone over the format before she left for the day. Stilted North American business school dropout language, the bare facts, nothing more, written in third person. If I were honest, I thought, looking over what I had so far, this would say: Oliver saw a girl on a bicycle. Oliver liked her and wanted to chase her bicycle. Dan got off the bus. Oliver didn't notice. Dan ran. Oliver chased him instead of the girl on the bicycle. Oliver apprehended Dan in front of a bakery. Oliver was disappointed with himself, but thought he saved the day. Oliver realized he was out shape.

I ended up with five categorical sentences that I left in a folder stapled to Alice's office door, feeling the opposite of studly and capable as I crossed the playground, intending to set out for home and searching for some reason to get excited about this. Carissa, Buck, and I had settled into a streamlined domesticity, cooperating our way through dinner, and whatever happened afterward in the way of entertainment, with a kind workmanship. Evenings with them were beginning to feel a little like changing a tire and even though I knew I contributed to this, I assumed I was the only one of us it bothered. They had each other, I had them, sort of, an uneven ratio. Carissa was still right about my needing a girlfriend, though I was usually so drained after a day at the school that I could barely string two coherent thoughts together for the friends she attempted to set me up with, all smart, all nice, all fine people with long irons in the fire and plenty of stuff to do on a Wednesday night aside from watching me drink three beers in two hours and lose to them at pool. Amanda may or may not have had a boyfriend now that the college term had started, but seemed to have been warned off me by Carissa in any case. Whenever she was working at the house, sorting books or packing them to ship, I tried to find a pretext for reigniting the beacon of interest she'd shown in me during tapas night back in June, or the night of the Spanish inquisition, as I'd come to think of it after the conversation Carissa and I had in the kitchen, a conversation that still didn't feel finished to me. Perhaps it wasn't a beacon of interest at all, I'd begun thinking, but a mirror reflecting what I threw at it, whatever I gave off that night and mistook for the beginning of something, when it was in fact the same more or less eternal flame of regressive self-doubt, simmering away in its dish of oil, while I chased its reflection through the night, into the pile of Amanda's dirty laundry. And months later, I'm still willing to be wrong about this in case I am actually wrong about this and her signals are just cruising beneath my radar and I am not a lonely person who, though he can barely catch Dan when Dan runs away from him at the bus stop, will doggedly pursue the figment of his own loneliness in order to escape it.

At least one of these problems is theoretically solvable, I thought, pausing at the rear gate to the playground. The school backed up onto a network of hiking trails through the foothills of Maybrick Peak. Sometimes we took walks as a class through the woods when the weather was nice. Tyler leading like an impatient scoutmaster, Dan bobbing shortly behind, Sasha strumming and dribbling, and Ellie, probably asleep in the sun back on the playground; the trails were impassible in a wheelchair and a little much for her on foot. I was surprised to find I was looking back on this memory of my first week or so at the school with fondness or something like it. If I had known then how I would feel now after letting Dan escape, I asked myself, what would I have done differently?

Probably made sure I could run after something, a student or a pretty girl on a bicycle, whichever, without embarrassing myself, I thought gloomily, glancing over the gate and up the trail, hooded beneath a piney arabesque. I had two hours of daylight left; might as well see how much work I needed to do to get this part of my life under control. It was either that or watching a fully clothed Carissa mess around in the garden and getting clawed by Agatha until it was time for dinner. These were not great options, but I was beginning to notice the hardest part of being an adult was creating options in general, good or bad, it didn't matter. Two crappy choices had to be better than one good choice I couldn't escape.

The worst that can happen is this will make me miserable in a new way, I thought, as I walked back inside to the school and began rooting through the plastic bins of spare clothing in the class bathroom until I found what I needed: a pair of Tyler's tent-like athletic shorts, and some sporty-looking sneakers that probably belonged to Dan. I didn't think I was doing anything wrong or unethical by borrowing this stuff to improve my vocational skillset. On the contrary, my ninety-day performance review with Alice was coming up. She was always talking about professional development opportunities, chances for setting and accomplishing goals, and had asked me to bring ideas on how to improve myself to our meeting. Beyond drinking less beer and reading more serious books, I hadn't come up with anything so far, but here I was, oddly ahead of the game, as I closed the playground gate behind me and set off down the trail in sportswear borrowed from my students.

When I arrived at the house on Winter Street two hours later than usual, slick and exhausted from stumbling around the trails behind school, there was a note from Carissa and Buck on the front door and a covered dish in the kitchen. They'd gone up to Burlington for a performance—Garrison Keillor masquerading as a bumpkin for an evening down at the waterfront, part of a maritime festival or something—and would be back later. They'd saved me some dinner; there was beer in the fridge. Obvious instructions for reheating followed.

Thanks, mom and dad, I thought, retreating with a serving

bowl of penne and vodka sauce and two beers to the back porch and shoveling the pasta into my mouth with a kind of miserliness, thrilled to be alone. The fact of the running was too new to be worth sharing and I knew it would be just another feather in Carissa's cap if she found out. I wondered when the responsibility for my lifestyle becoming less of an eyesore would once again devolve on me, or if I would be expected to credit every salutary decision I made from here on out to Carissa setting me up at the school. Keeping the running secret seemed impossible, but I thought I'd give it a try anyway, just to see what it felt like to keep it out of her purview and entirely to myself. I was still getting used to there being nothing sexual between us anymore and I was as okay with that as I could be while still waiting for things to swing back into hopeful ambiguity if anything changed with her and Buck. Meanwhile, the world was in front of me, it seemed, but I didn't like the feeling of someone mentoring me through it. My body hurt, but it was a small enough price to pay for establishing a new routine, some way to fill the hours I wasn't paid for other than mooning around the attic, messing with the cat and the philodendron, watching Carissa hunch like a peasant woman in the garden, and lamenting her lost semi-nudity.

Running to avoid this made as much sense as running to keep up with Dan and seemed to blend in with the generally upward swing of things lately. I was spending one or two nights a week out with Tracy and Pete, splitting pitchers of draft beer and improving my pool game. I'd recently begun reading through a stack of poetry Anne had sent back with Karen after she and Carissa drove up to North Hero with John the dog and which I'd ignored initially, worried reading John Berryman or Louise Gluck would make me feel stupid. Though after working at the Acheron Learning Center for a week, feeling stupid didn't bother me in the same way anymore. And I was no longer peeing in a plastic jug to avoid answering questions about myself, a definite symptom of micro-improvement.

Yes, things are on the up and up, I thought, my fork scraping the enameled interior of the serving bowl as I surveyed the empty yard, my current realm, for someone or something upon whom to leverage these newfound facts about myself. Nothing leapt out at me. No surprise there. Still, when I heard my phone vibrating from the pocket of the lumber jacket draped over a chair in the kitchen, I responded like it was a game show siren calling me to collect a prize, dropping the serving bowl into the flowerbed and nearly running straight through the screen door to get it.

"I'm at my granddad's place for the weekend and I started thinking about you," said Karen, evenly, suggesting nothing. I popped open a second beer, happy to listen for now. "And I realized I was worrying about how everything turned out. Are you okay now? Please tell me things didn't get worse after I left."

"They didn't get better immediately," I said, sipping, narrating, at home with this kind of catching-up. "But if you called for absolution, then yes, my child, no guilt need fall upon you."

"I've caught you in a good mood," said Karen, relieved, as if she expected to encounter a human shipwreck on the other end of the conversation. "I'm glad. What are you doing now?"

"I work at a school for autistic kids. They bite and scratch and run away. I started running today so I can catch them if I need to. Or flee, if it comes to that."

"You're really doing that."

"Yes, my love."

"I can't imagine it."

"It's true. Carissa got me the job. The principal is a friend apparently."

"Actually, that's wrong. I can see it. You're only ever selfish with people who you can afford to be selfish with. Otherwise, I think you probably have a big heart."

"A big lazy heart."

"Yes. That too."

"Was I selfish with you?"

"Not at first. But after you lost your house I noticed it."

"I'm sorry. I didn't mean to chase you off. Just the opposite, actually."

"You didn't, Oliver. If Carissa and Buck weren't there to help you sort it all out, I might have stayed around. Your summer was over though. So was mine. Are you living with them still?"

"For now. You remember that handsome sociopath in the straw hat who met us at my house the day we got back from North Hero?"

"Right. Henry the hotelier."

"Sort of, but yes, same person. I'm trying to avoid paying him to live in Acheron, but he owns everything, so it's hard. Buck doesn't need my money and I don't have any to give him anyway, so for now, it's working out."

"Maybe you should just drop your money in the sunhat and move on. You'd be happier by yourself, I think."

"I don't know if I can anymore," I said, wondering why people always assumed I didn't want them around. "He showed up at my parents', ostensibly to bring over my mail. We had words. I tried to hit him with a broomstick."

"I don't think I fully understand why you hate him, Oliver. You tried explaining it to me but you'd been into that honey-wine, I think, and I couldn't understand what you were getting at. I recall something about a dog or a pet policy."

"There's more to it than that," I said, thinking: is there? Let's see. "Here we have a small town autocrat who destroys whatever he can't control within the confines of Acheron County, though he's recently been expanding his dominion, which worries me. People say he's hated this town ever since his mother disappeared and everyone who lived here started thinking he had something to do with it."

"Did he though?"

"No. Or, there's no proof he did, at any rate. He was eighteen when she went missing and from what I've heard he was a creepy kid, but more or less harmless. I guess his mom worked for Mr. Castle, running the Herrenhof, so Henry went to work for him after finishing college or something, managing properties, buying up businesses, being kind of an enforcer for the Castle family estate, which he's now inherited, more or less, since the late Joshua Castle's son is kind of a dingleberry, from what I understand. But nowadays, I definitely think he'd dispatch her if he needed to, no problem there. He's dangerous and cruel when bored, I hear."

"None of that explains why you don't like him. Other than the dog thing."

"That isn't enough?"

"Not for you, I don't think. I can't imagine you sharpening your pitchfork over it, at any rate."

"What can I say, Karen. Every interaction I've had with him seems to suggest we will be enemies and as far as I can tell, that's one of two choices with Henry. The other is being a lapdog; there is no peaceful coexistence, because eventually you will have something he wants and he will come after you for it. That's why I quit my job at the grocery store when he bought it. Avoiding Henry is part of living here, if you're smart. But now he wants me to work for him, so I guess there is no escape after all."

"Doing what?"

"We didn't get that far."

"Is that why you went after him with a broomstick?"

"I think so. I was somewhat in my cups at the time, so there may have been other reasons."

"I miss you, Oliver," said Karen, sounding oddly refreshed, as if me rambling on about the trouble with Henry was exactly what she called to hear. "I really do."

"Well, you're in Randolph and here I am, in Acheron, as usual. Come visit. You could be here in half an hour. Carissa would love to see you."

"That sounds nice, it really does. But I'm with someone."

"You were last time, too. What difference does that make?"

"No, I mean, he's here with me. Ray. Ray is here with me, at the house in Randolph."

"So bring Ray. Ray can sleep on the downstairs couch."

"I decided not to sell it," said Karen, delicately skirting around what I'd said as if she hadn't heard me. It seemed I'd caught my bitterness over the whole Ray issue in the midst of a tea party, and was being offered a cup. Cream? One sugar or two? A biscuit, perhaps? I know shit fuck about whatever kind of friendship thing Karen wants from me right now, I thought. Every opportunity I'd had with Carissa to be a decent friend to her had gone haywire and she'd offered me plenty, all those lost chances to be an upright modern gentleman with a long enough view of things to not be surprised when a lead horse overtakes him or embittered by it ad nauseam, at the expense of almost everything else. Karen is offering you the option of acting mature about this, I told myself, as she continued talking. Don't be a slob. It didn't work with Carissa and it won't work now. "We're taking estimates, meeting with contractors, trying to get an idea of what we need to do to convert the place into a shelter."

"Shelter from what?" I asked, wondering what exactly Karen and Ray had to hide from.

"For animals, dogs and cats mostly," replied Karen, either mishearing me or forging ahead with the conversation anyway at all costs, I couldn't tell which. "I thought a lot about what your mom said at breakfast that one time, the morning after you got sprayed by the skunk. I told Ray about it. Using my granddad's house was his idea. So that's what we're doing up here. Figuring out what's next. It's a good feeling. I'd like you to be a part of it. You should come visit us if you can."

"I'm pretty busy around here," I said, loudly popping another beer. "But I'll try to do that if you want me to."

"Being in Vermont without seeing you doesn't feel right to me," she said. "Anyway, the lady from the zoning board just showed up to tell us what we need to go to get this place up to code or whatever. I don't actually know why she's here. Ray arranged it. But please, call me when you can come down. We're here for the next week."

I said I would and hung up, feeling as if I'd narrowly avoided making a fool of myself and not really understanding what a friendship with someone like me could offer someone like Karen, or Ray, for that matter. They were in the midst of doing something they expected to be proud of. What must that feel like?

*　　*　　*

Alice and I had begun sleeping together after my ninety-day performance review, a state of affairs Carissa was determined to treat as a mistake on my behalf after she found out about it. Any effort I made to correct this impression along the way or at least shift the blame for it back onto Alice made me sound like

I was either ethically bankrupt and a little out of control or too desperate to be anything but a windsock for the emotional mistrals of people like my boss. This was partially true. Quotidian loneliness, or the empty space in my life I wanted to fill with a woman of some kind, was taken for granted around the house on Winter Street. Whatever Carissa's friends, the people she set me up with, reported back, I knew it couldn't be encouraging. She never discussed any of it with me, but during the first week of October, I realized we were probably well into the tertiary tier of her friendships or the outer limits of people she knew and was willing to set me up with, when I ended up splitting a six pack of Red Stripe and going bait-fishing in some far-flung cove of Kranion Pond with a very nice lesbian named Theresa. We were mutually embarrassed, making it the most successful date I'd been on with anyone since Carissa began lining up the people she knew for me to disappoint, like a line of dominoes, I imagined, down they go, one by one. Theresa was gracious enough to admit Carissa may not have been aware of her preferences; it had been a while since the two of them saw each other. Middle school, it turned out. So, fine, I thought. No big deal. And, she added, Carissa was vague enough about the details to make the possibility of me being transsexual seem very real over the phone. I didn't know whether to apologize for being male or not being female, but we both agreed we'd been misled and managed to enjoy the remains of the Tuesday evening Carissa had chosen for us to meet, catching enough lake trout to cook over a camp fire on a deserted slip of private beach, the same beach, oddly enough, where I'd first seen Carissa emerging from the water. When I shared this with Theresa, she got a bottle of Wild Turkey out of her truck, poured some into a brace of tin cups and said if I wanted to go fishing again I should give her a call.

But later on, when I was still trying to justify the Alice thing to Carissa, I realized I had almost no idea how or why it began, and had skipped the questioning stage entirely, cruising instead toward wherever I'd been aimed like one of the rocket propelled grenades Alice's husband probably saw a lot of over in Afghanistan. At the time, a Friday afternoon in mid-October, I hadn't asked any questions, so couldn't answer any later on. All I had were facts: After early-dismissal, I'd hidden out in my classroom until I thought the building was empty, donned Tyler's shorts and Dan's shoes, and set off on the trails behind the school, shambling out of the woods forty minutes and four miles later, my shirt soaked through, the coda of an Indian Summer still overwarming the county like a plump hand cupped over the valley of Acheron. I hung my shirt on the cross bar of the swing set to dry and went straight for the garden hose coiled against the school building, alternately dousing my head and drinking dog-like from the nozzle. This was how Alice found me, at my most unselfconscious, very wet and a little sunburnt, gargling from the hose end like an overheated Doberman; an inauspicious prologue that would later confound Carissa when the facts, as I saw them, were related.

"You do have a home to go to?" said Alice, leaning out of the backdoor, suddenly lustrous in the midafternoon sunlight spilling through the conifers and over the hillside above the school. My immediate impulse was to stand still so she wouldn't see me. "I mean, this isn't something I should worry about, right? You showering on the playground after hours?"

"I was running," I said too brightly, the endorphins kicking my voice up a notch, pointing like a sailor spotting land toward the gate leading to the trail system. Alice didn't look in that direction, but focused on me instead, shirtless, bird-boned, and a little disgusting, I imagined.

"Are those Dan's shoes?" she asked, her eyes ticking over me, and the scene at hand, threshing something out. "And Tyler's shorts?"

"Yes, I borrowed them. I wash everything when I'm done."

"I'm choosing not to worry about this right now," she said, more to herself than to me, her gaze falling on some apparently neutral hinterland between us before rising again, finding me. "Actually, it's good you're still here. I was trying to waylay you this morning but the day got away from me."

"Did I do something?"

"Something else? No, Oliver. You've been here a month and a half. Time to discuss your performance. You don't look like you're in much of a hurry and it shouldn't take long, since you're new. Mind of we get this done?"

"Not at all," I said, clearly out of options as I sat with her at a picnic table beside the monkey bars, watching my wet t-shirt billow on the swing set and wondering if I should have made myself a little more decent for what was ostensibly a discussion between professionals. It can't go any worse than my interview, I assured myself as Alice extracted a four-page rubric with sections graded on a scale of one to five from her briefcase, slid a copy of this across the table to me, and, for whatever reason, popped the top button on her blouse. Here we are, getting down to business, I thought to myself, watching a couple about my own age walk a dog past the playground fence, hoping sitting shirtless and wet across from Alice didn't make me look a student who'd missed his bus to the group home.

"So, first of all," she began. "We're glad you're here and I'm very glad you're here. Inez and your team love you and most everyone else seems to think you're a great fit, so no pressure when I asked this next question. How do you think you're doing?"

"Well," I began, feeling as if I was about to retread some of the less steady ground I'd loped across during my interview for the job I was now excelling at, apparently. I imagined myself wearing a t-shirt with a question about how I was doing printed on it, and Alice's phone number beneath. A no sale sign seemed to obscure any objective personal analysis of the past six weeks. Once again, facts were my only ally in what was beginning to look like a war of attrition against taking responsibility for my recent decisions. What could I say for certain about how I thought I was doing? Inez had been shuffling me between Ellie and Tyler for the past month, so I'd spent a lot of time stumping in circles around the yard and unhitching hands larger than mine from my shirt collar. No big deal. Ellie liked to talk about food while ambulating, tuna, noodles, cheese, and that was about it. I felt I held my own well enough during these conversations and managed to keep her from running into the swing set while doing so, so good for me, a job well done. I'd even begun wheeling her to Grover's Market, my old stomping grounds, to buy snacks for the classroom. Things with Tyler seemed to be more or less on track as well. He'd recently begun some new goals, things I'd supported during staff meetings at the beginning of the month, not suspecting that cajoling him through them would become my daily responsibility. Inez saw the new routine as an ideal opportunity to get us working together and perhaps it was. We were now very familiar and a little tired of each other. Tyler had the odd habit of using a toilet to pee, but preferred to poop in his pants, so at the top of each hour of the school day, I sat on the edge of the tub with a stopwatch set for five minutes while he sat on the toilet six inches away from me, the two of us staring at each other like one of us was visiting the other at the county jail. If Tyler became anxious or uncomfortable, I showed him the watch. No one knew if he understood time, but he derived some sort of comfort from watching the numbers decline and knew he was finished when the thing beeped. If he did this four times successfully, I was allowed to give him a cup of soda or a handful of jellybeans, pictures of which were included on the visual chart I used to track his daily progress and entice him into the bathroom, indicating the prizes like a kind of scatological fairground barker every hour, on the hour. It was going well enough, I thought and the worst scuffles we'd had over the ritual of the thing always ended with me running away, out of the bathroom, and him unable to follow with his pants around his ankles. By the time I returned, he was usually calm enough to continue and if not, no jellybeans.

The second new goal was less tricky and offered us both a bit of a break from the strictures of the first. Shortly before lunch, I squeezed Tyler into a pair of latex gloves and walked with him around the neighborhood picking up trash, an activity that felt almost Zen-like after clocking him on the toilet. His goal was to collect ten pieces of garbage, but we usually exceeded this, since walking together was a low-anxiety activity for us both and made me feel less like his bathroom nemesis, daily water closet tormenter, cloaca persecutor, whatever I was or had recently become. If Tyler grew nervous or uncomfortable during the walk, he would usually take my hand. This felt both weird and special and drew an acute amount of attention to what he and I seemed to have in common, a mutual acknowledgment and acceptance of the world as a scary place, through Tyler was more forthright about it. I had to admit his outlook was definitely more honest and possibly healthier, than my own. I was little bummed out to realize I didn't have a hand to hold when things became overwhelming, or not the sort I wanted, and wondered if I shouldn't snag a page out of Tyler's playbook and become a little less choosy about who I derived comfort from, open myself to the overtures around me, Carissa, Buck, Karen, maybe even Amanda, who knew what would happen? I certainly didn't, though the difference between what the people close to me had to offer and what I had decided I needed from them seemed to be at the root of the problem. I wasn't entirely on board with it being a problem just yet. Still, holding the scarred and bitten hand of my mountainous and unpredictable student while we gathered litter together did me as much good as borrowing his athletic shorts after school to go running, though sharing this with Alice when she asked how I thought I was doing would probably leave her with more questions than answers or the kind of ambiguous answers that aren't easily bracketed by a scale of one through five. Facts, I reminded myself, before saying I thought I was doing fine—hoping it didn't sound like a wild guess—and mentioned my work with Tyler and Ellie, even adding something about recent afternoon forays into Sasha's lair, the sensory corner in Inez's classroom, to blow bubbles with him after lunch. Alice looked pleased. Thank god, I thought.

"You're about where we expect you to be, score-wise," she said, gesturing at the rubric in my hands. I flipped through it; mostly threes and fours, one five for punctuality. A solid B, overall. I could live with that. "I set up some goals for you on the last page, mostly professional development opportunities, getting more involved in the IEP strategies for your students, that sort of thing. Nothing to worry about, going forward. But before we finish, I'd like to ask if you have any personal goals you'd like to add? Is there anything specific you would like to work on over the next six months?"

"I think I should probably get better at poop stuff," I said, assuming this would sound like constructive professional think-ing until I noticed a kind of downshift in Alice's expression, like she'd just seen a bird fly into a window. "I mean, toileting in general. My comfort level is not where it probably should be yet and I feel a consistent dread whenever Tyler or Sasha need to be changed and cleaned up. I can sort of turn myself off and get through it, but I would like to be less flustered by the process."

"I was sort of looking for maybe a workshop suggestion, or certification program you might be interested in, something the school could facilitate you taking part in," said Alice, her pen hovering over a blank box on her copy of my scorecard, pre-sumably meant for my missing goal. "I don't know how to help you get better at what you mentioned. Poop stuff is poop stuff. It will become easier, I think, but wiping another grownup's ass will never become normal. If you started taking joy in it I might not want you to work here anymore. Was that your only idea?"

"I could say something else but it would be a lie."

"I'm writing 'will continue to develop direct care skill set,' " said Alice. I watched her put this down and slip the copy into her briefcase, snapping it shut and once again leveling her gaze across the table as if to show me that yes, she was a lovely woman, no doubt about that and clearly out of my league, no doubt about that either; the bare, essential facts of the matter, but also estab-lishing a wordless preface of sorts to what she said next. "Now that all that's over with, want to get a beer?"

"Yup," I said, standing in unison with her and walking inside to change out of Tyler's shorts and Dan's shoes.

I assumed Alice would drive us to one of the downtown bars, but we ended up at an out of the way, vaguely sinister place between the county dog pound and a water treatment plant, splitting a draft pitcher of something light and domestic on a newly rebuilt deck overlooking the Wendigo River. Part of it had been lost in the same storm that washed my house away, she explained cheerfully, after ferrying us through the clientele within, opposing camps evenly divided between people who worked with sewage and people who worked with stray dogs, with zero noticeable overlap, the kind of weirdly exclusive environment that would have terrified me if the deck over the river wasn't an apparent zone of neutrality and Alice not on familiar terms with the publican captaining the bar. She somehow secured our drink order by waving to him on our way outside, but he didn't appear to notice me one way or the other when he brought it to our table; Alice had to ask him for a second glass.

"I like it here," I lied, as we sipped slowly, listening to the river. It wasn't the sort of place I would have expected her to land on a Friday evening, but how many solitary, after work hours had I passed over a jug of tej at the Ethiopian restaurant, drawing wolves on a cocktail napkin with a pen I'd borrowed from the head waiter, stewing over nothing in particular, quietly ecstatic to be alone, yet out in the world, taking it in rather than taking part? It seemed we both had our sanctums, for better or worse, nooks to hide in and catch our breath. Even though the beer sucked, and the undercurrent of tribal war was palpable even on the deck I was pleased to be invited into her shelter.

"I don't have many places in this town where I can go to drink a pitcher of beer by myself without having someone remind me what they think about it," she said, glowering at the near memory of these malefactors over her beer glass. "If you have a job like mine, people believe they get a kind of say-so in how you live in your off hours. It's like they expect the people who deal with their kids all week to throw a candle party or build a birdhouse to unwind."

"I think the greatest North American fallacy might be the belief that what you think matters, or should matter, to people other than you. I've never been under your kind of scrutiny, but I think I prefer that kind of hubris, righteous self-appointment, morality policing, whatever you want to call it, out where I can see it. Just to keep track of things."

"Keep track of what exactly?"

"Current informers. Future executioners. Call it what you like. It always begins with nosiness, meddling, little condemnations, that sort of thing. From there, it's a remarkably short march to the gallows when they have their way, historically. The sound of human beings all agreeing at once on how things should be always reminds me of a headsman sharpening his axe."

"Inez told me she thought you might have hidden skills of some kind, potential we or you or both of us weren't using. I wonder if this is what she meant. Do you talk like this in her classroom?"

"Not categorically, no."

"Does what she said sound accurate to you?"

"Not really."

"Interesting. Would care for another beer?" asked Alice, standing up without waiting for me to answer and heading inside. When she returned with a fresh pitcher, another button on her blouse had become unlatched. This seemed like the proper time to ask about her husband.

"He's in the infantry," she said, slurping the head from her glass. The river burbled merrily below our feet. "Kunar province."

"So that's basically where you drive around waiting to get shot at?

"Not quite. They walk. Want to get out of here?"

"Get out of where?"

"This place. This bar."

"We still have beer left."

"I have beer at my house. I can make us dinner."

"That sounds nice, but not quite right to me," I said, thinking out loud, not necessarily worried about what was and wasn't right in the broader sense, but a little disturbed by how easily we'd spearheaded our way past the lingering and still very apparent, at least to me, problem of her warrior husband in some far-flung mid-east gutter protectorate waiting for enough things to explode so he could come back to Acheron while I fiddled around with his wife, my boss, back on the homefront; it was impossible not to imagine the stogie of my lust for Alice being lit off the smoldering tail feathers of a slightly raped-looking bald eagle.

"What does that mean?" she asked, not offended, no yet. Nearing it, though.

"Well, I suppose I don't feel right sitting here with you offering to make us a meal while he's over there doing what he thinks is his duty. And I'm a little ashamed of myself for pitying the ignorance of the man you married and probably love very much."

"Do you want to come home with me or not, Oliver?"

"Yes, I do, Alice. All the right impulses are there, but I'm still making that choice."

"What are you afraid of?"

"Getting what I deserve for it maybe. Or whatever the people you mentioned earlier, the ones who drove you out here, to this place, would probably agree I deserve."

"Current informers, future executioners."

"Right. Them."

"We have an agreement. He goes on a tour, I get therapy dick."

"Pardon me?"

"I disagree with what he's doing and he disagrees with what

I'm doing, but I will support him and he will support me, because we love each other very much, as you said. I promise no harm will come to you."

"What about at work?"

"You're serious?"

"Should I not be?"

"This isn't work-related."

"Well, okay then, I suppose. But one more thing," I said, reaching for my glass, but finding only the half-full pitcher and slugging directly from that. Alice watched, fascinated or appalled, maybe both. "This arrangement. It has the sound of a very logical, untested idea. I don't want to be the proving ground for it. Mr. Tryout. No."

"You want to know if I've slept with other people? Is that it?"

"Under the auspices of therapy dick, yes, that's right."

"If I said I hadn't, would that actually change your mind?"

"No, I don't think so," I said after some thought, wondering if this situation was ever really in my control, or if I was basically living in day to day in thralldom to the kind of impulses that either make people very happy or send them to jail.

"Well, since it's all the same to you," said Alice, taking the pitcher from me and finishing it off herself as a V of geese crossed the darkening sky above the river. "This isn't his first tour. I'm not using you to break anything in. And no one else was as tied up in knots about it as you are. I'm leaving now. Come with me only if you're finished equivocating."

She burped sharply and stood up from the table, clearly a little fed up, but not to any definitive point. I hopped the railing on the deck and circled around the building to the parking lot, a little afraid of plying the crew of dogcatchers and sewage men inside without her as a buffer.

Alice lived in a prefabricated log home up in foothills below Maybrick Peak, not far from Carissa's parent's house, thought I didn't realize exactly how close the two properties were until much later in the evening, after dinner and coition with Alice on a kind of rawhide futon on the sun porch. As she slept soundly in the back bedroom, I prowled the house naked, gnawing an ear of grilled sweet corn left over from dinner and sipping a glass of bourbon, neat, feeling at home in the place and used in a good way. Well used, I thought, negotiating my way through the kitchen amid a web of twinges; knees, lower back, left elbow for some reason, anything that bent. Alice had a pretty good idea of what she wanted from the get go, I suspected, and when the dam broke shortly after dinner, it was all I could do to keep up with her as we bopped and crashed around the sun porch, bringing down a set of drapes and overturning two or three smaller pieces of furniture, I'd lost count. The room looked like a wild animal had been turned loose in it by the time we were finished. Alice went to bed, tired from what seemed to me like a big day for us both, and I stayed up, tidying the sun porch and wandering around the rest of the house, listening to the low of ebb of Wynn Stewart on the living room stereo, her choice. It had been playing since we arrived. Not knowing what I wanted or being easily satisfied with whatever came my way, whichever, probably made all this easier and it was nice to finally find myself in a position where lassitude wasn't a handicap.

I rolled a joint the size of a Chinese finger trap on a cutting board in the kitchen, and walked through the living room to refresh my drink and throw a blanket over my shoulders, briefly noticing my reflection in a sliding glass door to the deck as I walked outside to smoke; a corncob clamped between my teeth, an overfull whiskey glass in one hand, puffy blunt between my knuckles, and a plum-colored bite mark bracketing the exact place where my neck met my shoulder. Also, I appeared to smile at myself around the corncob.

I may not know what I want, but I do know how to enjoy myself after stumbling over it, I thought, seating myself in an Adirondack chair and tugging the blanket around my head as I lit the joint, the smoke seeming to drape itself over the still air, the night silent, autumnal, a little eerie beyond the cast of the houselights. When something began rustling in the underbrush girding the yard, drawing closer to the deck by the sound of it, I half expected a clan of goblins or the headless horseman to emerge from the woods, a situation I wasn't prepared to handle but was interested in experiencing nonetheless. Encountering Menaces: The Oliver Himmel Story. Instead, a dopy-looking chocolate Lab came trotting out from behind some raspberry bushes and sniffed eagerly around the yard until it found something to roll in. A few minutes later, a flashlight beam swept through the forest and a voice shouted behind it, presumably calling the dog's name.

"Strummer! . . . Strummer! . . . Joe fucking Strummer!"

"Over here!" I called back, wrapping the blanket around my waist and pinching the remains of the joint in the corner of my mouth as I crossed the yard to where Joe Strummer was, rolling and gurgling in a patch of light from the living room window, and threaded my fingers gently beneath the dog's collar. "We're by the house! Follow the lights!"

"Thanks so much," said Carissa's father, emerging from the treeline in sensible shorts and a windbreaker, a flashlight swinging from one a hand, a lead from the other. He looked healthy, vigorous, not much older than the last time I saw him, though I couldn't remember exactly when this was. "Sorry to barge in on you in the middle of the night. We just picked this guy up at the shelter a few weeks ago and we're still trying to figure it all out."

"No trouble at all," I said, watching him stoop to leash the dog, not sure whether to wait for him to recognize me or go ahead and introduce myself, get it out in the open. "I was just . . ."

"You a friend of Alice's?" he asked, casually snooping, as he stood up with the dog in tow, though not waiting for an answer as he finally took it all in, the blanket slung around my waist like a dhoti, the damp joint hung crookedly from my bottom lip, and the mostly kernelless corncob I'd brought along for some reason swinging from my hand in a way that seemed to needlessly mirror the flashlight swaying from his wrist. Different men, different tools, I thought opaquely, as we shook hands. "Oliver! So sorry I didn't recognize you, man, how are you? Long time."

"Sure has been," I said, not sure what else to say. I didn't think I looked like the kind of person who knew how to nurture relationships.

"You know, I thought of you the other day. Buck came by the house with some record he wanted me to hear. *Out of Vogue*, I think it was called. You've heard it, right?"

"Yup. It's a favorite."

"I figured it must be. No one was putting stuff like that out in 1978. Take it from me. I was alive back then. Anyway, Carissa told me you guys were all living together in town, so I asked Buck to bring you along next time he comes by. The weather's still good enough to drag the speakers outside. We get quite a nice echo up here."

"I'll come by next time," I said, figuring I'd find an excuse not to by the time Buck got back from Massachusetts. He'd left the day before for some kind of non-profit summit or conference on one of the white-bread campuses in the Berkshires and was slated to return Monday. I glanced around the yard for something to pilot the conversation back into noncommittal terrain, but didn't find much.

"So you and Alice are friends?" asked Carissa's father, resuming his snooping.

"Pot?" I asked, offering the joint and tossing the corncob into the bushes, both as kind of diversion. Joe Strummer nearly dragged Carissa's father off into the woods after it, though he managed to snag the roach and calm the dog down long enough to take a deep hit before handing it back and thanking me, though not leaving, still waiting for answer to his question regarding Alice.

"It is the weekend and I think I deserve it," he said, rooted to the spot like a totem pole, going nowhere anytime soon, waving his hand generally at the dog. "Especially after chasing this moron through the forest for the past hour."

"Certainly," I agreed, offering the joint again, hoping a second round might send him on his way.

"I appreciate it, but no thanks. Any more and I'll be lost in the woods until morning. So, how do know Alice?"

"She's my briend," I said, narrowly avoiding calling her my boss, trying to shoehorn 'friend' in at the last minute.

"Your what now?"

"We're friends. I came up to help her out with something," I said. This had the weird effect of sounding both vague and specific, talking around the obvious or drawing a circle around it, and a little dumb, under the circumstances. Carissa's father hadn't seen much of me over the past years, sure, but he probably knew enough about what I'd been doing or not doing to know I wasn't some kind of journeyman Mr. Fixit, roving Acheron county for husbandless households with things to put right.

200

"Nice of you," he said, his eyes flicking glassily over the blanket girding my waist and the bite mark purpling my shoulder. I shifted away to conceal his view of this, and noticed a line of three parallel scratches crossing my chest like a bandolier, revealed to us both for the first time in the light from the living room window.

"She had some wood to stack," I said, no longer sure how I should stand to look less like a cicisbeo. "We had a few drinks with dinner. Didn't want to drive anywhere."

"I just helped her put away three cords last week," said Carissa's father. "I guess she must have got another one or two in."

"I guess so," I said.

"Never hurts to have a little extra wood."

"Sure doesn't."

"Something to keep you warm over a long winter."

"What?"

"I'm going to take off, now," he said, tugging Joe Strummer's leash, aiming himself toward the forest. "But Carissa is coming up for breakfast tomorrow, probably around nine. You and Alice should come by, have a mimosa. I'm making eggs benedict. I think we might listen to Prefab Sprout and play croquet if the weather holds out."

"Sounds good," I said, watching him tromp off into the woods whistling a tinny version of 'Prove It All Night', wondering what kind of satisfaction a man like Carissa's father could get out of blowing the thin lid off my cover. Whatever happened with Alice from here on out, the fact of it would be out in the open at the house on Winter Street, no way around that. The only real arrow left in my quiver, I figured, was the surprise element of showing up at breakfast with Alice in tow and act naturally in front of Carissa while secretly trying to live with myself between the mimosas and croquet. I didn't think Alice would go for it. Though we hadn't really discussed anything, brunch with the neighbors was probably beyond the parameters of therapy dick. I suppose there was always the chance the good doctor wouldn't say anything to his daughter, but I couldn't imagine not doing that if I were in his position. The only secrets I'd managed to keep from Carissa were the kind that didn't matter. I hadn't spent much time expecting that to change.

Alice and I didn't make it to breakfast the next morning. We woke up around 10, had coffee in bed, and went about dismantling the en suite bathroom as we had the sun porch the day before. She wasn't in any hurry to kick me out, possibly because doing so would necessarily involve driving me back to town. Either way, we had a brunch of our own on the deck, scrambled eggs, toast, cheese, Greek yogurt, some fruit, chewing and chatting as strains of *Two Wheels Good* rose from the direction of Carissa's house, echoing against the mountain wall behind us. The weather had apparently held out.

"A nice man," said Alice, raising her chin toward the trees, and the music bopping away above the meadow beyond them. "Of course, you know that. But I could do without the concerts. Sometimes it's like living beside a fairground."

"He was over here last night, by the way," I said, trying to make it sound offhand, not important, but still worth knowing. I'd debated sharing anything about meeting Carissa's dad in the yard, not really sure what kind of secretive aegis we were operating beneath, but figured if he was helping Alice do things like stack wood, it would probably come up eventually. Honesty is always easier for me when I'm forced into it, I thought, as the opening salvo of 'The Yearning Loins' erupted from the middle distance. "He was looking around for his dog. I thought you might want to know."

"Why? That happens all the time."

"Well. I was recognized."

"Oliver, we're not on the run."

"I know, but I just thought . . . I don't know what I thought."

"We're not going to go out for many meals in town or anything like that, but if someone wanders onto my property in the middle of the night and sees something they disapprove of, that's their problem, not mine. Besides, he isn't the type to worry about. He got so stoned while stacking wood with me a few weeks ago that he got lost in the forest on his way home."

"He said something about that. I thought he was joking."

"Two hours after I thought he'd left, I saw him through the kitchen window while I was making dinner, standing in the yard, scratching his head, looking like he'd lost true north. I fixed him a plate and we had a cup of coffee. Then I drove him home."

"Be that as it may," I began grandly, not really sure where I was going next. Someplace good, I hoped. "I suppose this kind of discretion is new to me. I'm trying to be a good whatever I am to you."

"That's very sweet, Oliver," she said, running a finger down the back of my hand. "But I have more at stake here than you. Let me worry about it."

"Okay," I said, as she began to gather the plates and cups, her bathrobe billowing open in the wind as she walked inside like a reminder, a brief flash of thigh, pubis, belly, breasts, or the composite shape of everything that seemed to be well in hand, yet also out of reach. I went upstairs to shower in the sacked-looking bathroom, and dress for departure. Alice had some things she needed to do with the rest of her weekend, I assumed, things that didn't involve me in my therapeutic capacity, and I had an average life to return to, a cat to feed, a plant to water. We left the house shortly after noon, and she drove me into town, idling at the curb outside the house at Winter Street, kissing in the cab of her pickup, making plans to reconvene on Sunday night, almost like a real couple.

From the outside, we must look like two very happy people, I thought, as I watched the pickup lurch around the corner of the street and immediately began wondering how much of this Carissa had seen as I turned toward the house and noticed her swaying in the hammock, her eyes apparently buried in a book, a Bloody Mary in a sort of vat balanced on a milk crate beside her, a libation waiting to be poured out.

Had we looked happy from where she was sitting? I wondered as I mounted the porch, watching her drop the book and fix me with the sort of studied expression the wise reserve for the functionally unwise, a kind of knowing fatigue or familiar disappointment, something I'd seen the tip of from time to time after moving in, which had always made me feel like a shabby apprentice kept on out of pity. She clearly knew or thought she knew everything and wanted to share her thoughts on the matter immediately. Fuck it, I thought, plopping myself in a camp chair across from her. Might as well get it out of the way now.

"How was breakfast?" I asked, helping myself to slug of her drink, not really sure where to go from here. Endure it. That seemed to be the only choice.

"I don't want to be mad about this, but I'm mad about it. Alice is my friend, Oliver."

"She's also my friend now, I think."

"She's also your boss, at a job you were able to get because I have a good reputation in the school district. I vouched for you, over other people who were way more qualified."

"That wouldn't be hard. Qualification-wise, I mean."

"So you see why I might be mad about this."

"It's not work-related, I assure you, Carissa.

"And she's married. I know her husband. He's a good guy."

"Does the phrase 'therapy dick' mean anything to you?"

"You're sometimes disgusting," she said, tossing her book aside and fleeing the porch, leaving her drink behind.

"Oh, fuck off, Carissa," I shouted through the screen door. "Maybe if you were happier you wouldn't spend so much time making us both miserable."

"I am happy, you shitheel!" she shouted back, reappearing in doorway, furious, but not opening the door, preserving a natural barrier between us, probably for the best. "The only thing that detracts from that is watching you bushwhack your way through the people around you, including me, including Buck, like you don't care or don't see us and maybe you don't, but that's no excuse for being a pig about what you want."

"Now, this is new to me," I said to her back, as she retreated once again into the depths of the house. "But as far as I can tell, therapy dick is about using someone to make yourself feel better about whatever you really want being far away or not around at all. You sure that doesn't sound familiar to you?"

No answer. I swigged the Bloody Mary and moved to the hammock, noticing a group of people who had probably come to see the foliage up in the mountains halted on the sidewalk, staring in my direction, brochures I'd written for Henry's tourism company, Releaf Tours, open in their hands.

"I wrote those," I shouted at them, gesturing vaguely in their direction with my drink, the soupy liquid sloshing onto my shoes. As usual, no one wanted to talk about what I wanted to talk about. They moved on, down the street, in the direction of greener pastures, leaving me with the problem of getting through the next twelve to thirty-six hours without coming to blows with Carissa. If the weather held up, as it seemed to be doing, I could probably sleep outside. Maybe Amanda would allow me to crash in her laundry again, but I doubted it. Karen and Ray would undoubtedly take me for the rest of the weekend, though I'd have to seriously rethink the past three months, try to end up on their side of things, Mr. Supportive of whatever they were doing.

It didn't sound like the kind of self-work I could get through during the forty-minute drive to Randolph. The Ethiopian place would have me until closing, I knew that, by which time maybe Carissa would have gone to bed, if I was lucky. Sitting around all evening, sipping tej and drawing wolves on the napkins sounded all right to me, but it was barely noon and they wouldn't open up until dinner time. What to do until then? The house was clearly off-limits and my car keys were inside, limiting my range. Go to the library; spend the afternoon flipping through magazines like a homeless person? Hike up to the college, see what kind of trouble I could get into with Amanda if she was home? Buy a six-pack of something cheap and go down to the river, skip rocks until nightfall? This also sounded sort of hobo-like, but the six-pack idea reminded me that I'd recently made a friend who I didn't have to worry about sleeping with or not sleeping with, a good person to call at time like this.

An hour or so later, Theresa and I were floating around another remote inlet on Kranion Pond in her canoe, our rods wedged beneath the thwarts, a nest of empty beer cans clinking around our feet as we watched the bobbers at the end our lines do not much of anything on the becalmed surface of the lake. Theresa hadn't minded picking me up at the house and hadn't asked why she'd needed to, though a general recognition of something having gone wrong on my end of things gave us a lot to talk around as we set out across the water. The day was a cool, primary slice of autumn in New England, with leaves turning on the trees around the lake, skimming the water as they fell and variegating the mountainside above, yellow to orange to red, colors that seemed to signify varying degrees of caution to me, perhaps because of the notices I continued to receive about my student loans. We'd reached the orange stage at the beginning of October, so I expected a red-letter day shortly after Halloween, once the dead had been rolled back into their sarcophagi, I imagined. A shame we couldn't bury a few loan counselors with them, but the enemies of man always seemed to be running loose, if studying with Dr. Norman had taught me anything. The world is a small place filled with people who will mostly all lapse into minor-league evil, at some point, I thought, rolling a joint with a beer between my knees, things I typically liked, trying to disassociate my personal crap from the foliage so I could enjoy it a little more.

"I met a girl," I said, lighting up and passing the joint to Theresa.

"I did too," she said.

"You go first."

"She's about ten years younger than me, a sophomore at the college. Having a phase. I don't expect it to last."

"The phase, or you and her?"

"Both, in that order."

"You don't seem bothered about it."

"She's really hot and wildly ignorant."

"Those are things that sometimes go well together."

"I love it. I have to listen to her jabber about micro-aggressions all day, but I get to spend the nights in her dorm room, listening to her say my name, over and over."

"May I sit in on that?"

"I'd maybe consider it if you weren't the kind of person who likes to be invited along on anything, no matter what it is."

"I've never thought of myself that way."

"People want to feel a little special, Oliver," she said, taking in line, recasting. "Your turn."

"She's married," I said, taking my cue from her, watching my line coil in midair and pierce the surface of a lake, settling at an acute angle to the water. "That's for starters."

"Okay."

"To a soldier. On tour."

"Semper fi."

"And she's my boss."

"Uh oh."

"Does the phrase 'therapy dick' mean anything to you?"

"Yes."

"Because I hadn't heard before yesterday."

"Sounds like you have a little job to do."

"I'm noticing I usually get only fragments of what I want over time, never the entire thing all at once."

"If the entire thing is shaped like a person, that might be why."

"Fuck," I said, the way some people probably say 'golly' or 'shucks' and more to myself than her, a sound of surrender. A loon cruising the far side of the cove wailed to itself as if it had received my signal.

We fished without catching anything until the beer was gone, and paddled back to the boat launch just as the sun slipped behind Mt. Abandon, leaving us in moody twilight as we loaded the canoe on the car and set off for town. On the way down the access road, Theresa asked what I was doing with the rest of my night, and I mentioned something about hanging out at the Ethiopian restaurant, so she suggested we get dinner there, an odd development. When she asked if the food was any good, I had to explain that while I wasn't categorically against eating there, I'd only tried the wine, which was very good. I hadn't known Theresa for very long, but she seemed like the sort of person who finds joy rather than terror in the prospect of a new experience, so I went along with it once we got to town, escorting her through a gauntlet of puzzled waiters, who had already parted to leave an open channel for me to reach the bar. I headed instead to Hodan's rostrum and requesting a table for two. This must be how things change. All at once or not at all, I told myself as I read the food menu for the first time, solidly out of my element, allowing Theresa to order for us when one of the still curious-looking waiters arrived to take it all down.

The meal turned out very well, I thought. Various stewed courses appeared: chickpeas, okra, and cabbage in berbere sauce, all poured over a flattened injera on a tin tray and eaten by hand. Theresa and I made pigs of ourselves, mowing through the spread as if we'd been working in a salt mine all day rather than drinking beer and shooting the shit in a boat on Kranion Pond. Hours crept by and when the food was gone, we migrated to the bar for desert, glasses of tej and crème brûlée. We were too full to talk much and Theresa settled into watching me draw wolves on the back of a beer coaster.

"I read somewhere that Stalin used to do this during meetings with his general staff," I said, watching her watch me. "I don't know why. And I think I read it in something by Martin Cruz Smith, so it could be made up."

"No, it's true," she said, finishing off her wine, slipping her desert dish toward a lingering waiter. "He used to fill the backgrounds in with a red pencil."

"Maybe they have one those behind the bar," I said, looking around for the bartender. "I should ask. I knew these were missing something."

"I have to take off," said Theresa, glancing at her phone. "I have a date with a young lady who is growing out her armpit hair for the first time. Do you have a place to go tonight?"

"Why would I not?"

"I picked you up on your porch in a day-old outfit after you said you couldn't meet me at the lake because your car keys were inside."

"Maybe I'm just lazy."

"I'm sure you are lazy, but if you need a place to stay, I won't be home tonight. I'm in the carriage house over by the ice-cream stand. My key is hidden in the lawn jockey's lantern."

"I love that you have one of those."

"My landlord does. He loves it. Nothing I can do."

"That's very generous. But I think it will be okay if I just stay here until they close and keep quite when I come in."

"She'll get over it if it's about what I think it is."

"What is that? And who is 'she' in this context?"

"What you told me in the boat. You know the rest, I'm not rehashing it for you, Oliver. Exiling someone is what people do when they can't do what they really want to them. Consider that maybe and walk softly when you're finished up here."

"Now I'm thinking I should cultivate a ruckus when I get home tonight, just to see what happens."

"I really do have to go. This was fun," said Theresa, leaning in to hug me. "If you were a women, maybe we'd be all set."

"If you ever need therapy dick," I suggested, as a waiter dropped the bill at my elbow.

"Funny," said Theresa, standing up, slipping the coaster with my drawing into her pocket. "You pay."

I watched her leave before returning to the wine and wolves. It seemed to be later in the evening and the restaurant was filling up, mostly with tourists who had come to see the leaves. I noticed Hodan seating some part of the group that had passed me on the porch earlier that morning and waved to them their at a table, which got me nothing, but felt good anyway.

As I lay in bed several hours later, after entering the house on Winter Street like a burglar, shoes off, avoiding loose floorboards and squeaky steps on the way to the attic, I lapsed in and out of sleep while lingering over the conversation with Theresa about what I wanted and the conversation with Carissa about bushwhacking, as she said, trying to lay the two side by side and dig out what they maybe had in common, if anything. Bottomless trouble seemed to lurk somewhere in there, the kind I hoped to avoid, but it seemed I had it pretty well boxed in, for the moment. At least I thought so, until I closed my eyes, trying to settle into the calmative sounds of the room, a branch ticking against the screen, Agatha purring between my feet, the beams wheezing toward settlement, but then a less familiar noise from the hallway -- the muted slap and drag of bare feet approaching from the stairs. And soon I saw Carissa standing in the doorway of my room in a t-shirt and panties, hair up, resting her forearm against the jam, one leg crossed behind the other like the hanged man on a tarot card.

Shit on a shingle, I thought. She seemed to be deciding something or waiting to be invited in, as vampires are said to do, a troubling comparison. The room was too dark for her to see me watching her, or much even beyond the outline of my body in bed, making the entire tableau all the creepier, a perfect opportunity to continue the shouting match we'd started earlier on the porch. I wanted to explain the general nature of my availability, as therapy dick or anything else and straighten out the record she seemed to have of my wanting her unconditionally over the past few weeks or years, I no longer knew which it was. And maybe add something about how I was just as disappointed with her as she was with me, maybe even more, and not for the reasons she probably thought, picking Buck all over again, big surprise, but because of what had her up here in the middle of night, hanging around outside my bedroom while he was out of town for the weekend. It was the one thing that us fucking wouldn't change, the thing that made us both weak, the thing that we recognized and probably hated in each other, but needed to be around in order not to be alone with it. I hadn't come up with a term for this yet, but I knew what it looked like in a primitive state. I'd seen it in Sasha's eyes when he grabbed Tracy's hair during art class; the terror of being abandoned in the outer space of your own head, adrift, alone, knocking into whatever is around. That seemed to be the end result of recognizing yourself in the careless decisions of someone else and wanting them anyway because of it and not because of it, and now we'd both bushwhacked our way to where we didn't want to be, good for us. Yelling at each other about it was like shouting into a mirror, I decided, so I closed my eyes again, finished imagining what it was too late to imagine with any sincere clarity and waited for her feet to sweep back toward the stairs.

*   *   *

I'm certain Buck immediately noticed something was wrong when he returned from Massachusetts on Monday night, but he gave it a week before saying anything to Carissa and me about it. Even then, we didn't get much past denial, the one thing the both of us could accidentally agree on. I felt bad for him, watching us throughout dinner the following Sunday, seated at the head of the table, Carissa on his right, me on his left, as she and I silently mowed through a vegetable lasagna he'd made and been excited about sharing with us, his head oscillating like a dog watching table tennis and finally clattering his flatware against his plate and half getting up when he couldn't stand it any longer.

"What the fuck is up with you two?" he asked. "Whatever it is, I can't take any more of it."

"Nothing," we said, in unison, eyes fixed on our food to keep from glaring at each other, I imagined.

"I leave for a weekend," continued Buck, "and it's suddenly like you two can't stand to be in the same room together."

"Carissa thinks I should only date the lesbians she sets me up with," I said, going out of my way to sound even-keeled.

"Pretending not to notice this is becoming a full time job," said Buck, wearily. "I already work from home. Please tell me what's going on."

"I've been thinking," said Carissa, twirling the stem of her wineglass, staring into her plate. "It's probably time for Oliver to be moving on now that he has his feet under him. I mean, how long is it reasonable for him to be here living for free? We're doing him a disservice, I think, cheating him out of full independence. But it's your house, Buck, so your call."

"I'll pack my things," I said, flatly. "Be gone in the morning. You'll never see me again if that's what you both want."

"Nobody is going anywhere because of me," said Buck, drawing himself up, towering over the table with a plate of cooling lasagna in his hand. "You guys are friends. Figure it out. Right now, I can't stand to be in the same with room with either of you. I'm eating on the porch. Fuck this."

We watched him leave the kitchen, swiveling back to face each other across the table after he'd gone, as if we were about to begin some kind of oppositional summit, the silent scream of our mutual contempt for one another seeming to take on the exact shape of the room.

"Slug," said Carissa.

"Witch," I replied.

"You're a human lesion. The more open you are the more disgusting you become."

"You'd be so lucky to fuck me," I said, downing my remaining wine, adding: "Again."

"I was lonely and desperate. The way you usually are."

"Harridan."

"Drunk. Clown. Sociopath."

"Well, this has been nice," I said, standing up from the table. "Now I have to go meet Alice at her place."

"Why don't you have another drink or three before you drive over?"

"I'll give her your best."

"I hope her husband waterboards you."

"When he comes back to town, maybe you can show him upstairs in the middle of the night. Help carry the bucket," I said, dropping my plate in the sink and walking out of the house, nearly passing by Buck on the porch without saying anything as he swung miserably in the hammock like a man hung out on gibbet, his dirty plate and a six-pack minus two between his feet. I halted, muttering something vague about seeing him tomorrow night, some standard placeholder valediction, and turned to go, hoping he wouldn't waylay me with anything significant, a long shot, I knew, even before he spoke.

"Before you leave, will you please help me understand what's going on here?" he said. It sounded like a kind of orison.

"I don't know," I lied. "Ask Carissa."

"I will, but did you . . . and don't take this wrong, Oliver, but you're not giving me any information here, so I have to ask. Did you . . . touch her or something?"

"What? No. Absolutely not. Is that what you think I do when you're not here? Lurk in the attic, trying to grope whoever's around the house?"

"I have no idea."

"You have no idea?"

"Well, I mean, I know you kissed her in the kitchen over the summer. I know about that. Look, I'm sorry, I had to ask."

"That was something completely different, it's over now and I'm sorry I did it."

"It's okay. I never was mad about it."

"How can that possibly be?"

"Well. We weren't really upfront about anything with you and I think I know how you feel about her, I've always had an idea of that and I care a lot about you both, so there wasn't much point in me being mad about it."

"I think you deserve a better friend than me," I said, reaching down between his feet, grabbing a beer.

"I'm sorry you feel that way."

I didn't know what else to say, so I left the porch, shambling down the walk to my car, tucking the beer in the console like a kind of plunder, and set off for Alice's house, feeling like a garbagy human being all the way there, not really sure what to do about it. Alice didn't know either, even after listening to me explain the parts of it that would make sense to her, so she made us Margaritas and we spent the rest of the evening hitting golf balls off the deck into the meadow between her home and Carissa's parent's house.

"Do you think I'm a sociopath?" I asked Alice later on, after we'd gone to bed, lying together in the dark, our bodies a question mark beneath the sheets.

"A sociopath wouldn't ask me that," she said, adjusting her pillow, dragging my arm across her chest, kissing my wrist, layering her comforts before sleep. Essentially the same thing I was doing, I thought. Brush teeth, turn off lights, make sure you're not a sociopath; the adult equivalent of checking for monsters under the bed. I'd never needed my parents to do this when I was a child, though nowadays I would've taken a beast or two hanging around in the odd closet or dark corner. That sounded like the kind of predictable problem I could steer around after a while.

Still, I felt like less of a villain after talking with Alice. I imagined Carissa back at the house on Winter Street, probably having some form of the same discussion with Buck, and, despite everything, I hoped she felt the same way.

*　　*　　*

By the time Halloween rolled around, the tension between Carissa and me had found a routine, mostly ignorable footing around the house and the three of us were almost able to enjoy putting together a costume for me the night before. Staff members at the Acheron Learning Center weren't required to dress up for the holiday, Alice had informed me, but it was always appreciated. A nice touch, as she put it.

Looking over my recent activities, I noticed a marked absence of nice touches and figured even if sleeping with my boss was a fine excuse for cutting corners, I was still the new guy to everyone else at the school and didn't want to single myself out as a slacker so early on. I'd seen press material from past celebrations; Inez as a scarecrow, Pete in some kind of werewolf outfit, and Tracy with a black mask, penciled moustache, and *sombrero cordobés*, appearing as Zorro, an interesting choice. The results of my performance review notwithstanding, I imagined myself dressed as myself in one of these photographs, part of some public relations kit beside my festive coworkers, like a reminder to donors to please keep giving; good help was obviously still hard to find.

Even so, I didn't want to shoulder the full responsibility of dressing like a kook to please others and spend the rest of the day having only myself to kick, so I gave over the choice of costume to Buck and Carissa, saying I had no ideas of my own. This wasn't entirely true. I knew Alice was going as a witch and thought it would be funny to show up at school dressed as broomstick, though I didn't see how this could be easily done, and worried I'd end up looking like hula dancer if I wasn't careful. And Carissa was the only person aside from Alice who would get the joke, a regressive possibility in light of the armistice we seemed to have struck when I asked her and Buck for help with a costume, something unambiguous, my only guideline, figuring as long as I didn't have to field any questions about what I was supposed to be, I'd be fine with whatever they chose for me.

Based on what was around the house, this turned out to be a pirate getup, essentially my interview outfit capped off with a tricorne hat Buck had for some reason and a cutlass Carissa had sawed out of a pizza box and wrapped in aluminum foil slipped in a belt, a sash actually—one of her scarves. Still, we all agreed, the costume looked incomplete. An eyepatch was out of the question with my glasses, and I didn't want to have to draw a grease pencil beard on myself first thing in the morning, so to make up for this, I stayed up until 1AM with Carissa, drinking box wine and making a papier-mâché parrot to fasten to my shoulder with wood glue or safety pins, we weren't sure which; whatever worked, she said. We didn't speak much and what we did say didn't stray far from the activity at hand, draping damp strips of newsprint over a bird-shaped mold she'd made out of more newsprint and masking tape, but it was nice to be doing something harmless together, an activity that would have made either of us seem crazy for disinterring what we'd silently agreed to bury for the time being in order to get through it.

She stayed up after I went to bed, painting the parrot we'd made, and got up with me in the morning to help attach the thing to my shoulder, a task we only accomplished after borrowing a staple gun from the neighbors. We were both running late for work, so she gave me a ride to school, a favor I was all the more grateful for after checking my reflection in the passenger-side sun visor, trying not to imagine myself walking to work with the goddamned bird on my shoulder. I looked stupid, but I expected that, and no more stupid than anyone else when I rolled into work. With the exception of Alice in her witch gear and Inez as a cowboy, the staff at the Acheron Learning Center all seemed to have slapped something together the night before. Pete looked like one of the three wise men from the Gospel of Matthew; he was supposed to be a ghost, he said, but couldn't find a big enough sheet to cover himself. And Tracy seemed hamstrung between a stage magician and coming as a Zorro again, no mask, and no hat this time, but a cape and moustache. She said she couldn't find all of her costume from last year. It was a mess and I was glad not to find myself at the extreme end of it either way, especially after buses arrived, their doors folding back to expel a crew of students mostly out of costume, oblivious to the holiday, with the exception of Sasha, who some jokester at the group home had managed to squeeze into a blood-red devil onesie, complete with plastic horns and a spade-like tail he had already begun to chew.

As we paired off me with Sasha, Pete looking like an oil sheik, tripping over his robes as he chased after Dan, Inez appearing as Buck Owens with Tyler in tow, and Tracy hovering around Ellie like an illusion was about to be performed—I noticed Alice snapping photos on the front steps and wondered what all this must look like to prospective parents when it was finally printed up and put in brochure form. Here at Acheron Learning Center, our staff are committed to celebrating things your kids couldn't care less about! Enroll now!

I was up half the night making a papier-mâché parrot with someone who hates me, I thought, trying to keep Sasha's tail out of his mouth as we circled the street on our morning walk. I have no right to be cynical about this.

The morning rolled along well enough, reaching a pleasant kind of stalemate shortly after snack. The wall clock in the classroom appeared to halt at 10AM, a fata morgana, but a familiar one. I knew that and wasn't worried about it. There was a party after lunch; one of the classrooms had been converted into a haunted house of sorts, plastic cauldrons of candy were standing by, as well as trays of pumpkin-shaped cookies and a kind of dipping and accessorizing station for caramel apples. If we could make it through the next two hours, there was enough food at the end of the line to keep everyone occupied until buses arrived. I didn't see an immediate reason to worry. Sasha and I had been getting along well enough since Inez put us together on Monday and after watching him brush his teeth like a violinist and slap through a set of questions about his mood and the weather outside—cloudy with a chance of rain—during homeroom, he'd settled into the

sensory corner beneath a weighted blanket, swiping at the bubbles I blew beside him and occasionally using an adapted sign
to request a song from me, swatting the place where my mouth
would be if I didn't move out of his reach like a leathered greaser
slapping a juke box. I'd worked my way through 'The Wheels
on the Bus', 'Twinkle Twinkle Little Star', and was now in the
last verse of 'Kids Don't Follow', the only other song I seemed to
know all the words to.

Kids don't follow
What you're doing
In my face and out my ear
Kids won't follow
What you're saying
We can't hear
Kids won't follow
What you're saying
In my face out my ear
Kids don't follow
What you're saying
We can't hear
What you say
Not tomorrow
Not today

"What the hell are you singing over there?" asked Inez, watching me from beneath the straw brim of her cattleman hat at a
table across the classroom. In a chair beside her, Tyler grimly
clapped together a puzzle, looking like a man under house arrest.
Before I could answer her, I felt a sharp tug on my shoulder, and
saw Sasha retreating beneath the blanket with Carissa's pirate

bird cradled against his chest. The air between us suddenly held a tang of urine. Tasks began stacking up, ordering themselves like soldiers on review. I leaned over, shifting the blanket aside, checking what I already knew; a damp patch like an unmapped continent darkening the lower part of Sasha's devil suit.

"Okay, Sasha," I said, trying to make it sound like I had something fun in store, while also raising my voice enough so Inez would hear me across the room. "Let's go to the bathroom."

I stood up and he stood up, all going well so far, though my parrot, the best part of my costume, was still clamped against his body, a little too close to the spreading wetness for my comfort. Maybe I was fond of the thing for what it reminded me of, amity or something like it between Carissa and me, our Treaty of Versailles, Peace of Westphalia, Pax Romana, whatever. It seemed to symbolize good things to come or at least boredom with the way things had been since Buck went to the Berkshires, a change all three of us needed. It wasn't Sasha's fault or problem that all this was tied up in the papier-mâché bird he'd snatched from my shoulder, but allowing him to chew it to pieces or pee all over it wasn't the right move either. Consistency, as Inez always said.

"Before we get changed," I began, hating myself a little for always relying on a first person plural pronoun to get most things done at work as I tugged the bird out of Sasha's grip, "can I have this back? We can't bring it to the bathroom."

Later, when Inez and I tried to pinpoint the exact moment things went wrong, I kept coming back to a sort of snapshot, unable to move beyond it: the back of Sasha's hand somehow in his mouth, the skin around a chewed-over callus already reddening around the teeth in his upper jaw, so fast it seemed to have skipped a frame. I almost didn't notice his other hand, suddenly coiling and jerking the loose fabric of Buck's shirt, my pirate/interview blouse, until a button a pinged against the window above the sensory corner. The clock on the wall read 10:15; the standstill was over.

I grabbed Sasha's wrist, throwing my other arm up between us in an exaggerated watch-checking motion to block his forehead, while Inez pulled his other arm out of his mouth, and drew it across her chest, holding him under the armpit and anchoring his wrist against her hip, trying to give me the time I needed to pry his hand off my shirt. The garment was already so torn that it looked like poncho, so I stepped out of it, slid my hand up Sasha's wrist to his shoulder, mirroring Inez in what I would later have to refer to in the incident report as a transport position.

"Outside," she said, glancing around the classroom. Dan rocked beside ayatollah Pete, getting through some deskwork and Ellie was still having snack with Tracy the Magnificent. Tyler looked on as if he had been abandoned at sea. "Pete, lock the door behind us, please."

We managed to get Sasha outside onto the playground before he dropped to his knees, which, according to our training, made the transport hold unsafe. We counted to three and let him go, a small, wet, furious man in a red devil suit, the both of us running in opposite directions. His hand instantly returned to his mouth as he stood, an obvious sign of more trouble on the horizon, his other arm held out from of his body like a sock puppeteer, not sure who to go after, but definitely deciding. He settled on Inez, pursuing her in a kind of ellipsis around the swing set, before changing his mind and heading toward me.

"I don't how to help you, I'm sorry," yelled Inez, as I led Sasha in a rough figure eight around the playground, trying not corner myself against the back fence and wondering what all this must look like to the people gathered on sidewalk to watch the show. A shirtless man in a tricorne hat fleeing a shorter, angrier man in a soiled Satan leotard while a cowboy looked on, apologizing to one of them. I tried not to look at the crowd, but ended up having to look somewhere else when Sasha broke from pursuing me to knock his head against the swing set— once, twice, and then I looked away, but the sound followed me, a bell with a moist and mossy tongue ringing. The crowd on the other side of the fence seemed to be mostly older, unemployed people in search of free midmorning entertainment or people with jobs weird enough to have Halloween of—except for Grover, who I noticed standing a little ways off, leaning on the hood of the dwarfish, fuel efficient car he'd driven as long as we'd known each other.

Almost ten years now, I calculated, waving. He waved back, looking apologetic, though this look quickly transitioned to one of warning and I noticed I couldn't hear the mushy bell ringing. Inez yelled something, possibly my name, and I turned around in time to see Sasha's face hurtling toward my face, like a baseball my father had once thrown to me in the yard of the house in North Calais, a baseball I wasn't prepared to catch and which I would see for the rest of my life whenever anyone threw anything at me, the memory of it smacking into my head and my mother running across the lawn to pinch the bridge of my nose, while my father looked on, sorry and probably with some idea of the larger impact of all this. The crowd groaned in canon.

I came to several minutes later in the third floor meeting area outside Alice's office, with the nurse the school kept on retainer shining a penlight in my eyes and nodding. What remained of the parrot was in my lap. I appeared to be in the middle of answering a question.

"Don't worry about that," she said to whatever I'd said. "No signs of a concussion, though I wouldn't go rollerblading without a helmet."

"No rollerblading," I agreed, nodding to myself and looking around the room. "How did I get up here?"

"You walked up on your own, apparently," said the nurse. "That was before they called me. And now, here you are. You may not remember much about it, at least for a little while. Your friend is going to take you for a CT scan whenever you're ready."

"My friend?"

"He's downstairs, waiting for you. By the way, what day is it?"

"Halloween."

"Okay. Where do you live?"

"In a house, not far from here."

"That isn't quite what I was getting at," she said, tucking away her tools, preparing to go. "But you seem like the figurative type, so I'll assume it's normal."

"What am I looking at?" I asked, peeling back a bandage over my heart and peering underneath. "Is this a bruise or a scratch?"

"I guess since you didn't have a shirt on, your devil buddy went ahead and grabbed you by the skin. For leverage."

"Did he hit me with something?" I asked, probing with my fingers toward the center of my face

"His forehead. Don't touch your nose. It's definitely fractured. Keep ice on it, take some aspirin. Happy Halloween," she said, getting up and leaning into Alice's officer doorway to say something before heading downstairs. I heard voices within, Pete and Inez, discussing something."

"As soon as the thing came off he was fine," said Pete. "Whoever put him in the devil suit should be fired."

"I'll see what I can find out from the group home," replied

Alice. "It may be something they were told to do by his parents. Where is he now?"

"Back in the classroom, eating candy with Tracy," said Inez, appearing in the doorway. "I'm going to head over there now. I don't see us going to the party, but I think he'll be okay until buses."

"Is that my blood?" I asked, gesturing at some vague reddish stains on her Western cut shirt as she came fully out of the office.

"Some of it," she said, looking at me, frowning, coming over for a better look, still frowning. "He opened up an old wound when he hit his head on your head. And the swing set. It happened a few more times after you . . . after he . . . Well . . . Are you okay?"

"Are the bars open yet?" I asked, standing up, as Alice and Pete came out of the office, swaying a little.

"Cover the mirrors," said Pete, *sotto voce*, to Alice, who appeared to be trying to remember what I looked like before today.

"I'm glad you're up and around," she said, making a call-me-later face as she handed over an Acheron Learning Center t-shirt, held over from last Christmas, with *HAPPY HOLIDAYS* written loud and clear across the chest. "Let's head downstairs. Your friend is waiting to take you to the clinic."

I followed them to the first floor, into the converted elementary classroom, festooned with orange and black streamers, spooky sound effects, and an animatronic grim reaper, similar to the one my mother and I had encountered in the pizza restaurant in Lake George. The thing emitted a joyful whoop as Alice, Pete, and Inez led me to where Grover was sitting with a group of three younger students, the four of them eating candied apples armored in marshmallow and sprinkles and drinking hot cider. He stood when he saw us, exchanging some words with Alice, a condition report no doubt, and nodded to Inez and Pete before taking my arm and leading us to the door. The reaper, sensing our departure, yowled from its corner.

"Which doctor do you normally see?" asked Grover once we were safely buckled into his Honda or whatever it was, driving down Clamence Street.

"Dr. Norman," I said, not really understanding the question.

"I don't think I know him."

"It's fine. I'm not going for a CT scan or whatever."

"You feel fine?"

"Actually, I feel like shit," I said, checking my reflection in the rearview mirror. I looked like shit too. Puffy bruised eyes, swollen, reddish nose, a couple of horizontal scratches across my neck, disappearing beneath my shirt collar, "but just take me home. No. Wait. Better idea. What time is it?"

"One or so."

"Take me to the Ethiopian place on Langdon Street. They should be open for lunch."

"If you like," said Grover, obligingly. "Mind if I invite a friend?"

"Just take me there please."

"You got it," he said, scrolling through his phone and placing it against the side of his head. "Change of plans . . . There was an incident . . . I'll explain later, or you'll see when you get there . . . Do you like Ethiopian food? . . . We're nearly there now . . . Twenty minutes? . . . I'll get you what I get . . . Right."

The restaurant looked as if it had just emptied out after a rush, so we had the run of the place. Hodan tried not to look at me as she led us to a seat by the front windows, which held a proscenium of glowing pumpkins. Grover ordered for us both and the third party he'd invited along the way, seeming to know his way around the menu.

226

"Come here often?" I asked.

"Bi-monthly, maybe," said Grover. "I saw you once, actually, over the winter. Tucked in at the bar. You looked busy with whatever you were doing. I had them send you a dessert after I left."

"You always understood when to keep your distance. It made working for you seem important," I said, feeling like Quasimodo as I nodded my thanks to Hodan, striding across the dining room with a glass of tej I hadn't ordered. "What are you doing now?"

"This and that. I manage the tour company on an ad hoc basis, more as a favor."

"Henry's company."

"One of them."

"I've always hated the name. 'Releaf Tours.' The vans drive by and I want them to explode, leaf peepers and all."

"I agree. If it hadn't been so initially successful, I would have lobbied more for a change. As it is, we have a brand, so we're stuck with it. Acheron is 'the foliage gateway' as I'm sure we're both tired of hearing from people who aren't from here. At any rate, we always need someone to write press material."

"Anyone can do that."

"You'd be amazed how untrue that is. We get a lot of art students who think writing copy is the same as a graphic design job. Have you ever seen a ten-page resume that's all internships?"

"I didn't know such a thing existed."

"I could have sworn it was delivered by flying monkeys."

"Thanks, but I don't want it. I don't trust Henry and I'm amazed you do."

"I wouldn't call it trust. Now that the grocery store is out of my hands, I have nothing he wants, or nothing he can own, at any rate. That's as close as he comes to thinking of anyone as an equal."

"Actually, I should ask your advice on this. He's been more visible lately, Henry I mean, showing up with a room key for the hotel and my mail, on one occasion. Wants me to work for him. Doing something unpleasant, I suspect."

"More unpleasant than what you're doing now?"

"It's a known quantity, Grover. I'm not afraid of my students. I'm afraid of Henry."

"You should be," said Grover, watching me over the brim of his water glass. "Though not for the reasons you think."

"You weren't just hanging out on sidewalk by chance today were you?"

"No, I was not."

"You came to see me."

"I did. I thought I might catch you on your lunch break," he said, setting aside the water glass, shooting his cuffs, shifting silverware, working his way up to something. "Maybe give you something to think about. Things ended up working out differently. Better, actually."

"You're friend, the one joining us," I said, watching a maroon Saab hatchback cruise by the window, shark-like, nosing around for a parking spot. "He sent you."

"I volunteered actually. I wanted to save everyone some trouble, including you."

"How is that?"

"Consider inevitability. A world where saying no only means you're waiting longer to say yes. This should scare you and I'm glad it does, because I think that means you understand what you will eventually have to do, though maybe not what waiting to do it means. He can wait without losing anything; you can't. I'm here because I care what happens to you."

"That's why you're tossing me to the wolves."

"There are always wolves to feed," said Grover, his eyes clocking something approaching behind me. "They only get hungrier."

"Gentlemen," said Henry, pulling out a chair and doffing his sun hat as he sat down between us. He folded his hands into a kind of vault beneath his chin, leveling a saurian, green-eyed gaze my way, taking it all in. "Does it hurt?"

"It's starting to," I said, verily.

"Grover, the scrip pad is in my glove compartment," said Henry, removing a hand from beneath his chin, dangling his car keys on a finger. "Please write out something for whatever Oliver wants."

"Sure, Henry," said Grover, taking the keys and leaving the table, passing a waiter approaching with our food.

"You're a doctor now?" I asked, unable to smell the meal appearing around me.

"I have a doctor," replied Henry, tucking in without much ceremony. "He had a problem with the Downing clan poaching on his land, riding ATVs through his meadow all night, that kind of thing. The game warden's a Downing. So are enough of the town cops to make it a hopeless thing to report. My doctor was a little stuck."

"Not for long, it sounds like."

"It was time for my annual physical anyway. We talked about problem solving. He sent me a box with a pie in it his wife made. The pad was under the pie."

"Like a tribute."

"Sometimes I think my only job around here is teaching people how to say thank you."

"Render unto Caesar . . . "

"It's nice talking like this," said Henry, sounding weirdly pleased, swiping at his mouth with a napkin and briefly locking eyes with the papier-mâché parrot standing at attention beside my wine glass, but not commenting on it. "You were a little less subdued last time."

"You were someplace you had no right to be, making threats I didn't need to listen to. You're lucky I didn't toss you on the fire."

"I should learn to pick my moments better. The element of surprise is like any other element. Useful when stable."

"I wasn't unstable, Henry, whatever that means, but I'm in enough pain now to make talking with you seem like just one more thing I have to get through before the day is done."

"Grover said there was an incident. Did you run into something?"

"Someone's forehead. I'm not sure how many times."

"Enough to make talking things out with you less of an auto-de-fé, apparently."

"Funny. I'm waiting until Grover comes back to leave. I still have respect for him even if he works for you."

"You've hardly touched any of this," said Henry, gesturing expansively at the food between us, half of which he'd already consumed while we'd been talking.

"I'm not hungry. And you're fingers have been all through it."

"What would you say," he began, ignoring me, vaulting his hands once again, the food momentarily forgotten, "if I told you Grover was the person who recommended you for what I need and that he is the reason you and I keep meeting like this? Would that change things?"

"No. Try harder. Or lie better. Whichever."

"Perhaps the issue here," said Henry, withdrawing a business card from his shirt pocket, scribbling something on the back, and sliding it across the table to me, "is that we're operating without a bottom line."

"Generous," I said, trying to keep my voice from popping up a register as I stared at the figure written on the back of the business card, a helpful figure, one that it didn't seem realistic to associate with me or any work I could hope to do; stability of a certain kind was suddenly within easy reach, no farther than the distance between the restaurant and the Acheron Credit Union or whatever foxhole Henry buried his money in.

"That's half of what I'm prepared to offer you for completion of the assignment. Half now, half when you get back, and a bonus if you keep expenses down."

"I think," I began, not sure what I was thinking, but grateful for the appearance of Grover, returning to the table with the bluish pad open on his palm and a pen at the ready—any diversion to give me some time to get it together and tamp down the sudden impulse to call it a day with Henry and give in to whatever he wanted.

"Specials today include Percocet, Oxycodone, Dilaudid, and Vicodin," he said, his expression changing as he glanced around the table, mostly at Henry. "I've interrupted something crucial, haven't I?"

"We'll see," said Henry, displeasure with Grover freighting his voice as he swiveled his gaze toward me like a set of artillery tracking a target. "Now that we've established a clear exchange of goods and services, I'm interested to hear if your perspective remains the same. Shall we talk, Oliver?"

"You took my book," I said, hoping to throw him off the trail for a while, at least long enough to remind the profit-oriented part of my brain what I was getting into. The figure on the business card seemed to leer at me from the tabletop. I flipped it over. Grover appeared to wince, a good sign, I thought.

"I did what?" asked Henry.

"I saw you. Up at my place after the storm. *The Honourable Schoolboy.*"

"Sorry. I hadn't read it in a while."

"But it was mine."

"I'll return it to you. It was an impulse."

"Thanks. I'm leaving now," I said, pushing back my chair, standing up, thinking: What am I doing here, talking with Henry Hoffmann on Halloween after having my face knocked in? I glanced across the table at Grover, who looked like he was preparing to abandon ship.

"I was hoping we'd get farther than this today," said Henry, clearing the last of the food neither Grover nor I had touched off the tray, signaling for the check. "I wish I knew what to do with a person like you, Oliver. I can't give you what you want if you don't know what it is."

"I know what I don't want," I said, knocking back the rest of my wine and grabbing the papier-mâché parrot from the table, tucking it into my pocket. "That's almost the same thing."

"I'm aware of why you don't like me," said Henry. "It's also how I know I'll be hearing from you again. Weakness always howls loudest."

"Your mom teach you that?" I asked, angling toward the door.

"I'll walk you out," said Grover, standing and following me outside. Henry remained at the table with his face in his hands, staring into the night gathering beyond the window like one of the Jack-O-Lanterns igniting up and down Langdon Street.

"That was stupid," said Grover when we reached the sidewalk. "You know why."

"You're both trying to wear me down. I don't like it."

"I'm trying to help you, but you seemed determined to dive headlong into suffering for something. I can't say what, but something that I don't fully understand and I'm not entirely sure you do either."

"Did you recommend me for this thing, whatever it is? To him? He said so."

"If I did, would that make any difference?"

"Nope. Happy Halloween. Make sure Henry gets back to the graveyard by sunup," I said, swiveling in the direction of home, a mask of dull pain covering my face as I slipped through waist-high divisions of children in costumes, feeling like I blended in well enough. Carissa was waiting for trick-or-treaters on the porch, dressed as Jessica Rabbit with a bowl of candy in her lap, and seemed ready to distribute some of it when she saw me shuffling up the walk. She stood up when she realized it was me, the candy bowl clattering across the porch, her hands finding my cheeks, probing them gently, her face so close our foreheads nearly touched, asking what happened, her eyes a little moist, I thought, but couldn't be sure, as she ran inside to get ice and aspirin, her red dress flying, sparkling. I heard small, excited voices approaching behind me, so I knelt and began combing the candy back into the bowl.

Alice stopped by an hour later, ostensibly to see how I was doing, still in her witch clothes. We sat together in the backyard beside the ruins of the garden and she watched me try to wrestle the lid off a family-size bottle of over-the-counter painkillers and talk with a plastic bag of ice cubes hung over my face like a feedbag, gifts from Carissa, who was back on candy duty and keeping her distance, I noticed. The evening had turned cool and snow was expected overnight; I noticed stray flakes caught in Alice's hair and on the brim of her conical hat as she leaned over to take the bottle away from me.

"I can give you the rest of the week off, with pay," she said, popping the top and shaking out some pills into my hand. "Maybe more, depending on whatever the doctor says. And you will see a doctor."

"Sure I will," I agreed, having no intention of seeing anyone I didn't have to see as I fished around in the grass by my chair for a bottle of Slivovitz I'd found under the kitchen sink, something to cut the chill and wash down the analgesics. Alice looked on for a moment before helping herself to the brandy. She wiped her mouth on her costume and set the bottle out of reach, eying me a little sadly.

"Your friend seemed responsible," she said. "I can't believe he let you talk him out of getting checked out. I should have sent you with Pete. I would have if we could spare the staff."

"It's not your fault. It was a trap."

"What?"

"Nothing. No, not nothing, but it would take too long to explain. Anyway, thanks for coming by. I promise I'll see a doctor soon. You don't have to worry."

"Are you dismissing me, Oliver?"

"No, Alice. But I'm in a bit of pain, as you can see, and I also have a lot to think about; things I can't really talk about—with you or anyone until I know how I feel about them and I don't want you to feel like you have to sit here with me while I figure it out just because I got hurt on your watch. I won't sue the school or anything, I promise."

"Do you really think that's what I'm worried about?"

"I didn't realize you were worried."

"We've had a good time together, I think," she said, taking my hand and turning it over in her own like something she'd found on a beach, a fossil or strand of driftwood.

"I suppose we have," I said, wondering why whatever was going on between us had suddenly become a dear memory, a thing of the past.

"You're one of the kindest people I've ever met."

"Thank you," I said, cautiously, on my guard. This had the proleptic flavor of a complement one person pays another based on the behavior they hope to see in them after delivering bad news, a kind of wish masquerading as an accolade.

"So the overall point is I like being here because you're here, Oliver. But if you want me to leave so you can stew over something private, I'll do that too."

"It's not private. I just don't know how to explain it."

"Try."

"Someone I don't trust wants to pay me do some work for him. There's a lot of money involved."

"Are you worried he won't pay?"

"No. I'm worried what he will pay me to do. It's an odd arrangement. I don't know whether to live in fear of what he wants or not doing what he wants."

"Take the money," said Alice, lightly, the bottle of Slivovitz clinking against her wedding ring as she raised it to her lips. "Worry about whatever else when you need to. It sounds like a good opportunity for you."

"Why for me? What does that mean?"

"Well, don't take this the wrong way, but what are you really doing here?" she said, her eyes flicking toward the house or the front porch, where Carissa probably still sat, distributing the last of the candy. Providing a straightforward answer to Alice's question seemed like the best way to avoid hearing whatever she thought she knew about that whole mess.

"Nothing I'm ashamed of," I began. "I go to work for you at

the school. I run through the woods everyday. I read a lot. I sometimes think about writing but never do. I feed my cat, or a cat, I
don't know who she belongs to, and water my plant. And I see
you, like this. I have everything I need to be comfortable for the
time being. Maybe my expectations are dialed a bit low since the
storm or maybe I just know what I can leave out now. Either way,
I think I've established some kind of baseline and abandoning it
to get even more tangled up than I already am with . . ."

"Could you leave me out?" interrupted Alice, suddenly looking very witchy in the glow from the kitchen window.

"I don't want to."

"What I mean is would you still have your baseline or whatever if I wasn't in the picture?"

"I'm not sure, but I doubt it."

"You know, people who are sick just want to be comfortable."

"No. People who are around sick people just want them to be
comfortable. It's different."

"Listen, this might not be the best time to bring this up, but I
can't avoid it with what we're talking about . . . "

"Ah. I figured something like this was coming."

"Something like this was always coming, Oliver."

"When does he get back?"

"In the next few weeks. His deployment is over. I'm not sure
when the next one will be, but Ray seems to think he'll be home
for a while."

"Who?"

"Ray. Raymond. That's my husband's name."

"No," I said abruptly, wondering if would just be me and the
Rays of the world from here on out. Being afraid of Henry suddenly felt ludicrous; he was one man, clearly up to no good, but
still just a single person with a known domain, whereas Ray or

236

Raymond seemed to be everywhere, with no telling where he'd show up next. Alice's husband wasn't a popular topic of conversation between us and Carissa had only mentioned him once as a kind of reliquary of guilt, so I didn't feel bad about not learning his name until now, though I felt a little unprepared to have so many nemeses stacking up all at once.

"No?" asked Alice, looking a little sorry for me, but a lot more sorry for herself, not that I blamed her; it was hard news to deliver. "Look, Oliver, I wish I could make this happen in a way that wouldn't disrupt your comfort or baseline or whatever it is, but I don't see a way that can happen. You're a good man and I'm very fond of you. Thank you for being such good company. You won't know how much I needed it or how grateful I am until you're separated from someone you care about more than anyone else."

"Right now, that's you for me," I said, not sure it was true, but figuring I might as well throw it out there and see what happened.

"That will change," she said, her eyes once more shifting toward the house and Carissa, I suspected, a topic I wanted to avoid at all costs.

"I'm going to do my best not to be bitter about this," I said, figuring it would be good practice for encountering future dead ends.

"I appreciate that."

"I'm guessing this will be the last time I see you."

"We'll, except for at work."

"Ah. Right," I said. That sounded like more practice than I needed. I was already living with Carissa, a person who wanted me sporadically and now I would continue working with Alice, who no longer wanted me at all. If there were a way to shoehorn Karen into this arrangement, I'd probably have all my bases covered in terms of carving out a miserable little life amid the rubble of the past six months. Dr. Norman had once shown a picture in one of his classes of a survivor from a bombing raid camping beside the graves of his wife, children, parents, and other people close to him who had been lost. I wondered if I was doing something similar by pitching my tent among the living dead, or living non-options, as it were. A grave is a landmark, I thought, fishing around in the frosty grass for the Slivovitz. Familiar horrors are at least familiar; it's nice to know where you are at the end of the day.

Alice seemed worried I'd pass out on the lawn and freeze to death if she left me outside and I was worried she might exchange some kind of one-sided condition report with Carissa if I didn't walk her to her truck, so we ended up bidding each other good-night on the front porch, beside a nearly empty candy bowl with a note beside it urging latecomers to take only one piece. I tried to kiss Alice, but she saw it coming and moved out of the way, accidently crushing the wire brim of her witch hat into the palsied bridge of my nose, a scene that would have been funnier if Isidore Castle, a gawky village idiot type who always seemed to be on the wrong side of his father's money, wasn't making his way up the front walk with a book from Henry, as promised.

"Tell him yes," I said, taking the book and slamming the door in his face as Alice retreated from us both out into the unhurried snowfall, her shoes crunching across the lawn, the night swallowing her when she reached the sidewalk.

Off to tend another man's cauldron, I thought nastily, as I climbed the steps to the attic, my face screaming from the brush with the witch hat, the handful of painkillers I'd taken earlier doing almost nothing. I would have worried more about making the wrong choice regarding Henry if every other choice I'd made

238

recently had turned out well. As it was, I seemed to keep circling back to the same pit of irredeemable longing and rocking at
the edge like Dan whenever we did a puzzle together. Whatever
Henry wanted me to do would probably be a vacation compared
to that.

*   *   *

I met Henry the next morning at his dead mother's house on Town
Hill Road, a spooky old Victorian ruin brightened not at all by
the table one of his handlers had laid out on the porch. Breakfast
was provided; fresh fruit, a bowl of yogurt, cheese, lox, bread,
and hardboiled eggs. It felt like a sort of last meal on earth or a
continental breakfast for victims of some inordinate hardship. A
stainless steel press steeped nearby, at the ready, steam from the
spout commingling with the smoke from a morning joint I was
puffing away at while Henry watched.

"Does it help with the pain?" he asked, spearing a cleaved bit
of cantaloupe on his fork, tucking it into his cheek. Chew, swallow, repeat. Apparently, none of the food is poisoned, I thought,
watching him eat. We're off to a good start.

"Not yet," I said. "It might be a tolerance thing."

"Normally I'd make you finish that out by the mailbox. As it
is, we have things to discuss, but I'm going to suggest you use an
ashtray before we begin."

"Your house, your rules," I said, draining the last bit of
my coffee and combing the ashes I'd gotten on the tablecloth
into the cup. Henry didn't look surprised by this and may have
even been expecting something like it; this seemed like the right
moment to make the mistake of thinking he and I were on the
same page, a conclusion it felt like he'd been urging me toward

since our meeting at the Ethiopian restaurant. What purpose could that possibly serve? I wondered, watching him across the table, sheltering beneath his sunhat as midmorning student traffic rolled past the house, up the hill, toward the college. Maybe Henry needs a friend, I thought, catching myself smirking at him absently.

"Are you going to eat anything?" he asked, gesturing at the barren plate beneath my chin.

"When it kicks in, absolutely," I said. "Why do you care?"

"I'd like a minimum of distractions on your end while we're discussing this."

"I can eat and listen at the same time. But if it's going to be like that, can you pencil me in for a bathroom break in half an hour?"

"Good, Oliver. I'm glad you can do two things at once. But before we begin, you should know that if any of what I say here leaves this table, your life will get very hard very fast."

"If you threaten me again, the price will go up."

"Instead of a threat, think of it as an observation of something causal. Gravity at work. A singularity. Lightening hitting the fire tower up on Maybrick Peak. You pick. A thing that happens because of something else, in other words."

"I don't know about you, but I'm ready to move this along," I said, shifting some food onto my plate as kind of ornament for my side of the table, a way to kick things off.

"What do you know about my family?" he asked, soundlessly settling his cup in a saucer.

"I know you don't really have one."

"That's true. What else?"

"I'm afraid you're going to go all wild-eyed on me if I mention your mom."

"Wild-eyed?"

"That's what people in town say you do whenever it comes up . . . "

"They probably have it right. Simpletons always know when to take cover."

" . . . But I feel like you want me to say something about it."

"Tell me what you think you know about it."

"Your mom," I began, feeling as if I was about to tip my hand in a game of cowboy poker, "disappeared on Halloween, back in 2010. Everyone saw her leave work at the hotel alone. Then she was gone. You lived by yourself, at this house, her house, where we are now, until you finished college and moved up to Mr. Castle's property to work for him. A lot people thought you had something to do with jer disappearence then and a lot of them still do. That's all I know, Henry."

"That's all anyone knows, including me," he said. "But what do you think?"

"Of what?"

"Of what people say about me. Do you think I had something to do with it?"

"No," I said. "I never did. You're a creep and a weirdo and I do think you're a little dangerous, but not like that, or not back then. And whatever you are now, you seem pretty proud of it. I'm sure you miss your mom since she probably made you this way, for better or worse."

"Interesting answer," said Henry, looking straight at me while refilling his coffee cup, another eerie gesture among many. "Do you remember someone named Denise Erlanger?"

"Nope."

"Christian and Byzantine Art. I believe you had the class with her during your junior year," said Henry, nodding his head up the hill toward campus. "I think the two of you did a joint presentation on some Ostrogoth church in Lombardy."

"The Arian Baptistry in Ravenna," I said, recalling the hour or two Denise and I had spent together in a downtown bar slapping the thing together the night before it was due and how I'd garbled my end of it the next day, missing my cue to change slides more than once because of the way her butt looked in a pair of cowboy-cut Wranglers as she stood in front of the class, discussing Theodoric the Great. She had the kind of dignified, slightly avian good looks that didn't normally stir me, though I remember feeling bewitched after our presentation and trying to find some pretext to invite myself over to the cabin she lived in out by Kranion Pond, a place I'd only heard rumors about. But I never got much farther than asking to buy her a beer when I saw her in town a few weeks before term broke for Christmas, our presentation already weeks behind us, my window of opportunity basically bricked over. Denise appeared to be in the middle of holiday shopping and seemed to think I was joking, though I couldn't see why, but said where she might be later if she decided to go out. I hung around there waiting for her until pretty late and ended up going home with a majorette attached to a visiting school's marching band who drank everything I had on hand in the cabin and wet my bed. The majorette and I had the best breakfast we possibly could the next morning, with the half-frozen sheets flapping on the laundry line beyond the kitchen window like a flag of quarantine, while I thought about Denise or how the night might have gone differently if she'd shown up, an unfair and unavoidable comparison to make and one I felt guilty about when I saw how embarrassed the majorette was. Denise didn't return for Spring term, so this turned out to be the last time I thought about her until Henry brought it up.

"So you know who I mean?" he asked.

"Yes," I said. "I remember her. What's she doing now?"

"She's in India. That's where you'll be going."

"Why would I do that?"

"She has something that belongs to me. To my family. I need you to get it back."

"What is it?"

"A vase."

"A what?"

"A vase. Chinoiserie styled, blue and white porcelain, with a little lid. I'll provide a photograph of something similar so you know what to look for."

"You want to send me across the world to get a vase with a lid?"

"It belonged to my mother."

"Is it valuable?"

"It's worth something, but that's not the point."

"What is the point, Henry?"

"It was where she left notes for me," said Henry, his eyes clocking toward the interior of the house. "When she was working. As you know, she worked a lot managing the Herrenhof Inn. I didn't see much of her. When I came home from school in wintertime, the house was so dark-"

"Just the way you like it."

"Be quiet, you fool," said Henry, not loudly, but with a sort of precision, a proto-warning spreading its leathery wings, preparing for takeoff. It was how I always imagined the generals I'd read about for Dr. Norman delivered their orders after looking over the maps, moving the pieces around, deciding who would die first between breakfast and lunch; every day is casual Friday for the butchers of men, I'd learned.

"I'm sorry," I said, not really believing the sound of myself apologizing to Henry, something I never thought I would do, but there it was, out of my mouth and on the record; it was turning into a morning, if not a year, of gloomy firsts.

"In summer the house seemed even darker," he continued, rolling forward in his former register, as if nothing had happened. I cautioned myself against designating this in my memory as a sign of graciousness in Henry. It wasn't that; he had things to discuss. "I wasn't a child then, but coming home to a dark and empty house made me afraid like one. It was the only place on the street without lights on. Emptiness haunted me. My mother knew this, so she would leave me notes in the vase on the mantelpiece. Nothing important. Where she was, what she was doing, when she expected to be home, that sort of thing. She would ask about school, whatever I was reading, remind me to eat dinner and not to stay up too late waiting for her to return. This was good for me. It gave me a reason to go inside and turn on lights. I left notes for her in the morning, before I went to school. It became the way we talked."

"Like a drop," I said, recalling John Barron and his tales of the KGB and instantly feeling like a dope, but not knowing how Henry expected me to logically interpret this new information about his life or the series of weird events that had made him who he now appeared to be: someone slightly more human maybe, or less happy, at any rate, than I'd always assumed; a sad, successful person in a dorky sunhat who also enjoyed spy novels and wanted to give me some money. I liked this new, workable imagining of Henry and hoped he wouldn't say or do anything to throw it off.

"I didn't think of it like that at the time," said Henry. "But after I started reading books like the Le Carré one I had Isidore return to you the other night, it made things seem heightened, in some way. As if our relationship had found its most vital expression through the passing of secret messages, like spies, yes, but also prisoners or people in love when they shouldn't be. Perhaps all three."

"Well, sure," I said, mostly out of words and beginning to feel a little yucky about what Henry was sharing with me. The nice man in the sunhat wants to give you some money, I reminded myself, hoping this would be enough to get through what remained of breakfast.

"I found all of them, our notes, after she disappeared," he went on. "She'd saved each one in the drawer of her nightstand."

"Moms save stuff," I said, hoping to pilot the conversation back toward more normal footing, expecting no help from Henry, or the nice man in the sunhat who wanted to give me some money and was maybe a little in love with his probably dead mother. "My mom still has all my artwork from preschool."

"They were in the vase when it was taken."

"You put them there?"

"It was the only place that made sense. She disappeared. I don't have a headstone I can visit. I had to make my own."

"So how did Denise end up with a vase full of you and your mother's collected correspondence?"

"I was away on business," said Henry. "And I never keep the house locked. People know I live here. It would be redundant."

"I asked 'how', when I think I meant 'why'."

"She wants me to leave Acheron."

"Never to return?"

"Something like that. She seems to view it as essentially a Robin Hood gesture on behalf of the townsfolk. Sell off whatever I can't return to them and be gone by the end of the year. Allow things to return to what passes for normal in this town."

"Where would you even go?" I asked, honestly curious

what other crevasses a person like Henry could imagine him-self flourishing in.

"I've recently become fond of North Calais," he replied, studying my face for either evidence of violence or fear, I couldn't be sure which. Either way, he appeared to be checking in on our power differential and, finding it still robust, felt comfortable continuing on with the conversation. "But it's irrelevant. I'm not going anywhere. And the vase isn't enough leverage to get me to go anywhere. However, I would like it back."

"I don't believe you."

"About what?"

"About any of this."

"It's not your job to believe me."

"What is my job?"

"It's not complicated. Go to India, find out where Denise is hiding my property. It's a delicate matter. She knows I want it back and has likely stashed it somewhere far from the orphanage."

"The what?"

"Orphanage, Oliver; a place for orphans. She's teaching them English, apparently, in exchange for room and board. It's some-where in Bihar. I'll get you the details later. Right now, the im-portant thing to remember is she may be expecting some kind of incursion on my part, so what I want you to recover won't be easy to find. You'll likely need to insinuate yourself to her some-how in order to get close enough to have a look. I'll leave how to do that up to you, but from what I know, the town is small and it won't be easy to hide. I would suggest using your previous acquaintance."

"How is that supposed to work? Hi, Denise! Remember me? We studied the arts of Byzantium together long ago! I'm here in India for no real reason and you're about the last person I expected to run into! Please take me to the orphanage where you live so I can poke around in your belongings! Don't you think she'll be immediately suspicious?"

"That would make anyone immediately suspicious. Fortunately, you have plenty of time to improve your story."

"How much time?"

"We'd like to get you on a plane to Delhi toward the end of November. So, three weeks on the outside. That should leave us enough time to get you a visa, allow you to settle whatever affairs you need to settle before you go, and put in your notice at the school, though we both know that won't be much of a problem for you."

"Oh, we do, do we?" I said, feeling like I might be inviting an outside view of myself I didn't want to hear. "What do you think you know about it?"

"The bar between the sewage plant and the pound has always been Alice's screening facility for therapy dick," said Henry, mildly tightening the sunhat's cord beneath his blockish chin. "I'm surprised you didn't know that going in."

"I don't like that you know that."

"Everyone knows that. Anyway, put in your notice on Monday or whenever you decide to go back to work."

"I haven't said yes to anything yet. What makes you think I will? This whole things sounds like it would be better handled by someone who does things like this for a living, one of those off-the-book fringe personalities you probably keep on retainer, someone like that."

"I don't know who you think I am exactly," said Henry, wearily. "Yes, there are always other resources I could use, but none of them are nearly as vulnerable as you. I understand how that must sound to you, but I'm not a monster, or not the kind you probably imagine. This is a delicate matter, as I said, best handled by a person with more to lose than he has to gain. I know there are things here that disappoint you. I've been watching them and you for years, but I also know you will always come back here so you can wait around in case something changes. So it almost goes without saying that if you want to remain a regular part of the landscape here in Acheron, you will go to India and help me solve this problem."

"Is that another threat? I can't even tell anymore."

"It's just the way things are now, Oliver. You can choose to be threatened by that or profit from it, or both. You have choices."

"When someone like you tells someone like me they have choices I don't feel like I have any."

"I feel like you might be waiting for a complement," said Henry. "Some reason or other why I want you to do this that doesn't have anything to do with the very good reasons I just shared with you. I would check with Grover if that's what you want or need."

"I think I'm just waiting for you to ask me if I'll do it or not."

"It sounds like you need a vacation," said Henry, pushing his plate toward the center of the table and standing up. "I think we're done here."

Henry stood, clearly waiting for me to leave now that he had what he wanted. Did I have what I wanted? I wondered, corralling the ashes from the tablecloth into my saucer and flicking this over the railing in to the flowerbed, as he looked on, stolid as a gargoyle. Not yet, I decided, standing up. But we appear to be past all that now. It seems to be mostly a question of what I can live with from here on out.

"What makes you think I miss her?" said Henry, meaning his mother. He stood halfway inside the door, watching me through the screen as if I'd come to sell him magazines, the question some kind of afterthought on his part, though it seemed like a measure of how far we'd come together since I arrived, a circle closing itself off for good.

"You mean aside from paying someone who hates you to go all the way to India to retrieve what sounds like the centerpiece of a real spooky shrine to her memory you probably have somewhere in there?" I asked, gesturing beyond the screen door, to where I guessed the living room probably was.

"You said you thought I missed her before you knew about that," he said. "No one else knows. I want to know what they see."

"The house," I said, waving at it with the remains of the joint. "You're three blocks from campus and a profit-minded gentlemen like you would rent the place out to students if you didn't have some reason not to. It's still your mom's house, I think, and that's why you won't leave this town, even if not leaving puts one of her lesser relics at risk. You can live without the vase, if you need to, but the house is non-negotiable. Speaking of which, can I use the bathroom?"

"You can go in the backyard, by the garden shed. No one will see you."

"How can I put this . . . I have to make a deposit."

"There might be a shovel or pitchfork or something in the shed."

"That's not really how I pictured it all happening."

"No one comes inside," said Henry, stepping out of the threshold, not bothering to latch the screen door behind him as he withdrew into the house's interior, confident I wouldn't follow. Fucking weirdo, I thought, tucking some of the linen napkins from breakfast into my pocket as I descended the porch steps to see what my options were out back. Part of me wanted to drop my pants and let it all go on the welcome mat as a lesson of sorts to Henry, my new boss apparently, who seemed to appreciate that kind of thing, people getting what they deserved or what he decided they deserved. That might be the big difference I should start getting used to. Winning was never all that important to me, but it was always nice to have it as an option rather than a memory.

As I turned the corner of the house, I noticed the shed Henry had mentioned and was about to head on over to sound out a good place for my excavation when I heard shouting from the sidewalk. Just past the fence, a stocky white woman who looked like she'd just fallen out of a deer stand was pursuing a tall, thin black man about my own age who I recognized as the bartender from the Ethiopian restaurant.

"I know where you're going!" she yelled, trying and failing to grab the tail of his shirt. "People been telling me all about her and you and what the two of you get up to after you close up! Don't think I don't smell her on you when you come in, saying you had to work late! I don't want to hear it! You understand me? Turn around when I'm talking to you! If you don't, I swear I'm through!"

"Bitch," said the bartender, without turning around, raising his voice, or altering his pace. "I'm going to the store to buy soup."

I didn't want to get in the middle of whatever was going on between them, but I also didn't want to appear rude. The bartender was a relative of Hodan's and had seen enough of me in varying states of vulnerability over the past few months to make him the closest thing I had to a guru in my life, so I shouted a greeting, inadvertently waving at him with the same motion I used to order a second or third drink, a kind of unfortunate Pavlovian reflex. This caught his attention and embarrassed us both. He continued walking, but the woman trailing him paused at the mailbox as if she'd stumbled on an ammo dump.

"Who the fuck is that?" she yelled at him, while pointing at me over the fence. "Who're all these people who know you? I don't know any of them! How come you never introduce to me no one! It's like you want to keep me a secret from this whole shitpot town! You ashamed of me? Is that why?"

Well, I somehow made that worse, I thought to myself, listening to the woman's voice trail off down the street as I slunk toward the backyard, wondering how long I should wait before showing my face at the restaurant. Life in public seemed to be catching up with me. Should I be searching for someone to blame for this or someone to forgive me for it? A second floor window slid open above me and a roll of toilet paper drifted to the ground between my feet in what seemed like a kind of answer.

"Put the napkins back where they came from," said Henry from somewhere above.

*　　*　　*

Ray, or Raymond as Karen had called him, turned out to be the sort of guy I would have liked very much if he wasn't such an obviously better choice for her. I'm not sure what I expected when I finally visited them in Randolph, but it felt like an important part of tying up the loose ends before leaving, or settling affairs, as Henry had said. I'd given my notice at the school, a move Alice seemed to expect; she said I would be welcome back any time, a possibility I tested after meeting with her by spending the afternoon sitting in pile of dead leaves on the playground with Sasha, singing Replacements songs to him as he strummed his lips and dug up the grass. There wasn't much to say, as usual, but there seemed to be no hard feelings on his end. Inez looked on inscrutably, though she lightened up a little later on when we went out for beers with Tracy and Pete and I gave them all an apocryphal version of the work I was doing for Henry, teaching English at an orphanage, according to me. Inez drove me home after we left the bar and when I asked if she'd like to come in for a drink, she declined in a way that made me feel like a goofball rather than a loser and seemed like the sort of thing I'd look back on fondly if I ever returned to the school.

Carissa was a little irritated with me for jumping ship after she'd gotten me the job, but didn't have much to say about it after I fed her and Buck the same line about teaching English at the orphanage. I was a little irritated by how shocked they seemed to be that I was up to something noble, even if it was a lie, but they both did their best to help me prepare. Buck dug out some books by Salman Rushdie for me to take along and Carissa got a guidebook on India from the library and began peppering our dinner table conversations with facts about the place I was going. Did I know Bihar was the poorest state in India? Did I know it's capital is Patna, a city with over two million inhabitants? Did I know Bodh-Gaya, the place where the orphanage and my final destination were, was situated on the banks of the Niranjan river, where Siddhartha or Buddha or whatever supposedly achieved enlightenment?

I didn't know any of these things and figured I'd learn most of them when I got to Bodh-Gaya and began stalking Denise. But since I wasn't working, avoiding Carissa's questions was becoming a full-time job and I was beginning to worry I might out myself as a fraud if I wasn't careful. Visiting Karen and Raymond nee Ray seemed like the perfect way to avoid doing this. I had a week to kill before leaving and there was only so much of it could spend running in the woods and hiding in the attic. My parents were also standing by for a visit before I left the country, nervous but excited for me to be doing something that didn't have an unfortunate flipside, my student loans momentarily forgotten. Between their house and Karen's place in Randolph, I figured I would be in the clear as far as Carissa was concerned. Hanging out with Karen and her boyfriend wasn't an ideal solution, but it would probably seem restful after living at the house on Winter Street for the past few months.

Ray didn't take long to break the ice, or the thin sheet of one-way glass I'd mentally erected between us upon arriving and was hoping to observe him through for the duration of my visit. Karen had gone to town to pick up stuff for dinner, leaving us alone, and I was helping Ray unload cages from the back of a newish looking pickup, the sort of vehicle I would have sneered at if it wasn't so obviously being used for its intended purpose.

"I know about you and her," he said, casually, over his shoulder while we were carrying the cages into the barn they had converted into a kennel. My first impulse was to run for it, but I held my ground, pilloried by curiosity. "And I don't have much of an idea of what you think about me, but I want you to know I think its good you came up here to see her, even so, and I'm glad to have someone helping me out with all this. It's a lot of work and I appreciate it. I just hope you aren't hurting over anything right now."

"What do you know?" I asked, setting the cage down.

"I know you were with her back in August. She told me about the storm and what happened to your house. I'm sorry about that, by the way. The rest of it's not a thing with me. I trust Karen. I don't think she would waste all that time with someone who wasn't worth it. Things with her and me, they didn't happen like that all at once. We both had things to figure out. Like I said, I'm glad you're here. It means a lot to her, I think."

"Okay," I said, not really sure what I could add to that or anything else, as I followed Ray back to the pickup. I looked around the yard, at the house, toward the barn, searching for signs of misery, but finding none. The property was cleared for what they wanted to do with it apropos of the zoning board and a general kind of forward momentum hung around the place, a constant suggestion of things in progress and ambition taking shape. Even if I didn't see what I was adding to all this, it was hard not to enjoy being there with them.

Having successful friends is almost like being successful, I thought after Karen returned from town and she and Raymond were preparing a stir-fry of some kind in the kitchen. I sat in an antique armchair in the living room, watching snow glide past the window, a bottle of wine between my knees as I paged through some of the books Karen hadn't sold to Buck, waiting to be fed, feeling a bit like the first inductee of the shelter they were preparing to open.

Over dinner, Ray and Karen asked about my trip, sounding excited for me, and I found myself coming entirely clean with them over it, not bothering to make it sound as if I had more to offer the world than I actually did.

"So you're working for sunhat?" asked Karen, amused, maybe worried.

"Looks like it," I said. "No way to avoid him. Or no, that's wrong. There are ways to avoid him. Just none I'm prepared to follow through with, I guess. Things are actually easier his way."

"Sunhat?" said Ray.

"It doesn't seem like a bad job for you," said Karen. "Just make sure you're not walking into something you can't walk out of. I don't think you'd hurt anyone, Oliver, but make sure this Denise girl doesn't get hurt over this. She sounds smart, but smart doesn't seem like enough with Henry. You're smart too and here you are."

"Here I am," I agreed, looking around the dining room for a reason to be there, a reason other than Karen.

"Have you travelled internationally before, Oliver?" asked Ray, trying to guide the conversation back into a common arena. "I don't mean that to sound one way or the other. Some people just don't find the time."

"I've been some places," I said vaguely, wondering if any of them had really prepared me for what I was about to do for Henry. Central America with my parents, the Yucatan, Belize, Guatemala, all visited when I was much younger—thirteen, fourteen, fifteen. I remembered wandering past slabs of jungle ruins, and following topless women on the beach outside our hotel, as workmen removed stones from the water so tourists like me wouldn't stub their toes when they swam. Canada a few times, or Montreal really, visiting a girl I knew at McGill, buying booze with her, scooting around on the train, eating shabby vegetarian food at a restaurant overlooking the Rue St. Catherine, getting stoned in a park and visiting the biodome. This felt like a big grownup weekend for me at the time. I'd given backpacking around Europe a shot shortly after graduating high school, or a three-month stint of escalating bad behavior abroad as I'd begun to think of it in retrospect, culminating more or less in unprotected sex with a rich girl from Johannesburg in a top berth on a ferry between Spain and Morocco. Charlene had shown me a picture of her boyfriend, Etienne by name, before all this happened, while we were still parked at bar in Algeciras, killing time before the boat left. He looked nice enough in the photograph, but had the logo of a popular shoe company tattooed on his bicep, a fact that for whatever reason made me feel less guilty about what happened with Charlene later on. She and I spent a few days knocking around Marrakesh with a couple of Canadian travel agents we met at the train station in Tangiers, drinking black Absinthe and smoking hash on the rooftop of our hotel between calls to prayer. At some point, and I don't know whose decision this was, we ended up paying someone with a van to drive us all out to the desert, where we rode camels through the ochre dunes and camped for an evening in a tent. I slept on a carpet and the desert was so dark after the sun went down that I nearly pissed on one of the camels in the middle of the night. By the time we got back to Spain, Charlene had to go back to Jo-burg, as she called it, and Etienne, probably a good thing, I'd decided, after spending a few weeks listening to her go on and on about the kaffirs back home, as she called them, and her belief that AIDS was a biblical plague sent to punish the wicked for their sins. It was nutty stuff and made her seem like she'd been trapped in an ice sheet since the first Boer War. After Charlene left, I ended up renting a car with the Canadian travel agents and driving around Portugal with them, visiting beaches, walking around castles, drinking a lot of dessert wine, something I could never get the hang of. We came back through Spain and eventually drove into France. They dropped me off at some shithole campground outside Nice where I met a hairdresser from southern California named Eve, who I followed through Switzerland to the top of Jungfrau, down into Italy, and back up to Austria and Germany without really getting anywhere. She cut my hair once in a public park outside the Capuchin crypt in Rome, but that was it. We got tired of each other somewhere outside Utrecht, where I dicked around until it was time for me to come home for Christmas and she left to go back to California. Amsterdam scared me too much to visit after nightfall. I fled to Centraal station as it began getting dark like I was being chased by a pack of wolves, high as a kite from my day in the coffee shops, my mind a mélange of paintings I'd seen: Rembrandt, Vermeer, Van Gogh, and mostly naked women standing in windows with red curtains. As my train unreeled from the station, I felt pretty certain I would have been safer in college, even after debarking back in Utrecht and scuttling through the snow to my hotel beneath the watchful eye of the Dom tower, its fourteen bells always seeming to toll six o'clock, a dark and unhelpful hour in winter. I met no one, so I took to spending my evenings ensconced in a Turkish tea lounge tucked away in one of the catacombs off the Oudegracht, the water in the canal a sheet of placid ice reflecting limited moonlight, smoking large joints with glass after glass of mint tea and reading a copy of *Dracula* I'd borrowed from the library at my hotel. I began identifying with Harker a little too closely during this time and started sending off stochastic dispatches to Buck every so often. He was in his first year at Acheron college and didn't respond to most of them. This bothered me until I returned home and he showed me some of the emails I'd sent him, ravings mostly, that didn't leave him with much room to add anything: in depth descriptions of paintings I'd seen and prostitutes I'd admired, a weirdly thorough description of the continental breakfast at my hotel, a sort of prose poem about the Dom tower following me down a dark street that prefigured the trouble I would have later on with Mt. Abandon. He told me he would have worried more if it he didn't know I was just experiencing what it felt like to be truly alone with myself for the first time in my life. I spent most of the time between Christmas and New Year trying to decide if he was right, but never reached a decision, though it seemed to bear out years later when I looked over what kept me in Acheron and thought of Carissa standing in the doorway of my room, awaiting some kind of invitation, and Henry smugly recounting what he thought was true about me during our meeting; that I would always come back to what disappointed me on the off chance it would change, because it was simpler, easier, more comfortable to do that than be alone with myself with nothing on the horizon.

Is it possible to dread your own personality without hating yourself? I wondered, glancing once more around the dining room, at Karen watching me simmer away over this question while Ray spoke lightly about some of the places he'd been recently. Croatia, Australia, a few weeks in Vietnam, and the fun he'd had thereabouts. Ice had gathered in the fanlight behind him and the fresh candles lit at the beginning of the meal were half spent. I suspected I might have somehow ruined the evening, though this faded as I helped Ray clear up later on. Karen had made a fire in the living room and was playing her grandfather's Herb Alpert records. The music made everything Ray and I were doing seem like part of a rakish, vaguely mean-spirited silent film.

"You've got a lot in front of you right now," he said, taking a stack of plates from me and arranging them in the dishwasher like a mosaicist. "I'm a little envious."

"Let's trade. I like what you have too," I said, not really thinking through what I was saying. "Sorry. I didn't mean that how it sounded. Not Karen. Well, no, actually her too, but more what the two of you have together. Or what you're doing with it."

"I knew what you meant," he said, pulling three stemmed glasses out of a cupboard, plucking a bottle of champagne from the fridge. "It's probably good that there's so much to envy around here."

I followed him into the living room where Karen was stuffing a log into the already roaring hearth while the Tijuana Brass Band tootled away in the background. We sat on the rug before the fire, toasting my excursion, the wind wailing against the windows in a way that reminded me of the sounds Sasha made on Halloween the day he fractured my nose with his forehead. I wondered why painful or embarrassing memories always seemed to creep in at times like this, moments when all appeared to be well, as if my mind had placed an embargo on happiness in the present. Perhaps this kind of contrast is the only way I know how to tell myself I'm happy, I thought, draining my glass, watching Ray kiss Karen's hairline, feeling a little ashamed of how reluctant I'd been to come see them.

*　　*　　*

Carissa drove me to the Greyhound station in Montpelier the day I was supposed to fly out. I was taking the bus to Boston and didn't want to leave my car at the park and ride for a month in the middle of winter. Henry had gotten me an evening flight out of Logan with one stop in Zurich, scheduled to arrive at Indira Gandhi International either very late or very early; I hadn't figured out the time difference and didn't know which it was.

I was pleasantly hungover during the ride to the bus station. Buck and Carissa had spent the previous morning and part of the afternoon making enough food to feed to the people they'd invited over to the house in Winter Street for the evening as a kind of informal send off. Amanda came with her roommate, who turned out to be Theresa's girlfriend, a fact I probably would have never known if the three of them hadn't shown up together. Inez, Tracy, and Pete were there with a few other staff members from the school. Alice made an appearance, though didn't stay long.

Hodan brought her family and several people from the restaurant who had the night off. Karen and Ray arrived from Randolph with a few jugs of cider they'd somehow found the time to press between everything else. Carissa's parents and Buck's dad came down out of the hills for a drink. Other people I didn't know trickled in and out of the house all night, with everything settling down around 3AM when Officer Roland showed up to ask Buck to turn down the Outfield record he'd been playing on loop and put out the bonfire Pete and I had made in the backyard, the light of which you could apparently see from the front of the house and which was beginning to scare the neighbors. I felt a little like I was going off to war, a feeling I liked, even after I tried to kiss Inez on her way out the door and slipped on the ice, ending up in a kind of heap by the bird feeder. She was too afraid I might try it again if she helped me up, so she just told me to have a nice trip and maybe she would see me when I got back.

A good party should leave you with a sense of manifold possibilities, I thought, spiking the coffee in my traveler's mug with a plastic in-flight bottle of unbranded scotch, one of three Theresa had left behind as a gift the night before. The other two were safely stowed in the front pocket of a daypack behind the seat, my only luggage for however long the job for Henry would take. He said a month, at most, so I had enough outfits to wear one per week, plus a toothbrush, spare set of glasses, passport, a cell phone with an international plan and $500 in cash, both from Henry, and a copy of the manuscript I'd written in North Hero. I'd left a second copy with 'The Campaigns of Belisarius: A Study in Avoidance' written at the top in Dr. Norman's mailbox with a note saying something about it being the best I could do and if he felt like cobbling it together into a degree for me when he got back, that would be fine. That was all of it. If my sojourn in

Europe had taught me anything practical—three months dragging around the sort of gear I could have used to summit Everest—it was the virtue of packing like a transient or someone who hopped freight trains from here to there. I remembered the man who taught me this. I slept in the bunk beneath his in a homeless shelter masquerading as hostel in some out of the way neighborhood in Glasgow. I had an excellent viewf the cemetery from my bed and was still suffering from a pathological affinity for Jonathan Harker, so in order to distract myself, I listened to my bunkmate share his theories about why black people had difficulty forming families. Tribal blood, he said. This seemed to be his favorite topic. No shuffling him away from it to ask how he managed to keep the single of set of clothes he owned in such good shape, even though he slept in them, and why his only luggage was a spare set of shoes, brogans I think, that he kept in black plastic shopping bag hung from the bedframe, but never wore. It was winter, so he lived out of libraries during the day and spent nights at the shelter, talking to me. A weirdly complete life, it seemed, one I came close to envying for its apparent mobility, when I'd watch him hoist himself out of bed each morning, and begin his aimless day, the shopping bag over his wrist as he tromped off down the frozen street, while I stood in line with my Long Trail getup, trying to find a place for it in the luggage room so my roommates wouldn't steal anything while I was out.

"I want to tell you something," said Carissa, merging into the right-hand lane as we approached the Montpelier exit. Ah, here it is, I thought, sipping my coffee. The coda. The conflict between us had reached a kind of saturation point and suddenly gone extinct without anything being resolved, so I had expected something from her when she volunteered to drive me to the bus stop, a lovelorn overture or earnest assessment of what we both knew and what she planned to do about it. The sense of possibilities held over from the night before seemed to demand something important from us both, though I was waiting for a cue from her. Last time I went out on a limb, she hacked it off, I said to myself, settling into my new role as I saw it, the man who waits and is rewarded. If only Henry could be here to see this, the smug bastard.

"I think I know what you're going to say," I said, hoping prescience would speed things along. I didn't want to have this conversation, the one I'd wanted to have since Carissa came back to town, in the parking lot of a bus station.

"I don't think you do, Oliver."

"I think I have some idea. He'll understand."

"Who will?"

"Buck. Everything suggests it. He cares enough about us both to make it kind of a changing of the guard."

"Changing of the guard? Are you serious? Do you know how that makes me feel?"

"Well, I'm sorry. I could have put it differently."

"I'm not some fucking outpost that you and he get to take turns patrolling. I can't believe I just had to say that out loud. I'm with him for good reasons the same way I'm not with you for good reasons. That's how it is. I'm beginning to wonder if you'll ever get used to it."

"You could have made it easier," I said, feeling as if what I'd expected of the next twenty minutes had flipped itself inside out to reveal a portrait of things as they actually were, not at as I'd predicted them to be. I imagined Henry sitting in the backseat under his sunhat, chuckling to himself. "I don't hang around your bedroom door scratching to be let in when he's out of town."

"No, you don't have any moments of weakness. At least mine have a beginning, middle, and end."

"At least I know what I want when I'm unhappy."

"I do know what I want, fuckface!" shouted Carissa, speeding down State Street past the golden dome of the State Capital building, flatly buffed against the gray sky above the town. "The only reason you can't see that is because it isn't you! It's like you're not used to sharing the world with other people, people who aren't what you want them to be. I don't want to be someone's bandage. I won't be yours."

"I love you," I said. It seemed to echo.

"I love you too," she agreed, sliding the car into a parking spot beside the bus station, a kind of spruced up doublewide behind a palisade of jersey barriers. "I think that's why we're both waiting around for things to change. It's good you're going."

"I would stay if you asked me to."

"Why in the world would I do that? Other people, Oliver. I'm one of them. Your bus is here."

"I know," I said, though I wasn't sure what I knew as I fished my daypack from the back seat. "What did you want to tell me?"

"I'm pregnant."

"No."

"Excuse me? Is that the first thing you can think of to say to me?"

"I don't know what to say. Is it his?"

"Of course it's his! Who the fuck else would I have baby with?"

"So you're keeping it?"

"This was a mistake," said Carissa, gripping the wheel with both hands and resting her head between them. "I am ashamed of myself for expecting more from you."

"I just don't understand why you're telling me."

"We wanted you to be the godfather."

"You both do?"

"It was a decision we made together. One I'll probably regret for the rest of my life. Right now, you're the only person who knows about this. So whatever you decide, don't tell anyone please."

"I don't know how I should feel right now."

"Most people would be honored."

"I want to handle this appropriately. So I think I'm just going to leave."

"Okay," said Carissa, sounding suddenly very small, hugging herself through the sweater of Buck's she wore, not crying, though possibly working toward it. She'd gained weight, I'd noticed that and that it looked good on her, and she'd stopped having wine with dinner or smoking weed with Buck afterward. I could have probably put this together if I'd taken the time, saved myself a blindsiding. People sometimes turn unrecognizably ugly when surprised and I felt like an ogre as I leaned in to hug her, letting my lips fall aimlessly against face, smelling woodsmoke and snow in her hair.

That went about as badly as an important moment can go, I thought, watching her car leave the parking lot as I boarded the bus and took my seat. I didn't like the look of things out the window as we got underway, barren fields snowed in, reels of black trees, ski slopes running down from the clouded tops of mountains in the distance, so I hid my head beneath my jacket like a bird drawing a wing over itself and cried silently until I fell asleep, dreaming of Mt. Abandon for the first time in a while, striding hugely through the dusk, searching for me in a place I no longer was.

I didn't feel any better by the time the bus drew up to Logan airport, but the standard rigmarole of checking in for my flight and getting felt up by a TSA officer gave me a sense of purpose to carry around with me like an extra bag or the single personal

264

item I was allowed according to a sign by the security line. I settled onto a stool at a bar in the terminal done up like an English hunting lodge while I waited for my flight to be called, glancing up now and again from the wolves I was drawing on my napkin, expecting to see an expanse of hill and dale outside the window and a tribe of lords in plus fours victimizing a fox, instead of the seemingly endless tarmac taking on the character of inland sea as the sun drew below the horizon.

Here I am, I thought, doing up the background with a red pen I'd borrowed from the bartender. Another grown up American taking up more space than he needed. I felt like I was part of a planned community of sorrow; the people around me, perhaps the people Carissa had spoken of, were all alone and on their way somewhere, all wrestling with the choice of the ugliness in front of them or the ugliness beyond, a kind of non-choice, like the one Carissa had laid before me when she dropped me off at the bus stop earlier that day.

I am not godfather material, I decided, while settling the tab and plodding off to my gate. Since Alice, I'd begun thinking of my penis as a wounded serviceman, a thought I was trying not to associate with her husband, but I didn't know where else it could have come from. If Buck and Carissa knew half the crap like this that's rattling around my head with no place to go, they wouldn't even ask me to get the mail, I thought as I boarded my flight, settling into the aisle seat I'd requested when Henry asked if I had a preference. It was a long trip; I didn't want to have to ask a stranger permission whenever I had to use the bathroom. As trays with complimentary champagne flew by, I briefly wondered why I hadn't used my limited leverage with him to negotiate a seat in business class, but abandoned the question. It seemed to speak to the part of my life that was crying out for a longer view of things, or some kind of endgame. But the idea of leverage was interesting and stuck with me. Now that Carissa was no longer a person to wait for, did I really have a reason to haunt Acheron the way I had for the past few months or years—depending on how Henry saw it—some residual spirit drifting between the school, the house on Winter Street, and the bar at the Ethiopian restaurant, a roughly isosceles triangle if viewed from overhead? It seemed I suddenly had more to gain than I did to lose from all this, a rare miscalculation on my employer's part and one he probably had no idea about. As Carissa had said, I was the first person she and Buck told about the pregnancy.

So: I'm free, I thought cheerfully, as the plane's engine thrummed and a stewardess announced the closure of the main cabin door. A fine time to realize it.

I drew the manuscript I'd written in North Hero out of my bag when the plane reached a cruising altitude, a little stumped as to what I could have been thinking by bringing it along as my only reading material. I packed this when there was still hope, I thought, weighing the pages in my hands. No, that's wrong. I packed this when I thought there was hope. There never was any.

I figured if I was going to spend the rest of the sixteen-hour flight time feeling sorry for myself, I might as well get on with it and investigate why. Maybe there was something I missed or maybe I would learn something new. Either way, reading through it wouldn't make anything worse. I can't remind myself any more of what I don't want to think about, I thought, flipping to page one.

IV.

"Other people's love is a little disgusting, why is it?"
—Lawrence Durrell, *The Black Book*

Carissa,

There are some things I never told you. I know that sounds unlikely after the scene I made in Buck's kitchen. Still, I thought I'd put some of them down here. You'll probably assume this is a selfish action if you ever read this. If we ever talk about it, I will agree with you.

*   *   *

When my parents decided to rent a camp on Kranion Pond for a month over the summer, I remember thinking it would last forever. After meeting you on the dock the first day, I hoped it would never end.

*   *   *

In some ways, it hasn't.

I remember trying to understand why you were dating Thomas when we visited him in Warren a week or so after I met you and Buck at the lake, a small, squeaky person who probably would have had a lot of tattoos and facial piercings if he was old enough to get them. This ended up bearing out later on, as I'm sure you know. I ran into him on Church Street during my final year at Acheron College; he was living in Burlington, managing a teen center, and looked like something between a ringmaster and a pirate in a musical review. But at the time, I assumed you saw something vital in Thomas that was invisible to me after spending the evening with him at the barn in which he and his retinue had slapped together a stage and mini ramp. His band played, Thomas whapping away on the drums as you stood by admiring him. I skateboarded on the ramp with Buck, who had driven us all down in his father's jeep, wondering if he was wondering the same thing about you and Thomas, but it was all too new for me to ask. It became clear later on that Thomas was a kind of scene-specific Lothario who you were willing to put up with for the entrée he provided into events like the shows at the barn in Warren. Though as we drove back to the lake that night, I felt a little stupid for wanting to see you with someone who matched the idea I had of what you deserved.

*   *   *

When it rained for three days straight during my second week at the lake, the three of us drove up to an indoor miniature golf course somewhere outside Winooski. I was unnaturally excited about this, but I recall being the only person who took the game seriously. I kept score like a dork while you and Buck hit the balls way too hard while yelling 'fore!' We ended up getting thrown out in the rain after one of you put a hefty dent in a replica of the Sphinx around hole twelve. I was disappointed, but felt like this was the price for existing outside the disordered fun you and Buck were determined to have. I still have the scorecard from that day; I won.

*　　*　　*

The first day after the rain stopped, I drank way too much with you and Buck at his father's camp across the lake. I don't think either of you noticed when I excused myself and stumbled out of the yard into the woods along the inlet, looking for a calm patch of shoreline where I could be sick without revealing my inexperience. I threw up in the water a quarter mile from the house, and watched the nebula of vomit undulate in the shallows until I felt better. When I looked up, I saw Buck's father in a rowboat with his head between the legs of a woman who was not Buck's mother. Her swimsuit was pulled to the side, and her head thrown back in the moonlight. I didn't realize I'd been spotted until a few days later, when Buck's father stopped me on the road between town and the lake. It was your sixteenth birthday and I was coming back with a present for you, a record by The Freeze I'd found in a shop off Clamence Street. Buck's father offered me a ride and asked if I liked to read. When I said I did, he asked me if wanted some books. Saying no was obviously the wrong answer, but I began wishing there was some kind of third option after he'd turned his jeep around at the fishing access, driven us back through town, and out onto the class four road where he lived.

The house was kind of hunting lodge built into the side of Mt. Abandon, seemingly insulated by thousands of books. Buck's father dashed around, pulling things off shelves and dropping them into a plastic shopping bag, while I sat in the kitchen with a glass of flat ginger-ale he'd poured me, watching a deer nose around some apple trees through the window. I thought it would never end, but when it did and we arrived back at the lake, I dumped the books he'd given me out on my bed, wondering if there was a theme I should be recognizing; Jim Thompson, David Goodis, James M. Cain. I read the jackets; lust, betrayal, and hopelessness seemed to be represented in equal measure. Consequences, in other words, though there was nothing threatening about Buck's father when he dropped me off. He said I should let him know if I ran out of things to read in a way that seemed to indicate we now had an ongoing partnership of some kind. This was first time an adult who wasn't one of my parents needed something important from me and I was very afraid.

*   *   *

He ended up marrying the woman I saw him with, as you know, a dental hygienist from Orange County. The divorce went through shortly before Christmas and wasn't pretty. Neither of us know much about that and Buck didn't say anything I thought I could share with you when he spent the holiday with my family in North Calais. Things were not great at the hunting lodge; his mother had departed, the hygienist was trying to make herself amenable, and Buck had been suspended from school for breaking the lacrosse captain's collarbone during a supposed shoving match in the parking lot. It wasn't Buck's fault. The guy was a known asshole and asked Buck if he could make an appointment with his new stepmom to have his teeth cleaned or something like that, so Buck put a dent the size of a dinner plate in the driver's side of the captain's truck. The guy took a swing and slipped on the ice, though the rest of his teammates said Buck shoved him. The end result was that Buck had to pay to fix the door and got to spend a lot of time at home getting to know his new stepmom. When his dad called my dad to ask if Buck could stay with us through New Year's, or until school started, I overheard enough of the conversation to have some idea what to expect. My parents did their best to make him feel welcome and we had a fine Christmas overall. I took him cross-country skiing and snowshoeing around my family's property, feeling underequipped to help him through whatever he was suffering from. He didn't say much about it, or nothing I'm willing to share with you, though you came up more than once. You should know that he apologized for what happened with you the last week at the lake, something I never expected to hear from him, because I didn't think he knew how I felt about it. We were sitting on the wooded ridgeline above my parent's house, watching smoke drifting from the chimney and sharing a thermos of mint tea and some tuna fish sandwiches my mother had packed us. I pretended I didn't know what he was talking about.

*   *   *

I'm guessing your half of that apology is still forthcoming. If you like, I'll pretend I don't know what you're talking about either.

*   *   *

Neither of you have anything to be sorry for. Maybe only you know that. Still, hearing what I didn't need to hear from Buck that day on the ridge made me feel like I wasn't as lost in myself as I would one day become, as you would one day become. The overall point here is telling me what I want to hear might be mutually beneficial.

*   *   *

Maybe you would feel better about everything if you knew about Britta. She was four or five years older than me, the sister of a girl I'd dated briefly in junior high. It didn't end all that well with her sister, but Britta continued to say hello to me when we passed each other in the school hallways until she dropped out in her senior year to hang out on the State House lawn in Montpelier. I ran into her often enough in town for us to have developed a kind of friendship, or mentorship, more accurately. She gave me tapes to listen to, smoked pot with me, and sometimes drove us to shows in Burlington in a Volkswagen Golf that sounded like a small aircraft on the interstate. I admired and feared her; she wore a studded black denim vest with a Disclose backpatch—a band I hadn't heard of until she played them for me—and pegged black jeans, no matter what the weather was, and always appeared to have just woken up from a long nap in the sun. At the time, she was the only woman I knew who didn't shave her underarms or legs, an oddity that both fascinated and repelled me. The people she hung around with on the State House lawn all looked as if they'd tumbled out of a boxcar, the sort of terminal lifestyle dissidents who are always on the sunny side of homelessness, just passing through, and who wouldn't leave the homes they'd forsaken without a jug of mouthwash to disinfect a fresh tongue piercing, a bottle of lotion to lubricate a new facial tattoo, or a length of laundry cord to leash their dog to a public bench for the day. Spending my summer with them on the State House lawn had the contained dangerousness of an adventure vacation, and bothered my parents enough to give me a curfew, though they dropped it after meeting Britta, who they ended up liking very much. Still, it may have been part of the reason they decided to pack me off to Kranion Pond for the better part of July, though this didn't end up preventing me from flying too close to the sun where Britta was concerned. A few weeks before I had to leave, she'd driven us to a word-of-mouth show somewhere outside Littleton, New Hampshire. We took a side trip to see GG Allin's grave, and when we reached the cemetery, I told her about what my parents had planned for me, the ruination of my summer among the boxcar children, as I imagined it. She told me a friend was lending her a cabin in the foothills outside Acheron until August. I should stop by if I decided to go with them, she said, as if the decision were up to me. Her choice of words made me feel like I had somehow graduated into a friendship with Britta, that she saw me as an equal of some kind, though an equal to what, I couldn't say. She left for Acheron a week or so before I did, the invitation hanging over me as I dicked around with her retinue on the State House lawn, feeling out of place without her there and little bit abandoned. I felt her absence keenly enough to wonder if she might be feeling the same thing about me, not love exactly but whatever comes after admiration, so I didn't waste much time when I arrived at Kranion Pond. After helping my parents unpack the car and get the house in order, I excused myself and walked the mile or two through the woods, up the side of Mt. Abandon, the lake winking at my back in the early afternoon sunlight, until I stumbled into the dooryard of the cabin. A deeply tanned, shirtless man with a vaguely tribal facial tattoo looked at me curiously from his seat on the narrow porch, strumming a

mandolin. Britta introduced him as Willow when she came outside, flour dusting the thighs of her black denim pants. She had
reached the bread-baking stage of anarchism by this point and
had also taken up the banjo. She and Willow had written some
songs, she said. Would I like to hear them? As with Buck's father and the books, there was no way to say no. While she and
Willow plunked away on the porch, noodling through a set of
six or seven songs that all sounded the same to me, with lyrics
about riding bikes, growing your own vegetables, and staying up
all night talking, I wondered if my life from now on would be a
series of questions with only one answer. After they completed
their set list, we smoked some pot and ate some bread, still warm
from the oven. I listened to them talk about a friend of theirs
who played the trumpet, someone they were hoping to enlist,
and watched Willow out of the corner of my eye, trying to figure
out his sudden position in Britta's life. Through the cabin door, I
saw one bed, the sheets disordered, and a beaten external-frame
backpack with a furled bedroll leaning against the wall beside it.
Looks like the only thing Mr. Willow unpacked was his instrument, I thought to myself, suddenly wishing I hadn't come at all.
I said something about having to be back for dinner and Britta
gave me a loaf of bread to take along, which I ended up feeding
to some ducks back at the lake, having no idea how to explain it
to my parents. She told me to come back any time and I probably
would have if I hadn't met you later that day.

*　*　*

That was also the day I stopped masturbating. I was worried I
might think about you, or that you would somehow know about
it when you saw me I can't remember which.

274

My favorite moment during those three weeks on the lake was dancing with you to 'Talking Bombs' on your birthday on the lawn at your parent's camp. We dragged the speakers outside onto the deck and the loud, propulsive music echoed off the far side of the water, redounding back from the darkness as if we were enclosed in a sphere of our own making, a comforting thought. If Thomas were not nearby, waiting to receive you when the music ended, the moment would have been perfect.

When I saw him in Burlington years later, I realized I had the inclination to blame Thomas for most of what happened at the lake, and that still seems to be the case as I write this. We had coffee and I sat on an unkind urge to tug the ring hanging out of his septum. We had to have coffee, because Thomas still wasn't drinking, had never drank or used drugs actually, as some kind of statement to the world at large. He was also a practicing vegan and when I looked at our tandem reflection in a shop window on Church Street, I had to admit he looked a lot better than I did. Shorter, but better. If he were any taller, I thought then, he would be unstoppable. I remembered him on your sixteenth birthday, watching all of us get trashed at your parent's lake house and wondered if it had been hard for him to see that and leave himself out of it. He put you to bed, and forbid me from rowing back to my parent's camp in a canoe, hid the paddle in fact, even when I got nasty and told him I was going home so I didn't have to listen to him fucking you all night. He seemed appalled and said: she's drunk, as if it were the most obvious thing in the world, which it was, at least in retrospect. I remember being utterly ashamed of myself as I followed him inside and passed out on a bathmat in the downstairs lavatory. He made everyone a vegan scramble or something in the morning and went back to Warren when it became clear we were all going back to bed after breakfast. Still, when I ran into him ten years later, I wanted to believe he had something to make up for, even though he was clearly just getting through it, as it were, the same as the rest of us.

*　　*　　*

I almost called you in New York to tell you I saw Thomas. I thought it would be a good way to remind you to apologize to me. I never did it because I realized an apology would mean I'd been right to demand one and I didn't want to be right about that.

*　　*　　*

Also: he rides a motorcycle to work now. It suits him.

*　　*　　*

I was a virgin when I met you. I'm sure you read this loud and clear, and at the time, this bothered me. The closest I'd come was with a girl who dressed up as a countess on weekends and hit her friends with a foam-rubber sword wrapped in duct tape. I'd gone down on her over Labor Day weekend, not really knowing what I was doing, but hoping if I tried enough things, one of them would turn out right. We'd met up at a Civil War reenactment near my house and I'd invited her over afterward to watch 'The Last Unicorn'. My parents were out when we arrived, though I hadn't known they would be, so the entire experience caught me off guard and was too new to make much sense of. Where do I go from here? I remember wondering after she left, not really expecting us to return to or refine the awkwardness we'd just engaged in. It was a practical question. I didn't have too many day-to-day options; I wasn't exactly unpopular at school, but I didn't know anyone who enjoyed the same things I enjoyed until I met you and Buck. There were Britta's friends, of course, though most of the young women who hung around on the State House lawn with her were a little scary and weather-beaten, not at all the sort of creatures I could invite over to my parent's house to watch 'The Last Unicorn'. The shorthand for what I wanted was: experience, though the longhand was experience with someone who didn't scare the bejesus out of me or support my parent's idea of a 10PM curfew. You were the first person who seemed to fulfill these criteria. I had no fixed idea of what I deserved from girls my own age and was willing to settle for almost anything before we met. As it stood, the prettiest girls I knew thought I was into witchcraft, a conclusion they'd worked their way around to after seeing me nosing around the countess, who wore period outfits to school on game days. Even after the events of Labor Day weekend, I didn't see a way to get out of from under that assumption, but hoped it might benefit me in some wildcard capacity in the long run.

*　　*　　*

This almost became true at a house party in Montpelier for the school's drama department over February break, when the captain of the cheerleading squad drank half a bottle of tequila and felt me up beneath a dining room table after everyone else had gone to bed. It was unclear what either of us were doing there;

we'd both been invited by a friend of a friend of friend, tertiary guests who suddenly had that in common. As she kneaded me, I noticed her spray-on tan beginning to rub off on the tablecloth, and the paler skin beneath. It was the middle of winter in Vermont, after all. We hadn't seen the sun since September. A chameleon is massaging me, I thought as she excused herself to go to the bathroom, a dorky observation that embarrassed me for how far it seemed to stray from the task at hand. I was almost relieved when I heard the sound of someone being sick nearby and found the cheerleading captain bent over the downstairs toilet in an attitude of prayer, the outside of the bowl striped with fake tan from where she'd tried to hold onto it. Her hair was getting into the water, so I held onto it while she finished throwing up and helped her rinse it out in the shower afterward. Spray tan and makeup clouded the water spiraling into the drain. After she toweled off, she looked like a different person, plainer, a lower average, someone who flew a little closer to the ground I loped upon. I realized whatever stages we'd skipped over to arrive at this kind of intimacy were not the kind we could make up for later on, even if we'd wanted to. Too much too fast too soon, I thought in a kind of jumble as we took a walk around the block together, hoping the cool night air might make us both feel better about most of what made her pretty being washed away down the drain, or what she thought made her pretty, at any rate. And what makes me pretty? I wondered, suddenly feeling naked beneath the down parka I'd borrowed from a hook beside the door before we went outside, the studded vest with the Nausea backpatch hung over a chair back inside the house. So we're both without our armor, I thought, trudging along beside the captain, who threaded her arm through mine and said something about how she was feeling a lot better and we could still do it if I wanted to. Do what? I asked.

*   *   *

The overall point here might be that if I could repeat my evening with the cheerleading captain, I wouldn't do anything differently. It meant I hadn't had sex when I met you, but I knew what to make of it afterward, when the artifice departs and the tent is taken down. This is still the hardest part for me. I don't know about you.

*   *   *

Actually, I think it's the hardest part for you, too, even if you don't. When we saw each other in Brooklyn, I was mostly interested in seeing you the morning after. It didn't work out that way, but you should know that's what I wanted.

*   *   *

This is more a note to myself, but: when I think about it, the reason Belisarius failed me probably had something to do with his marital issues. Antonina sleeping with her adopted son, the Thracian youth Theodosius. Whether fact or fiction, I couldn't seem to move past them.

*   *   *

You might find it interesting to know that the girl I went down on after the Civil War reenactment also moved to New York after graduating high school. She studied political philosophy at Fordham and made a name for herself in certain circles by establishing the first, and probably only, Marxist live action role-playing group. I'm not entirely sure how it worked, but I always imagined her in a kind of proletarian getup, battling it out with landlords and tallying up dialectical hit points in some shady corner of Central Park. I doubt you ever saw each other, but maybe I'm wrong. At any rate, I ran into her in town last Christmas and she said she was sorry I'd never asked her to finish watching 'The Last Unicorn', which took me by surprise. I should look her up if I was ever in New York, she said. As you know, I didn't end up visiting the city until my grandmother died later that year and you were the only person I called when I was there.

*　　*　　*

I'm not trying to tell you that I have options, or remind you of what I missed out on to be with you for twelve hours in Brooklyn. Still, it's hard not to wonder if I should have just saved us both a lot of trouble and finished watching 'The Last Unicorn'.

*　　*　　*

If I had, there would still be a lot of things you don't know.

*　　*　　*

Would you prefer that?

*　　*　　*

At one point during the last week, shortly before my family left Kranion Pond, the three of us climbed up Mt. Abandon. The trail led past Britta's cabin, but I didn't say anything to either of you about it. I think I wanted to believe I'd moved beyond the part of my life that needed her in it. This felt right. She had Willow, whoever he was, and their stupid folk music. I had you and Buck. You sat between us when we reached the top of the mountain, the valley spread out below us, the town a grid of gray amid endless green, and the lake a black mirror in the mid-afternoon sunlight. Our legs touched and stuck together. You asked me when you would get to see me again after I left and whether you and Buck could come see me in North Calais. I couldn't tell if I loved you and him separately or together, but I imagined the three of us occupying the same small island and how complete that would be.

*   *   *

Was it because we swam naked off Buck's dock the night before? Maybe. It was too dark for us to see much of anything, but we sat wrapped in towels on the shore afterward, the way we sat on top of the mountain a day later, passing a bottle of your mom's wine back and forth, newly aware of ourselves, it seemed to me. When Buck went to bed, I rowed you home across the inlet, the both of us wearing only his father's towels, though you left yours in the canoe when I dropped you off and ran naked over the beach and across the lawn to the house, laughing, ghostly, uncatchable. You may or may not know how long I sat in the boat before rowing away, wondering if I should run after you. I watched a light go on and off on the upper floor, your room, suddenly the only place on earth I wanted to be, even if wanting this made me feel I wasn't worthy of it. I didn't know how to respect you and want you at the same time.

*   *   *

I'm sure we can both agree I'm still figuring this out.

*   *   *

When Thomas dumped you the day before I was supposed to leave, Buck had already suggested I stay with him and his dad for the rest of the summer. It was a nice idea and my parents were happy with anything that kept me off the State House lawn during the warmer months. Our parents all knew each other at this point, had been to dinner and had drinks at each other's houses. There was no reason for my mother and father to say no. They were beginning to pack everything up when Buck came over in the late afternoon and told me what you told him about it: Thomas thought you partied too much and he didn't feel comfortable around you anymore because of it. He said he just wanted to be friends for now, until you got your life together; he only wanted to be around healthy people. Buck didn't seem surprised by any of this and may have been expecting it. He knew some of the people who hung around Thomas down in Warren and was aware of his reputation. The thing about only wanting to be around healthy people came up whenever he wanted to jump ship or board another, a kind of ideological catch-all. Apparently, he was already seeing someone else. Buck said you were pretty upset and he didn't know what to do about it, but you were going out to dinner with your mom in Burlington that night to talk it over and wouldn't be back until late, so it was out of our hands for the time being. I said something about not knowing how bad to feel for you, since I always thought you could do better than the little drummer boy from Warren. I thought Buck would laugh, but he just shrugged and said I was probably right about that, but it didn't mean you were hurting any less. I felt chastened as I watched him drag his canoe off the beach into the water, remembering the plans he and I had later to camp out on a deserted isthmus on the far side of the lake. We'd already cleared out the site and set everything up the day before, but Buck seemed to have forgotten about it. When I reminded him, he said he and his dad would be running errands in town for most of the evening, but he would meet me out there after ten. He shoved off, I returned to the house to help my parents pack, trying to be sad for you and happy for myself at the same time. I wasn't exactly sure how to go about getting what I wanted from you, but I knew Thomas stood in the way of it. I had already begun to love you, I knew that, but now that he was gone, I didn't think loving you was something I'd have to work around for the rest of the summer. I love you, I said to the mirror in the bathroom later that night, trying to ignore the boyish reflection mimicking me as I practiced on myself what I had decided to tell you. I knew this wasn't the same as actually telling you, but at the time, I wasn't worried about what you would say back. It never crossed my mind. I thought if I told you I loved you, spoke it aloud, you would love me too, like casting a spell or invoking a curse, depending on how you looked at it.

* * *

From my angle, fifteen years down the road, I'm inclined toward the latter.

* * *

I never said it, of course, not until much later. But at least now you know where it came from.

Looking back, I think the same overeager impulse that drove me up the mountainside to Britta's cabin the day I arrived at Kranion Pond was related to whatever made me set out early for the point where Buck and I had set up camp the day before. After my practice session in the bathroom mirror, I wanted to get things rolling and was considering telling Buck about it, asking his advice. As I cut through the water in a canoe toward the isthmus with the day ending around me, I was as happy as I can remember being at any point in my life. It was 8 o'clock and the wind was picking up, the water rocking the boat underneath me as houses began to peter out along the shore, the smell of grill smoke and the sound of music fading as I crossed into the uninhabited cove on the far side of the lake. A young man on a remarkable journey, this was how I thought of myself. As I neared the point, I noticed a canoe pulled up against the rocks and wondered if our campsite had been poached out from under us until I recognized it as Buck's. Maybe he got back from town early. I didn't think much of it, switching on my headlamp as I pulled my boat through the shallows and tied it off beside his, but something stopped me as I climbed the bank. I still don't know what it was, a sudden caution maybe, the kind of feeling I've learned never to ignore. But I ignored it then as I scrambled up the bank into the clearing, my headlamp fixing the tent pitched in its center like a spotlight and your bare, slightly sunburnt back through the open flap, rising and falling above Buck, who I couldn't see, but knew was there. You both saw the light from my headlamp and stopped, you rolling off him, trying to cover yourself. I didn't want to see anymore, so I switched it off,

no longer sure where to go or what to do. Who's there? one of
you asked, I can't remember who it was. It's me, I said, tripping
over something, a bottle of whiskey by the fire pit. One of you
said my name. You said something about not expecting me to
be there until later. I didn't say anything. I heard the two of you
talking as I turned to leave, but someone said my name again,
you, this time, and I stopped. You said I should stay. I heard you
leaning out of the tent to say it. It's okay, Oliver, said Buck from
somewhere inside. Come lie down, you said. I want you to.

*   *   *

I still don't know whether you meant 'to' or 'too'.

*   *   *

Or two.

*   *   *

I thought about turning back after I'd left the cove and the lights
of houses were already beginning to grow thicker along the
shore. The whiskey bottle I'd tripped over was open between my
knees as I paddled and my nerve was up, but I knew it would
fade if I turned the boat around. An isthmus was not an island,
I reminded myself over and over again as I rowed, as if this was
what kept everything about what I'd been invited into from being
what I wanted or what I'd imagined I wanted on the mountaintop earlier in the week. I knew if you and Buck really wanted me
there, you would have asked me to come along. And you hadn't; I
was an afterthought. I didn't mind being lied to about it. I would

probably have done the same thing. But I didn't want you to fuck me because you felt bad about lying to me and the possibility that you both pitied me as I rowed away fortified what was left of my nerve, though I didn't turn around and paddle back to the point. Instead, after tugging my canoe onto the beach, I passed by the darkened front of the camp my parents had rented, their car packed and ready in the driveway, and slipped into the woods a little up the road, switching on my headlamp after I was out of sight of the house. The bottle hung sloshing from my hand as I cracked along the trail up Mt. Abandon, my throat raw from either the whiskey or the lump that had set up shop in it after I beached the canoe. By the time I reached Britta's cabin I was crying and when she opened the door, I must have looked like a mess, because she immediately pulled me inside, took the whiskey away and gave me a glass of water. I tried to explain things to her in a way that would make sense, but she mostly ended up with a loose idea of me getting my heart broken somewhere down at the lake. This turned out to be all she needed to know. Yeah, she said. Willow left too. I asked why and she gave me a vague answer that sounded like a lyric from one of the songs they'd performed for me. I said I was sorry and she shrugged, sliding the whiskey I'd brought toward her across the table, accidentally knocking a measuring cup full of flour all over my lap. She apologized and started trying to brush it away, her hands already covered in it. When I said it was fine, I didn't care, she started pressing harder and slower and asked: what about now? I didn't know what to say.

*   *   *

It's not a happy ending, Carissa. Just an ending, one you

didn't know about. I know Britta felt bad for me, but I only realized this afterward. I had surprised her at the cabin the way I'd surprised you and Buck at the lake. I was still an afterthought.

*   *   *

I scared my mother half to death the next morning when she opened the back of the car and found me sleeping there, my headlamp still lit from the shaky trip I'd made back down the mountain around 5AM after Britta fell asleep. I didn't want to be rude to her and leave without saying goodbye or thank you or whatever I was supposed to say, but I also didn't want to be left behind at the lake with you. When I told my mother this or that I wanted to go with her and my father back to North Calais, she asked me why and I just said I changed my mind. It was a form of the truth and neither of them asked me about, even as I sat in silence on the way home, stinking up the back of the car with the residual scent of sour whiskey and Britta's armpits, I imagined. She bathed in the lake once or twice a week, I'd learned afterward. I was surprised by how little this bothered me. I could live with it, at any rate. I had to live with it, the same as everything else that happened.

*   *   *

I'm still living with it, obviously. That's why this exists.

*   *   *

Buck called me a week later to see if he could come down to Montpelier and skateboard with me. He did that and we didn't talk about what happened. We were having fun, so it didn't make sense.

*   *   *

You started calling me too. Just to talk. Not about what happened. I liked that, even if I couldn't figure it out. After a while, I stopped worrying about figuring it out. When you and Thomas got back together in September, I told you exactly what I thought of him and you agreed. We laughed about it.

*   *   *

After I got my license, I saw you and Buck more often. I began spending most of my weekends in Acheron, staying at your parent's house or with Buck at his dad's place. Sometimes we'd drive down to Warren to spend time with Thomas and his friends or all of us would caravan up to Burlington for a show. Two or three years passed like this, if you recall, a kind of stasis, one I suspect you were trying escape when you broke up with Thomas and left to attend school in New York. I'd always assumed you would go to school with Buck and me at the college on the hill, or perhaps I just hoped you would. Either way, I considered it a selfish action. I told myself this was because I'd gotten to know Thomas better over the years and felt bad for him, but the truth was without you nearby, I didn't know what to hope for.

*   *   *

I ended up blowing the admissions deadline and getting packed off to Europe to figure myself out while you and Buck began your inaugural terms as freshman. I came home feeling as if I'd learned a lot things about myself I didn't like and I wondered how many of them you already knew.

*　　*　　*

I think you're familiar with most of them by now.

*　　*　　*

When I started college after Christmas, I was miserable and overwhelmed. The only thing that kept me from dropping out was the possibility of falling even further out of step with you and Buck, who wasn't phased when I told him I was planning to move to New York after midterms. He asked if you knew about it and when I said no, he said I should probably run it by you. He didn't say why, but I knew he was right and that I couldn't do it; transparency has never been my friend. Imagining what you would say was enough to keep me at school for next four years.

*　　*　　*

Maybe Buck knew that.

*　　*　　*

We're getting into things you already know. I'm aware of that. I'm sure there are many things I still don't know and I'm fine continuing not to know them.

*　　*　　*

Britta turned up a few years ago at a poetry reading at a church near my parent's house in North Calais. I was there with them, she was there with her two kids, and we talked at the reception afterward. She looked fine, good even, maybe happy, or busy enough for it not to make much difference. She was married to a former professor of hers at UVM and was finishing a dissertation on Thomas Bernhard, someone I hadn't heard of, but Britta assured me I would like. When she asked what I was up to, the question stumped me. We walked out into the fields beside the church with plastic cups of wine as her children, a boy and girl, five and nine, she said, ran ahead. I remember thinking we probably looked like a very happy family to the people we'd left behind on the lawn outside the church. I couldn't imagine what kind of father I'd be without wondering what kind of mother you'd be, though, at this point, we hadn't spoken for almost a year and the last time we did, you'd been dating what sounded to me like an enterprising charlatan who edited fart sounds into videos of ballerinas leaping and pirouetting on stage and also ran some kind of kennel for performance artists, a group or organization he'd decided to call 'Marry a Black Dude // Grow Your Hair Out'. Your side of our last conversation took on the sort of free-associative, incoherent format he probably would have appreciated or tried to patent, and left me entirely in the dark as to whether I should continue trying to contact you at all. Even so, I thought of you months later, walking in the field beside the church with Britta, imagining what a family with you would look like or do to us. I wanted to ask Britta what her husband was like so I'd have something to weigh myself against, but as she raised her arm to chase a horsefly off her cheek,

I caught a glimpse of her bare underarm and decided I had dog-paddled out of my depth and it was time to return to shore.

*   *   *

If you've read this far, you probably understand I'm not trying to change your mind about anything.

*   *   *

I'd like to change my mind about a few things, but they seem to keep coming up.

*   *   *

For instance: I hope someday I can tell you I love you without sounding like I've been practicing saying it in the bathroom mirror.

*   *   *

On the other hand, I hope someday you can tell me you love me without it sounding unavoidable, the only logical result of how long we've known each other, aside from hatred.

*   *   *

Or indifference. This seems more likely.

*   *   *

One final note: Since beginning this, I've had experience with

islands and the kind of aqueous, Ovid-like isolation I once imagined for the three of us—you, me, Buck—but found the experience only valuable for what it made me miss back on land.

*　*　*

V.

"Are you ignorant of everything?"
"Yes."
"India?"
I admit . . .
"So you know nothing at all! I suspected! . . . Hm! Hm! You'll
have trouble!"

—Céline, *Guignol's Band*

AFTER TOUCHING DOWN IN ZURICH, I spent half of the two-hour layover hovering around a post-office in the terminal, wondering if I should send the manuscript to Carissa just to get it off my hands, but ended up staring through the window by my gate, watching dawn creep up over a black line of fir trees. Snow grayed the immediate landscape. The terminal had all the exacting, sterile order I expected of the Swiss, a nation I'd always thought of as being run by a league of militarized Aryan elves who spent all day in their workshops making clocks and machine guns.

Precision instruments for a precise people, I thought, glancing around me for signs of life. The nearest bar was closed and I had nothing to read. A potted plant beside my seat looked as if someone cared deeply for it, a possibility I found myself envying over and over as I flipped open the phone Henry had given me, wondering who I could call to offset the sense of banishment that had stolen over me since finishing the manuscript. There were only two numbers, an all purpose one of Henry's and one for his overseas contact, a person named Naphta, who would meet me at the airport in New Delhi and help me get where I needed to go. I could only remember two other telephone numbers off the top of my head; my parents, who would worry about me if I called them from Zurich to say I was feeling lonely, and Theresa, only because hers spelled out 'bad fuck' on the keypad.

Theresa it is, I thought, punching in the country code and following it with her number. She answered on the fifth ring, sounding suspicious and patiently listened to me deliver a greeting I only realized was way too loud and excited sounding after I heard my voice echoing back at me from the other end of the terminal.

"You're a smart guy, Oliver," she said. "So you probably know it's like 4AM here."

"I figured you'd be up and around."

"I'm in bed with someone. You met her like a day ago. I only answered because I didn't recognize the number and it freaked me out."

"Sorry to scare you. It's just, I'm here in this polite little airport, probably built with Nazi bullion and it's mostly empty and I thought of you. That's all."

"You remember I like girls, right?"

"I'm kind of like a girl."

"Only in the ways that would make you a pain in the ass to date. I'm mostly interested in moving parts at this point in my life."

"In some ways, I think that makes you the perfect person for me."

"I'm sorry. I know how much you probably want me to agree with you right now. I can hear it in your voice."

"I knew this was a mistake before I called. I think I hoped it to be a more exciting one."

"I have someone here. I'm being rude."

"Tell her I say hello. Tell her I hope her snake is well."

"I'll be sure to pass that along. Call me at a normal hour and I will be happy to discuss whatever's bothering you."

"What makes you think something's bothering me?" I asked, only getting halfway through the question before Theresa hung up. I couldn't blame her. She was in the middle of something. We both were, I suppose, I thought, looking around me at the people in variegated turbans and robes beginning to gather by the gate. A café appeared to be opening nearby. A sly-looking waiter brought me a coffee and a German language newspaper when I asked for something to draw on. He stood nearby, watching me squeeze as many wolves into the margins as I could with a pen I'd borrowed from him, sweeping away the cup and saucer when I was finished and murmuring 'der artist' as he took the paper, a term I found out later could either mean 'artist' or 'joker', depending on the context.

I slept on the plane to New Delhi, only coming awake when the wheels skidded to a stop on the tarmac somewhere after midnight and the stewardess announced our arrival in clunking, Raj-era English. The entire cabin smelled vaguely curried, an odor that grew into a kind of animus as passengers began hauling their belongings out of the overhead bins and debarking the plane. I stood like a scarecrow athwart two large families with seven crying children between them, feeling weirdly refreshed after my nap and eager to be on my way, though this feeling receded a bit after meeting Naphta in arrivals and following him outside into the anonymous atmosphere that seems to hang around major international airports, no matter where they are. He was a seedy, sinister little person, a bit older than me, exactly the kind of Igor I'd expect Henry to have on call. He'd costumed himself in harem pants and a kurta to pick me up at the airport, an outfit that would have looked just right on Dr. Norman, but made Naphta seem like he was trying to blend in with his surroundings after committing some nearby atrocity. He chewed betel nuts often enough to have a reddish mouth and teeth most of the time, as if he'd just taken down big game with his bare hands and devoured it raw, still screaming. After meeting him, it was hard not to feel as if I too was up to no good.

"You have all the details," he said after finding us a taxi, and boarding it with me. Two young men sat up front, both in their early twenties. One kept glancing backward from the passenger seat, past us, and shouting in Hindi at the driver, who would then honk the horn and sharply change lanes. "So you don't need me to go over them with you. I'm just here to get you where you need to go. If all goes well, you won't see me again after tomorrow morning."

"What happens tomorrow morning?" I asked, as the taxi shot between two semi-trucks, so close I could have touched the side of either through the open window.

"You get on a train. The Mahabodhi Express to Gaya. Might take twelve hours if it's on time, but budget for sixteen."

"I was hoping for day or two to see the sights," I said, not really sure what there was to see, not caring either, but definitely not interested in hopping on a train for a half a day after spending the last twenty-four hours in transit. Naphta ignored me, rolling his window lower and inhaling a burnt, slightly meaty odor from outside.

"Smell that?" he asked. "That's the crematorium."

Where did Henry dig up this ghoul? I wondered, trying not look at him directly as the taxi merged off the main road, passing through a large park and out into the streets of New Delhi. We drove past piles of building materials or rubble, I couldn't tell which, each guarded by two to three stray dogs, it seemed. Most shops had their shutters down for the night; a white fluorescent light spilled out of the few that were open at this hour, small places no larger than a storage unit, all containing three to five barefoot men in shirtsleeves and headscarves, cooking something or preparing to eat what they'd already cooked, moving their hands, squatting and talking. The car slowed as we entered a street that seemed to overlook itself, narrowing at the top as if drawn together by the laundry lines passing from window to window above.

"Paharganj," muttered Naphta, by way of explanation. I noticed people bundled in blankets outside their shops, asleep on the pavement, not stirring as the taxi rolled by. The night had begun to smell like spiced dirt and standing water as we stopped outside what was presumably my hotel. Naphta told the driver to wait and walked me inside to a desk with a sleepy looking clerk who surrendered the room key autonomically, as if someone offstage had yanked a cord attached to his arm.

"I'll meet you in the morning," said Naphta, after walking me up a flight of crooked stairs to the door of my room. He checked his watch. "It's 2AM now. I'll be here at eight. Your train leaves at ten, so be ready to go. And don't drink the water. Keep your mouth closed if you take a shower and if you have any open cuts or anything, cover those up before you do. I had the guys bring up a couple liters earlier. Use that to brush your teeth."

"Thank you," I said experimentally as he turned to leave. "By any chance, is there somewhere around here to get a beer or buy a book at this hour?"

Naphta either thought I was joking or didn't hear me or didn't care. I was suddenly alone with myself in the gloomy, windowless, airless stairway. The room wasn't much better. A single halogen tube hummed to life as I hit the light switch. The only furniture appeared to be a bed-shaped mound in the corner beneath a large curtain that concealed not a window but an oxidized iron grate with an industrial look, like something you'd expect to find on the side of a cargo ship. The bathroom had a hole in the floor to shit in and a faucet at ass level to spritz yourself afterward. A blue plastic bucket hung jauntily from the hot water nozzle, like an invitation to try it out. A turn of the spigot produced a hiss, but no water. The cold worked fine.

This is like indoor camping, I thought, slapping the light switch and settling into the blankets without undressing. The bedding seemed to have been thoroughly chewed over by whoever used it last, and smelled a little like the street outside. I was suddenly immersed in the kind of full-flavored squalor I'd only read about. Good for me. The room seemed to be inviting me to be depressed by it, an easy enough impulse to yield to on my end, but one that wouldn't make the hot water work or the shipside window screen disappear from behind the curtain. I hadn't been comfortable in familiar surroundings since midsummer. Why should I expect to be comfortable so far from home? I felt like I was asking the right questions, even if they led me around to wondering if I was so starved for something outside the closed, low-average circle I'd built around myself back in Acheron, that I'd put up with anything as long as it was out of the ordinary.

You're being paid a lot of money to relax your standards, whatever they might be and keep your head on straight, I told myself, swigging from one of three bottles of water aligned beside the bed mound, wishing they contained beer. I was restless from the flight, but too afraid of getting lost to leave the hotel, so I settled into a modified version of counting sheep; as each lamb vaulted over a split rail fence dividing the nighttime pasture I imagined for them, a tawny, red-mouthed wolf followed in hungerless, undeviating, eternal pursuit.

*   *   *

The next morning, I awoke to find Naphta sitting at the foot of my bed on the upturned plastic bucket from the bathroom, smoking a beedi—tobacco wrapped in a tendu leaf and tied with a string—and wearing the same outfit from the night before, harem pants, kurta, sandals, which made him look altogether like a kind of dissolute genie escaped from his lamp. Dust from the bed hung in a grid of sunlight from the non-window as I threw the blankets aside and stood up, freaked out, but trying not to show it.

"We're late," said Naphta, standing up, and kicking the bucket at me across the floor. "Have a shower or whatever you need to do. I'll meet you downstairs in five minutes."

How long was he watching me sleep? I wondered as I went into the bathroom, filled the pail, and dumped it over my head. I was used to a shower taking longer, but this seemed to be the only way to do things. I glanced around stupidly for a towel, but ended up drying myself off on the bed sheets, a choice that left me feeling less clean than I had before Naphta showed up. I was beginning to think of him as Henry's familiar. Probably the right impulse, I decided, as I left the room and walked downstairs.

We had breakfast on the roof of a hotel much nicer than mine as the street stirred below, the sounds of shopkeepers raising the shutters, motor-rickshaws roaring to life, bicycle bells ringing out arhythmically. We sat at a folding table beneath a striped canopy as if we were on safari, a dry heat building above us. Naphta drank black coffee and ate toast, appearing to read a fresh copy of the *Times of India* while rattling off some last minute details about what was expected me regarding Denise.

"The orphanage is on the other side of the river from the town," he said, his face concealed behind the newspaper as he spoke, another troubling bit of minor weirdness. "She has most of her meals there, but usually takes a walk over the bridge after her morning class. She teaches another class in the afternoon and seems to spend most of her evenings in her room or with the kids, though sometimes she'll have coffee in the square outside the temple complex by herself. There's no real order to it. Watch her long enough. You'll see what I mean. She takes biweekly trips to Gaya to pick up materials for her classroom, though these seem to happen whenever she can fit them in. Still, it's probably your best bet for getting what we need after you find out where she's keeping it."

"What do I do once I have it?"

"You call me. I'll send someone. Then you take the first train back here. I'll have you on a flight within twenty-four hours."

"About that. Any chance of getting bumped up to business class on the way home?" I asked, figuring I might as well start padding out my return journey now, while I still had something expected of me.

"Time to go," he answered, quartering the newspaper beneath his arm and standing up. I'll ask again when I call him with what he wants, I thought as he waited by the stairs for me to finish up. Make it a precondition of the handoff.

Before leaving the table, I opened the front pocket of my backpack, and removed a foil sheet with a course of anti-malarial drugs my doctor had given me, a course I was supposed to have begun before leaving the country, but between Carissa's pregnancy and the endemic fog of marijuana smoke in which I lived my life, it had slipped my mind; I'd only remembered now because of a sinister looking mosquito I'd noticed drawn on the front page of the newspaper Naphta had held between us. While he loitered by the exit like one of the forty thieves, I popped out the first pill into my hand, preparing to swallow it with the last of my coffee, thought before I could, he swooped in, plucking the pill and sheet from me in the same movement. It wasn't a violent motion, just a quick one and I wasn't sure what I had to say about it, even as I watched him read over the foil sheet like it was part of the newspaper still folded beneath his arm.

"Lariam," he said obliquely, flinging the medication off the roof, tossing the pill after it. "You're not taking that. We have work to do. Buy a net when you get there."

"A net?"

"Put it over your bed. We brought you all the way here to do something very specific. I'm not going to have you fuck it up because you're hallucinating or experiencing suicidal ideations or whatever. Let's go. You have a train to catch."

Reckless prick, I thought as I followed him down the stairs and out of the hotel, toward the New Delhi Railway Station at the end of the street. The gate was on the other side of a multilane, two-way thoroughfare choked with buses, cars, auto-rickshaws, bicycles, cows, and people who appeared to be in no real hurry to get anywhere, all amid the unrelenting sound of horns. I resisted the urge to hold onto the tail of Naphta's kurta as he waded through the disordered traffic like it was veteran's day parade somewhere in the Midwest, hugging the narrow median for only a moment before setting off again. He eventually landed us in the waiting area of the train station, where he left me beside groups of people sitting on blankets, picnicking and napping while they waited, to get me tickets from the tourist office upstairs. People stared and I stared back; it seemed to be normal here. A boy with burn scars on his face came up to me with his hand out, and waited patiently while I dug around in my pockets for something to give him. Just as my hand found a five-rupee coin, Naphta appeared, grasping my elbow, and hauling me to my feet with my hand still stuck in my pants. He said something I couldn't understand to the boy, who ran off, and rotated me toward the door to the platforms.

"Unless you want to be mobbed by retarded children," he said as we walked between several rusty-looking trains, searching for mine, "don't give anything to anyone ever."

"I don't think that boy was retarded. I think he had been injured in a fire or something."

"Weird-looking, at any rate," he said, releasing my elbow to light a beedi.

Reckless prick, I thought for the second time in fifteen minutes, after Naphta left me beside the second-class sleeper car I was supposed to board. I'm not sure what I expected the inside to be like, something held over from colonial rule, a private cabin with inlaid woodwork, brass lighting fixtures, velvet cushions, and a cozy sit-down bathroom off to one side. Instead, the car was essentially a hallway with alcoves along both sides containing six berths, three on each wall that passengers began folding down after it got dark. The bathroom was at the end of the car, the same bathroom I'd had all to myself at the hotel in Delhi, only now I got to share with the rest of my fellow passengers. The train was overbooked. Some of them didn't have beds, and hung out in the portico between cars or just stood in the aisle, watching the city fade away through the window, the tattered outskirt giving way to seemingly endless rice fields overhung by Palmyra palms and banyans. I'd managed to claim an upper bunk, which gave me a view of nothing except a row of defunct fans built into the ceiling, so I ended up sitting beside an elderly bearded sadhu in the breezeway, watching the green and brown land unreel through the open door. Every so often he would raise his trident and gesture at something with it, something that had already passed by the time I realized he wanted me to look at it.

Story of my life, I thought, shrugging and nodding at him, trying to get an idea of what passed for politeness on this side of the world. I had nothing to read and no one to talk to, so I spent most of the day waving at things through the doorway with the old holy man, the two of us shaping the roaring air between our hands like puppeteers. Toward evening, a chai wallah came on board, distributing sweet milky tea in clay cups from a huge stainless steel jug. Another man followed him with a basket, selling curried vegetables, potatoes and peas, wrapped in some kind of leaf. I sat with this food in my berth as it grew dark, nibbling quietly while passengers below let down their bunks and settled in for the night. The train clunked along the tracks, not going very fast, but since disengaging from Naphta, I wasn't in any hurry. He reminded me of a middle school classmate I'd carpooled with to soccer camp for week over the summer, something my parents had arranged, a mean-spirited clown who'd snuck dry cat food into my breakfast cereal one morning as a joke, barely holding himself together as he watched me chew through a spoonful of mixed grill flavored kibble soaked in skim milk. I'd returned fire a week later, the final day of camp, by slipping a sandwich I'd made with a turd from my cat's litterbox into his lunch. He'd taken two bites before realizing something was wrong, one more than it took me with the kibble something I wanted to remind him of but had to stay quiet about after he took a swing at me across the picnic table where we were eating lunch. The coaches had to pull him away from me and call both our parents to come get us. Even if I'd admitted anything, there was nothing anyone could really do to me over it, so I rode home early beside my father, who knew about the cat food in my cereal. You set yourself up for trouble when you mess with someone's food, he'd said impartially, closing out the topic and leaving me feeling triumphant about it.

But who was the reckless prick in that situation? I wondered, as I tucked my backpack beneath my head. I wasn't sure, but hoped all the things I was once proud of wouldn't eventually turn out this way. Nothing like two decades to take the sheen off a cat shit sandwich, I thought, rolling toward the wall.

*　　*　　*

The train clanked into Gaya junction the next morning, four to five hours late according to a student on the bunk below me. He was studying poetry at one of the city's universities and offered to share an auto-rickshaw to Bodh-Gaya, where his family lived.

"How far is it?" I asked, after we'd left the town and were speeding down a narrow, palm-lined road beside the river Carissa had mentioned weeks ago, the place where Buddha supposedly achieved enlightenment. It was now dry, I noted, as we sped along the bank.

"Maybe twelve kilometers," said Arun, with a kind of wobble of his head, a motion of contented uncertainty I would become familiar with over the next few weeks, like a shrug from the neck up. "Do you know the poems of Ovid?"

"Only the one about the satyr who gets skinned alive for hubris."

"Marsyas."

"Yes, I think so."

"He was considered very wise for a satyr. When Socrates is compared to him by Alcibiades in the *Symposium*, it is meant to be favorable."

"I see."

"He was also supposed to have invented the *aulos*, a kind of reed pipe, or picked it up after it was thrown away by Athena, and learned to play it."

"Why did she throw it away?"

"It made her cheeks bulge. The other gods made fun of her."

"Sounds about right," I said, as the rickshaw pulled up outside the gates of a Burmese monastery where Naphta had reserved me a room. I handed the driver some money, but Arun intercepted the bills and gave me half of them back.

"It is too much," he said, handing me my backpack as I stepped out. "This is a small town. People will know if you pay too much."

"Thank you."

"You must come meet my family after you are settled in. We live beside the temple."

"I'd like that. I live in this monastery, apparently."

We shook hands and the rickshaw, a kind of hornet-colored tricycle with a roof, four seats, and a lawnmower engine, sped off toward the center of town. I walked through the spired monastery gate into a large dirt courtyard with three tiers of rooms built around it. A few monks seated beside a small fire smoked cigarettes and watched something on a cellphone. Three dirty, well-fed dogs slept beneath a tree in the center. A rooster strutted out from behind the office, as I waited for my key, and disappeared behind a colonnade on the first floor.

I could live here, I decided, as I walked up a set of stone stairs to my room on the second floor, though I couldn't help but notice the place was full of people who seemed to have decided the same thing, stuck halfway, as they appeared to be, between enlightenment and wherever they'd fled from in order to find it, sun-leavened, glass-eyed individuals from California and New York City by the look of things. Most were dressed like Naphta, through some were in the maroon robes of acolytes, bald, mumbling and fingering prayer beads, or *mala*, as they are called.

Twenty-five hundred years of ongoing noble tradition, I thought further, as I entered my room, or cell; bed, desk, chair. That seemed to be it. But drop enough North Americans into it and you have kitsch overnight. Give us enough time and we'll make anything look like a cult. Yoga: another example.

Spiritual tourists. This was the term Denise would later use to describe the ranks of sandaled post-colonialists marching past the screened window of my room on their way to dharma studies. As far as roommates went, they seemed harmless enough to me, just people in costumes who thought they had figured out some part of the mess we were all in. I followed a couple of them to class a few times, figuring I should practice being inconspicuous for whenever Denise showed up, and sat in the back, listening to what was said with what felt like an open mind, though an open heart seemed to be required, something I wasn't sure I could manage on the spur of the moment. I gave up stalking the acolytes when I began envying their self-containment; it seemed like a step in the wrong direction.

*　*　*

I kept my head low the first few days in Bodh Gaya. The monastery was a quarter mile outside the town center and the Mahabodhi temple complex. It backed up onto a swamp, probably the last place I should have been hanging around after Naphta tossed my antimalarial drugs off the roof of the hotel in Delhi. I'd managed to find a mosquito net and a length of laundry line in one of the shops of the main square and spent the next afternoon stringing the thing up above my bed with pushpins, so as not to knock any holes in the wall, feeling spider-like as I wove my web beneath the single bare bulb in the ceiling. The power was cut off after ten most nights, so I'd bought candles to read with after finding a few books in a tourist shop that also sold private tours of the Taj Mahal in Agra and elephant rides. The books were shrink-wrapped for whatever reason, maybe to prevent damage or browsing, and not at all the sort of thing I would normally read; Joseph Conrad, Herman Hesse, competent writers who bored the daylights out of me, though I did find a copy of *Lonesome Dove* left behind in the lobby of a guesthouse where I stopped to ask directions and set about reading it in the backyard of the New Poli Poli café across the street from the monastery the same afternoon.

The New Poli Poli was directly beside the original Poli Poli, and appeared to be owned and operated by the same two brothers, though why they choose not to merge the tents of either business into one was a mystery, one I didn't explore too deeply after discovering that the New Poli Poli served beer my third day in town. From then on, I spent most afternoons in a rattan wing chair out back, reading and drinking Kingfisher out of a teapot, occasionally looking up from my book to stare at the dry riverbed. This activity explained itself, I thought, but a metaphor could be grafted onto it if needed. The New Poli Poli didn't have a liquor license, so the beer had to be decanted into something discrete, and a teapot blended in well enough. This didn't bother me at all; I began measuring my evenings at the café in the amount of teapots I'd made it through by the time I tightrope walked through the gate of the monastery across the street and slapped up the stairs to my room. I'd been stopped only once by a middle-aged Englishman in the hall on my way upstairs, one of the novitiates I'd followed to class, who rode a bicycle to the temple complex every morning with the kind of self-possession you could see from space.

"This is a Buddhist monastery," he said, leaning in, like he thought I might be lost. "Not a beach at Goa."

"So you want me to go away?" I shouted after him, already too far down the stairs to hear me. I went to bed, wondering why Naphta had stuck me in a swamp monastery with a bar right across the road. He must have known that would spell trouble.

It became more or less clear the following afternoon, when I glanced up from Lonesome Dove and spotted Denise crossing the bridge toward town, a bridge I had a nice view of from my rattan chair in the back of the New Poli Poli and had noticed often enough without realizing it led to the orphanage on the other side of the river. I had the immediate sense of being positioned, like a piece on a board. Had Naphta sat in this same chair, watching her as I was doing now? I wondered, clasping my lips around the spout of the teapot and tipping it back, trying to finish up in a hurry so I could catch Denise. A group of children kicking a soccer ball watched me do this unabashedly, and were laughing about it as I stuck my book in my back pocket and left the café.

Denise veered off the main road into town and up a hill through an area with a lot of Tibetan shops and restaurants. I followed her at distance, only realizing I was also being followed by two of the three dogs from the monastery after I was told to leave them outside by the headwaiter or whatever he was at the door of a place she'd gone into, Café Om.

"Please, sir," he said, gesturing at the two animals flanking me. "They cannot come in."

"They're not mine," I said, remembering my own struggle over this kind of thing with Henry years ago and how that turned out. "They followed me."

He didn't seem to believe me, but helped shoo the dogs away from the entrance long enough get me inside. One of them began to howl after the door was closed, though I was already seated by then, looking over a menu I didn't understand. Denise sat at the other end of the dining room with a guy I recognized from around the monastery. Was this a date? I couldn't be sure, though I made myself oddly jealous imagining it was as I ordered what sounded like a veggie burger and kept the menu to hide behind. She looked good, a bit thin, and not beautiful, but neither was I; it seemed unfair to go around expecting this from other people. Still, I liked the small wrinkles at the corner of her blue-gray eyes, the kind that formed when she forced herself to smile at her date, which I was pleased to see she seemed to be doing a lot. Her collarbone stuck out of her skin like a clothes hanger and I noticed a few filaments of gray in the dark hair she kept back, tucked underneath a bandana.

I probably wouldn't have recognized her if I didn't know what to look for, I thought to myself as my food arrived and I began plowing through it dutifully, not wanting to be rude, but too interested in watching Denise to eat much. I ate with one hand, and held the menu in front of my face with the other, stealing perennial glances at her over the top. Outside, the second dog started howling alongside the first, a somber, wolfish duet so loud in the uncrowded air of the dining room that it seemed to come from beneath the table. The headwaiter hovered by the door with a broom like a sentry, dividing his gaze between the dogs wailing in the street and the corner where he'd seated me, clearly replaying where, in his view, the evening had gone wrong.

Not my dogs, not my problem, I silently reaffirmed, peeking over the menu and accidentally locking eyes with Denise's dinner companion, the seat across from him now empty. His expression seemed to ask why I didn't have anything better to do, a good question, I thought, as I ducked back behind the menu in a kind of dumb reflex, thrusting my head deeply into the sand trap where I'd apparently set up shop for the evening, wondering where Denise had gone, but not wanting to leave my hiding place to have a look. It had been long enough since we talked that I didn't immediately recognize her voice speaking to me through the menu until I'd dropped the bill of fare to the tabletop and found her standing behind it, stirring a glass of what looked like yogurt, her business-like good looks the same as I remembered up close. Still not my thing, I decided, even as I tried to tease out the shape of her butt from the front, a kind of soulless fairground game that seemed to answer her date's silent question about whether or not I had anything better to do.

"He sent you," said Denise.

"Yup," I replied, not sure it was even a question, but feeling a little like a toothless saw as I tried to think of a reply she wouldn't immediately see through. Lying successfully was no longer an option, I knew that. But had it ever been? Henry said

Denise would probably be expecting someone like me to come along, and yet, he'd sent someone like me anyway. And here I was, making new enemies and failing to meet his expectations. I felt stupid in a new way and didn't like it, barely flinching when Denise tossed her glass of banana *lassi* in my face and walked toward the door.

"Clown," she said over her shoulder as she brushed past the craven-looking headwaiter on her way outside. The man she'd been having dinner with studied me for a moment longer before dropping some money on the table and following her, the dogs from the monastery squeezing past him when he opened the door to the street. They crossed the dining room to lie beneath my chair, lapping at the curds from Denise's drink dripping off my hair and glasses onto the floor, while the headwaiter looked on as if he was expecting the roof to collapse next, or maybe hoping for it, something to conceal the evidence.

"You really must leave now," he said redundantly as I passed him on the way to the door, the dogs padding after me, scabby animals with matted coats, licking their chops like jackals. They seemed to want me to be part of their pack and I felt bad for them because of it, though as I walked back to the monastery beneath a line of prayer flags snapping in the wind, I wondered how many times people had pitied me for the same reason.

* * *

I wasn't sure if Denise recognized me until a few days later, when she surprised me by showing up in back of the New Poli Poli. After the disaster at Café Om, I'd taken to spending the mornings with an older burnout named Krishna who lived in a shed in a small palm grove behind the café and would get me high if I brought him a soda. After breakfast, I'd knock on his door with a bottle of Fanta or Thums Up, and sit with him on his pallet, passing a chillum back and forth and having what I soon realized was the only conversation he knew how to have in English.

"Go to mountain?" he'd suggest, gesturing through the window of his shed at a humped eminence vaguely outlined across the dry riverbed. Krishna owned a pony and a cart and made extra money, or his only money maybe, by taking tourists like me for rides up there.

"No thank you," I'd say, still wary of mountains in general after what felt like a narrow escape from Mt. Abandon. No need to start all that again.

"Looking, seeing," he'd continue, the soft drink beading in his beard, his hands shaping the hazy air between us into things he saw from the mountaintop. "Good feeling."

"Yes," I'd agree. This was the part of the conversation I felt I understood best.

"Krishna pony happiest pony in town," he'd conclude, showing me a clipping from the local newspaper; I couldn't read the text, but the article included a picture of Krishna beside his pony hitched to a tasseled, two-wheeled cart with a yellow and red bonnet. I'd nod, he'd put the picture away, and we'd lapse into an enigmatic silence until one of us got hungry or fell asleep. After a while, the more or less closed circuit of our conversation left me wondering if Krishna expected me in the morning, or if it was new for him every time, and if so, how many different people he thought I was. Either way, I realized, this was the most even-handed relationship I could remember having with anyone in the last ten years, a thought that led me to wonder if I was cruising toward a kind of tee-ball version of enlightenment when the location of Krishna's shed was thrown into the mix. His house seemed to disinter the part of my life that had been washed away earlier in the year, with some of the baleful particulars removed; the mountain view was still there, of course, though separated now by a waterless riverbed that workmen used as a toilet in the morning, squatting far out in the sandy bottom as the sun rose.

Mt. Abandon could probably hop over that without a problem, I admitted to myself, though its Asiatic counterpart seemed more docile and easygoing—or at least less warlike. Krishna wasn't scared of it, at any rate; why should I be?

Good feeling, I reminded myself as I left the shed each morning, emerging from the palm grove and crossing the yard to the rattan wing chair behind the New Poli Poli, where I'd piss away most of the afternoon absorbed in the company of Augustus McCrae and Woodrow F. Call as they drove a herd of cattle toward Montana from Texas. They were mired somewhere in Nebraska when Denise appeared, sitting in the wing chair with a cup of Chai, waiting for me. I was reading as I walked out of the palm grove toward the café and probably would have sat on her if she hadn't said something first.

"Hi, Oliver."

"Denise; you're in my chair," I said, not irritated, just thinking out loud or saying what I saw as I closed the book and signaled to one of the brothers inside. He appeared a moment later with a teapot, two glasses, and a second chair. As I sat down beside her, Denise removed the lid of the pot and sniffed the contents.

"You should try spiraling upward," she suggested, watching me pour out a flat glass of Kingfisher, the beer almost the same color as the apron of sandy river bottom open before us, dotted here and there with workmen in mid-shit.

"I'm fine where I am, thanks."

"You seem to be. I've seen you out here everyday from the bridge."

"Coming to India has mostly been about finding new ways to do the same stuff I do when I'm not here."

"So why are you here?"

"It seemed like you had a pretty good idea the other night. Why are you here?"

"I thought I might be wrong . . ."

"Nope."

"And even if I'm not, I wanted to say I was sorry for the way I treated you after you were honest with me about it."

"Don't apologize. If you hadn't thrown your drink on me, I probably wouldn't have realized how hopeless this entire thing was to begin with. It feels a little like a practical joke I played on myself."

"It's not your fault. Henry gets sloppy when he's desperate, so he doesn't know that what he wants isn't even here. I'm not going to tell you where it is, but you can tell him where it isn't, if you like, whenever you report back."

"I'll run it up the flagpole when the time comes, but I'm not ready to go back to Acheron just yet."

"Even if you'd be doing essentially the same thing there as you are here?"

"Essentially, yes, but not exactly."

"Right," she said, watching me refill my glass. "With the east as your backdrop, all you need are puttees and a veranda to occupy at midday and you suddenly become a tragic figure, something out of Graham Greene, a dipsomaniac slowly going native."

"I've never read him," I said, a little annoyed by how closely this seemed to align me with people like the pompous English fraud across the street, peddling after nirvana like it was a bus he'd missed. "And I probably won't if he's the kind of writer who makes the people who read him think they know more than they actually do. I'll take that apology now."

"So what's your problem then?" asked Denise, sipping suddenly from my glass.

"I think I just don't know what to care about when I'm in a new place, so it's easier to focus on the same old things that exist everywhere. Food, shelter, disassociation."

"Beer at 11AM."

"Falls into the third category," I said, gesturing at the teapot. "Even when they stop bringing about joy, familiar things are at least familiar."

"I can't tell if you want me to think of you as funny or sad."

"I'll respect your choice either way."

"Why don't you come into town with me?" she said, taking the glass out of my hand and passing it and the teapot to a waiter loitering around the back entrance of the café. "I was just going to have a cup of coffee outside the temple and read a little, but if you come with me, we could visit it. I'm assuming you haven't yet."

"What temple?"

"The Mahabodhi temple," said Denise, slowly, as if she was waiting for me to say I was kidding about something.

"What's there?"

"Do you want me to tell you or would you rather go see for yourself?" she said, standing up and walking out to the street. I wasn't so manacled to my routine that following her into town constituted an unconscionable breach of some kind in the expectations I had for the rest of the day and I was pretty sure whatever I got out of it would be good for me. I hadn't been to town since the incident at Café Om, only getting as far as the samosa stand on the corner by the bridge before turning back and nodding off in the rattan chair facing the river around 4PM, my dinner half-eaten in my lap or dragged around the yard by the dogs from the monastery. Had Denise seen that? I wondered. I knew what I looked like after several days of jet lag that didn't seem to be going anywhere and was frankly astounded she'd recognized me at all, unless I always looked like shit and didn't know it. In any case, the hours of the day hung heavily on my mind and body, while the hours of the night were mostly spent pacing the roof of the monastery at three in the morning, wide awake, ready to begin my day, as the rest of the world slumbered around me. Boozing around the backyard of the New Poli Poli and getting high with Krishna probably hadn't improved things; I didn't have a mirror in my room at the monastery, but there was a fairly good piece of one above the sink in the hallway. I'd taken to avoiding it, or the hunted-looking, baggy-eyed, asymmetrically bearded person who glared out at me from the glass whenever I passed by; I knew I looked vaguely undead in bad lighting, so what could Denise possibly have seen in the flawless morning sunlight behind the café and wanted to drag along with her to the temple?

Some people collect burdens, I reminded myself, wondering if I wasn't one of them as we walked through the central market, past men in their shirtsleeves selling samosas and sweets made with condensed milk. Tiny overripe bananas in large bunches hung from the tin roofs of the stalls and bolts of fuchsia and electric green fabric flapped in the wind outside a tailor's shop. We passed a lot of men holding hands, emerging from banks of steam and smoke, talking seriously; the afternoons I'd spent walking like that with Tyler lumbering beside me rose up and receded with the aftereffect of something that may or may not have actually happened, a closed memory for the time being. At the end of the street, before we turned off into plaza outside the pink and yellow gate to the temple complex, I noticed a bull standing in a heap of trash, calmly chewing the tail of a downed kite. Sasha came to mind, gnawing his way through the stem of toothbrush during morning hygiene, one of my rubber-gloved hands cupped under his mouth, the other tapping beneath his chin so he wouldn't swallow the bristled head.

"What are you thinking about?" asked Denise as we tugged our shoes off inside the temple gates, shelving them in a kind of gatehouse at the base of the steps leading down from the entrance.

"My students," I said obliquely, as if Denise had an orchestra seat on everything that was going on inside my head. "I'm discovering I miss them."

"Come meet mine, if you like," she said, our bare feet slapping in tandem along the brick path, the temple rising two hundred feet above us, but seeming to grow as we drew closer. "I didn't realize you were a teacher."

"I'm not. More of a helper."

"Well, even if you're lying and this is some ruse Henry put you up to, I can always use help at the orphanage. The kids are fine, but they like new people. We've mostly been reading stories and pulling out vocab words. They're tired of it. I know that. They already spoke better English than most North Americans before I got here."

"I don't know what I could contribute to that if you're out of ideas."

"Did you bring any books with you, something you could read to them?"

"No. I have a manuscript, but . . ."

"That'll do. Come by with it tomorrow morning, around eight. Lunch will be provided."

"I'm not sure they'll like it; I don't even like it," I said, as we drew up beneath the spreading branches of a large fig tree seemingly sprouting from the base of the temple. Monks in prayer, assorted pilgrims, and a few people I recognized from monastery were arrayed beneath it. "What am I looking at?"

"The Bodhi tree," said Denise. "Supposedly a direct descendant of the tree Siddhartha Gautama achieved enlightenment beneath. He watched it for a week without blinking."

"Well, he was a rich kid. Probably had plenty of time on his hands."

"I think the salient idea here is that he gave up a life of security and comfort, or privilege, as the undergrads like to say, to achieve something more important. This is what the people here recognize, what they come here to learn about and celebrate."

"I think I would have preferred life at court."

"Jesters usually do," said Denise, gesturing toward the ground, the leaves overhead casting spades of shadow across our bare feet. "Consider where we're standing. Some people believe this place is the navel of the earth."

"The Greeks believe the same thing about Delphi; *omphalos* and all that. I suppose everyone has their own ideas about it. Some people believe the gate to hell is in Clifton, New Jersey."

"You're making me regret bringing you here."

"Please don't. It's nice to find one more monument that we didn't put up after killing something. So I'm glad you took me here to see the boogie tree; thank you."

"Bodhi Tree."

"What did I say?"

"I had a Korean roommate once," said Denise, backing out of the shade, angling toward where we left our shoes and the exit. "She used to practice her English on me like I was a wax tablet. Talking to you reminds me of that."

Was I not clear? I wondered, following her out of the gates and into the square outside the temple, where we sat on a bench outside a refreshment stand, sipping plastic cups of Nescafe with too much milk. As we were finishing our coffee, Arun appeared on the other side of the plaza, emerging from an internet café with a bundle of documents and few books beneath his arm; poems by a couple of central European bores from the last century, I noticed, as he came closer and sat with us, but also Lattimore's *Iliad*.

"I have gone through what no other mortal on earth has gone through," I quoted as he introduced himself to Denise. "I have put my lips to the hands of the man who has killed my children."

"He's been like that all morning," said Denise to Arun. "I can't wait to see what he says to my students tomorrow."

"It is the part of the poem most people remember," he replied cheerfully, ordering a coffee for himself. "I hoped to see you, Oliver. I still would like for you to meet my family. You must come to dinner tonight, both of you, if it is possible."

"I can't tonight," said Denise.

"Why not?" I asked.

"I have plans."

"What kind of plans?"

"I'm meeting a friend."

"That guy I saw you with from the monastery?"

"We're quickly approaching the part of my life that is none of your business," said Denise, standing up and turning to Arun. "I have class in twenty minutes, but it was nice meeting you and thank you for the invitation. Maybe another time."

"Of course," he said, watching her walk off toward the edge of the square and down the steps to the market, before turning to me. "So I will tell my mother to expect one person only?"

"Looks like it," I said, inadvertently sipping out of his coffee cup.

Later that evening, while casting around my side of town for something appropriate to bring to the meal with Arun's family, I received a call from Naphta, which I took on a wooden bench outside a teashop at the mouth of the bridge. The sun fading over the smoking shanties and Palmyra palms looked weary as people passed on the dirt track toward town; a man leading a bullock, a woman in a yellow sari sitting sidesaddle on the back of a motorbike, bevvies of monks in maroon and orange. The details were odd and new, but the general momentum of small town life was unchanged. Acheron abroad, I thought, as Naphta spoke. Minus college; plus temple.

"Let me tell you what I know," he said, as things clattered and moved in the background of wherever he was calling from. "I know we have two weeks on the clock and you're still knocking around in back of that café with the local space cadet and drinking the shit beer they have over here out of a teapot, reading cowboy stories."

"Sounds like you know everything," I said. "So what exactly are you calling to find out?"

"I'm not calling to find out anything. I'm calling to tell you to get to work. You've wasted a lot time, but not too much money, so far. If that changes, you'll hear from me again. Do your job. Find the vase."

"She knows. About me, about Henry. I don't understand why you didn't expect this to happen."

"We did. It doesn't change a thing. She's still taking you on long walks to the temple and inviting you to hang out with her students. Make something happen."

"How do you even know that? It was like six hours ago."

"Don't worry about that. Worry about her and what you're there for. Find the vase."

320

"Denise said what we want, what you want, isn't even here."

"So find out where the fuck it is!" shouted Naphta, closing out the conversation. I considered committing the phone to the dry riverbed, but walked around the corner and had a beer at the New Poli Poli instead as a kind of middle finger to what was still expected of me, despite how hopeless it looked. And I still had to figure out something to bring to dinner with Arun's family. I wasn't sure what the Hindu stance on drinking alcohol was or even if he and his family practiced Hinduism, but I knew I wanted more than one beer to get me through what remained of the evening, so I convinced the proprietor to sell me four large bottles of Kingfisher on the understanding I would bring back the empties.

"For deposit," he said, by way of explanation as I left the café with the beer secreted in my backpack, clinking neutrally as I walked the quarter mile into town. Arun's family lived steps away from the plaza where I'd met him earlier, in an apartment above the post office. His father was away in Patna on business, Arun explained after meeting me at the door and walking me upstairs. But his mother and two much younger sisters were at home. They stood beside an immaculately set table as he introduced them. I didn't know who to give the beer to and tried to present it to his mother, who didn't speak any English and didn't seem to know what I was trying to do with it, but she left the dining room and returned a moment later with a glass for me and one for Arun, I was relieved to see. She seated me directly between the two sisters, who both spoke perfect schoolbook English and used it to quiz me on popular features of the North American cultural landscape, things I knew nothing about, but felt I had to try and explain anyway, since all I'd brought to dinner was beer and myself.

"Have you ever seen Bryan Adams perform in concert?" asked the sister to my left, as her mother began serving the meal.

"No, I have not," I said, feeling like I was on equal footing with my two dinner companions until I realized the person I remembered as being Bryan Adams was actually a fatter version of Jon Bon Jovi with a stockbroker haircut, a kind of AM radio chimera.

"He will be coming to India to sing his songs," she continued. "I would very much like to go."

"Celine Dion lives on an island in a mansion," said the right-hand sister. "She will be selling it for fourteen million pounds sterling. That is a very high price."

"I agree," I agreed. Celine Dion rang a bell, though it seemed to correspond to the image of a battleship sinking with Gilbert Grape lashed to the prow, screaming for Arnie to come get him. That couldn't be right. The conversation continued on like this, a series of near misses that seemed to amuse Arun and went right over his mother's head. The food was the best thing I could remember eating that I didn't have to pay for; roti, dahi, dal, several different types of curried vegetables with and without paneer cubes, all served over a fluffy bed of steamed rice. I tried to complement my hostess during and after the meal and Arun helped convey some of this, though she practically pushed me out of the kitchen when I followed her with my plate and a few empty serving dishes, intending to help clean up.

"Please, it isn't necessary," said Arun as he guided me out onto a small balcony overlooking the street; he'd set up some chairs from the dining room with the remaining bottles of Kingfisher beside them. We sat there as it grew dark, drinking slowly and watching things clatter by beneath us. Arun talked mostly about poetry, reading some to me from the small collection he kept in his room. I tried to recite one of Berryman's *Dream Songs*, something about boredom meaning you have no inner resources, but botched it after the first few lines, the memory of the poem more a memory of the impression left on me by the words than the words themselves. Arun had a copy of the *Cantos* a cousin had sent him from Boston, heavily thumbed, which he handed over to me as if he thought I could explain it.

"I have been trying to make sense of it," he said. "Perhaps my ear is too formal."

"No, it's not you. It's a madman's book of common prayer."

"My professors agree with you."

"Fear god and the stupidity of the populace," I quoted, feeling smart.

"I think they are often the same," he said, sipping from my beer glass in what may have been an accident or a joke. I didn't ask.

*   *   *

The next morning, I trotted across the bridge as the sun rose, a clay cup of chai steaming in my hand and the North Hero manuscript tucked beneath arm, past the remote suggestion of villagers squatting in the riverbed to the orphanage on the far shore, the two dogs from the monastery padding after me, single file. The three of us stood outside the gates in descending order of height as I rang the bell, the cheerful three-story building beyond not at all similar to the Dickensian horror I'd imagined, or always associated with the word orphanage; it looked like something between a mid-range hotel and the student union at a community college. Denise let me in, but made the dogs stay outside. They immediately began howling as she led me through the halls and up a set of stairs to her classroom, the sound changing rather than fading, the architecture of the building funneling it like a speaking tube. Her students were already settled on a large carpet facing a table, two chairs, and a blackboard with nothing written on it, talking quietly somewhere between fifteen and twenty clean, well-fed children who all turned in unison as we entered the classroom. Denise introduced me—this is Oliver, from the United States—saying I was there to read them a story I had written and told them to listen well, because we would discuss it afterward. One girl in the back raised her hand and Denise nodded for her to speak.

"Please, miss," she said. "There is a terrible noise on the outside."

"Yes, Priti. It's just dogs."

"But, miss," asked a boy in the back, raising his hand after the fact. "Why must it be so loud?"

"They miss their friend," said Denise with zero irony, nodding at me to start reading.

"I would just like to say," I began. "If there are any parts of this story you do not understand, please stop me, or raise your hand, or whatever you do when you have a question or something doesn't make sense, and I will be happy to explain it as best I can."

"But did you not write it, sir?" said the same boy in the back, his hand shooting up *post facto* once again.

"I did . . . young man," I replied, cringing at myself, wishing I knew his name. "But sometimes all that means is that something has passed through you and there it is, on the page, daring you to make sense of it. Mocking you, even, with the possibility of meaning something, something important maybe, but not the promise. Ideas do not make promises. Only people do that."

"Thank you, sir," said the boy, seeming baffled. Denise tapped my arm, wanting me to begin. The howls from outside settled into

324

regular, foghorn-like intervals as I started reading, glancing up every paragraph or so to see what was going on with my audience. I expected to find at least one or two of them drifting off and was a little spooked by the compound raptness staring back at me whenever my eyes left the page. Initially, I tried to comb over the parts that didn't seem age-appropriate or translatable, but gave up after while; there seemed to be too many of them. Around mid-morning we took a fifteen-minute recess and released the children onto an open rooftop painted like a soccer field. Denise brought me a cup of tea and we sat on the sidelines, watching the children play.

"It sounds mostly not made up," she said, nodding toward the pages furled in the hand I wasn't using to drink the tea.

"It isn't. I never learned how to be creative in a vacuum."

"Well, thank you for sharing it. I don't know what the kids are getting out of it, but we'll find out when you're done."

We reconvened a few minutes later and I finished up with a little time to spare before the lunch that had been promised to me. Denise took over, standing beside the blackboard, the composite attention of the class shifting to her like a spotlight.

"So what do we think Oliver's story is about?" she asked, watching hands sprout here and there.

"Miss, I think the story is about the man not being able to marry the woman he wants to marry," chirped a girl in the front.

"And why can't he do that?" asked Denise.

"He does not have the resources, miss," supplied a boy by the door.

"That's true, Ravi," said Denise. "And why does he not have the resources?"

"I think it is because this man thinks too long about this girl," said Priti. "It is all he does, so he has no time to do anything else and because of this, he can't marry her."

"It is very sad," said the girl who'd spoken in front. "But I think it would make a good film."

"I agree," said Denise, without revealing which side of the girl's statement she agreed with. "It's time for lunch. Let's all say thank you to Oliver for sharing his work."

My work? I thought to myself, as the children flooded out of the classroom. I followed Denise out to the roof, where she introduced me to the other teachers and the director, Islam, with whom we would be eating. Lunch was boiled spinach and chapatti; nothing special compared with the spread at Arun's the night before. I'm thinking like a bum, I thought to myself, sponging the slimy roughage out of a tiffin with the bread, listening to Denise tell Islam about me while he stared into my face, as if he'd fitted me into one side of scale and was trying to find something else to complete the balance.

"If you would like to work here," he said, after we'd finished eating. "I can give you a job. No money, of course, but a place for sleeping and food for helping us with the children and cleaning up."

"Cleaning up?"

"Yes," said Islam. "Laundry, sweeping, and the toilets. There is much to do."

"So . . . a janitor," I said.

"I do not think I know this word," said Islam.

"Someone who cleans up after other people," supplied Denise.

"Yes, that," said Islam, wiping his mouth and standing up. "Please, think it over, Gulliver. Now I must go. It is nice to meet you."

"Gulliver," I said, watching him wander off to kick a ball around the roof with some of the children. "Educated abroad was he?"

"Don't take it personally," said Denise. "Or don't embarrass yourself by taking it personally."

"He obviously thinks I'm some kind of tramp."

"He's busy."

"Where is the toilet anyway?" I asked. "I might as well get a look at what I'm supposed to swab out for my boiled vegetables and floor space."

Denise gestured at door nearby, kind of in the middle of everything. I was hoping for something in a low traffic area, but didn't know how to get this across in a way that would leave her feeling sympathetic, so I went ahead with it, squatting in the stirrups and having what sounded like the loudest bowl movement of my life within conversational distance of her and the other teachers finishing their lunch. To make matters worse, she'd been joined by Mark, the guy I saw her with at the Café Om, who looked like he still had all the same questions about me when I emerged from the toilet ten minutes later like a man who'd been at war with himself.

"Heard you punishing that toilet," said Denise as he and I shook hands and exchanged names. "Good for you, Oliver. You show that fucker who's boss."

"I wouldn't be India if you didn't crap your pants once or twice," supplied Mark.

"I didn't crap my pants," I said, as he continued to talk over me.

"I just came by to grab my guitar," he said to Denise.

"You're not staying for the afternoon class?" she asked.

"I can't today. Going into Gaya to meet a friend at the train. He plays, too, though, so maybe he and I can put something together for the kids tomorrow."

"They'd love that," said Denise. "And I'd appreciate it. We're going to the temple tomorrow morning, around ten. You and your friend should come."

"I'll ask him," said Mark. "We probably will."

"I left my pages inside," I said to them, feeling a sudden need to excuse myself. "I'll grab your instrument."

"Thanks, brother," said Mark, barely glancing at me.

Smug fucking minstrel, I thought as I walked back to the classroom, Willow fresh in my memory after reading about him to the children. It's not that I didn't know what Britta or Denise see in guys like Mark or Willow; it's that I see it too and can't stand it. I combed my manuscript off the desk, feeling a little less proud now that I knew the children were used to better, Uncle Mark and his groovy tunes. The guitar stood encased in a corner behind the blackboard. On impulse I laid it on the desk and popped it open. The furzy bottom was thickly layered with condoms, like fallen leaves plating the surface of a still lake. I reclosed the case, and considering tossing it out the classroom window, or poking holes in some of the prophylactics. But did the world need any more of whatever Mark represented? I asked myself. I didn't think so, and settled for pocketing a few of the rubbers, though I was certain virile Uncle Mark would probably have given them to me if I'd asked and wasn't even sure what I would use them for at this point in my life. I left the classroom with the guitar dangling from my arm and the pages jammed in my back pocket, feeling hollow, almost translucent, the sort of person people only saw when they needed someone to fill time or clean out a toilet. I was also discovering slowly, and only by way of watching her with Mark, that I was attracted to Denise, or growing into an attraction to her, the kind of thing I would have been able to ignore if I had less time on my hands or more weed. But I'd been sent here to watch her, and now him by proxy, or the two of them drawn close together on the rooftop as I returned with the guitar, talking vibrantly over tea while orphans batted around a soccer ball in the background. It was like a scene from a not very good film, though not the one the girl in class had suggested, something enviable and utopian about existing deliberately, the sort of un-attainable fiction people are always striving to model their lives after. I dropped the case between them without a word, hoping to foster a natural boundary therein and give myself a break, if only for as long as it took me to reach the stairs. But before I got far enough away to pretend I couldn't hear her, Denise called out to me.

"You want to come with us to the temple tomorrow?" she asked. "Give the boogie tree another look?"

"Boogie tree?" said Mark.

"Yes," I said, then: "Maybe. No. I don't know."

"Ten o'clock if you change your mind," said Denise, swiveling her attention back on Mark, who had withdrawn his guitar from its coffin and was beginning to strum. Some of the children had drawn up beside him, requesting songs.

I don't need to see or hear any more, I told myself, fleeing down the stairs to the first floor, through the courtyard, and out the front gate. The dogs had tired themselves out howling away throughout the morning and were sleeping under the umbrella of a large banyan on the riverbank. I whistled and they awoke, just as the opening strains of a Cat Stevens song issued from the rooftop, something tautological about how you should sing out if you want to sing out.

What if you want to scream until your head explodes? I won-dered, as I began crossing the bridge with the dogs marching behind me. What then, Mr. Islam nee Stevens? A bitter though familiar yoke settled across my shoulders as I walked, one I as-sumed I'd gotten out from under after the conversation with Ca-rissa at the bus station, though it seemed to have only been in a torpid state since then, awaiting a new wellspring of resentment to reemerge, and thanks to Mark, I was back on common ground. I thought of how pleased with myself I'd been for only bringing along a daypack, traveling lightly, I'd told myself, while still dragging along the same old caravan of threadbare baggage, a line of dusty porters stretching back into the horizon, all the obvious things that made me the wrong person for someone else for Carissa, for Karen, for Alice, for Amanda, for Inez, for Anne, and now for Denise—things I assumed no one could see because I couldn't see them or hoped they would ignore because I could ignore them, but were apparently obvious to everyone who came within range of whatever I'd allowed myself to become or whatever I'd grown into, since the night I'd seen Carissa's sunburnt back framed in the entrance to Buck's tent, rising and falling, definitely moving, but held still all these years in my memory. Another word for this is: trapped.

So: we carry all the bad things we represent along with us, no matter what, I decided, as I reached the other side of the river and veered off toward Krishna's shack. Why did I think I could escape them by jumping to the other side of the world?

*　　*　　*

I was on the mountain with Krishna when the bombs went off the next morning, looking and seeing. The explosions were far enough away to sound like the footsteps I'd always associated with Mt. Abandon trudging after me and I waited for it to stride out of the yellow haze above the town across the river, coming my way. A thin plume of smoke rose beside the temple's peak in the distance and sirens began wailing in the distance. I glanced over at Krishna, sprawled in the shade of his horse, his hand frozen around the chillum he was about to pass my way when we heard the first blast, his eyes leveled toward the town below us.

There were ten devices, I learned later, spread in and around the temple complex, though at the time, I hadn't counted them and didn't know what I'd heard. It seemed to emerge the way serious things do, sudden and irreducible, parting the haze in which Krishna and I had passed the last twenty-four hours. After returning from the orphanage, I'd spent the afternoon in his shed and the night on his floor, only leaving to go to the cafe for food and sodas to pay my way. In the morning, when he'd suggested we go to the mountain, I didn't have a reason to say no, so we'd hitched up his pony and ridden over the bridge, veering left and up the side of the small peak I'd often watched through his window, stopping when the dirt track terminated and the pony was tired. He'd insisted I ride in the cart part of the way while he walked beside it, which made me feel like a janissary on his way to an execution, so I ended up hobbling along beside him with one hand on the pony's bridle, helping him guide the horse up the mountain. Denise crossed my mind, though not deeply, barely penetrating the membrane of substances I'd stacked up since leaving her and Mark on the roof of the orphanage the previous morning. I didn't feel good or bad; I felt nothing and wanted to keep it that way until I was extracted by Naphta and sent home.

But now something was happening, something I didn't understand and I needed a cue about how I should I feel or what I should do, though I didn't receive much of one from Krishna as he holstered the chillum beneath his kurta, clicked his tongue at the horse and began walking back down the way we had come. There was clearly something to dread, though he couldn't tell me what it was, so I followed him, growing more worried when we reached the bridge. People were flowing across it, heading in the opposite direction. The sirens were louder and a general murmur of unrest rose ahead of us. The traffic on the bridge was thickening. I almost missed Mark shuffling past the cart with his guitar beside one of the teachers I'd met the day before, who was speaking gently in Hindi to the children from Denise's class, coaxing them along toward the opposite side of the river. Mark had a crust of dried blood around one of his ears and down the side of jaw. His clothes, hair, and guitar case were covered in a thin layer of dust. He didn't seem to recognize me when I asked what happened, though I realized he was having trouble hearing me after the teacher leading the children made a gesture of forbearance and pointed to the side of his own head.

"Something exploded," said Mark, finally, after I'd leaned in and shouted my question into the ear that wasn't bleeding. "A couple of things blew up. I don't know how many. We were at the temple. Then we were just running, trying to get the kids out."

"Where's Denise?" I asked, too quietly. Mark just looked at me.

"It hit her here," said the teacher, pointing to a place above his eyebrow. "She is in hospital. In Gaya, at the medical college. They took her. Now, please. I must have the children get home."

"What hit her?" I shouted after him. The teacher ignored me, but the student's heads swiveled back my way, their constellated eyes seeming to pity me in unison. That's just great, I thought as I pushed my way through the crowd until I caught up with Krishna at the bridgehead. The orphans feel bad for me. I didn't know what to say to him, but he seemed to understand I needed to go and our time together was at an end. I gave him some rupees so he could buy himself a soda a limp gesture in light of everything, but the only one available to me and crossed the road to line of motor rickshaws idling outside the monastery, waving around a wad of money and shouting 'hospital' and 'Gaya' until I found someone to take me.

Denise was heavily sedated and sleeping soundly when I arrived at the medical college and lied my way inside, telling an ascending order of receptionists, duty nurses, and doctors I was her husband until one of them, a young, brisk resident, finally took me to see her. I stood with him beside her bed as he explained what happened. She was hit by a piece of masonry thrown out by the blast, he said. She'd lost a lot of blood from gash above her eyebrow, what the teacher had referred to earlier on the bridge and possibly had a fractured skull. Also, something was wrong with her eye, but they weren't sure what it was. They were watching for signs of internal hemorrhaging, but the prognosis looked good overall.

"But, she will be in some pain afterward," said the resident. "I think it is best if she is taken home. Have you spoken with the consulate?"

"Not yet."

"If you are not in a state to make arrangements for her, I can have one of my people take care of it. You flew into Delhi?"

"Yes."

"I will have someone call for you the consulate there."

"I think that would be best. Thank you."

"It is nothing," he said, wobbling his head ambivalently, looking from Denise, to me, and back to Denise. A bandage sculpted the injured side of her face into a sterile asymmetry. "How long have you been married?"

"Oh. Years," I said, trying to affect a certain weary fondness for the life I imagined us having together as man and wife.

"You have how many children?"

"None," I said, a little too proudly maybe, adding: "Yet."

"I have three," he said, mildly. "Two sons. Good boys."

"Congratulations."

"Thank you," he said, gesturing at a chair by the bed. "You may stay for now. Her belongings are in the drawer."

He left, and I sat in the chair, watching Denise breathe evenly beneath the thin white top sheet. I felt like I had done half of the right thing for her by coming here and stumbling into arrangements with the embassy, but there had to be someone else I should let know about this: parents, siblings, someone who cared as much or probably more than I did and would want to know if she was injured and far from home. I opened the drawer and removed her backpack, setting it on the floor between my knees. There wasn't much inside; spare bandanas, all smelling like her hair, a sweatshirt, bottled water, a photocopy of her passport and some American money in a plastic bag, and a copy of *Speak, Memory*, a book I'd never read.

I suppose I'll wait here until someone tells me what to do next, I thought, opening the book at the place where Denise had left off, the page marked by a piece of paper that drifted to the floor beside her backpack, landing face up. It appeared to be a luggage receipt of some kind; one piece, deposited at a cloakroom in the train station at Varanasi. I replaced the bookmark, and closed the book, holding the volume in my hands and alternating my gaze between it and Denise, snoring lightly in the bed beside me. I had given up on succeeding long before she told me the vase wasn't even in town and hoped I would make it back home with decent memories of the place Henry had sent me to fail. But things had suddenly changed, as they had earlier that morning on the mountaintop with Krishna. Henry would never leave Acheron. Even if Denise believed he would, that didn't make it any truer. And I didn't see how continuing to allow her to believe this could be more important than what I stood to gain from doing what

Henry wanted. Credit ruination and wage garnishment were on the horizon back home and probably would have been in place by now if I had a verifiable income. I saw the house in North Calais up for sale and Henry placing his bid, my parent's retirement a thing of the past, but not enough to make the near reality of it any less bitter for them as they moved into one of the low-income housing developments on Elm Street in Montpelier, bearing the cost of an education that had left me no smarter and may have actually made me dumber in terms of what it made all of us believe I deserved. Denise's students were right; I had no resources. But surely whatever she had against Henry wasn't worth what I had on the line. I was thirty, so it was too late to start over; the opportunity for new beginnings shears off after freshman year. But with the receipt for the luggage room in Varanasi, I had the chance to get out from under myself and all the people I was dragging down with me, a group in which I didn't include Denise. Perhaps, when all this was over, she would see that I'd thwarted Henry successfully and would even come around to my view of things.

And if not, I would always be grateful to her for telling me where I shouldn't look, I said to myself, as I tucked the book in my back pocket and left the hospital, repeating the scene I'd pulled earlier in the day in the medical college rotunda, waving around a wad of rupees and shouting 'train station' until I found a driver.

I arrived in Varanasi four hours later on the express train, pleasantly haunted by visions of a carefree Russian childhood spent chasing butterflies around vast provincial estates. I hadn't yet reached the part of the book where Nabokov's father was assassinated and the family sent into exile, so an equivalent wellbeing seemed within reach as I handed the receipt to the cloakroom attendant, who appeared moments later with a bulging shoulder bag.

"Enjoy your visit, Dennis," he said, stripping the tag and handing it over. I took the bag to a bench in the main terminal, figuring I should probably make sure it contained the vase before calling Naphta to come get it. At this point, a false alarm would probably have me on the first plane home, a place I wasn't sure I wanted to go without apologizing to Denise for what I was about to do, or had done. I was already looking forward to a point in the hopefully near future in which my recent actions would be irrevocable, especially after finding the vase intact within the shoulder bag, mummified in tape and several sheets of bubble wrap. I hadn't been instructed to check for the notes within, the selected letters of Henry and Winifred Hoffman, but decided to do this anyway, curious to see, or read, what kind of weirdness they'd gotten up to over the years and what about it had left my employer so desperate to recover its remains that he would send someone like me to find them.

Here I am, leading a marching band where angels fear to tread, I thought, as I scratched away enough of the bubble wrap to remove the lid, and tilted the entire vase into my lap to see what would roll out.

Ash powdered my groin. I gave the vase a shake; only more ash. So that's it, I thought, capping the thing and rewrapping it; Denise's last laugh. I wondered if she'd read the notes between Henry and his mother before burning them. I hoped she had; how could she not? I imagined him receiving the vase, hoping to review his missives in peace, only to find them existing as ashes, and in the mind of the woman who'd immolated them. It felt like the perfect plan to drive Henry wild and I couldn't wait to do my small part of it by seeing the thing home.

I couldn't imagine Denise not wanting things to turn out this way and imagining this made feel better as I left the train station, figuring I would find somewhere comfortable and interesting to call Naphta from. I didn't know much about Varanasi, but I knew the Ganges flowed through it and figured I might as well get a look at it before I went home. I'd spent the better part of my time in India staring half-drunk at a dry sand bed the locals used as a toilet, so my first look at open, flowing water after the rickshaw driver dumped me out on some steps leading down to the river left me feeling refreshed in a way I hadn't expected, or had given up expecting. I walked halfway down the steps and dialed Naphta's number, settling myself as far as I could from what looked like a kind of ritualized cookout on the bank nearby, robed men stacking wood in a rough rectangle, while another man circled it, chanting.

"It's a cremation," said Naphta, after I'd described what I was seeing to him.

"A what?" I asked, just as several men appeared bearing a body shrouded in white. "Oh. I see."

"You have the vase?" he asked.

"Yes. It's here with me."

"Good. Where are you?"

"In Varanasi, like I said."

"Yes, I know. It's a city with over a million people and an international airport. Can you be more specific?"

"I'm by the river. Sitting on some steps."

"Okay, you're going to have to do better than that. If there's a cremation going on, I'm going to assume you found your way to the ghats, and it's probably either Manikarnika or Harishchandra. Do me a favor: don't move."

"But, they've just thrown the body on," I said, as the men

positioned the shrouded corpse on the pyre. "I'm not sure I want to see that. Or smell it."

"Not my problem," said Naphta. "Just stay on the *ghats*."

"The what?"

"The *ghats*. The steps you're sitting on. Someone is on the way," he said, hanging up. Flames licked at the base of bier in my periphery, catching and smoking as the chanting kicked up a notch. I didn't want to be rude by pinching my nose shut, so I tried to only breath through my mouth, focusing on several women wading into the water below, submerging themselves and dispatching garlands of marigolds into the current.

Arun appeared to collect the vase, seating himself beside me on the steps. He watched me watch the ritual without saying anything, the materials between us, the smoke from the burning body drifting out over the river, graying the sunset.

"Manikarnika," he said, finally, threading his hand through the shoulder bag's strap. "One of the oldest in the city. It is believed that those who are burned here are liberated from the continuous cycle of birth and death; their souls are free forever."

"You got here fast," I said, trying for whatever reason not to seem surprised by it.

"We were on the same train."

"You've been following me."

"I was asked to watch you."

"I thought we were friends."

"It is possible to be friends and still do business, isn't it?"

"I don't know."

"I must pay for my education. You understand."

"Yes," I admitted, gesturing at the women below us. "What are they doing?"

"A *puja*," he said. "Showing reverence."

"So . . . a prayer."

"Yes. But one made from love rather than fear," he said, standing up, and removing his backpack, my backpack actually, from his shoulders and replacing it with Denise's bag. "I've brought you your things from the monastery. Naphta told me to tell you your flight home is leaving around midnight tomorrow. The BG express will be here in two hours. He said for you to take it. You will be back in Delhi by the morning. Now, I must go. I also have a train to catch."

"It was nice meeting you," I said, extending my hand. I meant it.

"Yes," he said, taking it. "I have family in Boston. That is not so far from where you live."

"No, it isn't."

"I will tell you if I visit them."

"Please do. You can get my contact information from Naphta."

"Indeed," he said, releasing my hand and walking back up the steps to the street. Watching him go, I realized I'd left Denise's copy of *Speak, Memory* in the side pocket of the shoulder bag, and considered chasing him down to get it back, but the smoke from the cremation was stinging my eyes, making them water, and I knew I must look like I was grieving over something. I didn't want Arun to think it had anything to do with him.

Arun's appearance left me with a different understanding of how Denise would probably see things when she woke up, if she hadn't already, injured and alone in a far away, rinky-dink hospital in East India, stripped by me of the one thing she was determined to keep hidden from Henry. I could look back on plenty of moments in my life where I thought of myself as a shitty person, though I couldn't remember a time when it felt so unequivocal. But as I drove back toward the train station, specifically disgusted with myself, I wondered if it was really all my fault. Was I taking on more of the blame for this than I actually deserved? There was only one person who could answer that question for me and after handing over a stack of rupees to my rickshaw driver and repeating the words 'bar' and 'beer' to him over and over, I ended up in a corner of the lounge at a Radisson behind the train station with a bottle of Royal Stag whiskey, waiting for Henry to pick up the phone.

"I think I told you never to call me on this number unless there is a problem," he said, after answering on the twentieth or thirtieth ring; I'd lost count after hanging up whenever he tried to send me to voicemail. "But as I understand from Naphta, all is well on your end, so we have no reason to be speaking."

"All is most certainly not fucking well!" I shouted, drawing an eye from the bartender across the room. "Why did it have to be Arun? You couldn't find someone else? I had dinner with his family! I liked them very much!"

"I'm not understanding your problem with this."

"I thought I made a friend."

"Oh. I see. Is that unusual for you or something?"

"It was mean, the whole thing. It didn't have to happen that way. It didn't have to be him."

"Naphta recruited him and arranged it."

"It doesn't matter."

"So if you really want to have it out with someone over this, call him."

"You don't care. "

"You're right. I don't."

"Because you don't have any friends."

"Successful people don't need them."

"So you don't know what it is to see yourself in someone who has hurt you and understand why they did it, even if you can't forgive them."

"Look, whatever was going on between you and Arun is none of my business, but it's probably illegal over there, so I would keep your voice down, wherever you are right now."

"I'm at the Radisson. In the bar."

"It sounds like you've been there awhile, thinking all this over."

"But that's not what I'm talking about; you put me in an impossible position."

"People like you always find their way into those positions, Oliver, whether or not I make them up."

"And people like you are always excusing themselves from the responsibility for the horrible shit they do by saying they just got there first; it would be someone else if it hadn't been them. I'd pity you if I could forgive you."

"I'm going to be generous and give you ten more seconds to explain what you want, if anything, before I hang up."

"I want you to tell me that it isn't all my fault . . ."

"That what isn't all your fault?"

"And that when she wakes up in the hospital in Gaya, she won't know that the world is that much more evil for her having known me, because it's really that she knew you, not me, that we both knew you. It isn't fair and I don't want to feel bad about it any more!"

"Who's in the hospital in Gaya?" asked Henry, the smugness in his voice receding a tick. "Oliver: who are you talking about?"

"Denise! Who the fuck else?"

"Tell me what happened."

"There was an explosion, a bombing at the temple. Something hit her head, a brick or a piece of the boogie tree, I don't know, the point is, what you made me do, what I had to do, I would never have had to do it if you hadn't set me up to have to do it and I want to hear you admit that. I want you to ask me to forgive you for doing that to me and to her so I'll be able to forgive myself, not right away, but eventually, even though I'll never forgive you, but I need to hear you ask. And I can't wait for you to see the ashes."

I don't know at what point Henry hung up, but I don't think he heard the last part of this, though I realized everyone else, the people sprinkled around the sleek hotel bar, heard it loud and clear when the bartender appeared with the doorman and asked me to leave.

"Please, sir, no more shouting," added the bartender, taking my arm. I agreed that it was time for me to leave and went to use the toilet while the doorman held onto my whiskey. Something clattered into the bathroom floor when I opened my fly at the urinal, a metallic nodule of some kind, roughly cross-shaped, that had somehow become lodged in the seam beside the zipper. How had whatever this was gotten there? I wondered, examining it in my palm with my arms held at a winged sort of angle by the doorman and bartender as they escorted me out past the gate. One of them handed over the bottle of Royal Stag I'd paid for when we reached the sidewalk, the pouring spout still intact, and I pocketed the artifact.

I had no idea what time it was, but I was certain I'd missed my train back to Delhi. That didn't worry me. I'd decided not to take it before calling Henry. Whatever happened from here on out, I thought I at least owed Denise a face to face explanation for what I'd done or why I'd done it, if only to remind her that even though she'd been right about me, there was still a small part of this within our control; we might never be friends, but we didn't have to let Henry make us into enemies. Arun and I seemed to have accidentally made this choice earlier on the *ghats*; it had to be possible with Denise. And somewhere between my third and fifth glass of Royal Stag, I'd begun imagining her awake in her hospital bed in Gaya, injured and alone, with nothing to do except wait for the embassy to get her out of there and decided that even if she didn't want to see me, I would at least be someone familiar to sit with while she waited. I didn't think I'd betrayed her trust, since she'd never invested me with it in the first place, but I hoped she would see that even after living up to her low expectations for me, we still shared a nemesis. Henry might be all we would ever have in common and I was okay with that, as long as she knew how sorry I was about it.

After getting kicked out of the Radisson, I walked back to the railroad station, hoping to catch a night train to Gaya, but was told regular services were either delayed or suspended because of the bombing and would resume sometime the following morning. Extra security measures were in place, a clerk assured me, as I swayed outside his ticket window. When I asked if he knew of a place nearby where I could rent a car, he wobbled his head and closed the shutter.

Probably the right answer, I thought, as I tripped out of the station, nearly falling on my face in front of a phalanx of motor-rickshaws when I reached the street. A not very well thought out plan about flying into Gaya began forming in my head, though I wasn't sure I could afford it even if they allowed me to board a plane in the shape I was in. Henry's original dispensation had dwindled to a serviceable but not very large sum, an amount I'd have to be careful with if I wanted to continue eating and sleeping in a bed and I wasn't about to call Naphta to ask for an airline ticket to send me in the wrong direction. Best to stay off his radar for the time being, I decided. My flight home wouldn't leave for another day, give or take, so I had enough time to get back to Denise before he came looking for me. Meanwhile, I was stuck in Varanasi until morning.

The Radisson was off limits, but I still had half a bottle of Royal Stag to close out the night, so I walked around the city until I found an English language bookstore, where I embedded myself in a quiet corner lined with orange-belted Penguin Classics, mostly fussy, mostly British, the kind of thing Buck enjoyed, leafing through them with one hand, gurgling whiskey with the other. This went on long enough without anyone noticing to make me feel like I had a every right to be there, doing what I was doing and when I was finally thrown out by the proprietor shortly before he closed up, I made a small scene in the street outside the shop that attracted the attention of two police servicemen and a localized group of young hoteliers who intervened on my behalf.

They were all the upper caste sons of families who owned hotels in and around the city—out looking for trouble, it seemed—and they invited me back to one of these to sit on its roof, smoke cigarettes, and drink the rest of my Royal Stag. One of them had a bottle of Smirnoff he appeared to be very proud of. Watching him open this is the last memory I have of the evening, though a few stray images came rushing back the next morning, when I awoke, shivering, dry-mouthed, and alone back on Manikarnika *ghat*, among them: searching my pockets for rupees to buy more alcohol for my new friends, and finding only the metal nugget from earlier in the evening. One of the young men plucked it from my hand, examining the thing for a moment before asking if it had fallen out. I said it had, misunderstanding his question. My uncle can fix it for you in the morning, he said. He is very good dentist. I will give you his mobile number. Tell him I sent you.

I don't remember how I felt after hearing this. I can only recall asking one of my hosts to point me in the direction of the river after being walked downstairs and out of the hotel and stumbling down the shuttered street until I heard water, half-rolling, half-walking down the steps to the bed of embers smoldering from the cremation I'd seen earlier, or another cremation, I couldn't be sure. I don't remember removing the North Hero manuscript from my backpack, but I can still easily recall watching the pages flicker, catch, and disappear on what remained of the pyre, joining the tributaries of smoke drifting south over the water.

*　　*　　*

I didn't reach Gaya until later that night. By the time I made it back to the railway station from the river, I'd already missed the midmorning train, so I bought a ticket for the afternoon line, and tried to sleep on a bench in the waiting room. I would have missed that train as well if the stationmaster hadn't seen the ticket sprouting from my back pocket and woken me up.

Because of the delays, a trip that should have taken four hours took nearly ten, most of which I spent in the vestibule between the passenger car and the toilets, watching a green and brown smear of landscape pass through the open door. The train was overbooked and it wasn't clear from my ticket whether or not I had a seat, but I managed to doze through what was left of the monstrous hangover from the night before with my back straight against the crosshatched metal wall, my legs folded beneath me, my hands at rest in my lap, in a posture of outward enlightenment. I still felt like shit by the time the train rolled into Gaya Junction, but in a way that was familiar enough to be almost comfortable, a workable gloom. Outside the station, I repeated my trick with the rickshaw drivers outside the train station, waving around my greatly diminished bankroll and shouting 'hospital' for what I hoped would be the last time.

The medical receptionist gave me a curious look when I announced myself as Denise Erlanger's husband, a look I didn't fully understand, though it left me with the sort of feeling I had just before seeing Carissa's naked back rising and falling in the tent, the kind of feeling I thought I'd learned then never to ignore. I thought I was doing the right thing as I climbed the stairs to Denise's room in the Gaya hospital; I remember feeling the same way the night I'd climbed the bank to the campsite on Kranion Pond, like the world had opened in front me just enough to steer myself through an unmapped section of it, the murky terra incognita between the things we want and things we can actually have, or what Nabokov said mapmakers used to call 'sleeping beauties'. I'd read that passage on the train to Varanasi and I wanted to share what I remembered about it with Denise if she was awake, hoping it might be a benign way to reinvent myself for her as someone who was harmless and worth being around. I planned on leading off with an apology for losing the book and was actually murmuring this to myself like one of the monks I'd seen around the monastery, rehearsing it, when I turned into the doorway of her room and noticed a familiar, broad-brimmed sunhat hung from the bedpost by its chinstrap, Henry sitting in the chair where I'd sat the day before, with her copy of *Speak, Memory* broken over his knee. He may have been reading aloud to Denise, who was awake, but staring at the ceiling, her left hand flat on the top sheet, the fingers laced through Henry's in way that looked uncomfortable to me, but somehow necessary for them, as if letting go would leave them both incomplete.

"Get out," said Henry without looking up from the book and

I obeyed, turning on my heel like I'd reached the end of a parade ground, walking back the way I'd come, down the stairs, past the now prescient-seeming receptionist, and out into the night. I still don't know whether Henry knew it was me in the doorway of Denise's room, but even then, I knew it didn't matter.

VI.

I MOVED OUT OF BUCK AND Carissa's attic in January, shortly
after New Year, and into the carriage house on Karen and Ray's
property in Randolph. The shelter was up and running, but they
hadn't fully disengaged from their lives in New York and needed
someone on site to look after things and manage the interns, two
veterinary tech students from the technical college up the road.
I spent days with the dogs—running them around a paddock
built in the backyard, cleaning out cages, delivering kibble—and
my nights working through Dr. Norman's notes on my thesis, a
hundred pages of passionless prose on Belisarius and his campaigns for Justinian against the Vandals in Africa and Ostrogoths
in Italy, with no mention of his wife or her supposed trysts with
Theodosius. I'd hammered all this out between Christmas and
New Year's Eve at my parents' house, a few weeks after getting
back from India and being paid for what I did there. Most of
the money went to the student loan companies I'd been fencing
with and lying to for the past couple years, leaving me feeling I'd
gotten almost nothing for my tuition, so I took the Belisarius box
back to North Calais after apologizing to Dr. Norman for the
what he had generously decided to call a prank the weird note
and the weirder manuscript I'd submitted to him before I left. So
my studies were more or less back on track and paid for, even if

I was receiving a degree I still didn't know what to do with in a field that depressed me. No one seemed to know how to make me feel better about this and after submitting the final draft of my thesis at the beginning of February, I stopped expecting them to.

Grover stopped by a few times over the winter to see how I was doing and took some of the dogs out with me in the woods behind the house. We didn't talk about India, Henry, or Denise. There didn't seem to be much left to say about it after he'd paid me back in December, a few days after Isidore, Henry's apparent aide-de-camp nowadays, had driven me back to Vermont from Logan Airport. This was the final arrangement of many Naphta had made after dragging me out of Krishna's shack when I didn't show up for my flight home. He'd flown with me from Gaya to Delhi and sat at my side in the departures lounge until my plane began to board, waiting outside the gate until it took off. The seat he'd gotten me in business class seemed like a thoughtful gesture, until I realized it had something to do with him bribing a stewardess to hand me off in Zurich to two bulky Calvinists who practically frog-marched me to my connection. Grover knew about most of this by the time he met me at the Ethiopian restaurant to drop off the check and looked nervous as he slid the envelope across the bar, where it came to rest beside a napkin covered in feverish-looking wolves and a half empty glass of tej.

"It's all there, plus something extra," he said, not sitting, but not leaving. "Naphta wanted to take out the cost of the extra flights and the other arrangements out of your end and Henry may have let me him do it if I didn't remind him that you finished up way ahead of schedule, even factoring in certain delays."

"Delays," I echoed.

"No need to get into it. All things considered, you did a good job."

"Who was in the vase?"

"I don't follow you."

"This ended up hitching a ride in my crotch, Grover," I said, removing the filling from my shirt pocket and placing it on the bar between us. "Who does it belong to?"

"Looks like just some pocket garbage to me."

"They were human remains. Don't lie to me again."

"I'd like to give you some money," said Grover, heaving himself onto the stool beside me and folding his hands into a kind of gallows beneath his chin. "Will you let me do that?"

"Was it his mother?"

"I don't see how that would be possible. Anyway, no one asked you to open it up."

"He said the vase was full of notes they used to write each other. Wouldn't you have done the same thing? I can't believe I believed that."

"That's also the information I was given. Denise seems to have burnt them."

"That's another thing. Why was Henry with her at the hospital? At least tell me that."

"They have history. The bombing complicated that history in a way none of us expected. The vase is only a vase, after all. Its history is limited."

"It's an urn, not a vase."

"Call it what you like. Thank you for helping us find it."

"Am I part of a crime now?"

"I know you probably want to hear something more substantial from me, but I don't have any answers for you aside from the ones we've both been given. I'm sorry."

"So they're both fucking crazy," I said, thinking it over, adding: "But they seemed happy when I saw them."

"They care about each other in their own way. She knows how to get to him. And to you, it seems like."

"I wouldn't say that."

"You went back to her when you didn't need to. That says something else."

"And yet, here I am. Where I usually am."

"Life is a closed track," said Grover, sliding off the barstool, buttoning his suit, combing the filling off the bar and pocketing it, preparing to leave. "Just between you and me, and don't breathe a word of this to anyone, I think she reminds him of his mother."

"The lady in the vase?"

"I'll throw this away for you."

That has to be my cue to get the fuck out of here, I thought, dialing Karen's number as I watched Grover leave the restaurant. She'd mentioned needing someone to manage the shelter when I'd visited her and Ray in October, even going so far as to show me the apartment they built upstairs in the carriage house. At the time, I hadn't thought much of it and even as I listened to Karen's phone ring, silently praying for her to answer, I wanted to believe things had been different back then and that something important had changed to make Randolph suddenly the perfect place to flee after my conversation with Grover. Though as I glanced around me, at the wolves drawn on the napkin, the honey wine in my glass, the slightly sympathetic expression of Hodan behind her rostrum across the dining room as snow drifted like ash through the arc of a streetlight outside the window, I had to admit they didn't look much different now.

I suppose we grow into what makes us unhappy, not out of it, I thought, as Karen answered brightly, suddenly, in exactly the way I'd hoped she would, though I didn't realize this until after

I'd left the wine and the wolves at the bar, and walked outside to hear her better, the snow billowing at my back from the direction of Mt. Abandon, hibernating darkly above the town.

*　　*　　*

Carissa had her baby in late June, a boy, ten pounds, six ounces, and I came up from Randolph when she got out of the hospital to meet my godchild. The house on Winter Street was swarmed with people, both sets of parents and some of their friends, people from the school where Carissa taught, Buck's friends from the nonprofit sector. The two of them knew so many more people than I thought they did fine, upstanding professional types, that I was shocked they'd asked me to be the godfather and a little humbled by it when I finally held the baby in the living room in front of everyone. Carissa watched me from a chaise lounge by the fireplace, enjoying her first glass of wine in nine months, and looking a little tired, but very happy. Buck was in the kitchen making margaritas, which allowed me to briefly slip into a fantasy about the child I held being mine instead of his, though it faded good-naturedly when he returned with a drink for me, setting the frosted glass on the mantel and seating himself beside Carissa on the chaise lounge. Yes, they looked right together, they always had, no getting around that and—even more so when I finally surrendered the baby to them, completing the picture, and walked out to the backyard to sit beneath the willow with Theresa, Amanda, and Amanda's roommate. The garden where I'd watched Carissa toil for the better part of last summer was off to a rough start, I noticed, the soil weedy and unturned, but everything else around the house seemed to be going well without me there, a thought that left me feeling happy and alone.

Alice showed up later in the afternoon with her husband, Raymond, who turned out to be one of the most genial and polite people I'd ever met in my life and who claimed to have heard a lot about me as we shook hands on the back porch, a possibility that left me feeling nervous and a little goblin-like after what had gone on between me and his wife while he was abroad, defending our freedom. I found Buck in the kitchen and made up an errand about needing to get more wine, though there were at least ten bottles held in reserve in the rack by the sink. Meanwhile, it was Raymond's turn to hold the baby and he was visible through the kitchen door, twittering to the infant in his arms and cavorting around the living room, a nice, stable person clearly at home in a world of adult responsibilities. I wasn't sure I could take much more of it.

"Yeah, go get some," said Buck, taking all this in with a glance. I thanked him and left the house, walking downtown through the dusky, quiet side streets of Acheron until I arrived at Grover's Market. I took my time inside, hoping Raymond would be gone when I returned, reading labels on anything that looked interesting, flipping through magazines by the registers, and having a long, mellow bowel movement in the store bathroom, a bathroom I'd used many times when I was produce manager and was pleased to find I still felt safe in. An hour rolled by like this and I was sampling things out of the olive bar, preparing to leave, when I spotted Denise in the express line. I froze, ducking back behind the sneeze guard like it was the menu at the Café Om, trying to get a better look. She'd gained weight since India, her hair was a bit grayer, and the eyelid on the side of her head that been hit by the brick drooped a little in a way that made her look slightly bored and very comely. On the conveyor, she set a pint of coconut milk ice cream, a bag of baby carrots, and a bottle of Riesling.

Normal groceries, I thought, not sure what I expected, but a little startled by how seemingly benign we had both become over the intervening months, I with my dogs and godson, and she with her ice cream, carrots, and wine. And what else? I wondered, as she paid and walked outside; there had to be more.

I waited a moment before following, the unneeded wine I was supposed to buy forgotten, trailing her at distance across Clamence Street onto Town Hill Road. The shopping bag hung lightly from her wrist, bopping against her thigh as she passed beneath streetlamps beginning to ignite, a trail of sodium vapor lights leading up the hill, toward the college. I had an idea of where she might be headed, but wanted to see it for myself. Still, I was surprised when I saw her produce a ring of keys and let herself into the house where Henry and I had first discussed her on the porch. His maroon Saab was parked in the driveway beside a newish Volvo with Vermont plates, presumably hers. The door closed and lights went on inside, something I couldn't remember seeing in Acheron as long as I'd lived there.

****

ABOUT THE AUTHOR

Joshua Amses is the author of three previous novels, and a graduate student in social work at the University of Montana.

About Fomite

A fomite is a medium capable of transmitting infectious organisms from one individual to another.

"The activity of art is based on the capacity of people to be infected by the feelings of others." Tolstoy, *What Is Art?*

Writing a review on Amazon, Good Reads, Shelfari, Library Thing or other social media sites for readers will help the progress of independent publishing. To submit a review, go to the book page on any of the sites and follow the links for reviews. Books from independent presses rely on reader to reader communications.

For more information or to order any of our books, visit
http://www.fomitepress.com/

More Titles from Fomite...

Novels
Joshua Amses — *During This, Our Nadir*
Joshua Amses — *Ghatsr*
Joshua Amses — *Raven or Crow*
Joshua Amses — *The Moment Before an Injury*
Jaysinh Birjepatel — *Nothing Beside Remains*
Jaysinh Birjepatel — *The Good Muslim of Jackson Heights*
David Brizer — *Victor Rand*
Paula Closson Buck — *Summer on the Cold War Planet*
Dan Chodorkoff — *Loisaida*
David Adams Cleveland — *Time's Betrayal*
Jaimee Wriston Colbert — *Vanishing Acts*
Roger Coleman — *Skywreck Afternoons*
Marc Estrin — *Hyde*
Marc Estrin — *Kafka's Roach*
Marc Estrin — *Speckled Vanities*
Zdravka Evtimova — *In the Town of Joy and Peace*
Zdravka Evtimova — *Sinfonia Bulgarica*
Daniel Forbes — *Derail This Train Wreck*
Greg Guma — *Dons of Time*
Richard Hawley — *The Three Lives of Jonathan Force*
Lamar Herrin — *Father Figure*
Michael Horner — *Damage Control*
Ron Jacobs — *All the Sinners Saints*
Ron Jacobs — *Short Order Frame Up*
Ron Jacobs — *The Co-conspirator's Tale*
Scott Archer Jones — *And Throw Away the Skins*
Scott Archer Jones — *A Rising Tide of People Swept Away*
Julie Justicz — *Degrees of Difficulty*
Maggie Kast — *A Free Unsullied Land*

Darrell Kastin — *Shadowboxing with Bukowski*
Coleen Kearon — *#triggerwarning*
Coleen Kearon — *Feminist on Fire*
Jan English Leary — *Thicker Than Blood*
Diane Lefer — *Confessions of a Carnivore*
Rob Lenihan — *Born Speaking Lies*
Douglas Milliken — *Our Shadow's Voice*
Colin Mitchell — *Roadman*
Ilan Mochari — *Zinsky the Obscure*
Peter Nash — *Parsimony*
Peter Nash — *The Perfection of Things*
George Ovitt — *Stillpoint*
George Ovitt — *Tribunal*
Gregory Papadoyiannis — *The Baby Jazz*
Pelham — *The Walking Poor*
Andy Potok — *My Father's Keeper*
Frederick Ramey — *Comes A Time*
Joseph Rathgeber — *Mixedbloods*
Kathryn Roberts — *Companion Plants*
Robert Rosenberg — *Isles of the Blind*
Fred Russell — *Rafi's World*
Ron Savage — *Voyeur in Tangier*
David Schein — *The Adoption*
Lynn Sloan — *Principles of Navigation*
L.E. Smith — *The Consequence of Gesture*
L.E. Smith — *Travers' Inferno*
L.E. Smith — *Untimely RIPped*
Bob Sommer — *A Great Fullness*
Tom Walker — *A Day in the Life*
Susan V. Weiss —*My God, What Have We Done?*
Peter M. Wheelwright — *As It Is On Earth*
Suzie Wizowaty — *The Return of Jason Green*

Poetry
Anna Blackmer — *Hexagrams*
Antonello Borra — *Alfabestiario*
Antonello Borra — *AlphaBetaBestiaro*
Antonello Borra — *Fabbrica delle idee/The Factory of Ideas*
L. Brown — *Loopholes*
Sue D. Burton — *Little Steel*
David Cavanagh— *Cycling in Plato's Cave*
James Connolly — *Picking Up the Bodies*
Greg Delanty — *Loosestrife*
Mason Drukman — *Drawing on Life*
J. C. Ellefson — *Foreign Tales of Exemplum and Woe*
Tina Escaja/Mark Eisner — *Caida Libre/Free Fall*
Anna Faktorovich — *Improvisational Arguments*
Barry Goldensohn — *Snake in the Spine, Wolf in the Heart*

Fomite

Barry Goldensohn — *The Hundred Yard Dash Man*
Barry Goldensohn — *The Listener Aspires to the Condition of Music*
R. L. Green — *When You Remember Deir Yassin*
Gail Holst-Warhaft — *Lucky Country*
Raymond Luczak — *A Babble of Objects*
Kate Magill — *Roadworthy Creature, Roadworthy Craft*
Tony Magistrale — *Entanglements*
Gary Mesick — *General Discharge*
Andreas Nolte — *Mascha: The Poems of Mascha Kaléko*
Sherry Olson — *Four-Way Stop*
Brett Ortler — *Lessons of the Dead*
Aristea Papalexandrou/Philip Ramp — *Μας προσπερνά/It's Overtaking Us*
Janice Miller Potter — *Meanwell*
Janice Miller Potter — *Thoreau's Umbrella*
Philip Ramp — *The Melancholy of a Life as the Joy of Living It Slowly Chills*
Joseph D. Reich — *A Case Study of Werewolves*
Joseph D. Reich — *Connecting the Dots to Shangrila*
Joseph D. Reich — *The Derivation of Cowboys and Indians*
Joseph D. Reich — *The Hole That Runs Through Utopia*
Joseph D. Reich — *The Housing Market*
Kenneth Rosen and Richard Wilson — *Gomorrah*
Fred Rosenblum — *Vietnumb*
David Schein — *My Murder and Other Local News*
Harold Schweizer — *Miriam's Book*
Scott T. Starbuck — *Carbonfish Blues*
Scott T. Starbuck — *Hawk on Wire*
Scott T. Starbuck — *Industrial Oz*
Seth Steinzor — *Among the Lost*
Seth Steinzor — *To Join the Lost*
Susan Thomas — *In the Sadness Museum*
Susan Thomas — *The Empty Notebook Interrogates Itself*
Paolo Valesio/Todd Portnowitz — *La Mezzanotte di Spoleto/Midnight in Spoleto*
Sharon Webster — *Everyone Lives Here*
Tony Whedon — *The Tres Riches Heures*
Tony Whedon — *The Falkland Quartet*
Claire Zoghb — *Dispatches from Everest*

Stories
Jay Boyer — *Flight*
L. M Brown — *Treading the Uneven Road*
Michael Cocchiarale — *Here Is Ware*
Michael Cocchiarale — *Still Time*
Neil Connelly — *In the Wake of Our Vows*
Catherine Zobal Dent — *Unfinished Stories of Girls*
Zdravka Evtimova —*Carts and Other Stories*
John Michael Flynn — *Off to the Next Wherever*

Fomite

Derek Furr — *Semitones*
Derek Furr — *Suite for Three Voices*
Elizabeth Genovise — *Where There Are Two or More*
Andrei Guriuanu — *Body of Work*
Zeke Jarvis — *In A Family Way*
Arya Jenkins — *Blue Songs in an Open Key*
Jan English Leary — *Skating on the Vertical*
Marjorie Maddox — *What She Was Saying*
William Marquess — *Boom-shacka-lacka*
Gary Miller — *Museum of the Americas*
Jennifer Anne Moses — *Visiting Hours*
Martin Ott — *Interrogations*
Christopher Peterson — *Amoebic Simulacra*
Jack Pulaski — *Love's Labours*
Charles Rafferty — *Saturday Night at Magellan's*
Ron Savage — *What We Do For Love*
Fred Skolnik— *Americans and Other Stories*
Lynn Sloan — *This Far Is Not Far Enough*
L.E. Smith — *Views Cost Extra*
Caitlin Hamilton Summie — *To Lay To Rest Our Ghosts*
Susan Thomas — *Among Angelic Orders*
Tom Walker — *Signed Confessions*
Silas Dent Zobal — *The Inconvenience of the Wings*

Odd Birds

William Benton — *Eye Contact: Writing on Art*
Micheal Breiner — *the way none of this happened*
J. C. Ellefson — *Under the Influence: Shouting Out to Walt*
David Ross Gunn — *Cautionary Chronicles*
Andrei Guriuanu and Teknari — *The Darkest City*
Gail Holst-Warhaft — *The Fall of Athens*
Roger Lebovitz — *A Guide to the Western Slopes and the Outlying Area*
Roger Lebovitz — *Twenty-two Instructions for Near Survival*
dug Nap— *Artsy Fartsy*
Delia Bell Robinson — *A Shirtwaist Story*
Peter Schumann — *Belligerent & Not So Belligerent Slogans from the Possibilitarian Arsenal*
Peter Schumann — *Bread & Sentences*
Peter Schumann — *Charlotte Salomon*
Peter Schumann — *Faust 3*
Peter Schumann — *Planet Kasper, Volumes One and Two*
Peter Schumann — *We*

Plays

Stephen Goldberg — *Screwed and Other Plays*
Michele Markarian — *Unborn Children of America*

Fomite

Essays
  Robert Sommer — *Losing Francis: Essays on the Wars at Home*